ALEXANDRA HAMER

To Be A Girl

ALEXANDRASAURUS

First published by Alexandrasaurus 2021

This novel is entirely a work of fiction. The names, characters and incidents portrayed in it are the work of the author's imagination. Any resemblance to actual persons, living or dead, events or localities is entirely coincidental.

Alexandra Hamer asserts the moral right to be identified as the author of this work.

First edition

ISBN: 978-1-7399060-0-9

This book was professionally typeset on Reedsy.
Find out more at reedsy.com

For Caroline - the Florence to my Emmeline.

Contents

Acknowledgement

A huge thank you to Clare Wallace and Vicki Le Feuvre, for their endless advice on how to make this novel better.

And the hugest possible thank you to my extraordinary wife, Caroline, for her unwavering wisdom, support, encouragement and advice, and for proofreading and reviewing ten year's worth of drafts ♥

I

The Right Person to Be

1

Thomas

One afternoon, right at the end of the summer of 1874, when I was four-and-a-half years old, I looked down at my thing.

Except it wasn't really mine. I mean, my chin was my chin, and my nose definitely belonged to me, but that thing between my legs, and its two accompanying articles felt quite foreign to me, as if they had been left behind by a stranger.

"Thomas, come and eat," shouted my mother.

That was the other thing – my name was Thomas, and although I knew it was a boy's name, I was still hoping that somehow, it might also be a girl's name.

"Right now," she added.

I walked into the kitchen, climbed onto my chair, and pulled a plate of sandwiches towards me. I wasn't hungry.

"Mama," I said.

She didn't reply – she was busy beheading a loaf of bread with a carving knife. The bread was tough and the knife didn't want to go all the way through the bottom crust, so she finished the job by tearing off the head with a twist.

"Mama," I said, a little bit louder.

"What?"

"Can... can my name... can a boy's name sometimes be a girl's name too?"

Mother put down the knife and grabbed both sides of the table as if she was thinking of picking it up to throw at me.

"What have I told you about these stupid boy-girl questions?"

"It *could* be a girl's name."

She closed her eyes for a moment to gather her temper, and once composed, she picked up the knife again and pointed it at me. "I'm going to breech you next week – and that'll put an end to this nonsense."

I didn't know what 'breeched' meant, but as she turned away to continue with the cooking, I looked at the back of her head and mouthed the words, "I'm not a boy."

* * *

The following Monday, when Mother returned from a shopping trip to London, I found out what it meant to be breeched.

"Right then, dress off," she said, "and I'll cut your hair."

Like most girls and boys of my age, my hair was long – beyond my shoulders, and Mother trimmed the frayed ends every few weeks, but this time, instead of the usual short tufts, large curls cartwheeled over my shoulders to the floor.

"Mama, that's too much."

"Shush," she said, snapping my head back into position with her fingertips.

I tried to reach up to feel how short she was taking it, but she hit my hand away hard.

"If you touch it, I will cut your stupid fingers off."

I locked my fingers together on my tummy to protect them, closed my eyes tight, and hoped as hard as I could that the cartwheels were smaller than they looked.

"There," she said, throwing the scissors aside. "Now then, let's see how these fit."

I opened my eyes as she opened a shop-fresh box and pulled out a pair of brown, woollen breeches.

I stamped my foot hard. "No. I want my dress."

"You're nearly five, child, and that is the correct and proper age for boys to stop wearing dresses."

"But I'm not a boy."

"Yes you bloody-well are. Now, you'll put these breeches on this instant."

I stamped again and looked her square in the face.

"I will not."

"Well, you nasty, ungrateful little brat."

Her hands snapped at my ankles like twin cobras, and whipped my feet off the ground. I landed flat on my back and started to kick at her, but she dropped on top of me like a wrestler, put her hand over my mouth, and pinched my nose shut.

I couldn't breathe, so I stopped fighting.

She stuffed me hard into the breeches, one leg at a time. They were stiff, and made of sharp wool that scratched at my legs. Next came a matching jacket, followed by rough buttoning, and then she held me by the scruff of my collar in front of the mirror.

"You're a boy," she said, "and there's the proof of it."

I only glimpsed my reflection for a second, and it wasn't really sadness I felt, or fear – instead it was a true and absolute rage, and I twisted my body round to scream right into mother's face.

She pulled back her fist and I cringed for a moment like a tennis ball waiting for the serve, then she hit me so hard across the side of my head, that I was knocked clean off my feet.

I'm not exactly sure what happened next, except that my mouth was full of blood, and my head was being held under the kitchen tap as mother yelled at me to wake up.

* * *

Geronimo was my best and only friend, and I absolutely adored him. He was stretched out on the Persian rug in a mote-sparkled shaft of sunshine, dozing in and out of a late-summer lethargy, and I lay nose to nose with him in my horrible, scratchy, boy clothes.

5

"Geronimo," I whispered. "What's it like to be a cat?" He half-opened his eyes, then closed them again.

"Do you know that father brought you all the way from the Far East on a big ship? You might even be from Japan, just like the girl in the picture."

The picture was a colour print called 'The Stray Shuttlecock' which hung on the front-room wall. It depicted a Japanese girl in a silk kimono who had come to retrieve a shuttlecock from her mother's sitting room. The mother looked disapprovingly at her daughter, just as mine did, but hers also seemed affectionate.

The girl was so pretty, and I would wander into the picture for hours, imagining that I was her – a happy girl, playing in a land of exotic wonders.

"I think I might be wrong in the head, Geronimo – like a mad person."

I lifted his paw to my face and nestled the tip of my nose between his toes and pad. The touch began him purring quietly.

"I'm afraid to be mad. Great-uncle Pollard, who used to shout at ladies' hats was mad, and they took him away to Bedlam. I don't want to go there – Mother says it is 'hell on earth' and people scream there all day and all night."

I made a tiny side to side movement with my head to bury my nose deeper into his hot paw, and looked over once more at the Japanese girl.

"I have to be a boy, Geronimo, and I don't know how."

2

Singular

"I hear you upset your mother, young man," said the Reverend Thomas Thomas with his head on a disapproving tilt, as he stood with my mother in the front garden.

I did not look at him as he spoke, but I can tell you that he was just old enough for his untidy hair to be thin, that he was lean, with a pink and grey face, and that he had an oddly fat bottom lip that I always wanted to lean away from.

"Yes he did," replied Mother, disapproving at me from the same angle.

I tried to ignore the 'he' by turning my attention to an ant on a stick I was holding. I closed one eye and observed it from as close as the open one could focus.

"Well, there is no greater burden than a thankless child," said the vicar, in the conclusive tone with which he liked to imply that a great truth had finally been demonstrated, and more importantly, a great truth that he had held true all along, and that we lesser beings were only just catching on to.

"Quite so," said Mother. "And had he bled to death, as seemed to be his intention, I would have had a thankless, dead child. And then what? I mean what exactly is one to do with a dead child? Does one call the constable, the doctor, or your good self? I haven't the faintest notion." She paused for a moment. "And then there is the expense, of course. No, it really won't do."

I could just begin to perceive the astounding, microscopic details of the ant – its tiny joints and feelers, its tiny bristles, and tiniest of all, the claws by which it was clinging to the stick.

"Not that expense is an issue for a widow of independent means, you understand," she continued, "but even a modest annuity should not be misapplied."

The vicar looked me up and down as if he was hesitating over a low-quality purchase.

"What concerns me most," he said, "is that he doesn't know a boy from a girl. That's really most peculiar for a boy of his age. I mean is he... well... you know... effeminate?" His nostrils flexed, as if he could smell his own disgust.

"No," said Mother. "In fact he's rather boisterous."

"I see," he said, stroking his baggy lip. "Then perhaps he's merely a simpleton."

"Certainly not," said Mother. "I'm sure I hardly need remind you that his grandfather Pollard, his *maternal* grandfather, was the headmaster of the Threeway School in Marylebone, and I can absolutely assure you that there has never been a simpleton in my family – not a single one."

"Mrs Stanton, the devil does not defer to such niceties as breeding when he infests the mind of a child. And of course, there's also his father's part in him."

"His father wasn't a simpleton either."

"I do not suggest that he was, but whilst the boy has fine, educated stock on your side, his father was of a more reduced background, being a common sailor."

Mother paused for a moment, her expression hovering between pride and injury, as the vicar leant down and spoke to me rather loudly.

"Now, here's a thing, young Thomas, look – it's a pocket watch of the finest quality. Now see, I press this button and... what wonders, eh?"

The button released a door that revealed a tiny choreography of golden cogs.

"Goodness," I said, momentarily distracted by the sight.

"Yes indeed – the inner workings of a pocket watch may be so fine that you wonder if the good Lord himself didn't guide the hand of the watchmaker. Can you tell the time yet, young man?"

"Yes I can," I said.

"Can you indeed?"

"It's quite true," added Mother.

I turned his hand to see the watch face. "The time is five and twenty past four," I announced grandly. "And, if you break your watch, you must take it to Mr Parkin who is a horologist."

"Well now," said the vicar, "'horologist' is quite a word for a four-year-old."

"I'm four-and-a-half, and ants have even smaller bits than your watch. And I can say thank you in Japanese – arigato."

With that he closed the little door and turned to Mother. "Well, he certainly seems bright enough... if a little queer."

Mother looked smug for a moment. "There is no doubting that he's a bright one, and heaven only knows where he finds so many words." Then her expression deflated. "But he's not at all like other children. He's really quite... well... singular."

The Reverend looked down at me again. "Do you know what singular means, young fellow?"

"Yes indeed," I said. "It means that something is very special and excellent."

They looked at each other with some amusement.

"Well," said the vicar, "that's certainly one definition."

3

African Tigers and Blue Penises

I had a sister – Elizabeth. She was three years older than me, and almost as much of a tomboy.

"Keep up, you stupid child," she said, as we walked the mile to school on a freezing morning in the November of 1883. I was now thirteen.

"No, I won't," I said. "This is my speed and you can slow down if you don't like it."

"Well, you're a nasty, hateful..."

"...Little brat," I said, finishing her favourite sentence for her. I was far too old to be called a brat in my opinion, but our relationship had not progressed in any way at all since we were little, so nor had the language she liked to use against me.

We always parted at the school gates without speaking – her to the girls' door, which had the normal, rectangular shape that you expect of a door, and me to the boys', which was larger, but shaped like a grave stone.

The boys' master was Dr Palfrey. He was squat and slimy, with bulging eyes, a wet pout, and an absolute inability to complete his shave. The worst thing about him though, was the drone of his voice, and the only way to escape from hours upon hours listening to it, was to annoy him enough to get myself sent out of the room.

"Whilst the coast of Africa has been mapped in great detail," he said, as he circled the map with the tip of his cane, "and indeed, a notable portion of the interior," now a smaller circle within the coastline, "there is still a great expanse in the dark heart of Africa, of which we know very little," and now a sharp crack on the Congo with the cane tip. "This is a place of impenetrable forests and great dangers, where a man might be crushed by an enraged elephant, or eaten alive by a tiger."

I raised my hand.

"What is it now, Stanton?"

"Please, Sir, there are no tigers in Africa, Sir." There were sniggers from the class. "Tigers are from Asia, Sir." I always caught him out on geography.

His bulging eyes now seemed barely retained in his head. "Are they indeed, young Stanton? Well boys, it seems we have a great explorer in our midst. And you have visited the dark heart of Africa to verify that fact, have you, boy?"

"No," I said. "But nor have you."

Everyone laughed again.

"Get out, Stanton."

"To the library, Sir?"

"That's right. And I'm sure your vast geographical knowledge will take you there with the same expediency by which it will deliver you to my office after school.

* * *

The library was usually empty during lessons, but I didn't mind being alone, or at least I was used to it. And anyway, I never felt completely alone when I had books around me – I loved them, factual ones in the main – geography, history, the sciences, but of all the books in the library, the one I most wanted to read was locked in a glass cabinet with various other volumes deemed unsuitable for open shelves in a school. It was called Gray's Anatomy.

I had tried picking the lock of the cabinet, and I'd even brought a hair-clip into school for that very purpose once, but the lock was a good one and I couldn't defeat it.

On this day however, whilst rummaging through the drawers of the desk

11

that only the teachers were allowed to use, I found the key – it wasn't even hidden really, it was just rattling around in its own little drawer asking to be used.

Once in the glass cabinet, I pulled the book out and replaced it with a similar-looking volume from the open shelves so it wouldn't be missed. I then sat in the furthest corner of the room and stood the desk lid upright so I could hide behind it.

The book was absolutely fascinating – full of the most detailed anatomical drawings and descriptions of the human body, and in a few minutes of skimming I had learnt all kinds of new words – 'aorta', 'metatarsal', 'epidermis' and 'clavicle', but then I found the chapter on reproductive organs and discovered something absolutely astonishing:

Girls do not have penises.

They don't even have testicles.

"Of course," I whispered. "Of course we don't – I knew it."

* * *

"Here's your poor sister waiting for you again," moaned Palfrey as he led me out of his office after my evening caning. "You see it is not just I who am inconvenienced by your behaviour," he said, as he buried his fingers bruisingly into my shoulder, "but also your sister, and no doubt, your mother."

'Neither of whom have penises,' I thought.

He shook his head in faux despair. "I really don't know what to do with you, Thomas. You are not without ability, and with a small application of effort, I don't doubt that you could rise to the top of the class, but still you persist in this puerile misbehaviour."

I watched his wet mouth for the strange end-of-sentence 'ooh' shape it would always settle into, but I made no reply.

"Well, I hope you're prepared for a life of loneliness," he said, "for no self-respecting young lady will want to marry you." To my surprise, I now felt a knot tighten in my stomach, but I tried not to show it on my face.

"For my part," he continued, with a shrug in his voice, "I can only warn you that you are on the very edge of expulsion. I doubt you will heed my warning but there it is. Now, get along."

* * *

In April of the following year, when I had just turned fourteen, Palfrey's warning came true.

I was hiding in the boys' toilet at the far end of the school – the one that no one used during breaks. I wasn't hiding from anyone in particular, it was just one of those days when I didn't want anyone to look at me.

On the windowsill was a small pot of blue paint that a decorator had been foolish enough to leave behind, and there was a brush lying across the top.

I considered the possibilities for a moment and then, without really knowing why, I painted a large, erect, and anatomically-detailed penis above the urinals.

I labelled the various parts with the correct anatomical terms in a fine copperplate – *'The Glans', 'The Shaft', 'The Foreskin', 'The Urethra', 'The Scrotum'* and *'The Testicles'*. Then I stood back to look at the horrible thing. My next instinct was to make it vanish by throwing the rest of the paint over it, but I hesitated... something about it being there felt right, as if I had detached it from my own body and locked it away in a painted image – like a magic spell or something, so I just walked out of the room and left the penis behind.

Twenty minutes later I was back in the classroom, imagining how it would feel to be in a mended body in a world of magic, when there was a knock at the door.

The school caretaker entered, and whispered something to Palfrey whose frown deepened by the syllable.

"Continue with your work, boys. I will return presently," he said, and glanced at me as he followed the caretaker out.

He was sure to know it was me. I wasn't frightened though – it was more a feeling of excitement, for whatever happened now would at least not be boring.

Moments later came the distant *wump* of a slammed door, then distant footsteps, followed by another *WUMP* closer this time, and then vigorous, stamping footsteps up the corridor towards us.

The classroom door burst open with such violence that a pane of glass was broken as it swung back against the wall.

Palfrey stormed towards me, his eyes bulging ahead of him.

He grabbed me by the coat, pulled me right over my desk, and dragged me bodily out of the class.

A few moments later, I landed hard at the base of the steps at the school entrance.

"Get out of my sight, you ghastly, horrendous, little beast, and don't you ever, EVER, attempt to enter this school again."

4

Emmeline

"Thank you, Thomas," said Mother. "Thank you very much for wasting my pitiful annuity on your private education. To think I could have spent that money on the comfort of a maid instead of keeping an ungrateful child in a very expensive school."

She looked at me with a whiff of disgust, as if she could faintly smell the painted penis.

"Your grandfather would despair," she said, as she turned away to continue washing dishes – a task she was performing in the style of a Shakespearean tragedy. "I don't know what you think will happen to your sister and I, stuck here in this wretched place. Don't you think you might have at least made an effort to better our circumstances? And that's not to mention the reputation you have gained for us in the town."

She dried her hands roughly and threw the towel hard onto the draining board.

"It's Monday," she said. "Monday is my day, and I won't let you spoil it for me, so I am going to London to see your Aunt Pollard." And she said this all as if it wasn't what she did every Monday.

* * *

I was now alone in the house with no particular thing to do, so I flopped in

15

the sitting room for a while, pulling faces into empty space and inspecting my fingernails in fine detail. Then I bored Geronimo with a game of string, chewed a doorstep of bread, and drank two cups of tea.

After that, I stood at the mantelpiece, looking at the only photograph of me in the house. It had been taken a few weeks before, and it showed me standing in my Sunday best, looking like a very normal young man.

Clothes – was that all it took to make me look like a boy? My whole self made invisible merely by an arrangement of fabrics?

I shoved the picture behind a vase and began to pace, wandering from room to room with my hands in my pockets, making scuff rhythms with my feet as I went – I paced the kitchen, the hallway, the kitchen again, then I went upstairs and after pacing the landing three times, I stood in my sister's doorway and contemplated the annoying tidiness of her things.

Her clothes were in there.

I frowned a little, then walked in and sat on her bed in front of the wardrobe – my hands still in my pockets.

After a little more frowning, I levered open the wardrobe door with the toe of my shoe and looked at her clothes.

What a different world she lived in – a world where those were the things you had, where it was normal to have them – a world where you could show people who you are, just by what you wear.

I started to pull the clothes out one at a time.

If I could put them on, I thought, perhaps I could look like me again – someone I hadn't seen in the mirror since the day I was breeched, but there were so many different things – petticoats, bustles, fastenings, laces, and I was afraid that if I got the sequence wrong, I would look less like a girl, and more like a stupid boy who ran into a washing line.

No, I couldn't do it. I put the clothes back as I'd found them, kicked the wardrobe door shut, and stormed out of the room, back into my normal life. Yes – 'normal life' as a 'normal boy' – what on earth could be wrong with that?

And then I started to cry.

How weak I felt. How absolutely hopeless... And then I felt angry about

16

feeling hopeless, and then I felt furious about being angry, so I stormed right back into Elizabeth's room.

I don't know why my hands were trembling – all I was going to do was put on some clothes, nothing more – just get undressed, and then get dressed again. Well, the clothes didn't belong to me, it's true, but I was only borrowing them, not stealing, and I wasn't going to damage anything.

The sequence of layers wasn't so difficult to work out once I got started – undergarments, then stockings, then petticoats, and I fumbled my way through without too many problems until I got to the corset. What an extraordinarily complicated thing it was – more like architecture than clothing and with twice as many laces to pull than I expected. It took me full ten minutes to work out that you pull two sets of laces towards the middle, and not one set from the bottom to the top. When I finally got it on, it wasn't just that I could hardly breathe, but I could hardly do anything else either – every movement being made as stiff as the corset ribs.

Now for the dress, and there were several to choose from, but I liked Elizabeth's green walking dress, so that's the one I climbed into. It sat somewhat deflated at the chest of course, so I placed a pair of rolled-up stockings underneath to fill myself out. Then I put on her best boater, and after a short hesitation, I stepped in front of the mirror...

For a moment I was blank and couldn't quite take myself in, so I closed my eyes hard.

When I opened them again, I saw myself – me, a girl, a young woman.

A tsunami of emotion rose through my chest and I put both my hands over my mouth to stop it flooding out all at once, but my eyes filled with tears, and little sobs started to leak through my fingers. They were happy tears though – welcome-home sobs, and when I finally stopped crying, I looked at myself from every angle.

I should have a name, I thought, but how do you name someone? After a person you admire? Or an ancestor perhaps? No one sprang to mind.

"Clara?" I said out loud. "No, not quite. Louisa? Yes – I have always liked Louisa as a name. I like Emma a lot too though. Actually, I prefer it – it has a nice sound to it, but... but there are so many Emmas in the world.

Perhaps Emily? No, better still, Emmeline – yes, Emmeline is the singular version of Emma." I looked myself up and down. "And it suits me – yes, I think I look like an Emmeline."

I walked up and down the room once or twice and tried sitting on the bed in a ladylike manner, but it felt somewhat forced, as if I were pretending to be a rather more delicate sort of a girl than I actually was. Then again, if I did not naturally have a ladylike manner, was that to imply that I really was a boy after all?

I did not want to think about that right now, I only wanted to… well, I didn't know what to do exactly, I only knew that I did not want to put the boy clothes back on. It was simply nicer being a girl, even despite the corset. And it was more than that – there was something deeper, something more profound, because for the first time in so many years, I felt like… like I was actually alive.

"Brown?" said Geronimo, as he appeared at the door. This was his friendly greeting and 'brown?' is the nearest I can come to describing the sound with its little rolled 'r' and its questioning intonation. I'm sure his catty mind had no opinion at all on my clothes, but I was now a girl in front of someone else and I froze for a moment.

He hopped onto the bed and flopped on his side. This was the position through which he expressed boredom, so I relaxed, dragged him on to my lap and made a big fuss of him. It was wonderful to do something so normal – an everyday act in the everyday life of a young woman – my life.

* * *

After two hours of quiet happiness, it was getting late and the risk of discovery had become too great so I was forced to return to my masculine disguise, but for the rest of the week I could think of nothing but the next Monday when Mother would go to London again, and all the other Mondays that would follow it, and every one of those Mondays found Emmeline looking back at me from my sister's mirror.

As the weeks went by I grew bolder and began to formulate a plan by which I might actually venture into the outside world as myself. It would certainly be dangerous, and it wouldn't do just to walk out of the house in Elizabeth's clothes because I might be recognised by the neighbours, so I needed to take the clothes somewhere else to change – some sort of hiding place where I could dress unseen, and be safe from discovery.

I began to scout for suitable locations and within a few days, I found an old house on Eastern Avenue, perhaps a mile from home, that was uninhabited and quite derelict. It was ideal in that it had a means of entry at the front, but also an exit at the back onto Parkers Lane, which meant that I would be able to enter as male from one road, and exit female into the other.

That following Monday, with Elizabeth's clothes in my carpet bag, I set my plan in motion.

I managed to get into the property easily, and once inside, the only trouble I had was putting on the clothes in the dusty room without getting them dirty.

Once dressed, I stood at the rear door, poised to go out, but quite terrified – it was one thing to think myself a passable woman in the safety of a bedroom mirror, but quite another to test her believability amongst the general public. I mean, what if I'm recognised? Or what if I'm attacked for daring to wear a dress in public? What if I'm arrested and taken to prison, or even to Bedlam?

I hesitated for perhaps twenty minutes, then I took the deepest breath that my corset would allow, and stepped into the world.

The first passer-by was a middle-aged man. I approached him, sick with fear, but he walked right by me without even a glance. I felt an immediate relief, but then also a disappointment because if he did not look at me, I couldn't know for sure if he saw me as a woman.

I did not have long to wait for another gentleman and this one did see me. Not only did he see me, but he smiled as he passed. My first impulse was that he had discovered me straight away, and that he had only smiled because he thought me such a funny sight. I looked around, fully expecting to see him standing there with his hands on his hips, laughing, but he was walking on, quite unconcerned.

At last I began to relax and soon passed several more people, none of whom betrayed any hint of suspicion – they only saw me – Emmeline – I was actually visible to other people and it was indescribably wonderful.

After only about half an hour, it was time to return to my dressing room, but the world was now fat with possibilities, and I already knew what my next adventure was going to be.

5

Strawberry Cake and a Dusty Hammer

The very next Monday, Elizabeth had a day off school so Mother decided to go to Brighton instead of London, and to take Elizabeth with her. They would be out at nine, and return at seven.

Elizabeth wore a blue summer dress, leaving my favourite green one behind, so as soon as they had gone, I was straight to her wardrobe, and then to my dusty dressing room in Eastern Avenue.

Once through the magic portal and into the real world, I walked directly to the train station – I was going to London for the day – a whole day of being me amongst the millions.

* * *

Harewell station was busy, and I approached the throng in a tangle of fear.

As I joined the queue, the lady in front of me turned and said, "Have you ever seen the like? Three windows and only one cashier, and people almost queuing out of the door. It really won't do."

"No, indeed," I replied, and that's how Emmeline spoke her first words in public.

The woman all but ignored my answer and attended to the little girl beside her, but I was glad of her indifference, because indifference was normality.

When I finally made it to the window, the cashier addressed me as 'miss' and I smiled at him.

"A day-return to Victoria please," I said, and he gave me my ticket and my change with a tiny hint of a wink.

* * *

As the train clunked out of the station, all my anxieties turned to excitement. I watched the suburban landscape steam past me, oblivious to its dreary greys, and only sensible to flashes of colour – crimson letterboxes, the blink of a yellow dress, a vase of flowers that burst gaudy and happy through a dirty window, and all I could think was how exquisitely beautiful the world is when your eyes are open to its wonders.

In no time at all, we arrived at Victoria station. I rushed through the concourse as if it were the wings of a theatre, and out into the raucous cacophony of London.

The throng was stupendous, and I wanted to throw my arms open to embrace it – brougham carriages, hansom cabs, omnibuses – dozens of them lined up in great rows outside the station, and at the same time, dozens more fought their way in and out, in a clattering argument of hooves and wheels, whilst fearless pedestrians picked their way through the melee.

The sound was immense, not only because of the traffic, but every voice was raised:

"Three a penny, Yarmouth Bloaters," shouts one man, "Here's ha'p'orths," answers a wandering confectioner, "Standard," another, and between them, shrill snippets of conversation like, "I'll wager five pounds that you're wrong." or, "Come along do, Edward."

And the city smelt wonderful – of smoke and horses and manure, fried fish, perfume and dirty hair. Indeed it was as great an assault upon the nose as it was upon the eyes and ears combined.

I did all of the following things in London: I stood outside Buckingham Palace and wondered if the Queen was at home; I sat on a bench in St. James' Park and watched a boy chase squirrels with a stick; I walked up to the doorway of a fancy hotel as if I were a guest, only to turn away at the last moment with a smile for the doorman, and when I reached Piccadilly, I went into a teashop called 'The Stanhope' and had a cup of tea with an outrageous slice of strawberry cake.

And I spoke to people too – anyone that I could find reason to: I discussed the weather with an elderly lady as I helped her cross to the Burlington Arcade; I asked at the tea counter in Fortnum and Mason about the difference between Darjeeling and Assam; I enquired after a policeman for directions that I already knew, and I tapped a complete stranger on the shoulder just so that I could apologise for having mistaken her for someone else.

I soon began to notice two distinct differences between the way that people normally acted towards me as a boy, and the way they were now acting towards me as a woman – one negative, and the other positive.

The negative was that people were less inclined to give a woman space on the pavement, so I continually needed to step out into the road as I walked, and it was both men, and other women who blocked my way.

The positive, paradoxically, was that people are friendlier to women – I was often smiled at, doors were held for me, and other women would talk to me quite freely. I couldn't remember a single instance in my life as a boy in which a lady I didn't know voluntarily discussed anything at all with me.

But then there came a third difference that I began to notice in my inter-actions with men, which was that they can be extraordinarily patronising. Sometimes this worked to my advantage – for example, in Fortnum and Mason the man at the tea counter was at great pains to explain the intricacies of tea fermentation in slow detail. This was all very interesting to me, for it was a subject I knew little about. On the other hand, I found it distinctly irritating when he would not let me smell the lapsang souchong for fear that it was "too potent for the delicate sensibilities of a young lady."

* * *

After two breathless hours, I reached the far end of Piccadilly and there I came upon the premises of Mr Robert Brinkley, Photographer.

I entered without hesitation, and a thin and tidy young man greeted me.

"Good afternoon, Miss. Have you come to have your likeness taken, or to pick up your photographs?"

"To have it taken," I said.

"I thought so," he replied with a glint. "I'm quite sure I would have remembered, had you had been here before."

I smiled – it was a pleasant surprise to be flattered in this way, but it was also quite funny to imagine how he would react if I told him my little secret.

"May I take your name, Miss?"

"Emmeline Stanton," I said, and it sounded quite wonderful out loud.

"Here is a list of our prices, Miss Stanton. You will find us very competitive. Do please take a seat and Mr Brinkley will be with you presently."

"Thank you," I said, and I took the price list to the seating area.

A few minutes later, the front door opened and a young woman entered.

I could not see her face from my position, but she was wearing what I took to be a very expensive walking dress in a muted rose colour. The dress was very muddy about the hem – much more so than happens from walking along the street, and she was carrying two quite large and heavy bags.

"Ah, Miss Bright. And a very good afternoon to you," said the young man with a slight bow as she approached the counter. "I finished framing your photographs not ten minutes ago. Could I trouble you to take a seat for a moment whilst I wrap them?"

"Oh, yes, thank you," she said, almost apologetically. "I am a little early, so please don't inconvenience yourself."

Her voice had a creamy music to it, and none of the presumption you might expect of such an expensive dress.

As she took the seat opposite, she glanced at me, and the moment I saw her face clearly, I think I just about fell in love. It was quite the most complicatedly delicious face, and I'm not sure how to begin my description:

She was mostly eyes – enormous, wet discs of dark hazel, and you could see her sparkling behind them as if you were watching fireworks through sunglasses. She also had a little pout with her top lip slightly ahead of the bottom one, as you might see in someone who is trying not to cry. And yet, at the same time, her expression was gay and bright and quietly mischievous.

In truth, I could not call her beautiful by any conventional notions of beauty, but for me, she had the loveliest face that I think I had ever seen.

She set her two bags in front of her, one of which clunked as it hit the floor. "Excuse me," she whispered, almost to herself as she opened one of them and pulled out a small book. She placed the book on the seat beside her, but then, from the same bag, and to my astonishment, she lifted out a large dusty hammer. This extraordinary object, she then placed in the other bag before lifting both to test the balance of them.

Satisfied, she sat back down, and took up her book.

I was worried that she might notice me staring so I looked to the side. There was nothing in particular to see to the side, so I frowned thoughtfully at the skirting board to imply that I'd seen a skirting-board anomaly of some kind, but that seemed a bit strange, so I deepened the frown a little to make it look like I was having deep and complicated thoughts that had nothing to do with skirting boards.

Then, out of the corner of my eye, I saw her hold the book to one side for a moment to look me up and down.

"Here, they are, Miss Bright, a very nice set, I must say."

She jumped in her seat as the young assistant placed her package on the counter, then she glanced at me.

"Excuse me," she whispered, then made a little embarrassed cough as she rose to collect her goods.

At that same moment, the door to the studio opened and in burst a quick, tubby man who was all exuberance and bushy mutton-chops.

"Miss... Percival isn't it?" said the man.

"Miss Bright," said Miss Bright.

"Of course it is, and a very nice set we've made for you I think." He then looked at me expectantly and I was announced by the assistant:

"Miss Stanton, Mr Brinkley."

"Miss Stanton, I am charmed. Please, do come through." He held the door for me and bid farewell to Miss Bright.

I stole a final glance at her as I left, and in return she gave me a little smile. I held that smile, along with my breath, as I followed Mr Brinkley down the corridor to the studio.

* * *

It was a surprisingly large room. The roof had been converted to glass along one half and the camera sat on its tripod in the centre. At the end hung a large painted backdrop of an idyllic country scene. Many props were scattered about the room – palm trees, Greek pillars, park benches, a giant Chinese vase etc.

"A simple portrait is it, Miss Staunton?"

"Stanton, but Yes," I said.

"Of course it is – I do apologise. Now then," he said, stroking his chin theatrically and looking about at his props. "Where on Earth would you like to be? I can do you the English idyll, as you see here, but also Ancient Greece, Ancient Rome, Cairo, with the pyramids included, or even Darkest Africa – complete with tiger." He indicated an ancient and exhausted stuffed tiger in the corner of the room and I laughed aloud. He took no offence and laughed with me.

"I should love to have something oriental. Can you possibly do Japan?"

"Why certainly – I have the very thing."

He wrestled with the English idyll, displacing it from a hook and rolling it up. Then he went to a large stack of rolled backdrops, and with a great commotion hung another up for me.

"Miss Stanton, The gardens of Nijo Castle in Kyoto, as depicted by an artist who has seen them with his very own eyes. Will that do?"

"It will do very well indeed," I said.

As I took up my position, I wondered what scene Miss Bright had chosen, and then I thought how much I would love to have one of her pictures to take home with me.

"Might I suggest a more sombre expression perhaps, Miss Stanton? To give the portrait its due gravity."

"I am afraid I cannot, Mr Brinkley – you have me on the happiest day of my life and I do not think I can muster a sombre expression."

"Ah, young love is it?"

My smile enlarged a little, partly because it was a little bit true after seeing Miss Bright, and partly because he could have no idea just how singular his sitter was. "Amongst other things perhaps," I said, before adding, "But you really oughtn't to ask such questions."

He gave a playful smile with a little bow of apology. "Quite right, Miss Stanton, quite right. And given present unmentionable circumstances," he winked, "I shall gladly break with tradition and capture you with a happy countenance."

And so my portrait was taken.

* * *

The photograph would not be ready until the next day, but I paid in advance with the last of my money, and the assistant said I could return for it whenever it was convenient.

"Thank you," I said, and hovered for moment… "Um… may I ask a question?"

"Certainly, Miss Stanton."

"The lady who was here to pick up her photographs… in the rose dress."

"Ah yes, Miss Bright. She's quite famous you know. She…" The front door opened just as he was finishing his sentence. "Ah, Mr Percival, do come in," he continued. "Would you excuse me, Miss?"

"Oh, certainly," I said.

And so I left, knowing only her surname, that she was quite famous, that she carried a big, dusty hammer in her bag, and that she had the loveliest face I had ever seen.

6

Deuteronomy

After three perfect hours in London I had to return to Harewell to allow enough time to get changed before Mother and Elizabeth got home. We had to change trains at Otford and that meant a twenty minute wait, so I decided to walk into the village as a happy little extension to a day which had finished too soon.

The village itself was pretty, with a big pond in the middle. I stood by the pond in the sweet, country-summer breeze, as ducks splintered the sunshine on the water, and dandelion seeds floated past me like sleepy fairies.

A man was sweeping the pavement nearby. I glanced at him and smiled politely. He was a butcher – I could tell from his apron. He took my smile as an excuse to stop pushing his broom and to lean upon it instead.

We watched the scene together in silence for a moment, then he said, "Not such a bad life on a day like this, don't you think, Miss?"

"Yes," I said. "It's quite perfect."

I'm not sure how long we stood there, perhaps only a minute or two, but I remember thinking what a precious thing it is to exist, and to have another human being know it.

* * *

I was back at the station in plenty of time for my train, but just as we were about to pull out, there was a loud metallic clunk and the train stopped dead.

I couldn't afford a delay.

After ten long minutes, the conductor came through the carriage.

"Bit of a problem with the engine, I'm afraid," he said. "But the driver has promised we should be on our way in another ten minutes or so."

A full thirty minutes passed before we finally tugged out of the station, and that put me well behind schedule, but if there were no more delays, I was sure I could still make it home before Mother and Elizabeth.

As we finally pulled into Harewell, I jumped off the train before it had stopped moving, and ran as fast as I could to the derelict house in Eastern Avenue.

As soon as I was in, I grabbed my carpet bag with my boy clothes in it and...

"Up here, Angus," shouted a man from upstairs, after hearing my commotion. "They want us to start with the front bedroom. You better bring the crowbars up."

I didn't move.

"Angus?"

There was a pause, and then footsteps.

I burst out of the house like a startled deer, and took off down the road with my carpet bag in my arms.

There was no time to find anywhere else to change, but I was fairly sure I could still beat Mother and Elizabeth home if I ran all the way.

I must have looked like I'd robbed someone as I entered our street – running with my head tucked into my neck to hide my face, but by my calculations, I had made it with ten minutes to spare.

After sprinting up the garden path, I all but fell into the house...

...and froze.

There they were – Mother, Elizabeth, and to add an extra dimension of discomfort, the Reverend Thomas Thomas himself.

They all froze too, and we stood there in an icy photograph of mutual horror until Elizabeth broke the silence.

"Mama, those are my best clothes. He will ruin them."

Mother looked away from me, sat gently down in the armchair before the fire, and stared into the flames with no facial expression at all. The vicar looked at her with exaggerated concern, then put his hands on his hips and glared at me.

"What on earth do you think you are doing, young man?" He puffed his chest up a little and took a step towards me, pushing his bottom lip ahead of him as if he meant to fight me. "Well?"

"You wouldn't understand," I said, holding my ground.

"There is nothing to understand but that you are a degenerate," he said, his voice considerably raised. Then he pointed a shaking finger at my still deflated mother. "Because, not content to shame your poor mother and sister with your disgusting, perverted vandalism of the school, you now bring wanton perversity into their very home."

"I am neither perverse nor degenerate," I said, raising my voice to match his. "I am singular, and far more complicated than the likes of you could ever understand."

"The likes of me, you say? Then would you argue with God?" He leant close enough that I could catch his spit in my face, "Deuteronomy, chapter twenty two, verse six: *A woman shall not wear that which pertaineth to a man and neither shall a man put on women's garments, for all that do so...*"

I stepped even closer and cut him off sharply with the completion of the line, "...*for all that do so are an abomination unto the lord thy God.* And I think you will find that it is verse five, not six."

He backed off slightly by leaning away from me, but I moved into the space he created so he stepped right back to the fireplace, shaking his head as he went.

"And I am not a boy," I said. "I know I am not a boy, so the verse does not apply."

The vicar looked to Mother, still shaking his head. "He is quite mad, he really is quite mad."

There was an uncertain quiet for a moment, at the end of which Mother rose from her chair, and stood before me.

Her expression was still blank.

She looked into my eyes very calmly, but with a faint squint, as if she were pondering a stranger in the distance. Then she raised her fist and hit me across the side of my head as hard as she could.

I stumbled, deafened in one ear, and bleeding from a bitten tongue.

"Get them off," she growled, and I ran from the room holding my face and crying.

* * *

The explosion of that Monday evening settled as an inert, grey dust over my life, and rendered all emotion muted and flat. For several days, Mother and Elizabeth would neither speak to me nor look at me, and I sensed that they would not reply if I spoke, so I lived silently and alone with them.

I lost all sense of time and routine in this grey landscape – I would fall asleep at strange times, sometimes waking in the middle of the night on the sofa, and sometimes in the middle of the day on my bed.

I was not completely alone though – Geronimo took great advantage of a warm body to sleep on at unusual times, and I would often wake with him curled against my back, or draped over me like a stole.

After perhaps a fortnight of isolation, I noticed several visits from a telegram boy, and then, quite suddenly, Mother spoke to me:

"Go and pack your things, you are going to your Uncle Walter in Naples."

I tried to speak, but could only find a whisper: "When?"

"A cab will come for you at five tomorrow morning. Your tickets and itinerary are in here." She handed me an envelope, and without looking at me, she left the room.

31

II

My Own Flesh and Blood

7

You Have Only Yourself to Blame

On the morning of my departure, I sat on the sofa clutching my carpet bag with both hands, trying not to tremble. Geronimo was out somewhere, and Mother was in bed, but Elizabeth had gotten up at four o'clock to prepare some food for my journey.

I did not know whether she was acting upon Mother's orders, or upon some small remnant of sisterly affection, but I did know that I was extremely glad of her presence.

"You have only yourself to blame, Thomas," she said, "but perhaps Naples will be a new start. And you certainly won't inconvenience Uncle Walter in the way you have Mother and I – he simply won't tolerate it." She paused to give me a glance of warning through the kitchen doorway. "He's not a tolerant man, Thomas, and he will have very strict expectations of you." Then she returned to preparing the food.

"He's only one step below an ambassador, you know," she added after a minute or two. "He might even be an ambassador for all I know, and if you apply yourself you might end up with a position at the Foreign Office."

"I don't want a position at the Foreign Office."

She shook her head. "It's your life, Thomas – throw it away if you want to, but you will soon be a man, and will have to make your own way in the world. It would be as well to enter manhood at an advantage."

She wasn't looking at me, and I mouthed the words, 'I will never be a man

- I will die first.'

There was a knock at the front door. My heart thumped in my chest like an echo of the knock, and cracked open a great hollow of butterflies.

Elizabeth walked over to me with the bag of food. "That'll be your cab, Thomas – here's something to eat along the way. Now then, don't dally, pick up your carpet bag, and resolve to better yourself."

I stood up but my legs could hardly bear it.

"Well, goodbye, Elizabeth." I said, extending my hand. "And I'm sorry about your clothes."

"Goodbye," she said, without touching me.

Never before had I felt a desire to embrace my sister. She was my last familiarity, my last moment of home – I wanted to climb into her arms and hide there, deep and warm in some safe little corner of a childhood I'd never really had, but there was no embrace, and the next I knew, I was floating in a daze along the garden path towards the cab, numb to the normal sensation of my footsteps as if the path were made of cushions.

As we made our way towards the train station, I watched all the world I knew float into the past, and I cried about it, silently – no sobs, no grimace, a sort of a cold cry, but with an ocean of hot tears pouring out of it.

* * *

By noon, I was on the steamer from Dover to Calais, standing alone at the stern of the ship, clinging to the handrail with all my might as if trying to stop myself falling backwards into the rest of my life.

Everything was changing so fast – my home, my family, even the food on my plate would be different now, but all those uncertainties were drowned into insignificance by the sound of Elizabeth telling me that soon I would be a man. Of all the changes in front of me, the one I feared most was puberty. I had feared it for a long time now, but had buried that fear deep in the back of my mind in the same place you keep the knowledge that one day you are going to die, but now it had been drawn fully into the open by the gravity of so many other changes, and it cast its shadow over all of them. Even in the next few days my voice might break and be ruined; even in the next few weeks I might see beard hairs crawling down my cheeks. And if not in the next few weeks, then soon – very soon, and that will be the end of me, trapped in someone else's life for as long as I can bear to live it.

* * *

By eight that evening I was at the Gare du Nord station in Paris looking for the platform for my night train to Turin. I had forty minutes to spare, but after studying the departure notices for some time, I could see no reference at all to my train.

Maybe there is no train, I thought – maybe I am homeless now, and in a foreign country – maybe that was Mother's plan – to dump me far from home in a place where I might just starve to death.

On the edge of panic, I asked a porter in English for directions, but his reply was completely unintelligible. Another man replied in German, and another in what sounded like Italian, but then I saw a woman selling a paper of some kind called La Citoyenne. I noticed her because she wasn't the usual type who sells papers, in fact she looked rather well-to-do, and that made me think that she might speak some English. Or maybe it was just that I wanted my mother, and she looked a little bit like her.

"Excuse me, Miss," I said, trying to look like I wasn't crying, "Do you know what platform I need for the 8:40 to Turin?"

"Typical man," she said.

I couldn't quite take her reply in, so I pretended I had misheard and tried again: "The 8:40 to Turin, Can you help me?"

"Why should I?" She looked directly into my eyes, daring me to argue with her.

"I need to catch a train you see… to Turin, but I…" She continued to glare. "I'm only fourteen," I said, in desperation.

"So in seven years you can vote."

"Vote?"

"Yes, vote – you will have the right to vote."

She's one of those suffragists, I thought – a woman who wants equal rights for women. I had heard of them, but never met one before.

"I have no objection to women voting – none at all." I glanced at the station clock. "Do you know my platform, Miss? I really need to know."

"Typical man – you want me to speak when it is convenient for you, but otherwise I should remain silent?"

"No, I told you, I have no objection to women voting at all… or… or doing anything you want to – I really don't."

"Buy La Cityoenne, and perhaps I will believe you." She held out a paper.

I looked at the clock again, then back to her defiant face and felt immediately angry. Twice she had called me a typical man, and now she wanted money from me – money that I could not spare, and for a paper in a language that I couldn't even read. I wanted to argue back at her, but there was no time, so I turned away and tried to find someone else to help me.

"Excuse me, Sir, do you?…" He ignored me. "Parlez Anglais, Madame?" She shook her head and pushed past. "Sir, I wonder if you can…" Another rebuttal.

"Hey, English boy." It was the suffragist again. I looked round. Her face had taken on a sort of disparaging pity. "You are in the wrong station," she said. "You need the Gare de L'est." She pointed to the station entrance. "Go out through the front, turn left, then right and down the stairs – it's a ten-minute walk."

"Thank you," I said, trying to express the full depth of my gratitude with my eyes before running for the station entrance.

* * *

The night train was horrible – a hard, wooden bench in a bumpy carriage. I did sleep intermittently, but kept having the same nightmare in which I was paralysed, and being carted away in a dustbin full of black hairs.

When dawn finally arrived, it brought Miss Bright to mind, and my mood lifted a little. I imagined a compartment for two – we had the curtains open, and were watching the sun rise over an exotic landscape.

Well, she had smiled at me at the photographic studio, which meant that she liked me, and surely, the people that you like are just the sort you travel with. We could be on the grand tour perhaps, two ladies on an adventure, and then I imagined a kiss, and I smiled and frowned about it at the same time.

I kept Miss Bright with me all the rest of that day – we shared my packed lunch, we discussed everything from the geology of the Alps, to the various species of wood that the carriage was made from, and that second night, I leaned my carpet bag against me, and imagined it was her.

This time I didn't have nightmares, but I woke up once in the small hours frowning about that kiss again, and trying to decide whether it was the strangeness of two women kissing that made me frown, or the knowledge that no woman would ever kiss me unless she thought me a man. In which case I would probably never find out what it's like to be kissed.

8

Napoli

Two days later, at dawn, I finally reached Naples, but despite the morning sun, the station was dark and forbidding – full of lurking men and unpleasant smells, and as there was no-one to meet me, I kept my head down and walked through quickly.

I had an address to follow so I exchanged my English money for lire at the station entrance and hailed a cab.

"Via Dei Tribunali," I demanded authoritatively, in a rather ludicrous attempt to give the impression of a self-assured Englishman with whom it would be unwise to trifle.

The cab lurched away and was soon into the most appalling mêlée of traffic that I had ever experienced. I clung to the side for my life.

"Deutsch?" shouted the cabbie over the din.

"English," I shouted back.

"Welcome to Napoli."

"Thank you," I said. "Is the traffic always like this?"

"Of course, very very busy. You like?"

"Not really."

"Then you must learn to like, or Napoli will make you crazy."

We travelled on for about 10 minutes then jerked to a stop.

"Via Dei Tribunali start here."

I climbed down and paid him.

"My English very good, yes?"

"Yes," I said.

"You should hear my French," he exclaimed, and with an "Au revoir" he cracked his whip and broke once more into the throng like a charioteer into battle.

* * *

Via Dei Tribunali was a raucous hazard of filth and noise. At road level was a theatre of shops, food stalls and costermongers, as busy as Oxford Street at Christmas, and yet so narrow in places as to barely let two small cabs pass each other.

The buildings on either side were shabby, tall, and painted in faded washes of terracotta and yellow ochre. They seemed to lean inwards under the weight of the thousand washing lines that hung between them. Ironwork balconies overlooked the hubbub, and people chatted from one to the other whilst attending their washing, or sat in quiet contemplation of the confusion below.

Some sections of the street stank of rotten cabbage and rotten fish, but then you would reach another section that was hazy with the most exquisite smells of cooking – of fresh herbs, fried onions, steaming shellfish and baked bread. My stomach was exhausted by the continuous fluctuation between temptation and revulsion.

I must have walked half a mile or so before I found Uncle Walter's house. It looked rather more modest than I had expected, being just another in the line of tatty buildings that ran the length of the street.

Sitting outside it was an absolutely destitute woman – boot-black with dirt, and holding up an emaciated baby to passers-by. I had seen the destitute in England, of course, but how unutterably desperate seemed these two discarded rags of humanity.

I looked at the limp child and its hopeless exhaustion, and I felt a kind of shock. I am not sure why I felt it – perhaps recent events had left my emotions at a higher pitch than normal, but I wondered how I had the audacity to bemoan my life at all when this tiny child seemed to have no chance of one.

I took the remaining lire out of my pocket and held it out to the woman with the warmest smile I could conjure. She put the child gently in her lap, took the money from my hand and stuffed it into her bodice. Then she reached towards me with both hands.

I thought that she was asking for more money and I turned my pockets out to show her that I had none, but she shook her head and indicated that she wanted my hand. I held it out and she took it in both of hers, placed it very gently against her cheek, and smiled the most profound 'thank you' right into me.

It was the first time in several days that I had felt my existence worth anything at all.

* * *

I took a deep breath before ringing Uncle Walter's bell, and I took a few more deep breaths before the door was opened by a middle-aged maid with a tight, stony face.

"Thomas Stanton?" she asked with a broad Italian accent.

"Yes," I said.

"Benvenuto. Enter please."

We walked up several flights of stairs with each landing seeming to belong to a different residence.

"Does Uncle Walter own the whole building?" I asked.

"No, he rent the top floor."

It was chilly and damp inside the apartment – tiled floors and tall ceilings. It was also sparse and the decoration tired – not quite the residence of an ambassador, nor even of someone 'one step below an ambassador' as Elizabeth had described him.

The maid took me to a door, and behind it I could hear two men talking. She knocked and an Englishman's voice said, "Enter."

"Il ragazzo, Signor Pollard," she announced.

"Thomas," exclaimed Uncle Walter, beckoning me in with one hand and holding a glass of whisky in the other. "Splendid fellow, do come in."

I entered.

"This is my nephew, Thomas Stanton, Signor Grimaldi. He will be stopping with us for the present, and we are very much looking forward to having him."

"Benvenuto a Napoli, young man," said Mr Grimaldi, who was a fat, tidy businessman with thickly curled hair.

"Thank you, Sir."

He looked at my uncle. "Shall we say midday at Gambrinus then? We can finalise matters there."

"Splendid," said Uncle, gaily patting Mr Grimaldi on the back as he left, and adding, "Don't forget your wallet, eh?"

With Grimaldi gone, Uncle put his drink down and looked me over from top to tail with his hands on his hips and a big open smile which I returned.

He was perhaps forty-five, not tall, but very broad and sturdy, like a rugby player in a suit. His nose was bent somewhat to the right but his smile favoured the other side a little more, making a balance between the two features. He certainly had the Pollard family look about him, but I fancied he had kinder eyes than any of my other relatives.

"What do you make of him, Maria?"

"He look a fine boy, Signore," replied Maria.

"Thank you, Maria – that'll be all," he said, and she exited quickly, closing the door behind her.

He looked me up and down a few more times with a twinkle, then he stepped forwards.

I thought he was about to shake my hand, but he made a sudden rush and punched both fists sharp into my chest, grabbed my lapels, and stumbled me backwards across the room until my head cracked so hard against the wall that a rush of pins and needles fizzed through my limbs.

He pushed his face right into mine, compressing my head against the wall with his forehead, and squashing my nose flat with his.

"Do I have your attention, Thomas?" His voice was very still, his eyes

43

now utterly dead.

"Yes, Uncle."

"Good," he whispered, and he clamped me there silently for what felt like ever.

"You stole from your own sister."

"I, I only borro…"

"I despise a thief."

His breath was so close that I could not only smell the whisky, but could taste the eggs he had eaten for breakfast.

"Would you like to know what I despise even more than thieves?"

"Yes, Uncle."

"Inverts – filthy, disgusting, little inverts like you. And I promise you this, my filthy monster – if I ever catch you dressed as a woman, trying to seduce me, trying to coax me into your grotesque desires, I will fuck you, and then I will kill you. Do I make myself clear?"

"Yes, Uncle."

"This is Naples, boy, life is cheap here."

"Yes, Uncle."

There was another dreadful, dead-eyed pause, and then, quite suddenly, he released me.

"Splendid," he said, reverting so quickly to jovial affability that I had to rely on the pain in my chest and head to confirm that I had not imagined the last few moments.

"And how was your journey?"

"F… fine," I said. "We had a delay coming into Naples but… but apart from that it was very… fine."

"Ah, yes – we are rather plagued by landslips on that line. Anyway, I'm a busy man, Thomas, and I doubt our paths will cross a great deal, but there is a good education for you here, and if you play your cards right, you might even progress to a position at the foreign office."

"That would be wonderful, Uncle."

"Splendid, splendid. Maria." The door opened – she had been just outside. "I'm to the office, Maria. Deal with Thomas, please."

"Si, Signor Pollard."

And without further interaction, he left the room.

* * *

My room was dismal – damp air, brown walls, thin mattress, no pictures, no lock on the door, and that night, despite the exhaustion of travelling for three days, I lay awake into the small hours.

Only three weeks ago, I had spent the happiest day of my life, wandering through Piccadilly as my true self, and now, in so short a space of time, I found myself trapped in a pit that I must share with an appalling monster who can't decide between fucking me and killing me, and all the time waiting for puberty to crawl over my body like a black mould.

9

A horn-shaped charm

I was to be educated within the apartment rather than at a local school, and Signora Mazzotti was my appointed tutor. She always wore black and an irritated frown, and would elbow into my room every weekday morning, smelling of coffee and street air.

She was polite, if sternly so, and made no small talk. She would mark my work quickly, and with little tuts as if it was full of mistakes, but it wasn't, and sometimes I wondered if perhaps that was why she was tutting. Once the marking was done, she would take out more books from a bag, and issue brief directions:

"You copy this – page ten to thirty-two. You read this, all of it – you do all sums in chapter four, five and six of this. All instructions are written here, you understand?"

"Si, Signora."

And then off she would hurry in pursuit of some other irritation.

The work was easy, but I applied myself to it meticulously because it gave me a sort of escape – a little bit of every day in which I could forget my troubles, or at least talk over them in my head.

When I ran out of school work, I distracted myself with the two books I had brought with me from England – the copy of Gray's Anatomy which I had stolen from the school library, and a sort of encyclopaedia called Enquire Within Upon Everything which contained everything from the recipe for curried oysters, to the best method for changing the water in which leeches are kept.

When I wasn't distracting myself with studying or reading, I would often pace about the apartment, wandering barefoot on the cold tiles, from one dim room to the next, sometimes for hours on end. And I talked to myself a lot whilst pacing – partly to reassure myself that my voice had not broken yet, but also to argue aloud with Mother and Elizabeth – trying to persuade them to let me home.

During one of my walks, I heard a crash – ceramic, like a fallen vase, and then the sound of a chair going over, so I sneaked along the corridor, towards the noise.

"Bloody thing, let me kill it, let me kill it."

I glimpsed Uncle Walter through a slightly open door, his back to me, stamping repeatedly on a little grey bag of feathers and blood. I stood back and to one side to avoid being seen while I listened.

"I say, steady on, Pollard, it's only a pigeon," said another English voice.

"And now it's a dead pigeon."

"But really, you might have simply let it back out of the window."

"I cannot abide birds, Pearson – filthy verminous little beasts. And by the way, you may consider my feelings for, and intentions towards Signor Grimaldi similarly."

"Marseilles is an awfully big place, Pollard – even an idiot could hide in it, and Grimaldi is no idiot."

"Nevertheless, I will find him."

"Well, I don't see how."

"What do you think the police are for?"

"The police? Well, they aren't there to service your personal vendettas."

"I'm with the foreign office, Pearson, and when a distinguished diplomat asks for help in tracking down a foreign undesirable, the local police are generally only too happy to help."

"But really, Pollard, over a few lire?"

"No one steals from me, Pearson, no one – not ever. I will find him – I can absolutely assure you of that."

And he full-stopped his statement with three wet stamps.

I tiptoed back to my room as fast as I could, and I didn't leave it again for three days.

* * *

Uncle Walter's Apartment was the scene of frequent wild parties. I was not invited to them, but listened to the goings-on from my room or from the corridors.

I would hear men arrive individually through the early evening, but the women always came later, and in a raucous group. There would be clinking and giggling and playful screams, which became more and more shrill as the night wore on. Eventually, the men would begin to take the women on excursions to other rooms.

I knew full well the mechanics of sexual intercourse from my anatomical studies, but I had no idea what it sounded like until I came to live with my uncle.

Different men had their own particular vocalisations – one always made a sort of hooting sound that I have only otherwise heard from a woman giving birth. Another gave a triumphant laugh that turned to a descending cry at the critical moment. The girls, in return, would make sounds of exaggerated pleasure and faux amazement.

Uncle Walter's sounds were darker though. I would hear him walk the woman along the corridor, all charming wit, but a few minutes later, he would be coughing staccato abuse – a single word with each thrust:

"Filthy. Ugly. Dirty. Bitch." And with each full stop the bed bruised into the wall.

The girl's sounds would gradually diminish throughout this pounding, before returning as small, frightened cries.

One night, I heard him slap a girl three times, and splittingly hard, if the sound it made was any measure of the force. Right after the slaps came a clatter, then a short scream that was all of a sudden cut dead.

I peeped out of my door as two of Uncle's male acquaintances ran into the room of the scream.

"All right, Pollard, that'll do, that'll do," said one who then led him out of the room by the arm.

He complied, but screamed abuse back over his shoulder. "Filthy wretch, you think you can make me do things? I will kill you. Do you hear me? I will find you and I will fucking kill you."

"let's get back to the fun, eh, shall we? There's a good fellow," said the man, continuing to pull him up the corridor.

"Filthy Italians," he mumbled to the man. "Think they can make an Englishman do things, I'll kill him for it." Then he looked back at the room again. "Do you hear me? I will find you, and I will fucking kill you." And then they disappeared together, back into the party.

The other man who had entered the scream room now peeped out to check that all was clear before bringing out a boy. He didn't look any older than me – fourteen or so, delicate and pale, crying quietly and holding his throat.

As they passed my room the boy dropped something without noticing. It was a necklace with a charm on it – a red, horn-shaped charm, about an inch long.

I opened my door enough to pick it up.

"Um… excuse me," I said.

They stopped, and the boy looked round – his long eyelashes were all clumped together with tears and his neck was scarlet and raw.

"Your necklace," I said, holding it out to him.

"Il mio cornicello," he whispered, taking it gently from my hand. "Grazie – th… thank you."

The man glanced at me, and then at my door. "Best get back to your room then, lad," he said, before leading the boy away.

* * *

It was clear that the longer I stayed in this house, the shorter my chances of survival. Not that my life amounted to much, but it seemed preferable to die slowly at home from the effects of puberty, than to die violently in this awful place, so I needed an escape strategy, and I felt my best hope was was a letter home:

* * *

October the 11th, 1884.

Dearest Mother and Elizabeth,

I have now been in Naples for a full month, and am missing you both terribly. It is so unlike Harewell here, and really quite a dark place despite the Italian sunshine.

I have had a lot of time to reflect upon my behaviour, and I now realise how much of a burden I have been to you both in the last year. I write now to humbly apologise for all the distress and embarrassment that I have caused.

Mother, will you please also pass my apologies on to Reverend Thomas – I did not mean any of the hurtful and meaningless things I said in the fluster of being discovered.

And Elizabeth, I do so hope that I did not damage your clothes in any way. If I did, please let me know the bill for repairs, and I promise to send you the same as soon as I have it.

You will both be happy to learn that sending me here has had very beneficial effects, for I have been no trouble at all to Uncle Walter, and my teacher, Signora Mazzotti, is constantly amazed at my great progress in maths and Italian. I'm sure you would both be very proud of me.

So, now that I am such a very reformed character, you can have me back with no fear at all for my future behaviour.

To which end, with your permission, I would like to return at the soonest opportunity, and would be very grateful if you could make the appropriate arrangements.

I miss you both terribly, and remain your REFORMED, and very loving SON and BROTHER,

Thomas.

* * *

I wasn't reformed; I wasn't a son, or a brother, and I had learnt nothing here other than that my uncle was a murderous lunatic, but given that my family were the ones who sent me to this awful place, I saw nothing wrong in trying to manipulate them into getting me out. All I could do now was wait and hope.

* * *

Two months later, on Christmas night, the carousing was festively extravagant. There were more people, more bottles, more squeals, and more banging.

In the small hours of the morning, just as I had begun to doze through the noise, my door suddenly opened. I sat up sharply and held the sheets up to my neck.

"This is the lad," announced my uncle, as he led a fat man into my room, the two of them holding candles.

"What do you want?" I asked, the hairs on my back and arms rising in stiff fear. They did not reply but held their candles up to me.

"My goodness me," said the fat man. "He is a pretty one isn't he?" He reached over and patted me on the shin through the sheets. "Don't be frightened" he said, as I slid my leg away.

"This is the Norwegian Consul-General, Thomas. He's a very important man," said Uncle Walter with a maniacal grin. "And, he wants to bugger you." Then he shouted bitter, whisky-fume laughter at me.

"Come now, Pollard, don't frighten the poor creature," said the consul, pulling Uncle a little away. "I wanted a peep, that is all. Let's return to the fun and leave this delightful creature to his beauty sleep." He then led Uncle and his whisky laugh back out of my room.

I quickly pulled on my trousers and shirt, but was shaking so much I could hardly do up the buttons.

A few minutes later I heard footsteps approaching.

51

The door opened and it was Uncle Walter again, but this time alone, and in the light of his candle I could see that his eyes were now dead.

He walked directly to me, grabbed my face about the jaw and pushed my head back hard against the wall. The flap of skin between his thumb and forefinger slid into my mouth and prickled my tongue with salt.

"Let me make this very clear to you, my grotesque little invert. If the Norwegian Consul-General wants to fuck you, then you will bend over and accommodate him like the degenerate that you are. Do I make myself clear?"

I was gagged by his hand and could not reply so he slid it up my face, grabbed my hair and banged my head backwards again.

"Well?"

"Yes, Uncle."

He repeated "Yes, Uncle" back at me, before finally letting go of my hair and walking away.

As he reached the door, he turned back and stared at me for a moment. I looked down at my feet.

"That's a coy look," he said. "Very coy – looking down like that." He paused, then took a step towards me. "You think I am so easy to seduce? You think you can make me do things?"

At that moment, the consul general put his head round the door.

"Do come along, Pollard – you can't promise a single malt and renege – I am quite drooling in anticipation."

* * *

December the 27th, 1884.

Dearest Mother and Elizabeth,

It has been over two months since I wrote to you, and I can wait no longer for your reply. I will assume for now that either my letter to you has been lost, or yours to me. I have therefore determined to make my own way home. I will acquire some money by whatever means I must, and will take the cheapest route I can find.

I do not know how long it will take, but I think I might be able to get a place on a ship sailing to Marseilles on January the 15th. From there it is only a short trip across France and the Channel.

I will see you very soon,

Thomas.

* * *

Three weeks later, a reply came:

Jan. 9th, 1885.

Thomas,

Mother and I have considered matters very thoroughly in the light of your unwelcome begging letter. You have no one to blame but yourself for your predicament. Mother will not have you back, and we are quite happy with things as they are.

We therefore absolutely insist that you give up on returning to England. It is time for you to make your own way and become a man.

Please do not trouble Mother or myself further with your childish pleadings. We don't want you.

Elizabeth.

10

How Absurdly Convoluted This Becomes

I was staring at the shape of my hand through my bed sheet, stretching out my fingers so that it looked like the hand of a skeleton beneath a shroud. Then I drew my fingers into a fist, as if the skeleton had woken from the dead.

The fist was about the size of Geronimo's head, and I began to form my fingers into a pair of cat's ears. How lovely it was to imagine him there, hiding beneath my bedclothes – something he had always done because he liked to sleep in my smell.

I turned his head towards me and whispered, "brown?"

There was a knock at my door.

"Si accomodi, Maria," I called, but it was not Maria, it was the Norwegian Consul-General and he quite filled the door frame.

"Dear Boy," he said, "please do not be even slightly alarmed." I was more than alarmed but there was nothing I could do about it – if I told him to go away, I might face the wrath of Uncle Walter; if I allowed him in, I would likely face a buggering.

"Look," he continued, indicating the door theatrically with his hand, "I will leave the door open, and I will sit on this uncomfortable little chair beside it."

I still couldn't reply.

He sat himself into the chair and placed both hands on the silver top of his cane. "My dear boy," he said, looking at my frightened face, "if I wanted to ravish you now, I could do so with ease, being at the very least, thrice your size. I want only to talk a little." Then he smiled rather gently at me.

"Very well... Sir."

"Please, call me Atle."

I could see him more clearly now than in the candlelight of Christmas night. He was fat but not grotesquely so, his cheeks were full and plum-pink, his mouth thin, and above it sat a sparse moustache of sweat beads. His hair was Norwegianly blond and longer than most, and he parted the floppy fringe of it to one side, as if framing the scarlet pimple on his forehead.

He smiled again and then leaned forwards a little. "Thomas, let me begin by stating quite clearly that I know what you are – I know about your little excursions 'en femme' and, more importantly, I well understand boys who have such needs."

I felt my cheeks catch fire.

"It is really not so unusual to be a little effeminate you know," he continued, "nor indeed for a boy, or even a man, to wear a dress – I know several men who like to impersonate women from time to time, and they are amongst the most entertaining fellows I know. Indeed..." He looked out of the door conspiratorially and leaned forwards again, "I'm something of a 'tight-lacer' myself on occasion. Are you shocked?"

"No," I said, but I was.

"And, if I may be direct," he tapped his cane on the floor and looked me in the eyes, "I also know of the love you feel for other men, and as such I would like to make you an..."

"But I don't feel love for men."

"Oh, but you do, and if you do not realise it yet, you soon will, as the passions of manhood begin to inflame your childish heart. And I can tell you, Thomas, that when you embrace your inversion, there is a whole charming little world of pleasure to be had. One must be discreet of course, but do believe me when I say that you are not alone in your needs, and nor do they necessarily destine you for unhappiness."

There was silence for a moment.

I felt absolutely naked, as if having my bottom examined by a doctor, but he clearly said I wasn't alone in my needs, so he must know others like me, and perhaps that meant I could talk about these things to him.

"Um… these men who wear dresses," I said, "do they feel themselves to be women inside? That God has made a terrible mistake and placed a woman within the body of a man?"

"No, no, they are not mad – the clothing is merely an expression of their effeminate nature – the same nature that brings them to love their own sex.

"But…" I took a deep breath, "That does not describe me," and then I began to whisper aloud. "I do feel that I really am a girl, and not only that, I do not love men."

He laughed. "To believe that you are a girl is a mere confusion of youth. That you love men is something that you will discover in time – I'm quite sure of it." He smiled expectantly, as if he thought I was about to admit that he was right after all.

"I must say, I do not really feel very confused – I simply feel like a girl."

He leaned back in his chair and we had silence again for a few moments. "Well, it would indeed be a pity if you turned out to be the other sort."

"Other sort?"

"Yes, dear boy, there are two sorts of men who wear dresses. The delightful inverts that I have just described, and the rather more tedious fetishists who are normal men in all but the fact that they derive a naughty thrill from feminine attire."

"These 'other sort', do they love women then?"

"Invariably."

"Well, that could be me except… except I do not feel the naughty thrill that you describe – I feel quite blandly normal when dressed as a woman."

"Oh, Thomas, that is really not at all interesting, and frankly it is a little queer, but perhaps we should expect these confusions from someone of your tender years." He leant forwards. "Tell me, have you ever actually been in love with a woman? Honestly now."

"Yes… yes I have… in a way. Her name is Miss Bright, and she is famous for something – I'm not sure what though."

"Really, Thomas, a childish infatuation with a celebrity hardly counts. No, my instincts on these matters are never wrong – sooner or later, you will find yourself drawn to an inverted life and all the lascivious fun that it entails, I am quite sure of it."

I frowned at my feet. "Actually, I have met her, and she smiled at me. Anyway, I do not think that I want to be inverted – it is just not how I imagined I would live."

"Then, pray tell, how did you imagine that you would live?"

I hesitated for a moment then said firmly, "I think I will live as a woman or I will die."

"Then you do imagine that you will love men."

"No, I mean as a woman... um... as a woman who loves women?"

"A man living as a tom? Well, how absurdly convoluted this becomes."

"A 'tom'?"

"Yes, yes – a tom – a woman who loves women," he said.

"And such people exist?"

"Well of course they do."

This news was quite stunning, and I wanted to reiterate it aloud. "So a woman can love a woman – I can love a woman and yet still be one myself."

Atle shook his head and rolled his eyes. "This is all really quite simple, Thomas – you are not a woman, you are a boy who likes to wear a frock, and the only question before us is whether you will turn out to be the inverted sort or the dressing-up sort, and I already have my opinion on that. Frankly, I did not come here to discuss your juvenile confusions, I simply came to make you an offer."

I shook my head but he held his hand up.

"Hear my proposal in full, and then you may agree, refuse or defer at your leisure. Now, plainly put, you are a very pretty little thing, and I would like you to come to my home where I will show you a splendid wardrobe from which you may choose anything you like. I will pay you one English pound for the pleasure of watching you put on a dress and then disrobe. If you will allow me to pleasure myself a little whilst you disrobe, then two pounds will be yours. If you will kiss me once undressed, three pounds."

He then gave me a sly smile.

"There are ways that you might increase this little consideration to four pounds and, if you are a very daring boy, five. I doubt your Uncle makes that in a week."

I could think of no reply, my mind being in a crumple from the collision of possibility and disgust. He raised his finger.

"Do consider it. I am in no particular hurry, my apartments are not far away, and you need only come to the rear entrance and inform my staff that you have a delivery for Atle." He stood up. "And thus, I will leave my card, and bid you adieu." And with a little bow, he left.

* * *

"The filthy wretch," I whispered to myself, but how astonished I was by our conversation – there are women who love women – this surely must be me.

And yet, how can I explain my body? No, it's impossible, everything points to confusion – that I am nothing but a peculiar man, possibly even of the 'other sort' that Atle described.

Could I live a life as that other sort? Loving women and yet on occasion, dressing as one too? Perhaps with time, I could settle into it – I might marry a nice friendly girl who would tolerate my urges, and it wouldn't be so awful, would it? Or perhaps, Atle's first instincts were correct, and I would become the inverted sort of man instead – a man who loves men. What an extraordinary thought.

I stood on the balcony and looked down at passing men to see if there were any at all that I might consider attractive. I could see that some were prettier than others but even the prettiest had no particular effect on me.

I tried to imagine embracing their broad, muscular backs and kissing their rough lips. The thought was mildly unpleasant, although I could imagine being able to do it – same as I could probably eat a raw egg if I had to.

Think of a pretty girl on the other hand – think of Miss Bright in particular, and I could happily feel my hands on her little waist and our sweet strawberry lips together.

The more I thought about pretty girls… well, about Miss Bright, the more it would excite me, and I began to feel a sort of ache about it in my trousers.

Perhaps this ache was one of Atle's 'passions of manhood', but if it was, then it also meant that the dreaded masculinisation of my body may already have begun, and death, therefore, was almost upon me.

11

One of Either Sort

Two weeks later, Uncle Walter returned from a trip to Marseille. I was looking for dark hairs on my top lip in the mirror with a magnifying glass when he put his head round my door.

"Hello there, young Thomas, and how does life treat you today?"

"Very well, Uncle, thank you," I said, lying of course. "I hope you... I hope you enjoyed your trip abroad."

"It was splendid – a successful hunting trip shall we say."

My stomach turned over – he must surely have caught up with Mr Grimaldi.

"Now then," he continued, "you are to attend a ball at the Norwegian Consulate with me this evening. How does that sound?"

"Um, very nice – thank you. I um... what should I wear?"

"Not a ball gown, if that's what you were hoping, ha ha. Maria will bring you a suit, and you will owe me ten lira for the rent of it."

"Yes, Uncle."

"Be ready at eight."

"Yes, Uncle."

Atle was clearly behind the invitation, but I was not particularly afraid of him after his appearance in my room, even if I knew I might have to spend at least some part of the evening politely declining his advances.

* * *

I was ready as instructed, and for the first time since I arrived in Naples, I stepped out of the house. A cab was waiting for us and I climbed in.

There was some hesitation as the cabbie struggled with an uncooperative strap between the horse and the carriage. Uncle Walter stood over him with his hands on his hips offering chirpy suggestions in Italian.

As I waited, I looked towards our building and saw that the destitute woman was still there, and to my surprise the child was still alive, but in the five or so months since I had seen them, the poor creature had grown very little, if at all, and the woman now seemed almost undone.

She was looking at me through half-opened eyes, and when she saw that I was looking at her, she smiled. It was only a tiny smile, more with the eyes than the mouth, but it was the second time that this utterly wretched soul had given me the one thing that every other person in my life except Geronimo had withheld.

She pointed to the baby, then pointed to her mouth. I nodded my head and held up my hand to signify 'later'. I am not sure if she understood this vague signal, but she seemed to settle a little into the dirt, and closed her eyes.

The strap problem resolved, we were soon on our way.

A few minutes into the short journey, Uncle Walter, who had, for the most part, been silent and still, suddenly placed his hand on the inside of my thigh, very near the top. It was there only a moment before he lifted it away, pulled it back, and then punched me violently in the shoulder with it. I yelped and recoiled.

"Weren't expecting that were you?" he said.

"No, Uncle," I replied, my eyelids flickering in anticipation of a second blow.

"Splendid," he replied and the cab halted. "Here we are then, Thomas. Let's have some fun, shall we?"

"Yes, Uncle."

61

* * *

He immediately disappeared into the crowd and I found a little table in a corner from which I could watch everything in solitude.

There were perhaps a hundred people. They were all well-to-do types – gentlemen and ladies, elderly dowagers, a few officers, but there were also lots of younger guests.

One woman, aged perhaps eighteen, was so perfect in every aspect, that she could have been a painting come to life – her hair was a thick, glossy chestnut, her skin was translucent olive, and the perfect curves of her body were all enveloped in platinum satin.

It seemed to defy all the laws of probability that so many lovely features could accumulate into a single being, and I felt quite certain that the only way such a woman could even exist in the world, was for some other poor woman to go without.

I looked down at myself, at my flat chest and my narrow hips, all wrapped loosely in an ugly, bland, man's suit, and all I could look forward to was that I would soon begin to fill it with muscle and body hair.

I took a long drink of red wine and hoped to lose myself in it.

"And what do we have here?" It was Atle. "Don't you look a picture in your little suit?"

"Good evening," I said with the sourest expression I could curdle, "and thank you for inviting me."

"Oh dear, we're not a happy fellow, are we?"

I realised that I was being rude, but I couldn't quite care enough about it to apologise. "I'm quite all right, thank you, just… a little tired."

"Well, you enjoy the view and the wine, and if you can bear it for a couple of hours, the main bulk of the guests will be leaving and you may then join me in a more intimate party." He raised a finger, "Not alone, dear boy, there will be a small, select company and you will be amongst friends."

"Do I have a choice?" I asked.

"Of course, and you may leave immediately if you so desire."

I felt I had now been too rude, even for my bitter mood.

"Thank you," I said with an apologetic smile. "I will come."

"How delightful."

I did not know what sort of an event I had volunteered for, but in truth, I didn't much care as long as it was a distraction from my thoughts.

* * *

About two hours later, as promised, most of the guests left. Uncle Walter followed them, but he passed me on the way out and leaned very close to my ear.

"You owe me ten lira for the suit. You will pay for it tomorrow."

"But I have no money at all, Uncle."

"Then I suggest you find some."

"But by what means?" He was absolutely still at this moment, and I could feel the hairs on my neck rising under the spell of his dead eyes.

"Oh, Thomas," he whispered. "Your life dangles by a thread." And then he left.

* * *

Shortly afterwards Atle reappeared. "Thomas, dear boy, you are as good as your word. Do follow..."

He took me along a grand corridor and into a cosy drawing room, within which were perhaps twenty drunk and lively people.

"Here is Thomas – a new friend," he announced. There was a little cheer of greeting and I smiled awkwardly.

"Welcome, friend," slurred a tall and sturdy man whose face was partly obscured by a floppy fringe of curly hair. He put an arm around my shoulder. "I am Christophe," he said. "I am an atheist and a sodomite, though neither is a requirement of the other."

"How very true," said Atle, lifting Christophe's arm from my shoulder. "But let's not crowd the fellow."

Christophe's hand stayed on my shoulder for a moment. He smiled very warmly at me – a pause of kind reassurance in his eyes, and said, "You're safe here, Thomas." Then, he lifted his hand away in an exaggerated gesture. "Quite right too, Atle – he's far too pretty for a big old brute like me, so now I will stagger back to Antonio, fall into his delightful arms, and hope that he will forgive my flirtations."

On a sofa nearby, a large man placed his cheroot into the corner of his mouth and held his arms open to Christophe, who, as promised, fell into them with a desperate swoon, spilling both their glasses of wine.

I had never seen men behave this way before. I had seen drunkenness of course, but they were actually sitting with their arms around each other in an intimate embrace.

I began to relax a little. Perhaps I was safe here amongst these extraordinary people – people who know as well as I do what it is to have a secret.

"You do realise, Thomas, that you are most awfully pretty," said Atle.

"No," I said.

"Oh yes. You know, in Japan they have a name for pretty boys like you – 'bishounen'."

"Have you been to Japan?" I said.

"I was at the Norwegian embassy in Tokyo for a year."

"I do envy you that – it's a country I have always dreamed of visiting."

"Well, Bishounen do fare rather better in Japan than in Europe, and I don't doubt you would have many admirers. But come," he looked across the room, "I want you to meet two friends." He cupped his hand beside his mouth to whisper, "One of either sort if you take my meaning, and a word to the wise - we always defer to a person's presentation here, so do be sure to say 'she' and 'her'." He cleared his throat. "Thomas, may I introduce Giulietta and Munchy."

Before me, sitting on a sofa, were two men dressed entirely as women. Munchy was wearing a crimson silk dress and I think her corset must have been very tight indeed to make such a tiny waist. She took my hand immediately and gave a pained expression to Atle.

"Oh so pretty, I hate her," she said, with a very French accent. Then she looked to me again and said, "I am delighted to meet you, you beautiful boy, come and sit with me and Giulietta."

The four of us sat together.

"Now then, ladies, I am going to disclose a little confidence here," said Atle. "Thomas has been known to wear a dress too on occasion." I felt myself turn scarlet.

"Oh, I can't bear it," exclaimed Munchy before smiling at me in agony and saying, "Too pretty, really."

Giulietta tapped Munchy on the leg and indicated that she wanted to swap seats so that she could sit next to me. She was quite bit older than Munchy, but although her dress was more conservative, it was still very fashionable. She held out a hand to shake mine, but shook it firmly as if concluding a business deal.

"I am pleased to meet you Thomas. How do you find Napoli?"

"Quite overwhelming," I said.

"Ah yes, but not all of Naples is like the Via Tribunali. I am from Vomero – we are a little more civilised up there. And please, do not feel embarrassed," she said, earnestly. "Wearing a dress is nothing here."

"Thank you," I said, "but I have not done so for quite a long time now."

She nodded knowingly. "Yes, you know, I used to feel so disgusted with myself that I went years without doing it, but in the end, it is no more than a little fun, and why should we not have a little fun in life?"

"Indeed why not?" I said with a smile. "And... may I ask a personal question?"

"By all means."

"Have you always known that you were really a woman inside? Even when you were a child?"

"I am a man of course, but you mean to ask how old I was when I first indulged in this little passion? Well, I cannot remember clearly, but I was perhaps thirteen or fourteen."

"So you do not feel that you actually are a woman?"

"No," she said, with a slight frown. "Do you?"

"No," I scoffed, "but I remember once thinking that I was. I soon got over it though."

We laughed together for a moment, then she said, "Life can be a mite confusing for such as we, can it not? Although, I have certainly wondered what it would be like to be a woman. I suppose every man has."

"And how did you take to the idea?"

"Well it might be fun to try for an afternoon and to see what the sensations were, if you take my meaning." She winked, "but frankly, it wouldn't do to be without a…" she nodded at my crotch.

"Quite so," I said, and we laughed again. She leaned over to Munchy.

"Munchy, Thomas here wonders if we have ever thought what it might be like to be a real woman, with all the parts."

"A real woman? Well, that would mean I could entice a real man into my bed." She laughed then put her hand on my knee, "But what fun could I have with him without a cock?"

We all laughed again. "But could you not enjoy him as a woman might?" I offered.

"Women do not enjoy sexual congress, Thomas. You can ask Giulietta's wife about that."

"Munchy please," laughed Giulietta. "You really go too far."

* * *

From here the evening ran quite pleasantly: Munchy was very entertaining – several times she gave the room a very coarse song, and accompanied the lyrics with some really quite obscene dancing. In between the songs she would be very rude to some of the guests, but in such a brilliantly witty way that no-one could take offence.

It was extraordinary to think that I could dress as myself amongst these people and no one would think any the worse of me for it. And yet, what would be the point if they are going to see me as a man in a dress rather than who I really am?

Not that I could really blame them for that – after all, it was now becoming clear that I was the only person in the world who actually felt the way I did.

12

Lascia Ch'io Pianga

Later that evening, just as I thought the party was dying down, Atle made an announcement:

"Friends," he said, whilst standing at the door with one hand on the knob. "Here's a very special treat for us." We all went silent and he opened the door dramatically. "I present, Il Maccari."

There was a cheer and a round of applause as an exceptionally tall man… or woman… no, definitely man, of the most unusual proportions walked into the room. His torso was actually quite short and fat – it was just the extraordinary length of his legs that made him so tall, and with his cape tossed over his shoulders, he looked like a giant heron with a belly full of fish.

"Who is he?" I whispered to Giulietta. "Is he a… a 'he'?"

"Have you not heard of Il Maccari?"

"No."

"He is a singer, the last castrato they call him, he's really quite famous."

"Castrato?" I said.

"Yes, a genuine castrato."

"You mean actually castrated?"

Giulietta's answer was cut short by Il Maccari himself:

"My good friend, Atle, asks a song of me," he announced, "and Atle always gets what he wants." His voice struck me immediately – it was very high and distinctly female. Everyone cheered.

There was a piano at one end of the room with a pianist already installed and Il Maccari took his place beside him.

"I feel quite in the temper for Handel," he said. "Would Lascia Ch'io Pianga be to everyone's liking?"

I did not know the piece, but I cheered with everyone else until we all fell expectantly silent.

It began as a beautiful, mournful sequence of chords from which seemed to fall a sorrowful and familiar melody. Perhaps the melody itself was familiar, or perhaps I only recognised the sorrow that it so eloquently expressed.

At the dying of the opening chords, the music lay still for a moment. Then Maccari took a breath and began to sing.

It was the most exquisite sound that I have ever heard, and it floated and fluttered over our broken hearts with a perfect mastery of the air.

My eyes filled with tears almost from the first note, and by the time we were at the end of it, I was sobbing and could hardly care who saw.

"A handkerchief here," cried Munchy. "Il Maccari has stolen another heart."

"I do apologise," I said, "but I think that was just about the most beautiful thing I have ever heard."

I took a handkerchief from Christophe, and when I had dried my eyes, I found myself looking directly into the face of Il Maccari himself. He took my hand, and kissed me on the knuckles.

"It is a pleasure to sing for such a sensitive soul."

Not only had he the voice of a woman but also the complexion, for although his skin had wrinkled a little into middle-age, it was so very soft, and he had no hint at all of a beard. It was not an attractive face – not by any means, but it was certainly constructed of the best feminine materials.

"Thank you so very much, Signor Maccari. I never knew that a man could sing so high."

"You have never heard a castrato sing?"

"No," I said.

"It was his first time, poor child," said Maccari to the room, and everyone nodded knowingly.

"I think I should love to have such a voice."

"Yours is still unbroken, but to retain it as such… well that costs a little more than you might be willing to pay." He made a snipping action with two fingers, and all the room laughed together. "And there is little call for a castrato now, that is why I am the very last one – a tired curiosity from the past." He looked mournfully at everyone, and they all shook their heads in firm disagreement with this assessment. "You are all too kind."

* * *

A little later, Munchy was entertaining the room again with an entirely different sort of song, and I took advantage of the distraction to draw Atle into a corner.

"I must know more about castratos, Atle. Where might such an operation be performed, and how much might a person pay for it?"

"Dear boy, the plural is 'castrati', but you must put these thoughts out of your head. Castration alone does not produce a voice like that. It requires many years of training and diligent practice."

"But the pitch, he sounded like a woman – his voice has not broken."

"Well of course – that is the very purpose of the castration. But, Thomas, you really are not a woman, and castration will not make you one. Also, there is an even greater price to pay than your testicles."

"Money? How much?"

"A price extracted upon the body." He looked around to be sure that Maccari was far enough away. "You have seen his bizarre shape, so unusually tall with those ridiculous stilts for legs. That is how they all look, and they all have those fat bellies."

He leaned closer to whisper. "Not only that, but those who have been left a cock by the castrator, have the most sorry little sausage that cannot rise even to the most tantalising entreaties. So whilst castration might give you the voice of a woman, it will not give you the body. And who would believe you a woman at six feet tall?"

"But there must be something that could be done against such complications," I said.

"If there were, I am sure they would do it."

"But if I did not eat too much, how then could my belly become fat? And perhaps there is some way to stop legs from growing so long."

"By what possible means could you deter the growth of your own legs?"

"I don't know," I said. "Some sort of brace perhaps... or weighted skirts or... well... something."

"Thomas, you are a very pretty boy, but you *are* a boy."

"Well, we'll have to agree to differ."

"On whether you are a boy, or on whether you are pretty?"

"Am I really pretty?" I said.

"Yes, Thomas, very."

"But femininely so?"

"That I cannot deny, though most boys of your age have a feminine aspect to their faces."

"The trick will be to retain it," I said.

"I should very much like to kiss it."

He suddenly seemed rather close.

"Atle, no, I don't want to."

"Shame really, you might have made ten lira for a kiss, which is a sum of money I fancy you have need of." He rubbed the lapel of my hired suit between his thumb and forefinger, and I felt my shoulders sag a little under the disappointment.

"I don't suppose you would simply lend me the money would you?" I said.

"Neither a lender nor borrower be. No, I offer a simple transaction, and on rather generous terms I might add."

I did not want Atle to be my first kiss, but nor could I face the risk of making Uncle Walter angry.

"What would be the required duration of the kiss?" I asked.

"What a romantic question. I think I might demand at least a minute."

"If you say thirty seconds I will do it."

"Christophe," shouted Atle.

"Yes?"

"You have a second hand upon your pocket watch do you not?"

"I do."

"Good, then count off thirty seconds while I kiss this beautiful boy."

A small crowd now gathered to cheer Atle on.

"Set…" said Christophe with one hand raised. "Go!"

Atle's face loomed towards me as if I were studying a pink fish through a magnifying glass. His lips were wet and took position not upon mine but around them, forming a seal as if he meant to inflate me.

The audience counted down the seconds:

"Thirty, twenty-nine, twenty-eight…"

His jaw began to work up and down as if he was sucking the blood from a wounded knuckle.

"Eighteen, seventeen…"

And then his tongue entered my mouth. This I was completely unprepared for. It was an incongruously pointy thing, like the tail end of a slug, and as it slid towards the back of my throat I felt myself gag.

"Ten, nine, eight…"

I could not breathe and tried to back away, but his hands reached around me – one to the back of my head and the other to my buttocks which he pawed and kneaded.

His fingers crawled steadily into the cleft of my bottom, as he pushed my hips forwards to rub my genitals upon his thigh.

"Three, two, one."

There was a cheer and I took a huge breath.

"There, you see, Thomas, not so bad was it? Perhaps you felt a little thrill of naughty possibility?" I could think of no answer. "Well, it was your first kiss, dear boy, which might perhaps be likened to your first glass of whisky – it seems not altogether pleasant at first, and yet there is something in the taste of it that sooner or later tempts you to a second glass."

* * *

The revulsion crawling up and down my back was still not able to distract me from the hope that I had found at this exotic party – the hope that I might arrest the terrible masculinisation of my body through castration.

I had no idea how it was done, or who could do it, but tonight I had met someone who had actually been through it, and if him, why not me?

I was determined to get as much information from Il Maccari as I could, but to my immense frustration, he left the party before I had the chance to speak to him. However, I did manage to find out from other guests that he was currently appearing in an opera called, Il Crociato in Egitto at the Teatro San Carlo, so I thought that if I could find the teatro, I might be able to approach him there.

* * *

The destitute woman was still crumpled in the same dirty heap when I arrived back at Uncle Walter's building. It was three in the morning and I was very drunk. The woman was fast asleep, as was the child.

I had managed to appropriate some food for them from the party, and had it in a bag. I had tried to select foods that were filling, but that would also keep for a few days – cured sausages, candied fruit, bread and the like.

I reached forwards to nudge her awake, but it seemed better to let them have the benefit of sleep at this hour, so I placed the bag very gently beside them.

How incongruous it felt to stand over this hopeless pair when I was so full of hope for myself – to be juxtaposed with a head full of wine and possibilities, against their futile and malignant famine. I had my ten lira in my pocket, enough to feed them for a month or more, and yet its ultimate purpose was for the obscene triviality of hiring party clothes.

I reached into my pocket to take out a lira or two, but instead I took out the whole sum and tucked it into the bag of food.

I had no idea what I would say to Uncle Walter tomorrow, but the world seemed so full of possibilities right now, that I didn't doubt that I would think of something.

13

Not Yet, Uncle

The following morning, I awoke hungover and terrified – I had given Uncle Walter's money away.

I ran to the window and looked down to the street for the woman. She was gone, so there would be no getting it back now.

"He's going to kill me, he's going to kill me, he's going to kill me," I whispered, over and over again, waiting for an idea to interrupt me as I paced the room.

"I have to get out."

I went to the window, but the drop was sheer, and there was no way to climb down. Even if there was, where would I go? I tried to imagine fending for myself on the streets of Naples – stealing food, or maybe finding work somehow. Or maybe I could make it all the way back to England, even if I had to walk and swim. But even in England, where would I go?

I looked down at the place where the destitute lady usually sat. "Perhaps I will just starve to death. No, I can't run away to starve – that's not the answer… but I can't stay." I started to pace again. "He's going to kill me, he's going to kill me…"

I sat on my bed and picked up Gray's Anatomy to distract myself for a few minutes and give my brain a moment to catch its breath. I went to the section on male genitalia – after all, I had much research to do with my upcoming plans for castration.

"Exactly how would a doctor perform a castration without killing the patient?" I mumbled to myself. "It's the spermatic artery that worries me – it runs straight from the aorta here," I pointed at the diagram, "and down to the testicles, here, so cutting through it would surely make for a profuse and probably fatal bleed. It'll kill me, it'll surely kill me... Uncle Walter is going to kill me..."

I shook my head and opened my other book – Enquire Within Upon Everything, looking for any advice I could find on treating blood loss. 'Alcohol may be applied to a wound to inhibit bleeding,' it said.

"That might help me – I should make sure I have plenty of alcohol to hand so I can apply it to the surgical wound... or the injuries from Uncle Walter, because he will try to kill me – he said my life is dangling by a thread, and he will do it, I don't doubt he will do it."

I stood up again. "I have to get out, I have to get out."

I quickly dressed and threw my few belongings into my carpet bag, then I stood frozen at my door for several minutes unable to bring myself to open it.

The problem was that Uncle Walter's room was only a few yards along the corridor and I would have to walk past it to get out of the building.

"If he hears me, he will kill me. He will certainly kill me."

I stood with my hand on the door knob for at least twenty minutes before I finally found the courage to turn it.

There was a small creak as I pulled it very slowly open, and I peeped outside.

He was sitting in a chair in the middle of the corridor, facing directly towards me. He had been waiting.

"Do you have it?" he said.

I couldn't speak – nothing would come out, so I backed into my room.

I heard his footsteps coming up the corridor towards me.

I stood next to my bed and waited.

"Do you have it?"

"Not yet, Uncle," I said, chirpily, "but I can pay you back in one month with interest – fifty percent."

He stayed in the doorway, leaning on the frame, and examining me, inch by inch.

"Eighty percent?" I suggested.

Now he walked towards me, but not looking at my face – his eyes were focused somewhere vaguely about my middle.

He came right up against me, chest to chest, then reached round the back of my head with his left hand and gripped my hair.

He turned his own head a little to the side, almost as if he were listening to me breathe, then he slid his right hand, slowly down the front of my trousers.

He stopped, for a moment, but then he pushed his hand further until he touched the root of my penis with his fingertip.

I heard my voice, not a word, just a sound, as if a doctor had caused some small pain during an examination, but the moment I made it, he pulled out his hand, let go of my hair, and left the room.

I remained fixed in place, breathing tiny little breaths from the top of my lungs, listening to his footsteps along the hallway.

They slowed, and then they stopped.

I'm not sure if I breathed at all for the next few seconds.

Now footsteps again, – fast, heavy, getting louder.

He kicked my door, back open and strode directly for me.

"You dare to seduce me? You filthy wretch."

He swung a right hook, catching the side of my head with his wrist. It was only a glancing blow, but the fear of it knocked me to the floor.

Now he aimed a stamp at my head. I threw up my arms to protect myself. The edge of his heel caught me sharp in the armpit.

He stamped again and again, aiming for my head each time as if it were a kitchen rat.

"Please, Uncle," I screamed.

I tried to crawl under the bed to shelter. He stamped on and on – the blows falling, one after the other, down the side of my body.

I pulled my legs under the bed, but he turned it over, so I curled into a ball as he started to aim solid kicks at my back, again, and again, and again.

In desperation for my life, I turned and grabbed his foot – he fell and we both scrambled to our feet.

I ran at the door, but he caught me by the collar and spun me back onto the floor, then he threw himself on top of me, clamping my throat in his hands.

I pulled at his wrists with all the strength I have ever had, but could make no impression on them. The stiff tips of his thumbs pushed my windpipe flat and I felt as if my head was going to burst.

I looked into his eyes to beg for my life.

His expression was calm – mildly interested, as if reading a newspaper. He did not look directly into my eyes, nor did he avoid them, but looked past them as if they were of no particular significance.

The world began to drift away in muffled sounds and sparkling lights, and then something remarkable happened – I cannot account for it, but for that brief moment I felt quite relaxed, quite indifferent to my predicament, and to my life – it was the feeling of a warm summer's afternoon by the river, a glass of lemonade, the smell of nettles, a skylark and a warm breeze… and then I disappeared.

14

If You Take His Things

Why has the bed fallen over?

That was my first thought when I opened my eyes and saw it lying on its side. There followed several seconds where my mind had so many unfamiliarities to contend with that it could make no sense of any of them, but then my memory rushed in all at once, bringing with it the terror that Uncle Walter might still be in the room, just beyond my sight, daring me to be alive.

I lay absolutely still.

If I jump to my feet suddenly, I thought, right at this moment, and run for the door, I might surprise him enough to effect some sort of escape, and if I could just get as far as a public place, I would be safe because he surely wouldn't kill me in front of other people.

I counted down in my head from three, then tried to leap up.

Two things happened at once – the first was that my entire body was so stiff with pain that I could not lift myself beyond a seated position, and the second was that I saw he was not in the room after all.

I glimpsed movement in the doorway and my heart stopped, but it was Maria – she was peeping in at me with her hand on her chest. I had the impression that she might have been there for several minutes, perhaps too afraid to enter and find a corpse, but she now stepped briskly over to me and helped me onto a chair.

"He has gone out," she said, glancing over her shoulder, "so you must leave right now. There is a place you can go to for a few days, but you must go now. I will get food – you can take it with you." She clapped at me. "Quick quick." Then she hurried out.

It was the most enormous effort to move – sharp stabbing pains ran all down my right side, and there was a deep ache in my back when I breathed in. My right hand was swollen, making it difficult to lift things with it, and my right thigh could hardly bear my weight.

The worst of the pain was from my neck – the skin was burning, but beneath that it felt like I was wearing a tight collar of inward-pointing spikes, and deeper still, thick lobes of ache radiated into my head and chest.

I worked my tongue around my mouth trying to lick the blood off my teeth but it was too painful to swallow and I spat a mouthful of red saliva and black clots onto the tiles.

I picked up my carpet bag and checked that it still had all my things inside. Never before had the having of more things seemed so vital to survival – things one could trade, and eat, and live in. Why had I not collected more things in my life?

As I limped my way down the hall, I passed Uncle Walter's study. There was a silver cigarette case sparkling on the table. That was a thing I could have – a thing I could sell for enough money to get me through a few days at least, so I took it, and then I took his silver picture frames, and then his silver ink pots, which I first emptied over his desk.

One of his drawers contained a small cash box so I took that too, and all these tradeables, I stuffed into my carpet bag until, as a final goodbye, I dragged the drawers out of his desk and with my good hand, I threw them right across the room.

I hurried as best I could towards the front door where Maria met me with a bag of food.

"Go down Via dei Tribunali until you find Via San Gregorio Armeno – the street of the nativity figures. At bottom you will find a vico – how you say in English, an 'alley', it called 'Vico Figurari'. Look for small blue door. Here is the key. It is a store room only, but it is mine. You stay for a few days, until you are strong enough for leave the city, but you must leave the city."

"Thank you, Maria," I tried to say, but only a whisper would come out of my strangled throat.

She ignored the 'thank you' and continued.

"But this most important of all, Thomas – you must keep away from the police – you hear me? Stay away from the police."

I nodded.

"Signor Pollard, he always use them to find people. He do it many times."

"I understand."

She stuffed the bag of food into my carpet bag and saw the trinkets I had stolen. She paused, then looked deep and hard into my eyes.

"If you take his things, Thomas, he will kill you." And she shrugged at the end of the sentence to dismiss any other possibility.

"I have no choice," I whispered. "And he wants me dead anyway, so what difference can it make?"

She shook her head dismissively. "Then if you get out of Napoli alive, hide, change your name, because he will come for you Thomas, and he will not stop 'til he find you."

"I understand – thank you".

I hobbled down the stairs as quickly as I could, intensely aware that I might meet him coming up them at any moment. The closer I got to the street, the tighter the knot of tension pulled, and in the last few steps to the door, it was so taut that it drew all the pain out of my injuries and allowed me to actually run down the street, even with my bag.

A little way along, the pain returned, but I forced myself into a nonchalant walk so that I could avoid drawing attention.

It was quite late into the night by now – I did not know the exact hour, but the darkness helped to conceal me, and by dead reckoning I took a slightly circuitous route, hoping to make myself more difficult to follow.

Eventually I found my way to the blue door in Vico Figurari.

Once inside the pitch-black space, I locked the door, crouched into a corner, and cried, and cried, and cried.

15

The Cell

That night I slept in little respites between the pain and the cold stone floor. Every so often there would be a noise outside, and I would wake terrified that my uncle had discovered me. I would then lie absolutely still, straining my ears for the faintest sound, until eventually, I would drift off again, sleeping for a few more minutes until another noise, or nightmare, or shooting pain startled me back into attention.

Dawn finally came through a small opaque window at the back of the room, and for the first time I could see my surroundings. It was very like a jail cell, but full of old furniture and various objects that Maria must have disliked too much to live with, but not enough to throw away.

I tried to stand up, and collapsed immediately into a heap of pain. Nothing on my right side was working properly, and it took me three more attempts before I managed to pull myself to my feet. I then limped across to a small mirror that was propped up next to the window.

One of my cheeks was a bluey-pink and the whites of my eyes were dotted with the scarlet speckles of burst blood vessels. There were similar broken vessels beneath the skin of both cheeks. My neck was horrific – not so much the sides which were a deep and mottled red, but at the throat there were monstrous purple-black blotches which bore the vertical marks of his thumbnails.

I was terribly bruised all over my back and down my right leg, and it still hurt my back to breathe, but I decided that if the pain were due to an internal rupture of some kind, then the bleeding into my body would probably have carried me off by now.

It was also very painful to speak, and I had hardly any voice at all. In this state I would not be able to test my voice for signs it was starting to break, and I was afraid that the injury itself might somehow precipitate the breaking.

I rummaged through the cell for things that might be useful. There was a solid-silver letter opener – rather a good one I think, and it was fashioned after a stiletto knife, so I could use it to arm myself against my uncle, or anyone he might send after me.

I also found some clothes in a leather case, including an old dress. It was fairly ten years out of fashion, but it did have a high collar which would shield the worst of my neck injuries from view.

Once dressed, I put all the things I had stolen from my uncle into a basket, ready to sell, except for the money box – I couldn't sell that without a key, so I prised it open, hoping to find money.

There was a necklace inside – it had a red, horn-shaped charm attached to it.

My stomach rolled over.

It was the necklace of the boy that Uncle Walter had attacked at the party – the one he had promised to find and kill – a promise he must have fulfilled.

That poor boy – I could see him so clearly, his eyelashes clumped together with tears, his strangled neck, red and raw, and I could see Uncle's sharp feet, stamping on his frightened face, stamping on my face... stamping, stamping...

I heaved, but nothing came out.

There was a watch in there too with the name 'Carlo Grimaldi' inscribed on the back – that was the man he vowed to find in Marseilles, so he was surely dead as well.

And there was another souvenir – a lock of dark hair, but not cut hair – it was pulled hair, because the roots were still attached. It didn't come from the boy – his hair was much shorter, and it wasn't from Mr Grimaldi – his hair was white, so there must have been a third victim, at least.

How close I had come to having some possession of mine, or even some body part placed inside this tiny coffin. The thought of it made me heave again.

I decided to keep the things – they were at least evidence to use against him if ever it came to some sort of trial, so I tucked them all into a little pocket in my carpet bag.

* * *

A few minutes later, I was standing at the door with the basket of goods in my hand, trying to gather my courage. The last time I had been so frightened to go outside was before my first excursion as Emmeline, but this time, instead of being in fear of ridicule, I was in fear for my life.

I took a deep breath and stepped out.

Walking itself came as a shock – it was very difficult to persuade my injuries to cooperate with me, and every time my right foot touched the ground, pain shot from my knee to my shoulder, and stabbed every spot in-between.

I managed to limp to the nearest market, and amidst the cacophonous sparring of fishmongers and fruiterers, there were several stalls selling bric-a-brac that I thought might be interested in my things.

The first trader I approached gave a dismissive snort and held up one finger for a lira. I shook my head at him and moved on quickly. Two other traders offered similarly disparaging amounts, the best being two lira. This would simply not be anywhere near enough for any of my purposes.

With a fourth trader I attempted to barter – I asked for fifteen ("quindici") in the clearest voice that I could scrape out of my throat, but he seemed to take immediate offence, and made his return offer of two lira in an openly hostile manner by standing up and dragging his gaze from my eyes down to my feet and back up again.

At this point, I had only been out for fifteen minutes or so, but I was already exhausted – perhaps from the effects of walking in pain, or perhaps my body was expending so much upon the repair of itself, that little energy was left for walking about, so I decided to give up for the day and headed back to the cell to rest.

* * *

I awoke at dawn the following morning, and lay there as the orange light ripened to lemon, trying to think through my predicament. Perhaps a market was not the best place after all, or perhaps I needed to polish the goods to make them look shiny and tempting, or perhaps I just needed to learn how to barter.

But really, I knew that my biggest problem was selling them as a woman – people would always just assume that my mind was inferior for being a female one, but it wasn't – I had outwitted my teacher, Dr Palfrey, and the Reverend Thomas plenty of times, and many other men too.

Then I remembered the suffragist woman at the train station in Paris who had made me wait until the last minute before telling me where to find my train. I had thought her terribly unfair, but perhaps, thinking I was a man, she only wanted to show me a little of the unfairness she puts up with everyday. Suddenly, I quite liked her, and I wanted to be a suffragist too.

Well, regardless of how things ought to be, I had to deal with them as they actually were, so with the most bitter reluctance, both for the self-betrayal, and for the great risk of being recognised, I headed back out into Naples in my Thomas clothes.

My injuries were no better, but I took breaks every few minutes to help sustain my energy, and I eventually found a little shop selling second-hand goods and antiques of a superior quality called Vecchio Vesuvio. After a deep breath to gather myself, I entered the shop, and strode to the counter like the confident, painless young man I was not.

"Bongiourno," I said, in a rather well-to-do English accent.

"Deutsch?" asked the proprietor, examining me over his pince nez.

"No, English – parla inglese?"

"Of course. How may I help?"

"My mother and I are returning to England in the next few days, and we are keen to alleviate ourselves of some excess baggage. I have a few items here that might be of interest to you." I took them from the basket and set them out along the counter for him.

He looked me up and down before examining the objects and I wondered what he made of me – my male clothes were of good quality, but I was more than a little dishevelled and visibly bruised.

"Hmm, silver – not so popular these days," he said. "The frames are good however, and I may be interested for the right price. How much do you hope they are worth?"

"Well, as you point out, they are good frames. Shall we say ten lire the pair?"

He frowned at them.

"Not so much I think. But let me see these others. The cigarette case is interesting, very English, and the ink wells, well, they are rather mediocre. I might give you thirteen for the lot."

"If you will call it fifteen, I'll shake your hand on it," I said, holding mine out to him.

"Fifteen then." We shook, he paid me, and I tried not to let my profound relief show enough to spoil my confident-young-man charade.

* * *

Opposite Vecchio Vesuvio was a second-hand clothes shop, so I went straight inside to find a replacement for Maria's old dress – something inconspicuous that I could hide in, and travel in.

Within a few minutes of rummaging I found quite a nice brown walking dress, a boater, and a pair of black boots that were only a touch large. The lady who ran the shop seemed very stern – there was no hint of a smile about her. She looked me hard in the eye and said,

"Tre lire."

It seemed quite cheap to me so I gave her the money without question.

"Grazie," I said, as she handed me the clothes, but she didn't acknowledge the thank you, or make a reply – she just focused her irritated expression on re-folding any clothes I had disturbed in the rummage.

As I grabbed the door handle to leave, I saw two policemen standing outside Vecchio Vesuvio, about to go inside.

I leapt backwards, knocking over a hat-stand and hid out of view to one side of the door.

The shop lady looked at me, then looked at the policemen.

Her expression still didn't change, but she raised her palm to indicate for me to stay hidden as she watched through the door window.

She was helping me.

I mouthed the word 'grazie' to her, and tried to show her with my eyes how much I meant it, but her face remained solid.

As soon as the policemen had disappeared, she pulled the door open, stood aside and nodded me out.

I ran. I don't know how I ran with my injuries, but I did, taking extra turns, left and right to make myself harder to follow, and I did not stop until I was back in the cell.

* * *

The following morning, I tested my voice. It was harsh still, but now it seemed deeper – the masculinisation had begun, and I was out of time.

16

Pizza Marinara

After peeping up and down the alley outside the cell to check for policemen, I limped out in my new dress, and made my way directly to the Teatro di San Carlo to find Il Maccari, the castrato. The theatre was a fine building with a grand portico of stone reliefs. There were posters outside for Il Crociato in Egitto and a little way down the poster it announced 'Il Maccari, L'ultimo dei Grandi Castrati!' which I took to mean something like 'Il Maccari, the last of the great castratos'.

It was still only ten in the morning and it seemed unlikely that he would be here this early, so I waited across the road in a position from which I could see all the entrances.

* * *

It was about half-past twelve when I finally saw him – not approaching the theatre as it happened, but glimpsed in the lobby of a hotel nearby, and I caught him just as he stepped into the street.

"Signor Maccari, Sir, I... I am so sorry to trouble you."

"No trouble at all, my dear, I always have time for my public."

He spoke rather loudly as if to announce to passers-by that he was being admired.

"Would you care for a photograph? I dare say I have a few cartes de visite on me," he said, reaching into his pocket and making a great show of his *prononciation française*.

He clearly did not recognise me.

"We met a few nights ago, Sir."

"Did we indeed? And did you enjoy my performance?" He directed this question again at volume to the public at large.

"Very much indeed – you sang at a party at the Norwegian Consulate." This I said very quietly, trying to coax his volume down to mine.

He looked at my face closely. "Yes, I think I might recognise you, what name was it?"

I looked around and leaned a little closer "It's Thomas – I was the one who cried when you sang."

I winced as if waiting for a bang. He did frown at me for a moment, but then smiled very kindly.

"Well now, don't you look a picture."

"I do apologise for my appearance, but I am so desperate to speak to you, sir – I think you might be the only man in the world who can help me." Maccari deflated a little and nodded his head as if my statement was somehow disappointingly familiar.

"I am for lunch now," he said, quietly, and with none of his previous theatricality, "why don't you join me?"

"That would be lovely, thank you very much." And we walked away together.

"Do you like pizza?"

"I don't know. What is it?"

My question stopped him still.

"You've never had pizza? How long have you been in Napoli?"

"About six months I think, but I haven't been out much."

"Well then, Thomas, you are bound for a treat, but I can hardly call you Thomas looking like that now can I."

"Oh, well it's… um… I'm Emmeline, Sir… if you don't mind."

"As you wish, Emmeline – a very pretty name."

"Thank you." We continued walking.

"Your voice is very hoarse, my dear, I hope you don't have a cold – I really can't afford to catch it."

"Not a cold, Sir," I said, "it's an injury." He glanced at my throat which I had thought was fully hidden by my high collar, but the way he winced suggested it wasn't.

A few minutes later we entered a restaurant of sorts called Pizzeria Mastunicola.

I had been expecting something rather more grand, as might provide a lunch worthy of an opera singer, but it was quite stark really – the walls were tiled, but the tiles were not holding on to them very enthusiastically; the tables were ill-matched, some marble-topped, some wood, and both varieties were well chipped about the edges.

The smell though, was quite wonderful, and I recognised it immediately as the bread, tomatoes and herbs that had so often haunted me on the balcony of my room at Uncle Walter's apartment.

The staff seemed to know Maccari, and a waiter led us to a table, but it was of no better quality or position than the others.

"Due marinari," said Maccari.

The waiter nodded an 'of course', then shouted in Neapolitan, "Duje marinàr," and three cooks who were standing before a huge domed oven, shouted back the same, but in comically high voices. I looked at Maccari, who rolled his eyes, but then he shook his head at me very slightly.

"Don't let it trouble you," he whispered, "it's normal – normal for castrati."

It seemed quite extraordinary to me that anyone would mock a voice of such exquisite beauty. I looked at the cooks and one of them made a two-fingered snipping gesture at me whilst indicating Maccari with a nod.

At that moment, the waiter, or perhaps he was the manager, shouted something like "Basta." rather crossly at them, and they returned, smirking to their work. He then came to our table and, with a little bow, apologised. Maccari laughed it off immediately, patting the man on the arm.

In perhaps no more than three minutes, the waiter appeared again with two large plates, upon each of which was a huge, tomato-drenched flatbread.

"My dear Emmeline," said Maccari, "you are about to taste pizza marinara, one of the finest dishes in Europe. Now then, tear off a piece of the bread while it is still hot and give me your impression."

"Oh," I said with my mouth full. "It's so soft."

"And yet possessed of an infinitesimally thin crust?"

"Yes, and... smoky."

"But now try it with the tomato."

I had not had hot food for days, and the tomatoes were piping rich and sweet and sharp.

"It's absolutely delicious," I said with a hot dribble on my chin, and it was delicious even though the swallowing of it was so painful.

"San Marzano tomatoes, from the slopes of Vesuvio, fresh garlic and an excellent olive oil."

"And thyme?" I ventured.

"No," he said, raising a long, slender finger, "wild oregano." Maccari was clearly in love with his food, and his belly was the declaration of that love.

We ate ravenously and said little more until our plates were empty.

"That was unspeakably lovely," I rasped with my hand on my throat to soothe the pain, "I wish one could buy pizza in London."

"Please no," he said, laughing. "An English chef would make a disaster of it – pizza must always remain a Neapolitan secret."

There were now a few moments of uncomfortable silence, before Maccari took a mouthful of beer and looked me straight in the eye.

"You want to find a castrator, don't you."

"Yes," I said, leaning forwards pleadingly. "How can you know that?"

"I have met two people like you before. You will tell me that you are really a woman, but somehow trapped in the body of a man, yes?"

I looked around again. "Well... yes," I said, astonished that he could know this much of me, and even more so that there were others like me.

"Don't do it – it is not the answer," he said, with his head tilted forwards slightly and his eyebrows raised – the expression of a mother warning her child against a sharp object.

"There is no other answer," I said. "And if I don't do something in the next few days, my voice will be lost forever, and I will grow a beard, and so many horrible things will happen to me. I cannot contemplate it – I cannot survive it."

"And if you have castration, your body will end up like mine - tall and incongruous, and people will laugh at you. You will be no more accepted as female than would a woman with a beard."

"Well... I have not yet worked out what to do about that, but maybe I will think of a way to stop it happening."

"You can't."

"But at least there's a chance in it – it is my only chance."

"Nor will castration give you the organs of womanhood – you will never have children, nor satisfy a husband. Indeed any man that experiences you intimately will know you right away as a fraud."

"I don't want a man to experience me, and... and I am not a fraud," I said in a shouted whisper. "I am Emmeline, and whatever deformities God has imposed on me are... are superficial."

"But no woman will want you either, Emmeline – no one wants a castrato – you will make yourself completely unlovable. Can you really be alone for the rest of your life?"

I went to speak, but nothing came out.

"You're crying," he said, and I wiped my face.

"Well it's..." I wiped my face again and looked away. "I'm used to being alone. But at least... at least with castration..." I frowned and leaned towards him. "If puberty gets me, then I will be completely invisible. That's the thing – you see it's lonely not to be loved by another human being, but it's even lonelier to be invisible to all human beings. Do you see what I mean?"

Maccari shook his head gently. "Shall I tell you what befell those two others like you?"

"Yes."

"One died during the procedure, as half the boys who underwent it did. Indeed, when I was castrated with two other boys, only I survived of the three. The other man... or 'woman' as you prefer, was already fully grown when he underwent the procedure. He hoped that it might somehow reverse his masculinity and allow him to live as a woman. It did not, and six months

90

later he cut his own throat with a broken bottle."

Again I couldn't speak for a moment, I just looked at him with my mouth open, waiting for the right thought to come out.

"Look," I said, "I cannot deny that those are terrible stories, and I cannot deny that my path is probably futile... and lonely too, but at least with castration there is some small hope. I mean, 'probably futile' is surely better than 'certainly hopeless.'"

Maccari gave me his kind smile again. "I have lived this life, Emmeline, and I have lived in some of the dark places that you are so determined to enter. I know that nothing I say will dissuade you, but I hope you understand, that in good conscience, I could not let you attempt such a thing without first warning you of the consequences."

"You are very kind, sir, and thank you – your warnings are invaluable."

"The truth is that I do not know if there are any castrators left, for it has been illegal to castrate since 1870."

"The very year I was born," I said. "How ironic."

"If you want to try the man who castrated me, then look for Carlo Colombo on Vico Lungo San Matteo in the Spanish Quarter. I do not know if he is still there, nor even if he's still alive, but that is the only lead I can give you because it is the only one I have. And you should know that he is not, by any means, a doctor."

"Thank you so very much," I said.

"I say again, Emmeline, it is not an easy life for a castrato – the only ones that I have known to make a tolerable life of it, are the very few like me who have made a success of their voices. I do not honestly think that you can live as a woman, not for long anyway, and that is the truth, but if you survive the operation, I suspect that you might continue as you are now for perhaps two or three years before the distortion of your body begins to draw attention."

"Three years is not so bad," I said. "It's three more than I would otherwise have had."

17

Spermatic Artery

The Spanish Quarter had nothing about it that was salubrious. The buildings were similar to those on Via Dei Tribunali, but more decrepit and more over-looming, and a foul miasma seemed to hover in the streets like a dying breath.

Vico Lungo San Matteo was narrow, and seemed darker than the other streets. I asked an elderly woman for Carlo Colombo. She didn't answer but beckoned me along a way and took me to a door. She knocked it fearfully hard and yelled "Carlo." There was no answer so she yelled again "Carlo, na' visitatric." There was a chesty cough from inside, and the elderly woman nodded me at the door before walking on.

A few moments later a very small, and very, very old man opened it enough to reveal half of himself.

"Signor Colombo?" I said.

"Sì."

There was nothing to do but come straight to the point:

"Castratore?"

He waved me off dismissively. "Nun, illegàl."

"Per Favore," I pleaded, taking out my money.

He held out both his tremulous hands to me palm down. The joints of his fingers were like oak galls, choking the dead twigs of an old tree.

"Nun pòzzo," he said.

It was clear that he would struggle even to cut up his dinner with his crippled hands, and if I wasn't mistaken, he was also blind in one eye.

"Is there another doctor?" I asked. "Altro medico?"

"Nun," he insisted, "illegàl." Then he leant his shoulder into the big black door and pushed it shut.

I just stood there, blank for a moment.

"That really is the end of it – the end of me," I whispered.

I felt strangely calm about it, as if there was nothing to fight any more. My voice had shown no improvement this morning so it had probably been too late anyway. I had no friends, no family, and every reason to be alive had now escaped me.

I found myself walking through the Spanish Quarter, wondering how the end of me would come. Should I simply stop right here, sit in the gutter and wait quietly for death to arrive? Or should I hurry it along by some means?

I could think of no reason to prolong it, but the moment I fully acknowledged that fact and stepped from passive death to active suicide, I also stepped from calm to fear.

I tried to reassure myself that once dead, there will be no fear – that fear itself was simply another horror from which death would alleviate me. But as the logic of my suicide became more and more persuasive, so the fear of it became more and more debilitating, and I cursed Uncle Walter for not having had the strength in his thumbs to finish me off.

* * *

Eventually I found myself at the docks. Journeys began here, journeys ended here, and I had brought my small life all the way from England, ready to off-load it like a sack of fertilizer.

It was a place that presented many opportunities for suicide. I could just slip off the quay, into the water and drown myself, but it seemed so frightening to suffocate in the khaki cold of the water. I could hang myself by a rope and choke – there were plenty of them lying about, but surely that too was suffocation, and by more painful means.

Or, I could take out Maria's letter opener and open an artery with it. Thanks to Gray's Anatomy, I knew just the insertion points that would provide the greatest flow of blood.

How ironic it was – a few hours ago, I was seeking the insertion of a blade to save my life, and now I sought the same to end it. I should have castrated myself, I thought – it would probably have killed me, and if it had, then all well and good, and if it hadn't...

...yes, that was the thing, what if it didn't kill me? What if I castrated myself and survived, and got my three extra years of life?

It was a stunning idea. Could I actually do it myself? Remove my own testicles? It seemed plausible, especially with my medical knowledge. I would need a scalpel or a good razor, a needle and silk thread for sutures, and some alcohol to discourage bleeding.

Well why not? The outcome would solve my problem either way.

Could I do it though? Could I actually cut away a part of my own body with my own hands? Could I tolerate the pain? Could I tolerate the horror? I certainly would not like to see it done to anyone else, so how much more horrific to see it done to me?

These were questions I could only answer in the act, so I headed for the market to purchase everything I needed for my experimental operating theatre.

In addition to the razor, the needle, the silk thread, and the alcohol, I bought some cotton gauze, a pair of towels, a dozen good candles for extra light, and by luck, I also happened upon a magnifying mirror.

I turned towards the cell, now quite certain that what I was about to attempt was nearly impossible, but equally certain that I was going to attempt it on account of the 'nearly' part of impossible. If I did manage it, then I should certainly never need any further evidence that I was singular.

As I walked, I found myself fascinated by the normality of the people I passed, and I imagined myself stopping one couple for a chat:

"Lovely evening for a stroll," I imagined saying to them.

"Yes," says the man. "I am taking my wife to purchase a pair of gloves.

And yourself, Miss?"

"Me? I am off to a tiny store room to castrate myself with a razor. Good evening."

I laughed aloud at the thought of this exchange, but laughing aloud when alone in public seemed to hint at insanity.

Am I indeed mad? I wondered. Was I simply a very disturbed young man, deluded about his sex, and about to mutilate himself, perhaps even to death? It was possible, it was surely possible, but if I was insane, how would I know? Can the insane know that they are insane? Perhaps, if I survive, I will be able to unravel that little mystery, and if I die, then it matters not either way.

En route I tried to think my way through the procedure:

To simply slice off the entire complement of external parts would surely kill me, and in no time at all, so that could be immediately dismissed as an option. Slicing off the whole scrotum would be perhaps marginally less bloody, but really, for now, my argument was with the testicles, so I decided that the most survivable method would be to extract the testicles through small incisions in the scrotum, then tie off the spermatic artery with the silk thread before cutting the attaching vessels through.

* * *

Once back at the cell, I laid everything out in careful order.

The alcohol was an English gin – 'Old Tom' – two large bottles of it. I had been very surprised to find it in Naples, but I knew it was strong, and therefore ideal for my purposes.

I allowed myself a mouthful to settle my nerves, but no more as I did not want to cloud my mind or fumble my fingers. It tasted awful.

I now entered a very meticulous and precise frame of mind. I took off my dress and folded it carefully. I then laid out a towel to sit on, placed the lighted candles in tidy symmetry on either side of my lap, and propped the magnifying mirror on a rolled-up towel between my legs.

As I took the razor in my hand, my heart began to thump at my chest like a frantic neighbour beating on the door of a smoking house.

I paused for a moment, and decided that perhaps I should begin by washing my genitals in gin, and perhaps my hands, and the razor too so that all the surfaces concerned would be coated in the haemostatic fluid. This done, I took up the razor again and hovered with it for a moment, not quite sure how to begin.

I felt the scrotum carefully. I would have to make an incision big enough to extract the testicle, but I first needed to decide the best position and angle for the cut.

If I cut at the bottom of the scrotum, the testicles would be at the limit of their extension before exiting the hole, making access to the suspending vessels difficult. So I chose the side of the scrotum, and fairly high up.

I held the skin taught with one hand, and reached down once more with the razor.

I placed the corner of the blade against the skin and made the tiniest scratch.

It stung so I stopped and lay back for a moment.

How on earth can I do this? I thought. Every instinct is against me, as would be the advice of even the most reckless observer. For that matter, was I really sure I even wanted to do it?

How does one quantify sureness? If I'd had to express it as a percentage, then I would have said that I was perhaps eighty-percent sure. Was that enough? I didn't know.

I sat up and tried again, but again I failed and lay back. Another attempt ended the same way and I began to cry – what a bizarre horror story my life had culminated in.

I tried to visualise myself in a man's life – a strong man, handsome, steady, a good income, a wife, children perhaps. For a moment it seemed almost tolerable, but then I imagined myself naked before a mirror – a large, square-cornered, hairy, snorting, leathery man, with big hands, and a fat, hanging cock.

I sat up again and held the razor once more in place. I growled and began to breathe in and out through my teeth with great rapidity, and then I pushed the razor through.

My God, it hurt – an acidic, wincing sting that prickled right up my back, but I pushed the blade on in a single slice for more than an inch.

There was blood, but not as much as expected, and I drizzled some Old Tom over it to inhibit the flow.

The gin turned the sting into a burn.

I threw my head back, blowing in rapid puffs as if trying to extinguish a fire on the ceiling.

As the burn subsided, I returned to the incision.

I now needed to squeeze the testicle out through the hole.

It began to emerge like a bloodshot, blind eye through a tight eyelid, as if I had awoken the monstrous thing with my intrusion.

I began to hesitate over the pressure, but suddenly, almost of it's own accord, it popped out.

The horror immediately gave way to an instinctive calm, and self-preservational concentration.

My studies came to me with clarity – I noted the pale, tubular vas deferens which transports sperm away from the testicle, and I could see the spermatic artery which offered my principle threat of haemorrhage.

I took a length of silk thread, and tied it three times around the vessels to choke their supply of blood, then picked up the razor again.

This next act – the cutting through of the vessels, would be my Rubicon then – the very act of castration.

I held the vessels over the blade and closed my eyes for a moment.

"Dear God, help me."

And with an upward snap I cut through.

A pain shot up into my abdomen as if I had been kicked, but it was not so painful as to deflect me, and I cast the testicle aside as if flicking the contents of a sneeze off my hand.

More gin, more burning and puffing, and then to the other side.

Again the first cut was the greatest effort. This right testicle was somewhat smaller than the left for some reason, and exited without argument. I tied off the vessels, and again I hung them over the razor and cut through.

Immediately there was a problem.

I did not know the cause – perhaps it was that I looked away for the cut and sliced too close to the silk, or perhaps I confused the knots and they simply fell open, but I was suddenly and profusely bleeding.

I poured gin again, but there was no discernible effect on the gushing blood and a dark pool began to spread out from my crotch.

I took more silk thread, but now I could not find the artery – it had contracted back into the scrotum and everything was drowning in blood.

I took the razor and doubled the length of the incision so that I could get a thumb and forefinger in the hole, but it was almost impossible to distinguish structures in the hot flow.

For a frantically long time, I struggled to retrieve the vessels, but at last, I caught the end of the artery between the nails of my thumb and forefinger.

By now my head was light and dizzy, and I knew there may be little time left.

I pulled another length of silk, and in a spinning, floating fumble of effort, I finally managed to pass it around the vessels and tie them off.

I do not remember anything beyond that moment.

III

Despite All Contradictions

18

Mine to Keep

When I first awoke, I was not at all sure what had happened or where I was. I tried to sit up, but my heart was racing very fast and I was so dizzy and weak that I fainted.

This pattern of waking dizzied with a racing heart before fainting, continued perhaps for a few hours or perhaps for a few days. I know that I drank a lot of water, and that I also ate some bread. I do not remember eating it, but I do remember that when I finally awoke in a fit enough state to remain awake, there were lumps of bread scattered about me with bites out of them.

But the bread is not the thing that I most remember from that more lucid awakening – the thing I recall above all else is happiness. It was really a very simple happiness – a quiet contentment – I knew exactly what I had done, and that I was alive, and I knew that right now, the world was better than it was before.

I tested my voice, and I could immediately feel that a lot of healing had taken place – it was a little rough, but the pitch was right – female pitch – it wasn't broken.

I then sat up and looked at the horrendous carnage that lay about me. There was so much blood – much more than I thought a person would have in them, so much in fact, that it seemed quite funny and I laughed out loud, but the laughing hurt my ribs so I had to stop myself.

What's more, I had been rolling about in it all during my restless delirium so my legs, arms, back and shoulders were all caked in it, and my hair was standing up in a stiff red headdress. I tried not to laugh again.

There was still some Old Tom in one of the bottles so I used that to clean the blood from the surgical site – it did not sting, at least not much, which I took to mean that some sealing of the wound had already taken place. Once cleaned the wounds looked reasonably happy – not too inflamed or swollen, and not weeping.

It was at this moment that I saw one of the little prunes that had been a testicle. This sight did squeeze a little retch out of me, and a second retch came when I noticed that some of the bread I had bitten lumps from was smeared, or rather soaked in blood – I had therefore eaten some of myself.

Perhaps though, it had been nutritionally beneficial to return some of that lost blood home – it may even have been why I was still alive, and anyway, was it really any different to eating a black pudding sandwich? Again I laughed out loud, and again I stopped myself because of the pain in my ribs.

I now spent perhaps an hour gently cleaning the blood from my body. I did not hurry the task, but took it at a gentle and faintly ritualistic pace. It felt therapeutic – as if I had taken the mud bath at a spa, and was cleansing it gently away.

I then went to the mirror and inspected my uncle injuries. I could see that things had certainly improved – the burst blood vessels in my eyes were fading, scabs were flaking, and the blacks and purples on my throat were now fading to browns and yellows, but this was already enough exertion to exhaust me, so I decided that I would do nothing more with the rest of the day than recline, eat, and perhaps read a little, so that's what I did.

* * *

It was two days more days before I felt strong enough to attempt my escape from Naples. I cleaned the cell first and placed all as I had found it. I also wanted to leave some money for Maria, or at least a letter of thanks, but didn't dare do either, as I had no idea how much money I would need myself to get back to England, and I feared that a letter might fall into the wrong hands and endanger her. She had also left no instructions for the key so I decided to push it under the door as I left and hope that she would have a spare.

I always felt vulnerable leaving the cell, but to now push the key out of reach, and cut myself off from my last refuge, was like stepping backwards into darkness. I couldn't linger on such dark feelings though, for if I was going to survive, I would need to retain a strong and positive disposition. I nodded to myself and began to feel almost pugnacious about it, as if fate had sent me a bully, and I was determined to give him a bloody nose.

As I began to walk, I felt very conscious of my surgically altered body – lighter somehow, not from the loss of two little balls, but from the loss of the weight from my heart. I also began to sing quietly to myself, just to feel the female pitch of my voice – something which had only been on loan to me before, but which I had now paid for in blood, and was mine to keep.

19

Like a Cat from a Mastiff

I had already decided that my best route to England would be back the way I came, and now I wasn't even apprehensive about the journey, because in my new body, with my real voice and a positive disposition, I felt I could do just about anything I set my mind to – a solo expedition across Europe was nothing.

After a short diversion to the market to buy food, I headed for the train station, but then I realised that I still had Maria's silver letter opener in my carpet bag – I had been carrying it since I found it. She had all but saved my life, and I couldn't bear the idea of stealing from her, so I decided to take a short detour back to the cell to slip the letter opener under the door.

As I turned into the alley, I noticed some men – two of them it looked like, but they were in the shadows and the sun was in my eyes so I couldn't see them clearly. Normally I would panic to see men in the alley and turn around, but not today, not in my pugnacious mood, no – I was going to simply walk past them as any other woman might, and if by some chance they are Uncle's men looking for me, then they are looking for a boy named Thomas, and I am neither.

As I got a little closer, I realised that they were actually very near the cell.

A few steps more, and I could see that they were right outside it.

Then the sun went in and I saw their clothes – uniforms – policemen.

My new-found courage evaporated, and every instinct now screamed at me to run, but that would only mark me out as their prey, so I had to keep walking forwards, feigning nonchalance.

As I closed upon them, my heart began to pound hard against my sternum. The cell door was wide open and both policemen were stood with their backs to the street, hands on hips, looking into the cell.

'Don't look, don't look,' I whispered in my head, but then I thought it would look odd not to, for who wouldn't be curious? So as I passed the door to the cell, I glanced inside, and there I met the dead gaze of Uncle Walter.

I looked away instantly and kept walking. "Don't run, don't run, don't run," I whispered, as I strained my ears for approaching footsteps. It was impossible to differentiate the sounds behind me from the flap and rustle of my skirt but I could feel his proximity lifting every hair on the back of my neck as it reached along the street towards me.

At the end of the street, I took an Orpheus glance back, and saw him standing outside the cell, a policeman either side of him, and all three watching me go.

The moment I turned the corner, I ran like a cat from a mastiff, but the street was an impossibility of potholes, stalls and pedestrians, so I kept tripping and barging into people who yelled abuse back at me.

A hundred yards into my run, I looked behind. They were chasing – all three of them, and I heard myself cry out.

A few yards more and there were steps to my right – a door – an open door – a church door.

I do not know if I tripped or collapsed, but my palms slapped the marble floor inside the church doorway as I winded myself over my bag.

A hand reached down to me. It was a priest in black cassock. He looked into my eyes and I gripped his hand with all my strength.

"Please," I begged. He looked at the entrance to the church, and keeping hold of my hand, he shut the door and locked it. Without a word, he led me along the side of the nave and stood me in a confessional box.

There was a firm knock at the church door.

"Si, si, un momento," he called out, and then he spoke to me – very quietly, and in English:

"What trouble are you in, child?"

"I have done nothing wrong, really I have not, but they mean to kill me… please."

He searched my face for a moment, then looked at the bruises on my neck.

"Very well."

He pointed towards a small door on the other side of the nave.

"I will let them into the church and I will take them through that door. When you hear it shut, you must leave the church immediately."

There was a knock again. "Si, si," he shouted, then he pulled the purple curtain halfway across the confessional door, just enough to cover me. "Do not close it," he said, "or it will not look empty." Another knock and he was gone.

I heard the church door unlocked, and the first voice was Uncle Walter's:

"La ragazza," he said, not threatening but pleading – it meant 'the girl'. The Italian from that point was fast and further confused by the echo in the church, so I could not grasp the whole of it. I heard the words 'daughter' and 'desperate', and there were some lies about young love and a broken heart.

The priest interrogated them firmly but politely for several minutes, and all the time my uncle playing the frantic father. Gradually the priest began to soften – he was saying "si, si" again, but gently now, and with a tone of understanding and agreement, as if he had been entirely taken in by my uncle's lies.

Finally, he said something about 'hiding' and told them to follow him.

I could not tell if their footsteps were approaching, so I crouched, ready to burst out and knock them all down like skittles, but then I heard a door open – the small door – the priest had trusted me.

The moment it banged shut, I ran for my life - out of the church, and sprinting in a zig-zag through several streets and alleyways to put space and confusion between Uncle and me.

I decided to head straight for the train station. Then I decided that of all places, I should not go to the station, for he would surely have been expecting me there for days – he probably had people lying in wait. Thank goodness I hadn't gone there earlier. The docks then, I thought… no, for again, he will surely be watching all main points of departure.

But there was another route out of Italy – another train – one that travels up the East coast instead of the West. I knew that I could get onto that line at Benevento, and I knew that to be somewhere North-East of Naples, so, taking my bearings from the sun and the position of Vesuvius, I set off.

* * *

After walking hard and fast through several miles of tangled suburbs, I expected the city to gradually peter out – that there would be a steady sparsening of buildings, but the edge of Naples came quite suddenly, and there was a moment when a single step took me from city street to country track. It was beautiful country too – humming and dry, and in the far distance were hills – soft, rounded, and wooded in short, dark green. I finally began to relax a little, slowing from a rush to a steady pace.

I walked right through the long afternoon, and I reached my first signpost for Benevento at dusk. It said nineteen miles. I was afraid of the dark, but this was a distance I might cover in a night so I decided to keep walking for as long as my nerve held.

It held until about midnight when I was almost knocked to the ground by a red deer stag bursting out of the woods and across the path not five feet in front of me. I stood quite immobilised with shock, as his deep scent passed over me and followed him into the woods, but when all was still again, I laughed in the way you do when stepping into cold water, then tiptoed off the path and climbed under a low tree to hide from the rest of night and its creatures.

* * *

I left my hiding place just as the Eastern sky began to glow a little with dawn. I think I had slept intermittently, but it was hard to differentiate dreams of sleeping in the woods from actually sleeping in the woods, for the one was as surreal as the other.

I walked through a fresher, cooler morning, before finally reaching Benevento around midday. The train station was not difficult to find, but I entered cautiously, wary of the small chance that Uncle Walter had a man looking out for me even here.

It seemed fairly deserted, so I went to the ticket office. I decided not to ask for a ticket as far as Paris, nor even to Turin, for I did not want to leave such an obvious track for Uncle and the police to follow. Instead I bought a ticket for Foggia which was not very far, and then at Foggia I would buy a ticket to Turin, and at Turin, a ticket to Paris and so on, all the way back to England by separate, unconnected tickets, and then... And then what?

20

A Good First Impression

Three days later, I almost arrived at Victoria Station. It seemed highly unlikely that my uncle could have anyone waiting there for the Dover trains, but I didn't care to take the risk and decided to get off a stop early at Clapham. And anyway, I had no particular need to reach Victoria, for it was not as if I would be taking the onward train to Harewell. No, my new life would begin in London, and Clapham was as good a place to start as any.

My biggest priority was to find employment – everything would depend on me finding an income. But first a couple of practicalities – I changed my remaining lire to pounds at the station, and I also needed to find somewhere to stay – a lodging house of some sort. I looked for someone to ask, and found a porter pushing an empty trolley along the street outside the station. He was tall and thin, with a great broom of a moustache, and he had a friendly look about him.

"Excuse me," I said.

"How may I help, Miss?"

"I wonder if you might be able to point me in the direction of a lodging house."

He looked me up and down, but politely.

"Might I enquire, Miss, are you looking for accommodation at a particular price? I mean to say, Miss, that where to go, all depends upon your means."

"I see. Well, to be candid, my budget is minimal."

"Right you are. Then may I suggest you head towards Chelsea. You will find many reasonably-priced establishments there, and they're not all bad I hear."

"Thank you very much."

As I turned to walk away, he spoke again.

"Beg pardon, Miss."

"Yes?"

"If you don't mind me asking, is it your first time in a doss-house? I mean lodging house of course." The accidental appearance of the term doss-house caused him to scratch his nose awkwardly.

"Yes it is," I said.

"Then might I suggest, Miss, that if budget allows, you find yourself one with cubicles? It is much the nicer way to have a little privacy."

"Cubicles – thank you, you're very kind."

"Not at all, Miss – stayed in a few myself, and always glad to point a young lady in the right direction."

It was a great relief to have made a good first impression in England as Emmeline – an ability to do that could surely only be of benefit to me in my new life, but it also brought home just how few people had ever actually liked me. My family certainly didn't – not any of them.

There was Maria in Naples – she had helped me, indeed she had all but saved my life, but perhaps that was only out of a sense of morality, for she was never warm, and I don't think she smiled at me once in the whole time I was there.

Atle did like me, but not in the way that I wanted to be liked.

Then there was the destitute woman – she certainly liked me, although… although perhaps even that was only the effect of my having helped her rather than any affection for me as a person.

Still, I had made a good first impression here in London, and I had done so as myself rather than disguised as a man, and perhaps that meant that people would take more readily to Emmeline than they ever did to Thomas.

And not to forget Miss Bright of course – she had liked me at a glance, I was sure of it. Yes, perhaps people just needed to see me for who I really am.

* * *

By the time I reached Chelsea, it was early evening. There were indeed many lodging houses, just as the porter had promised, however, most were for men only, and several hired rooms by the hour rather than the night. Of the houses catering to women, fourpence a night was the cheapest rate to be found, but a cubicle could not be had for less than sixpence.

I entered a moderately clean-looking establishment on a narrow street – it was called The Turks Row Home For Single Women.

I was greeted a little way inside the door by a large lady sitting on a wooden chair – her legs splayed apart. She was leaning back as if she were pregnant and taking a moment's rest, but she looked to be in her fifties, so pregnancy was unlikely.

She wished me a pleasant, "Good evening," and then continued with, "Dormitory or cubicle, dear?"

I was by now very short of money, but I decided that I should still heed the advice of the station porter.

"A cubicle please." I said.

"That's sixpence a night."

"Then I can afford three nights, but I hope to find employment tomorrow so I'm sure I will look to extend my stay."

"That'll be one shilling and sixpence for now then, my dear."

I handed over the money, and it left me with only fourpence.

"Much obliged," she said, and popped it in a pocket of her apron, then she opened a large ledger and scratched a few details.

"What name is it please?"

"Stanton, Emmeline Stanton," I said.

"Two 'm's?"

"Yes." And there it was – my full name written down in a book, despite my uncle and in defiance of my mother.

"Supper's at eight so you're in time for that. We only have respectable ladies here of course, and needless to say, men are not allowed on the premises under any circumstances, other than they might be a fireman or such, come to save us all from a fiery death."

"Of course."

"Well then, Miss Stanton, you may call me Mrs Buckler." She handed me a key attached to a large brass token with 'C 12' written upon it. "The cubicles are to be found on the second floor and twelve is at the farthest end. Go on up, and I hope you will find The Turk to your liking." Then she smiled, and I felt that I had made my second good-first-impression of the day.

The building was somewhat in need of attention – one of the stairs seemed safer stepped over than upon, plaster was missing in several places, and there was something of a pondy whiff to it all, but it was nowhere near as bad as one might have expected of a so-called 'doss house'.

As I passed the dormitory on the first floor, the smell of pond was drowned by the smell of people, but on the second floor – the cubicle floor – the smell was lighter, I suppose because the smells were held within the cubicles and only let out when a door was opened.

Cubicle twelve was a tiny affair, little bigger than the bed, and a smaller space even than my Neapolitan cell, but I had only myself and one bag so it would do. The sheets were clean but the mattress was not. I turned it over but found the other side more stained than the first, so turned it back again. It was dry though, so whatever had been excreted upon it was now incorporated into the fabric and should hopefully remain there.

At supper, I sat with some twelve other women. We were served Yarmouth bloaters, which I prefer to kippers because they are not so salty, and there was also bread, butter and tea.

I had the impression that few of the inmates knew each other, and little was said between us as we ate. Everyone looked tired, but the woman directly in front of me looked so exhausted that I thought she might collapse into her food at any moment.

On the train from Dover that morning, I had imagined myself having quite a pleasant time in London, working in a hat shop or something like that, but then, lots of young women probably move to London thinking the same thing, and the truth was that I had never worked – I had barely even done any school work, never mind the kind of physical labour that leaves a person in a state of collapse by supper time.

How on earth was I going to do this?

21

If Only I Could Sew

Just before I left the following morning, I asked Mrs Buckler if she could offer me any advice on finding work.

"What are your skills, my dear?"

"I have none in particular," I said. "I read and write, I know some science, some geography, and some medicine."

She laughed. "And where on earth would a young lady acquire such informations, pray tell?"

"Oh... I read all manner of things in books."

She paused, and looked me up and down. "I dare say you do, but what practical skills do you possess? Can you sew?"

"Only in the most basic way I'm afraid."

"Well then, what previous employment have you had?"

"None."

"Do you have a character reference?"

"No."

She shook her head. "Well, you might try Westaways. It's an employment agency for ladies on the Brompton Road. They mainly supply governesses, but I hear they also have lesser positions. Aside from that, I can can only suggest that you walk about the town and enquire wherever you can."

"Thank you," I said, "I will certainly try Westaways."

There was something about the way she had said, "I dare say you do," that gave me a feeling that I was now slipping away from my good first impression to the more usual dislike, but I also felt sure my accomplishments would be very useful to an employer – a knowledge of science could be helpful in almost any form of business; geography might help in an export or import department, and surely a little medical knowledge could prove invaluable if someone was injured at work.

When I reached Westaways, I stopped at the door for a moment to tidy my reflection in the window. There I was again – Emmeline – me looking back at me. The site of my true self was always a peaceful thing, as if my reflection reached right through the glass to embrace me and welcome me home. I did look a bit tired – there were shadows under my eyes but I smiled to myself, and that made me look much brighter.

* * *

"I have come in search of a situation," I announced to the receptionist with a big smile.

"Are you on our books?"

"No, I'm not, but I should like to be."

"What name is it please?"

"Emmeline – Emmeline Stanton."

"Very well, Miss Stanton, take a seat and Mrs Angelico will see you presently."

Presently, Mrs Angelico called me in. She seemed quite elderly, and her hair was tied back tight, as if trying to arrest the descent of her features.

She looked me up and down before speaking.

"Now then, Miss Stanton, I will ask you several questions, and we will establish thereby, whether you are suitable for our recommendation."

She took out a notebook and a pencil.

"Your date of birth?" This had me momentarily perplexed, for I was dressed as a somewhat older woman than my actual years. "...Well?"

"Um... the fifth of March, eighteen... sixty... eight." I added two years to make myself seventeen, but keeping all other details the same.

"Are you sure?"

"Quite sure."

"Then do try not to hesitate – it makes you appear untrustworthy."

"I apologise."

"You don't look quite seventeen, I would have said sixteen at the most," she said, squinting at me.

"I am seventeen," I insisted, and she made a doubtful note of it.

"Now then, what are your qualifications?"

"Well, I know some science, some geography, and a little medicine," I said.

She put down her pen and looked at me with a mixture of amusement and disgust, as if I had broken wind.

"Let's confine ourselves to the relevant shall we?" she said.

"I thought such knowledge might be very useful."

"Do you sew?" she asked, completely ignoring my explanation.

"Not really, no."

"Do you play the pianoforte?"

"No."

"Do you cook?"

"I'm afraid not."

"Do you have a character reference?"

"None."

She took off her spectacles. "What was your previous position?"

"I have not had an occupation before but, um, I'm quite singular – I mean to say that I learn quickly, and am very adaptable. I am really rather desperate for a position, Mrs Angelica."

"Angelico."

"Sorry."

She closed her notebook.

"Miss Stanton, you have somewhat the demeanour of a governess, but none of the required qualifications. Indeed you have no more qualifications or references than one would expect of a scullery maid."

"I see, and are there any positions for scullery maids?"

"There are, but not for ladies of your demeanour. Essentially, Miss

Stanton, you are both under-qualified and over-qualified, and I do not think you are suitable material for Westaways."

* * *

Well, it was a setback, but the day wasn't done yet, and nor was I, so I spent the afternoon wandering about Chelsea trying every conceivable place in which a young woman might be respectably employed – hat shops, florists, pubs, laundries etc, and when I had exhausted Chelsea I extended my searches to the neighbouring areas of Knightsbridge and Earls Court, but all to no avail. There were several positions to be had as a seamstress. There were also a number of positions in service advertised, but none for a woman with no domestic skills or experience. There were also factories of various sorts that took unskilled female labour, and these might have offered my best opportunity, but none of the ones I enquired at had any vacancies.

I finally returned to the lodging house late in the evening in a state of anxious exhaustion, knowing that if I failed to find work tomorrow, I would have one more night in the comfort of a bed followed by complete destitution.

* * *

The next day began with similar disappointments, but I finally had a bit of luck when a pub landlord told me that Barclay Perkins, an enormous brewery in Southwark, was taking on both male and female staff today. It was my last chance, but a good one – surely.

I was not entirely sure where Southwark was, other than it was East of me, and far enough away that I had not been there, but I asked directions and must have walked and half-run perhaps four miles to reach it. Once there, I followed the signs to the relevant offices and joined the long queue of prospective employees.

I counted eighty people ahead of me which was not good, but the brewery was so large that it seemed it could accommodate all eighty with ease. And surely, some of those ahead of me would be unsuitable.

People were escorted into the office one at a time, and interviews were brief, but once I had counted only seven women exiting with satisfied expressions, a ginger-haired man put his head around the door and announced, "No more women – men only now please."

The female part of the queue deflated to a collective sigh, and my stomach rolled over in dread.

When I had begun to live as myself, I had not really considered that changing my sex would so diminish my opportunities. How stupidly naive I had been. I mean, why couldn't they employ just as many women as men in a brewery? I might concede that physically, we are the weaker sex, but brute strength is not the only strength, and I'm sure we are able to work just as many hours as any man.

Once again I remembered the suffragist at the train station in Paris, and I decided that from now on, I too would call myself a suffragist. It was a strong word, and I would need all the strength I could find if I was to survive what was coming.

22

The Tentacles of Lecherous Men

"Very pleasant to know you, dear," said Mrs Buckler the following morning, as she took back the key to C 12. She put it in a drawer, mumbled something to herself, then picked up a broom and left the reception without looking at me.

I am not sure what I expected her to do other than that, but for a moment I imagined her saying, 'Would you like me to be your mother now? Then you needn't pay for the room.'

"Yes please," I said, aloud.

The real Mrs Buckler, upon hearing my voice, put her head around the door.

"Ten o'clock has gone, Miss Stanton, please leave the premises, thank you."

* * *

I looked up at the sky as I walked out of the door. I had never perceived the sky as the absence of a roof before, and there was nothing but a puff of cloud between my head and forever.

I tried to focus my attention upon immediate necessities, the first of which was food. So, with the fourpence I had left, I bought a loaf of bread, a pound of raisins, and the biggest piece of cheese that the remainder would stretch to. I would have to make it last as long as I possibly could, so I put it straight in my bag, and promised myself that I would not eat a single mouthful until this evening.

I spent the rest of the day as I had the previous ones – enquiring everywhere I could for employment. My searches took me Eastwards through Lambeth and Bermondsey, then North through Whitechapel until, late in the afternoon, I found myself at Spitalfields Market.

I had asked for work at perhaps two stalls when I became aware that a young man was following me. I glanced him up and down. He was a beastly-looking thing with his lower front teeth missing, leaving his lower canines to stand out like pig tusks. But he was also incongruously tidy, for he was clean-shaven, his boots were shiny, and his clothes looked rather expensive.

He smiled at me, but darkly, as if the smile was all for himself.

He disappeared for a moment then as I passed a quiet corner he reappeared and stood in my way.

"Pretty thing ain't ya," he said.

"Let me pass."

"No need to be uncivil, darlin'."

"Blocking my way, Sir, is uncivil."

"If I doesn't block it, how am I to discuss business matters with you?"

"Business?"

"That's right, darlin', pretty little thing like you 'as no need to go begging for work."

"I am not begging, I am merely making enquiries. Now stand aside, Sir, or I will scream for help."

He moved closer, blocking me in completely, then he took the cheroot out of his mouth and stared at me through the tobacco plumes with the eyes of a dead pike.

"You won't scream," he said, his breath a tepid vapour of tobacco and tooth decay.

I knew that look – it was the same dead stare of my uncle and I froze.

Without breaking his gaze, he reached into a pocket, pulled out a card, and pushed it into my hand.

"Now, you can go on looking for a position in the market, and sleepin' where you can, and starvin' too I don't doubt. Yes, Darlin' – starvin', for if you ain't starvin' now you soon will be. But come and stop with us at Sixteen Exeter Street, and you'll do a pound a night with that soft little face. Think it over, why don't you."

And with that he walked away leaving the card to curl in the sweat of my hand.

A pound a night, now that would be good money, I thought. And how surprised the punters would be to find a little penis smiling back at them at the denouement. I laughed to myself to hold back from crying, and then I cried anyway, just a little.

* * *

Within a couple of hours it was dark and I had no idea what to do about it. At first everything was quite raucous – people tumbled out of pubs and into music halls, then out of music halls and back into pubs – they laughed, they sang, and they cheered, with the general temperament being one of boisterous fun. But as the night deepened, the mood darkened – the laughing and singing gained more bark and snarl, and encounters turned to fights at the slightest contradiction.

The men in particular became steadily more menacing – in the early evening, a few had whistled at me or made lewd comments, but by the small hours the comments had become passing gropes and offers of money for revolting services.

I had never anticipated just how much unwelcome attention a young woman alone on the streets must endure. The men were so unspeakably relentless – it was like a madness in them, as if their entire existence revolved around the pursuit of women.

* * *

By about three in the morning, I managed to find some peace on what seemed like a fairly well-hidden bench in a corner of Green Park. I was exhausted. I took my Thomas coat out of my bag, wrapped it around my shoulders and closed my eyes.

I have no idea how long I slept, but a sudden clack of wood against the bench woke me with a start. I jumped to my feet, and there was a policeman standing behind me with his truncheon resting on the back of the seat.

"Not here, Miss."

"I do apologise, I was just taking a small rest – not sleeping, I wasn't asleep, I just closed my eyes for a moment."

"Why don't you go down the embankment? Then you won't keep getting moved on."

"Yes, I will do that – thank you, and good evening," I said, and walked away as wakefully as I could.

"Not that way, Miss. You want to head down there." He pointed with his truncheon. "Keep on until the river, then turn left and follow it North and East for a couple of miles – you'll be amongst your own there."

"Of course, thank you," I said, following his instructions but with no clear idea of what he meant by 'my own'.

* * *

It was very cold by now – my body was dead tired and my feet felt as if I had spent the day stamping instead of walking, but after an hour or so, I caught the scent of homeless hair and urine, and shortly after that I finally found myself amongst 'my own' – a great encampment of homeless and destitute people, scattered along the embankment beyond Waterloo Bridge.

It was very crowded, and yet surprisingly still because most of the people were asleep. There were some benches, but they were already full – each one had at least six people sleeping on it in seated positions, and many others were sitting against the walls that ran along the embankment.

I walked very quietly through them, and as I did not want to be noticed or engaged with, I stood in a dark corner where the embankment wall met a monumental plinth.

I was now too hungry not to eat, so I opened my carpet bag quietly, tore off a chunk of bread and pushed it into my mouth. Then I opened the bag of raisins and stuffed some of them in with it. The resulting mush was the very same mush you get from eating a teacake, and, after pizza, it seemed to me about the most delicious thing I had ever eaten.

For the next several minutes, my troubles took a rest and left me in a tiny world, made entirely of food.

* * *

At some uncertain time, deep into the early hours, I opened my eyes from a standing doze and became aware of a man meandering along the embankment in my general direction – his head was down, and his face was reduced to a nose between the high fence of a collar and the low brim of a hat.

Every so often he would stop at a woman, nudge her awake, and then mutter something to her. The three that I saw him approach all waved him on – two with indifference, the other with some annoyance.

I sank into my corner as he came near and I stood very still, hoping that he wouldn't notice me, but the corner wasn't dark enough.

He looked at me from my crotch up, and when he saw my face, his own seemed to illuminate from behind its collar fence.

"How much to suck me?" he whispered.

"I... I..." I couldn't find the rest of the sentence.

"And don't go elevating your price just 'cos you got a pretty face. Shall we say tuppence? Thruppence then. Come on, darlin', give us a suck."

I turned my face into the corner so he couldn't see it, and the moment I couldn't see him, I found my voice.

"Leave me alone," I said, loud and firm, and now that I could speak, I had the courage to turn back and look him in the face.

He paused for a moment to glare at me.

"You mouthy little bitch," he said, lunging forwards, grabbing the sides of

123

my head with his hard hands and sealing me in with his body like a coffin lid.

He pressed his mouth against mine, and I felt his sour tongue poke into my mouth – I tried to block it with my own but it was too strong. Nor could I kick him or force him away from me. He reached down to his trousers but had some difficulty with his flies so had to break away from my face to look down.

I took the chance to scream and flail at him.

"Shut it," he growled, bringing a fist up from his crotch and holding it under my chin. "Or I'll shut you up for good."

A voice came from a nearby bench.

"For the love of God, woman, will you please give him his fun, we're trying to sleep here."

I screamed again, "GO AWAY."

He tried to clamp my mouth shut, but there was now a general murmur of irritation from people nearby, and the man on the bench spoke again:

"God help us, she ain't going to suck you mate, now fuck off or you'll 'ave my fucking fist to suck on instead."

The man immediately let go and scurried away.

It was suddenly very quiet. I wiped my mouth and spat every last spit out of it, then I steadied my shaking hands against my face and began to sob.

"Quiet there," came the voice again, but more of a mumble.

Vision after vision of Uncle Walter flashed before me, but I made no further sound, for although I convulsed with each sob, I closed my throat and covered my mouth with my hands to press the pain deep inside me where no one would hear it.

* * *

The next day, my second as a homeless wanderer in London, found me a great deal more daunted than the first.

I spent the morning working as hard as I possibly could at finding work, but by mid afternoon, the constant rejection, the tiredness, and the rising hunger left me exhausted. I found myself another park bench and risked a short nap, but I felt no better for it, and afterwards I simply sat there, devoid of motivation as the afternoon wasted into dusk.

I decided to try to eat a little – get my strength up for what was to come, but when I opened my bag, I realised that I actually had something inside to sell by which I might pay for a few more nights at The Turk – my Thomas clothes.

I took them out and laid them across my lap to inspect them.

As Thomas I would have been safer here – men would not have threatened me, at least not in the same repulsive way, and I would have been employable – yes, I could have worked and supported myself, even started a business – I could have made my way.

And then it occurred to me – what was to stop me putting these clothes back on as a disguise, just for a while, and thereby regaining all but my testicles? It was a prospect not far short of prison, and with similar connotations, but Thomas was the nearest thing I had right now to a safe place.

Yes, I could pretend to be Thomas, I thought. I know that I am Emmeline and that can never change – I will just be acting for a spell, maybe only for a few days until I have some money and can devise a plan by which to return to myself.

It would certainly be a great failure to go backwards in this way after all that I had been through, but was it really any more abhorrent than the prospect of another night fighting off the tentacles of lecherous men?

No – if I can castrate myself to be Emmeline, then I can surely survive a few days in disguise to keep her alive, so I hid myself in some bushes in a corner of the park and changed.

Once back on the streets, it was not long before I caught my reflection. It was a hateful sight. I think that perhaps, in the back of my mind, was the idea that somehow I would still look female – a woman in fancy dress – even that I might have to struggle a little to convince people that I was male, but no, I had all the appearance of a boy, and he broke my heart.

23

Cat-Spit, Kipper-Fingers

For the next several weeks, I slept at the Embankment, and I learnt to get there early enough for the chance of a seat on a bench, which, although painful to sleep upon, was so much warmer than lying on the pavement, both because of the insulating wood, and because of the body-heat of your neighbours.

I did not speak to my fellow rough-sleepers any more than I had to, for what is the point of making friends when living in disguise? Instead, I kept to myself, and myself to the background. I was lonely, of course, but I was so accustomed to loneliness by now that it had almost become my friend.

My biggest problem was hunger – a relentless, tormenting rodent that gnawed and gnawed at me, hollowing me out from the middle with blunt teeth, and the filling of that expanding hole became my absolute obsession. There were a few soup kitchens about the city, but the quantities of food they served were quite meagre, and you could never fill yourself up.

After three or four weeks, I finally got so hungry that I resorted to eating food that someone else had discarded. It was a sandwich – I had watched a man on a park bench take a bite from it while he argued with his lady-friend. As the argument gained momentum, he placed the sandwich on the bench, one half leaning against the other as if it had been set out for display by a chef.

"Leave it, leave it, leave it," I whispered, as if I was praying to him, but then I thought that the prayer might only draw his attention to the very thing I wanted him to forget, so I whispered, "Argue, argue, argue," instead.

His temper continued to rise and the woman dismissed his every protest, until finally, tired of listening, she upped and stamped away. He followed, taking his tirade with him, but answering my prayers by leaving the sandwich behind.

I could hardly breathe for fear of his turning round to retrieve it, but when he was perhaps ten yards away, I sprinted for the bench, swiped the sandwich up and shot away.

I did not look back, nor did I stop to eat it, but rather pushed it into my mouth as I ran, breathing in great snorts through my nose as I did so. My God, it was absolutely delicious. I do not even know what the filling was, other than delicious.

From then on, I ate whatever discarded food I could find, as long as it seemed fresh enough that it wouldn't make me ill, and it was a short step from eating discarded food to stealing fresh food when the opportunity arose, or indeed when the opportunity could be created.

Thus, as scavenger and thief, I survived, except to say that one doesn't really survive destitution – you measure your success only in the slowness of your decline, but you do decline, and day by day you become thinner, more weary, and ever more despondent.

I did continue to look for work, but as despondency and famine infect you, they become visible to others in the slope of your shoulders and the shadows beneath your eyes, and you look less and less a viable prospect. Each refusal then deepens your despondency and the deeper it grows, the more likely the next refusal, and so on. Eventually, I stopped asking for work altogether and begged for money instead.

* * *

By the end of May I had been homeless for three months and had lost at least half my natural weight. I had taken to napping against a tree on the inland edges of the embankment. It was a grand and motherly tree – an elm

I think, and there was a gap the size of my bottom between the roots. The tree hid me from the other homeless people, and with a newspaper beneath me it was warmer and more comfortable than the benches to sleep against.

I'd had some luck that afternoon, stealing two fat kippers from outside a hotel kitchen after taking advantage of an inattentive delivery man. I had eaten one of them a few yards from the hotel, but the other I had saved for this evening and relished it in the seclusion of my tree before falling asleep.

In the small hours I was awoken by a tiny rough tongue against my hand.

"Geronimo," I whispered, and without opening my eyes I ran my fingertips over his head and along his back. "Dear old friend, how have you been?"

He purred, and each time my hand ran over his head, he would push it up into my palm as if he were trying to lift a trap door.

As long as I kept my eyes closed he was Geronimo, and I was at home and all was well.

He licked at my fishy hands; he even took a tentative bite at my little finger to see if it was kipper all the way through. It didn't hurt, for a cat knows what's yours and what's kipper by the give in it.

"I have missed you so much, my little kitty," I said, and with my eyes still closed, I started to cry. "I have missed you the most – more than Mother and Elizabeth."

The cat climbed onto me, settled into a ball in my lap and kneaded at my thigh.

I wiped my cheeks with my cat-spit, kipper-fingers and we dozed off together, keeping each other warm and at home for the rest of the night.

24

Heron's Eggs

When I awoke near dawn, the cat was gone. I stood up, took a final look at the scattered poor of the Embankment, then turned for Harewell and home.

Well, why not go home? I was living as a man now after all, and surely, when Mother and Elizabeth see my destitute and masculine state, they will take me back. I mean, it is easy enough to reject someone by letter when you have a thousand miles between them and your conscience, but to look into the eyes of your own starving flesh and blood – well, that should provoke the compassion even of my family.

Then perhaps, if I can get myself full, and well, and employed, there might still be some time left to be Emmeline before I turn into a long-limbed castrato monster.

I nodded to myself. "Yes," I whispered, "I'm going home."

* * *

I knew Harewell to be twenty-five miles from London, and I knew roughly the direction. It was a formidable distance to contemplate in my current state, but every day was daunting now, so what difference would that really make?

By midday, I had at least made it into the countryside, but I was already exhausted, and by dusk I was so weak that I fainted twice. I simply could not go any further, so I staggered into a field, in the deep corner of which was a stack of wet hay. I climbed into it and hoped that I would somehow find the energy to continue in the morning.

It was a clear night, and cold for being clear, but the hay was tepid with fermentation, and gave me a little warmth.

I lay there listening to the sounds of the countryside. It was so very different to London – there was a stream nearby glubbling over boulders, while above it, a tall stand of elms whispered the breeze. In the far distance I could hear cows, but every so often I also heard a nearby snuffle which I took to be a hedgehog or perhaps a rat. All I could think was how much I wanted to eat the hedgehog, and the rat, and the cows. Even the trees sounded tasty.

I did try to chew on the hay, but the damp had made it bitter, so I just curled up around my stomach and wondered if my empty corpse would be found in the morning, or whether it would just rot away with the hay so that no one would ever know what became of me.

* * *

I woke up at dawn feeling a tiny bit better, as if sleep were something I had eaten. The grass was sparkled with dew and I washed my face in it before walking down to the stream at the bottom of the field to drink.

The stream opened out into a large pond, and as I emerged onto the bank, a heron took fright and made a great flap of flying off. What a beautiful thing to see, I thought, and what a wonderful meal it would have made.

The water was clear and tangy, and I had not realised quite how thirsty I was until I began to suck it in – I opened my mouth wide into the water and gulped, even chewed at it. All it lacked was a little milk and sugar… and perhaps a cake on the side.

After that, I sat back on the bank for a moment preparing myself for the walk ahead, but then I noticed that the heron had been nesting – not in the trees as they normally do, but in the fork of two fallen logs that leaned out over the pond. And there were eggs in the nest – big eggs, big, sky-blue, beautiful eggs, and four in number.

It was an easy matter to wade in a little and steal them, an easier matter even than buying eggs from a shop, and no, there were not four, but five. I felt I should leave the last one for the heron but I could not – I was too hungry. And besides, it was still spring and she would soon replace them.

I cradled the eggs back to the wet haystack, took out Maria's letter-opener, tapped a crack in one, and taking care not to lose a single drop, I broke it into my mouth. I barely had a moment to taste the contents before they shot down my throat like a frightened rabbit.

Two more eggs followed down the burrow, and the remaining pair I wrapped carefully in my Emmeline clothes – saving them in case I had another moment of weakness today.

* * *

I finally made it to Harewell in the early afternoon – a nice spring afternoon. I had only been gone perhaps nine months in all, but it felt like a lifetime, and ancient memories materialised from every corner:

There was the tree that Duggan had ring-barked with a pocket knife – it was a crab apple tree, but the fruit had been sweet. Here was Mr Carstairs' house, where Mother and I once had tea with bulging, hot-cross buns. Beyond that, the lamp post beneath which a cabbie had died of a heart attack after choking on a chicken bone.

Eventually I reached the corner of my road, then at last, my home. It was beautiful – a dusty cake of a cottage – the venue for all my previous springs, and all the other seasons of my childhood, and I had to stop at the gate for a moment to cry about it.

I looked up at my bedroom and there was Geronimo – my little kitty, his nose against the window and his eyes crossed as he tried to persuade them to focus on me instead of the glass. He did look funny, and in a few minutes he would be in my arms, and then I truly would be home.

The door was open and I entered without knocking, for this was where I lived. I could hear a familiar voice through the sitting room door – it was Elizabeth, and then Mother's voice too.

I opened the door softly, just enough to put my head through, and there they were.

"I have come home," I said, in teary triumph, pushing the door fully open, and in my head we all rush towards each other to embrace, but in this real sitting room, this real family only glare at me. Not so much a glare, but a look of shocked surprise that steadily reconfigures itself into a glare, and then they both stand up together.

Elizabeth's face now expresses anger amidst the shock, but mother's is anger knotted with… well, it looks rather like hatred.

I break the short silence:

"Is there something I could eat?"

And in my head the glares break into smiles and they say in a chorus, 'Of course there is.' But not in this real moment where Mother, in a low growl says, "How dare you show your face here – how dare you."

"You will leave immediately, Thomas – immediately," said Elizabeth, "or we will call the police."

I froze, open-mouthed for a moment.

"But… but I have nowhere to go, I have nothing… nothing to eat. Please, I will be no trouble, things can be just as before… please?"

Mother stood up.

"Get him out of here." Her voice rose from a whisper to a scream as she pushed Elizabeth at me. Elizabeth, following through the momentum of the push, pinched a hold of my arm and marched me sharply at the door, and once we were through it, Mother slammed herself shut in the sitting room.

"How could you, Thomas? How could you? That poor woman."

"Wait, Elizabeth, please, what woman?"

"Don't feign ignorance with me. Uncle Walter was here not three weeks ago looking for you – he told us everything."

She pushed me on to the doorstep.

"What did he tell you? Who is this woman?"

"The maid, Thomas – Maria – the one you beat half to death."

Poor Maria, what had he done to her?

"It's a lie, Elizabeth, I promise you, and I absolutely deny it. Uncle Walter is a madman."

"No, Thomas, Uncle Walter is an ambassador – you are the madman – you are the one that despoils our school, that parades about the town dressed as a woman, that steals your own uncle's silver, then beats and strangles his maid. We don't want you, Thomas – we don't want you." Then she punched me off the doorstep and onto the path.

"But he is a murderer, Elizabeth – I promise you. He has killed three people that I know of, and he meant to kill me too. Probably still means to."

"If I had any sense," she added, "I would lock you in a room and send a telegram to Naples."

"But I have proof – I have the things he took from them – from the victims – a necklace, some hair, a watch." I held up my carpet bag.

"But neither will I deny that you were here," she said. "He means to find you, Thomas, he is absolutely determined – he even has our photograph of you to show the police what you look like. As for me, I will give you this one chance to run, but nothing else. Now go, and if you value your liberty, never return."

"I am starving, Elizabeth, please, if there is any value left in sharing your blood with me then please – I will leave, I will leave right now and never return, but please, I am starving, and I will die of it if I do not eat something soon."

She slammed the door and I fell to my knees. I thought for a moment that I was going to cry again, but I didn't and instead, I stood back up and began to walk away.

As I reached the end of the path, the door opened again and Elizabeth threw a whole loaf of bread at me – right at me, then three apples and a lump of cheese, slamming the door shut, even before the square cheese had stopped rolling.

I scooped everything into my bag and started up the road.

"Brown?"

It was Geronimo. I knew what he was doing – he was following me. It was something he did – trotting along the path behind me as if I had kippers.

"Brown?"

I dared not look round – I could not take him with me, and I could not bear to say goodbye, so instead I walked on, my gaze fixed upon the path.

Soon I passed the crab apple tree again, and I knew that he never followed anyone beyond there.

I listened for a final 'Brown?' but there was none, and I walked on, eyes fixed ahead, cold upon my course.

I thought only of the food in my bag – my mouth aching in anticipation of it, and the moment I left the boundary of the town, I slid out of sight into a dry ditch and stuffed myself so ravenously that I almost choked. Once I had eaten all that my stomach could stretch around, I lay on my side and slept like a snuffed candle.

* * *

When I awoke, I immediately rose and started my journey back to London. My stomach was full for the first time in weeks, but my mind was empty – I did not care what had happened, nor did I not care – I simply walked, like an automaton.

By nightfall, I had made it back to the stack of tepid hay. I climbed in, closed my eyes, and my empty mind dozed off again in short time.

* * *

A storm blew in during the night, exciting the trees all the way up to a creaking roar. It must have built steadily, for my sleep was not disturbed until some confluence of wind currents managed to snap a large branch with a gun-shot crack.

The shock of the sound also cracked open my blank mind, and in that instant I knew that I would never see my family again, and knowing it, I felt it, all of it, and all at once.

I did not attempt to stifle my grief, but howled it back out and into the roar of the wind – I shouted my sobs like a frantic child, screamingly, unhindered by disapproving mothers, beyond punishments and beyond reproach, and I cried and cried and cried until it was all out of me.

* * *

By dawn, the wind had spent its anger, and the atmosphere had settled into a sulking drizzle – the bird songs were muffled by the mist, and everything smelt of boggy peat.

I went to the stream to drink and frightened the heron again.

"Sorry," I whispered, as she landed a little way up stream to watch me. "I was most awfully hungry you see – so hungry that I think I was dying of it."

I tore off a large piece from the remainder of my loaf, then waded into the water and placed it on the nest.

"I'm done for anyway, Heron, so you might as well eat it – maybe lay some new eggs."

I waded back to the shore, and looked back at her.

"I don't believe in magic, or curses, Heron, but… but if you cursed me for stealing your eggs, then you should know I was properly punished for it."

The heron remained absolutely still in her pool with an expression blank enough that my imagination could impose upon it anything from gracious acceptance, to the simple alert of a tiny brain.

"Well, there it is," I said, and with that, I turned and continued on my journey back to London.

* * *

Two days later, I climbed onto the stone guard rail of Waterloo Bridge and looked down into the cold, fast water of the Thames.

Emmeline had destroyed my life, and I hated her. I had only tried to give her life, and in return she had left me to face slow starvation in abject solitude.

Whatever time I had left, I did not want to spend it with her, so I took her clothes out of my carpet bag, and dangled them over the water.

"Goodbye Emmeline Stanton," I whispered, "and good riddance."

I let go and watched her fall softly into the khaki water. She didn't sink right away, but floated for a few moments, before a coal barge came blind from under the bridge and drowned her.

"You, boy."

I jumped down from the railings and grabbed my bag.

A slim, well-to-do gentleman of perhaps forty stood before me, leaning on a cane. He was not Uncle Walter, and he was not a policeman. In fact, he was clearly more than well-to-do – he had that sheen of wealth – a look you can't pin down to a single clue, but that wealth exudes like a perfume. I hated him immediately.

"There's no law against climbing on the guard rail," I said.

"I didn't say there was."

"Then what do you want?" I said, wishing I had the energy to punch him in the face for being so comfortable. "Your type never give money, so you must have some other reason for bothering me."

"Do you recognise your betters, boy?"

"Yes," I said. Do you?"

I detected a tiny hint of a smile, as if he were trying not to laugh.

"Laugh – go ahead, I don't fucking care."

He didn't.

"You're very thin," he said. "How long have you been living like this?"

"Three or four months, give or take – hard to keep track."

"Do you drink?"

"None of your business."

"Educated?"

"Autodidacted."

"Ha – priceless. What is your name?" he said.

"Geronimo," I said.

"Your *real* name."

By now he had me somewhat distracted and I decided to give a proper name, just to see what he would do with it.

"Ger... ald... Nimmo," I said, "it's Gerald Nimmo."

"Well then, Nimmo, have you a mind to work?"

"Work?"

"Suppose I were to give you a job," he said. "What then?"

I scratched my nose. "Why would you do that?"

He reached into his pocket. "I take it you read?"

"Yes," I said.

"Then take this card, and present it at Ardea's Meat Products first thing tomorrow morning. It is not pretty work, and I dare say it will not fill that sharp little mind, but it is honest work, and it will put food in your belly. What do you say?"

The card read:

Mr Jacob Ardea.
Ardea's Meat Products Ltd,
The Metropolitan Cattle Market,
Islington.

All I could think was that a job would sustain me, and all the unhappiness I felt at this moment would continue... indefinitely.

"I don't know what to say," I said.

"How about 'thank you'."

"But a job would sustain me."

"Precisely."

I frowned at the card, but my mind had crumpled.

"Whose were those clothes?" said Mr Ardea.

"They were Emmeline's."

"Your sister or mother?"

"You might say my twin."

He nodded knowingly, but mistakenly so. "We all lose people, lad – you'll get over it in time." And after another pause he added, "I'm going to give you a day's pay in advance because I rather fancy that you will appear tomorrow. Here is enough for a lodging house and a good meal. If you're wise, that is exactly how you will spend it – a full belly and a good night's sleep will put you in good stead for a solid day's work. Don't disappoint me – it's six shillings a week if you show willing."

As he walked away, I sat down against the railings, cuddled my bag and cried, but without really knowing whether I was crying out of relief or dismay, or both.

IV

The Female Universal Electrical Emanation

25

Ardea's Meat Products Ltd

T hat night, I took a lodging house in King's Cross – a men's lodging house. Whether it was better or worse than sleeping rough, I'm not sure, but the fact that I was spending some of my money to sleep there meant that some stupid part of me was going to take up Mr Ardea's offer.

I took a bed in the dormitory rather than spending extra on a cubicle. The smell was urinous and heavy with armpits, and manly men were everywhere. I suppose they were no more manly than the average, but there was something about getting amongst them and sensing the obligation to behave as they did that made their manliness seem so dense and oppressive. I sat on a free bed and tried to look manly too, but I felt more like a flower in a field of dirty-bottomed bullocks.

* * *

At around six the following morning, I arrived at the market in the foulest possible mood. The market itself was an enormous place covering many acres. I walked in through ranks of cattle pens, and a remarkably similar arrangement of smells and sounds to those that I had experienced overnight.

Given the wealthy sheen of Mr Ardea, I was not surprised to see several buildings with his name on. Outside the buildings were fleets of delivery wagons and vans, and their teams of horses.

One main door seemed to offer an office. I hovered outside it for a moment, not quite sure what to do, and then I saw my reflection in the window.

I looked male.

"Because you are male, you fucking idiot," I whispered. "So go and be one, and I hope it fucking kills you."

I entered the office. There was a desk, and behind it a man with a comb-over raised his palm to hold me still while he finished counting on the fingers of his other hand. He then scratched something into a ledger before looking at me expectantly. I thought he might say 'Can I help you?' or something like that, but he just stared at me, waiting for me to react to his expression.

"Apparently I work here," I said, and handed him the card Mr Ardea had given me.

He put it aside without looking at it.

"Nimmo, is it?"

"Yes."

He didn't reply, but walked to the door and shouted, "Mason."

A few moments later a thuggish young man appeared, wearing an apron that was absolutely drenched in blood. He was big – haggard-looking, his tiny black eyes overshadowed by a great fist of a brow.

"What?" he said, in a voice that sounded like the bark of a mastiff.

"Got one of Mr Ardea's good deeds for you – name of Nimmo. Start him off on the usual."

He looked me up and down.

"Bit fucking thin, ain't ya?" he said, and then he laughed.

"Get on with it, Mason," said the man behind the desk.

I followed Mason out of the office across a stretch of mud to a brick building, and was at once in a large room – stone-floor, tiled walls, with a line of marble-top tables along either side, and a gutter running down the middle to a large drain.

The aroma was very strange – it was like the smell of a butcher's shop, but beneath that was the smell of fermenting grass, like damp hay cooked in beer, and it might have been tolerable if it wasn't for the smell one layer below that, which was a mixture of eggs and excrement.

Piled upon the tables were mountains of offal, and attending to them were perhaps seven or eight men who pulled out various organs from the piles, cutting them away from extraneous tissue and depositing them in organ-specific pails and buckets.

Mason grabbed the back of my collar, as if holding me up for inspection. "This fucking useless skelington is Nimmo, lads." Everyone looked round, and some of them laughed,

"I mean, look at the fucking state of 'im," said Mason, giving me a shake. "He ain't gonna be no use to no one."

I felt nothing – I just looked at their mouths and listened to the sounds.

When they stopped laughing I said, "So what do I do?"

"Pick up a fucking knife and do what we do," said Mason. "And don't get in the fucking way or I'll cut yer knackers off and drop them in the bollock bucket."

"They ain't dropped out of his belly yet," said one of the men and they all laughed again.

* * *

The work was not difficult and I grew accustomed to the bloody unpleasantness quite quickly, but I avoided talking to my colleagues – they were nothing like me and I wanted no part of them.

Mason though, was difficult to ignore – he would pull faces at me while I was working, or rather, he would pull one particular face, and always that face – it consisted of a raised upper lip, flared nostrils and a loosely protruding tongue. I think it was supposed to represent a sort of crazed disgust, and it revealed a line of cracked teeth in his upper jaw that had, no doubt, been broken by a well deserved punch in the face.

But I was also strangely indifferent to his abuse – I didn't feel anything really, not even that I was actually there – I was just watching a life from afar – the life of a pathetic man called Gerald – a man in whom I had no interest at all.

* * *

For nine months I continued with my work at Ardea's Meat products, indeed beyond nine months, but I draw a dividing line at the nine-month mark, because that was when something happened.

"I need someone to take this to head office in Piccadilly," said the man from the office, whom I now knew to be called Mr Cunningham. He was holding up a ledger.

"I'll go," said Mason, before pulling his usual face at me on the grounds that he thought I would want to go myself.

"You can't even read," said Cunningham, then he looked round the room at his options and settled on me. "Nimmo – you take it."

"I can't stand Piccadilly," I said. "Make Mason do it."

Mr Cunningham was already walking towards the door with the ledger held in the air for me to follow. "Get your coat on, Nimmo," he said.

As soon as he had left the room, Mason held his knife in the air, sideways-on to show me the full blade.

"I'm gonna cut your fucking throat when you get back," he said.

"I wish you fucking would," I whispered, as I followed Mr Cunningham out of the door.

* * *

It was a wet mid-morning when I arrived at the Hyde-Park end of Piccadilly. I had deliberately avoided this part of London since that one perfect day as Emmeline – at first I had avoided it because it was the happiest place in the world and I didn't want to taint it with my homelessness, but now it was haunted by a dead Emmeline, and my hatred of her.

"Fuck it," I whispered, and started walking.

Within a few yards, I passed the Stanhope teashop, where I had eaten strawberry cake and immediately felt sick. I crossed the road to get away from it, but then I passed Fortnum and Mason where I had learnt the difference between Darjeeling and Assam. "Fuck your tea," I whispered. "And fuck you, Emmeline." I started to walk faster and faster – the memories of that perfect day chasing me like a pack of dogs, and each one biting another piece out of me until I found myself running full pelt, all the way to the Ardea office at the far end of Piccadilly.

I burst through the door and stood panting in the reception.

"You look like you've seen a ghost," said the clerk at the desk.

"A ghost and its dogs," I said, handing over the ledger.

"Do you want to sit for a moment before you go back? Catch your breath?"

"No," I said.

I stepped back out onto Piccadilly, and there, right in front of me on the other side of the road from the office, were the premises of Mr Robt. Brinkley, Photographer – the shop where my picture had been taken in front of a Japanese backdrop on that perfect day.

I had never seen the picture – my life had completely dissolved before I got the chance to retrieve it, but that meant it was still in there – a piece of Emmeline still existing in the world – the very last piece, keeping her alive – alive to taunt me and laugh at the disaster she had made of my life.

If I could get my hands on the picture, I could destroy it, I thought – tear her into little pieces, burn her, and make her go away. "Yes," I whispered, "I must have it."

I crossed the road and entered the shop.

There was already a family at the counter – the father was discussing the prices in minute detail, so I took a seat and waited. It was the same chair that I had sat in before, which meant that in front of me was the chair that Miss Bright had taken.

I had thought of her so many times since then – she was always my romantic fantasy, and to return here, to the very place, was to bring her vividly back to mind – her enormous eyes, the muted rose dress that so tightly embraced her, and the big dusty hammer in her bag.

And I remembered her looking at me – that glance from behind her book, and into which I had read all manner of wonderful intentions.

"Can I help you, sir?"

I jumped.

The family had gone, and the man behind the counter was looking at me expectantly.

"I have come to pick up a photograph taken... about a year and a half ago. It's all paid," I said as I approached the counter.

"Do you have your slip?"

"No, the slip is lost. It is a photograph of my sister," I added, then turned my face down in a slightly bereaved manner. "She is no longer with us."

"You have my sincere condolences." He was the same thin and tidy man who had flirted with me last time, but he was nowhere near as friendly as I remembered him. "Unfortunately I can't let one go without the slip."

"You must have some record of my payment?"

"We will have a record of the payment itself, but not of who made it, and without the slip I'm afraid you have no say in the matter."

"But people must lose their slips all the time. You surely have some procedure in place to cover such eventualities."

"If you were the person in the picture, then we could easily verify the matter of course, but when the subject is not present, we can only decline, for how would it be if the true owner of a picture were to find that we had given their likeness away to a stranger?"

"My sister is dead – she cannot come in to verify her likeness."

"Which is most regrettable, but my hands are tied."

I glared at him for a moment, then I turned to leave, but realising something, I continued my turn right back round to the counter. "You said that you could verify ownership if the subject were present."

"An impossibility in this case."

"True, but my sister looked so much like me, that I am sure you will see we can only be brother and sister."

The door to the studio burst open and Mr Brinkley entered with all the breathless exuberance that I remembered from our previous meeting.

"Mr Brinkley, I appeal to you," I said, holding out an arm to encourage him towards the counter.

"Appeal? What's this, what's this?"

"He's lost his slip, Mr Brinkley, and I have explained the terms quite clearly."

"Are you in the picture, young man?"

"No, but it is of my sister, my deceased sister, who looked so much like me that I'm sure you will see the resemblance."

"Let's have a look then shall we? What name was it?"

"Stanton, Emmeline Stanton."

He began to flick through the 'S' drawer, and soon pulled out a photograph with its associated paperwork and inspected the image.

"Could you describe the young lady?"

"She is standing before a Japanese backdrop – the gardens of Nijo castle in Kyoto. Oh, and she is smiling in it."

He looked again at the picture, then at me (I forced the same smile) and then back at the picture.

"Why, you are the very spit of your sister, and she is indeed smiling – most irregular. I rather like the idea of smiling in photographs." He considered for a moment then nodded firmly to himself. "I am happy to let you take her away."

"Thank you very much, Sir," I said.

He gave the picture a final look. "A very handsome young lady she was, if you don't mind me saying so. How very sad." And then he handed it to me.

I looked at myself.

And I saw myself.

Emmeline.

I put my hand over my mouth and tried not to cry, but within a moment I was sobbing.

"You must miss her terribly," said Mr Brinkley.

"It's more than that," I said. "I can't live without her."

26

What is this female testicle?

That night, after work, I bought clothes – second-hand and dirt cheap – a dress, combinations, a corset etc, and I also paid the extra for a cubicle at the lodging house.

When I closed my cubicle door, I took out my new clothes, and without hesitation, and despite the perilous proximity of men, and despite my thinking that it was probably an ill-judged idea, and despite my previous determination to abandon my life as a woman, I put them on.

This is not an easy thing to do in a sixpence, lodging-house cubicle – I had to perform the entire act lying on my back like an escapologist locked in a box. But I did it, corset too, and once dressed, I just lay there, calm and happy, inhabiting normality, and shortly after, with warm ease, I fell asleep.

The next night, I did the same, and the next night, and the next, and then I thought to myself, what about Sundays? It's my day off, and I could spend the whole day as myself – it would be wonderful, and all I would need to do is to find somewhere to change.

That following Sunday morning, I was out early with my Emmeline clothes in my carpet bag, searching frantically for a space to change in, and feeling as if every minute spent in search of facilities was another minute lost from my life, but eventually I found a little gap in an alleyway formed by the poor co-ordination of two teams of builders, and I stepped inside.

The moment I stepped back out, and into the world as myself, it was so exciting that I hardly knew what to do with myself, but I mainly just followed the promenaders in parks, and sat on benches to watch the world go by – very ordinary Sunday activities, but if ordinary can be perfect, it was perfectly ordinary, and I savoured every moment. I mean, sleeping in my own clothes was one thing, but to be amongst other people – to actually exist to them and be part of the human world, was to be truly alive.

* * *

My life continued like this for several weeks, until one Sunday afternoon in the middle of May, when I caught my reflection in a shop window and saw that the gap between the hem of my skirt and the pavement was growing.

I had known full well that it would happen eventually, just as Il Maccari had warned me, but to actually see my limbs lengthen – to see the beginning of my deformation into a lanky, castrato freak, was to see my approaching death.

That night, in a state of panic, I filled my carpet bag with bricks and held the bag in my arms for half an hour, and I did this diligently every night for a week until I realised that whilst it might reduce the growth in my legs, it might also increase the growth in my arms.

The next solution I tried was a sort of brace in the form of a long leather belt. This I wrapped around my bottom and knees to prevent my thigh bones from growing in the night, with the idea of creating something similar for my arms too if it worked, but it was so painful to wear, and cut such deep welts into my knees that I abandoned the idea for fear it would cripple me.

And then I ran out of ideas.

I could make no sense of what was happening to me – why should an absence of testicles make my arms and legs grow? I mean, women do not have testicles, so why do their limbs not also grow excessively long? Come to think of it, how do girls become women at all? Where do their breasts, and hips come from? It's clearly not simply from an absence of testicles, for if that were the case, I would not be so repulsively shapeless.

And then it struck me, that just as testicles turn boys into men and restrain the growth of their limbs, so there must be something inside girls that turns them into women, and restrains their limbs too – a sort of feminine reflection of the testicle.

I was electrified by this realisation. What is this female testicle? Where is it? How does it work? And it took only one evening buried in Gray's Anatomy before I worked it out – ovaries – they were the magic organs – they had to be, I mean both testicles and ovaries were pale balls; both were supplied by arteries that emerged from exactly the same place, and both were the organs by which babies are conceived. They were so similar in fact, that the connection was undeniable.

But how did they actually work? If I could work that out, maybe I could save myself somehow. At first I conjectured that an exotic feminising or masculinising serum leaches out of them and circulates around the body, but then I decided that the more likely scenario was some sort of electrical emanation, radiating out from the testicles and ovaries, and for at least three feet in all directions so that it could reach the extremities. Either way, I needed to get hold of some ovaries as soon as possible.

Short of breaking into a morgue, I could see no way of obtaining human ovaries, but then I began to wonder if there was some small possibility that male and female emanations were universal to all species – in short, that there was a universal female emanation, that would make udders on a cow, but breasts on a girl.

The danger was clear – that to expose myself to the emanations of the ovaries of a cow, for example, would be to risk becoming somehow cow-like.

I did not imagine that I would turn into a cow as such, but it seemed quite possible that certain cow characteristics might develop – perhaps freakish swellings where the udders would be, or a great thickening of the fingernails as they became more hoof-like. And what of my mind? Would I begin to experience intellectual deficits as the bovination took hold?

With no other options before me, I decided to risk it. I stole a pair of cow ovaries from work, and that night, I sat in my cubicle with them in my hands.

I tried for a moment to feel the emanations through my palms and fingers, perhaps as a tingle or vibration of some kind, but nothing. I listened to them too in case there was an electrical hum, but again nothing. It could be, I thought, that the emanations are beyond human senses, but it could also be that the ovaries are already as dead as the cow they came from, and will only work when living in a living body.

If they were dead, then so was I, so I could only work on the assumption they were alive. I held them fast against my abdomen by wrapping a length of cloth about my middle, and then slept very badly with hoofed and horned nightmares.

The following morning there was no change and nor was there after several weeks of using fresh ovaries every night, so I decided that the only thing left to try was to put them right inside me by swallowing them.

My instinct was to cook them first, but to cook a thing is to change it – indeed, when a person suffers a burn to their hand, the hand may cease to work entirely, so why would heat be any less damaging to ovaries? I therefore resolved to eat them raw.

I thought that I could probably swallow one in quarters, so four swallows every night with four more in the morning and that would be the unpleasantness over with. This meant that I would have to cut them up, and I realised that might also destroy their function, but unlike the destruction that comes from cooking, cutting them up leaves the substance of the ovary itself unchanged. And besides, I simply could not fit a whole one down my throat so there was no other option.

My first attempt got halfway down my throat before my stomach squeezed it back up in disgust, but I tried again, and this time successfully.

For several weeks nothing happened, but then something – something quite remarkable, for whilst at work, I noticed that my nipples were sore, and when I examined them, I found them strangely hard – as if there was a dried pea behind them. Now it could have been that I was suffering from some sort of nipple disease, but I had never heard of such a thing, and I had no other symptoms of illness.

I watched the peas closely over the coming weeks and gradually they

151

changed, growing in size very, very slowly until they were hazelnuts, and then they became softer like grapes. In a few more weeks the grapes ripened, becoming softer still and fatter, and steadily, like a ripple through a pond of custard, the swelling spread outwards, building all the time in volume.

It was so hard to see the difference day to day, but over a week or two it was clear, and in a few months I had acquired for myself two small but very true and happy breasts that were clearly and definitively open to no other description than 'breasts'.

This was about the most wonderful thing that had ever happened – every night and every morning I would hold them in a state of happy disbelief, and as they continued to plump, I was soon able to fill the bodice of my Sunday dress without resorting to padding.

And the wonders did not end there, for I also stopped gaining height, and the circumference of my hips increased by an inch and then two inches, and it was not that I was getting fat either, for my waist measurement remained the same.

I had yearned for my missing body as a mother might yearn for a missing child, where every day begins and ends with a pining emptiness, and every potential joy is muted by loss. But now she had come home, and it was both wonderful, and indescribably normal.

27

By All That's Fuckin' Holy

I was able to hide the changes to my body from the men at work quite
easily – I wore a tight under-shirt to hide my chest, and the loose
and heavy clothes of a man were just the thing to hide my figure. But
there were other changes that were more difficult to hide – these were the
changes to my face, as the texture of my skin became softer, paler and more
translucent, and I think the apples of my cheeks became more plump. My
hair changed too, becoming thicker and more silky.

I do not know whether it was the sum of these changes, but I seemed
to have gone from having an androgynous face that had served as both
male and female as required, to a face that only looked female, and when
I dressed as a man, people would give me odd looks – they would glance
at my face first as one does when passing a stranger in the street, but then
they would glance down at my body, paying rude attention to my chest and
groin, before looking back to my face and frowning.

This frown would sometimes be innocently curious, but on other
occasions it would turn to a stifled giggle, and occasionally I was given
a very stern glare of disapproval, or even hatred. This was not a look that I
was used to receiving outside of the family home.

Entering and exiting the lodging house with a female face was also
becoming quite dangerous, but I kept my head low and my collars up,
and got in and out of my cubicle with as little attention drawn as possible.

The offal sorters at work seemed less observant at first, perhaps because the change was so gradual, but after a while they began to frown at me, and then to make comments.

"Where's yer beard, Molly boy?" was popular, and on one occasion, Mason said, through his irritating face, "I'm gonna cut yer knackers off, Molly boy, 'cos you ain't fuckin' using em."

It was all light-hearted enough at first and I would laugh it off in the manliest way I could muster, but steadily the mood began to darken, and as it darkened the comments grew fewer until they stopped altogether – I was moving from a subject of ridicule, to an object of disgust.

On a Friday in December, I arrived at work to an altogether new atmosphere. The silent stares had been replaced by excited, giggling glances that looked to me, then to Mason, and then back to me.

I had no doubt at all that something unpleasant was about to happen, and I was waiting for someone to tip a bucket of guts over my head or something, but at eleven-thirty-three (I remember the time precisely having just looked at the cattle market clock-tower through the window) Mason grabbed me from behind, spun me around, and fixed me against the table.

Everyone else stopped work to gather round and watch.

Mason was strong, and there was little I could do but stand there and hope that whatever infantile prank he was planning would be over quickly and with no harm done.

"We think yer a girl," he sneered.

"Really," I said, suddenly very aware of my unbroken voice.

"And we mean to prove it."

At a nod from Mason, three of the men moved in quickly and pinned me stiff.

"How dare you touch me, get off me, all of you – I've done nothing to you."

"Go on, Mason," they shouted.

Mason started to unbutton my jacket. "Go on, get it open," they shouted, so he stopped unbuttoning and started ripping whilst I desperately pulled against the men restraining my arms. Once my jacket was open, he ripped down my under-shirt in a single tug.

And there they were, my precious breasts – two pale, glowing globes, lighting the room like holy orbs and stunning all to silence.

Mason grabbed them both in his bloody hands.

"I told you, I fuckin' told you it was a girl." Then he started to bounce them up and down roughly whilst nearly choking on his exaggerated cackle.

"GET OFF ME," I screamed, and so hard that my voice broke into silence in the middle of it. I craned my neck trying to bite at his hands.

"Titty boy wants to bite me does she?" He grabbed the hair on either side of my head. "You wanna bite me do you? You little fuckin' freak."

Several others reached in now to maul at my breasts, hard fingers, sharp nails. I screamed again and again until a massive hand clamped itself over my mouth, splitting my top lip against my teeth.

"Reckon it's time to teach this little freak how to be a proper woman," said Mason. He reached down, sliced open my fly buttons and dragged my trousers down to my thighs.

And there it was for all to see – the inappropriate accompaniment to my breasts – my small, childish penis, bowed in shame before its audience, and for the second time in my ordeal there was silence.

"By all that's fuckin' holy."

Again silence.

"Do it up the arse then, or you won't get your money off Pollard."

There was a cheer and I was spun on to my front, my face in a pile of liver.

"Go on, lad."

Turning my face to one side I managed to scream again: "HELP ME. PLEASE, DEAR GOD." And at once the reply came:

"YOU WILL CEASE."

It was Mr Ardea, and I was immediately released.

I clawed at my trousers, pulling them up to cover myself whilst closing my ripped shirt with the other hand. Mr Ardea held out his hand to me and I shuffled across to him. He placed the hand on my shoulder.

"Are you all right, lad?"

I nodded.

"It's not a lad, Sir, it's a freak – tits and cock, Sir."

"You will all get back to work immediately and I will decide later if any of you are to keep your jobs."

With his hand still on my shoulder he led me outside.

* * *

He took me through the office to his own larger office behind. There he sat me on a chair, handed me a towel and a glass of brandy, and asked me once again if I was all right.

"I think so, Sir, no harm done… no harm done."

I lifted the towel to my face to wipe off the liver blood, but the moment my face was in it I began to cry. I tried to stop myself but I couldn't, and I leant forwards into the towel in quiet convulsions.

It was at least ten minutes before my tears had run their course, and then I just sat there with my face buried, the whole horrible world muffled away by soft cotton. I felt strangely calm in this little cloud – nothing outside of it seemed to exist, none of the evils, nor Mr Ardea, nor even my body.

When I finally emerged into the bright office, Mr Ardea was sitting at his desk, leaning a little to one side – his hand on his hip and his other elbow on the arm of his chair.

"Better?"

"Much better – thank you. I… I really don't know how to thank you."

"You've no reason to thank me – I won't tolerate such behaviour on my premises, and would have acted on anyone's behalf in such a situation."

"Well, thank you all the same."

After a short silence he said:

"You know, Nimmo, there are more people like you in the world than you might imagine."

"Like me, Sir? That seems unlikely."

"You may think so, but I have a medical acquaintance of some note, who once mentioned to me that he has, on more than one occasion, attended the birth of a child who, well, how might one express it? A child whose construction is somewhat ambiguous."

"In what way precisely, Sir? – I have some medical knowledge."

"It is sufficient to say that in some cases, it is by no means clear whether one should announce a boy or a girl."

"Fascinating."

"So you see, you are not so unusual after all."

I knew that I was not quite what he described, for there was no apparent uncertainty to my sex at birth, but for the moment it seemed best to let him see me that way.

"How are these cases resolved?" I asked.

"Well, I think it is usually accepted that such a child would be doomed to an impossible existence, and that the kindest thing to do is to let nature take its course. However, I am told that on occasion the parents do not take to the suggestion that their strange offspring should be left to expire, and instead make their best guess as to the poor creature's sex and raise it accordingly. Perhaps this is your own story?"

"I was raised a boy, but I have turned out to be a girl."

"In which case, why do you live as a boy, and a not particularly convincing one at that?"

"I have tried to be myself, Sir, but it is so difficult when you are homeless, what with the way men are and everything. No offence, you understand, but…" I nodded towards the sorting room as my explanation.

"None taken. I would call it a wise strategy, except that you fail rather miserably to portray a man – your whole demeanour is quite inappropriate, even without your feminine appearance. Not quite sure why I didn't see it when we first met."

"Thank you." I laughed a little.

"So, I'll wager the clothes that you threw into the Thames were your own?"

"Yes, Sir."

"And the name you gave – Emily – was your name?

"Emmeline, Sir, yes. And my surname is actually…" I now felt sure that if I could trust anyone with my surname, it was him. And I wanted him to know it – to exist as myself to him. "…my surname is Stanton."

"Well then, Emmeline Stanton, as you have been wronged upon my premises, I feel that it falls upon me to make amends and help you along. I'll tell you what I'll do – a good friend of mine, George Crean, runs a little biscuit factory in Bermondsey. He employs many young women, and I'm sure I can persuade him to find space for another. Here's the address of the factory – Reamer and Crean is the name."

He scribbled it down for me.

"And I suspect you'll find, that if you present yourself on Monday morning, they will be expecting you. In addition…" he reached into a pocket and counted out some change, "…here's ten shillings to see you through until Monday."

I took the address and the money with my head bowed in gratitude.

"I really don't know how to thank you."

He dismissed my thanks with a wave of his hand and I stood up to leave, holding my trousers together.

"Will they hold for your journey home?"

"I think so. Um… I was just wondering, Mr Ardea, Sir – is it your intention to mention to your friend that I am not quite… well… not quite right?"

"Certainly not, and if you can keep your little…" He nodded at my crotch. "You realise, Emmeline, that it's a spinster's life for you?"

"Yes," I said.

"You really must never allow yourself to form a romantic attachment."

"Never," I said, but there was such a weight of loneliness in the word that I could feel myself start to cry again. I coughed and shook my head. "Men are of no interest to me, Sir."

"Glad to hear it. Well, off you go then. And on Monday, don't, for heaven's sake, arrive dressed as a man."

28

You Will Exkoos an Unusual Requess?

That evening, I claimed my bag from the lodging house, put my Emmeline clothes on, and set out for Bermondsey in search of a lodging house for Ladies.

I could no longer pose as a man – the events of that morning had proven that fact beyond question, so from now on I would be myself, whatever the consequences.

* * *

It was early evening when I walked into Bermondsey, and I had travelled only a little way along Grange Road when I noticed a sign in a sweet shop window that read:

Room for rent.
Apply within.
Very reasonable rates.

I had not thought to try for a room in an actual house, and no doubt it would be far too expensive for me, but as no price was given on the notice, I saw no harm in knocking the door to find out.

I was taken aback by the speed at which my knock was answered.

"Yes?"

"Good evening," I said, "I am sorry to trouble you. I have come about the room."

"Dear Lord," said the woman, "I only hung the sign up half a minute ago."

"Oh – then I am the first."

"Come in then, Miss...?"

"Stanton."

"Well now, surely you jest," she said.

I felt my stomach somersault at the idea that she had seen through Emmeline to Thomas. "But... but I am Emmeline Stanton," I said.

"But we're Stantons too. Where are your people from?"

"Harewell – South-East," I said.

"No, we're North London. Mind you, I don't doubt that we probably share an ancestor at some point in the depths of history."

"I don't doubt it at all," I said.

She ushered me through. She was a trim lady, quite proper, neatly dressed, with a clean pinafore, and her hair in a kempt pile upon her head. She was perhaps thirty, a pursed mouth, a humped nose, and large eyes that had sleepy lids like a medieval portrait.

"Are you employed locally?"

"I start at Reamer and Crean on Monday."

"Most people around here call it Creamers. Half of Bermondsey works there – it's a very good start for a young lady. Now then, I should point out that the room is very small."

"The size will not be a problem, but I must first ask the price."

"Five shillings the week, all found, and paid in advance."

This was somewhat more than a lodging house, and if I were to earn the same amount at Creamers as I did sorting offal, then it would be quite difficult to pay for it, but how lovely it would be to live in a house again.

She showed me into the room which was indeed very small, and yet it hardly seemed so to me, being perhaps three times the size of a lodging house cubicle. There was a window overlooking Grange Road, a small chest of drawers, an iron bed, and even a picture of the queen on the wall.

It felt like a home – a real home.

"I'll take it… if you'll have me," I said.

"Yes, why not? You seem a decent type, and you are a Stanton after all."

I reached into my purse for the money.

"You will have breakfast and supper every day," she continued, "that's included, but you will have to eat in here I'm afraid, as we have but the smallest of tables downstairs, and with my husband and daughter together there is no space at all for a third."

"That will be quite satisfactory," I said.

"The chest of drawers makes for a very serviceable table mind, and I will set it for you."

I handed her the five shillings.

"Thank you kindly, Miss Stanton," she said. "I'll leave you to settle in, and I'll bring you up something to eat in a little while. We've nothing fancy mind – will you eat curried oysters?"

"That would be lovely, thank you."

* * *

My own room – a proper room in a house, a clean house, a clean bed, and a solid door with a key – my key.

After dinner, I lay on my bed with something like happy anticipation of the future – finally I could truly live as myself all day, every day, and who knows, it might even be quite enjoyable to work in a biscuit factory.

But such happy thoughts only kept me company until sunset, for as the night crept in through the window, so it dragged visions of Mason and Uncle Walter in with it, and they sat in the room with me, daring me to fall asleep.

It was near two in the morning before I finally nodded off, but at the very moment my mind let go of consciousness, I saw myself face down in the offal, and Mason poised to violate me with his huge knife.

I sat up startly to throw the vision off, and it was at that moment that I heard something in my head – an echo from this morning – yes – "Pollard"

161

– that was it – "Do it up the arse then, or you won't get your money off Pollard."

I didn't know which of the offal sorters had said it, but the name, Pollard must surely have referred to Uncle Walter – he must have paid Mason to rape me... no, no, no, he could not have found me, not with a false name, I must have misheard – no one said Pollard... and yet... and yet I heard it, I heard it distinctly – Pollard – yes – it must be my uncle – it must. And if he knew where I worked, perhaps he now knows where I live.

I mean, what if he or Mason or some other of his minions has followed me here? Mason could easily have followed me – perhaps just dismissed from his job, his mind bloody with revenge, or maybe Uncle Walter paid him to follow me, like he paid him to rape me.

I got out of bed and turned the key in the door to make sure it was all-the-way locked. It seemed sound, but what if the mechanism had not fully engaged? What if, when I had locked it, I had locked it wrong – half-done the job, or turned the key the wrong way?

I lit a candle and held it close to the lock so that I could see the shiny bolt protruding across the gap between the door and the frame. It was there – the door was locked, it was certainly locked. I tried the handle anyway, four or five times, just to be on the safe side, then I went back to bed and wondered if I was going insane.

* * *

The following morning was a Saturday, and as much as I wanted to spend the whole day hiding in my room, I had another problem to contend with – having left Ardea's Meat Products, I no longer had access to ovaries, and would have to go out and find someone who could supply them to me.

I put my ear to the bedroom door and froze there for perhaps ten minutes, trying to hear the breath or creak of someone waiting in the hallway. I heard nothing, so I turned the key a fraction – still nothing, so I took a deep breath and opened the door.

No rapists, no murderers.

I suffered the same hesitation when I reached the front door and might never have gotten out of the house at all if it wasn't for Mrs Stanton arriving back from a shopping trip and opening it from the other side.

"Oh, good morning, Miss Stanton," she said.

"Good morning, Mrs Stanton," I said, trying to join in with her laughter about the shared name.

She stood aside to let me out of the door and I took my momentum from that to step into the street.

I drew another deep breath, pretending to be taking in the air rather than steadying my nerves.

"Mm, very fresh, today," I said.

"You look awfully nervous, my dear."

"Oh no, I'm fine – really."

"It's always a bit daunting – first day at a new job."

"Yes," I said, "I suppose it is. Oh but this isn't my first day – I don't start till Monday."

"Oh yes, that's right. Well, enjoy your walk anyway, dear – it'll settle your nerves."

"Thank you, I will," I said.

I walked briskly at first, poised to run. Then, a few yards along, I turned a corner and hid for a moment before peeping back out to see if anyone was following me.

There was no one. Well, there were people, but ordinary people going about their ordinary Saturday morning – not abusive offal sorters and homicidal diplomats – just people.

I began to relax a little. I mean I really couldn't be sure that I heard the name Pollard at all – not in the confusion and desperate intensity of the moment. No, in fact I'm sure I didn't hear it – I couldn't have. I laughed a little to myself – me and my scientific mind, letting irrational fears, magically transplant my uncle a thousand miles. I shook my head to loosen the fears and resolved to focus on the job at hand instead – ovaries.

* * *

163

The logical place to find ovaries was a butcher's shop, so I went into the first I found, but when it came to asking for them, I couldn't quite bring the words out for fear that I would somehow be exposing my secret, so I walked out with nothing.

I felt I needed a lie – some tale that would justify my strange request and lead the butcher away from the truth, so I wandered about Bermondsey for a while looking for another butcher and waiting for an idea. Then, as I approached the premises of Geo. Cowles, I hit upon the very thing – I would pretend to be foreign:

"Good mornink, Mr bootcher," I said, rolling my 'r's for added effect.

"Good morning, Miss."

"You will exkoos an unusual requess?"

"Certainly, Miss, how may I help?"

"I come from Iceland – a very colt kantry and far away. In my kantry we haff special dish we call ovumpioff. We haff for brekfast every day. For ovumpioff we need, um, how you say in Engleesh – ovary of cow. Can you supply?"

"Ovary you say? I'm not sure what sort of a thing that is."

"It lies near womb – like two leetool eks."

"Eggs?"

"Just so."

"Cow eggs – well I'll be," he said, scratching his head.

"And I need two fresh, every day."

"Well, Miss, I will speak to my supplier, and if such a thing can be extracted from a cow, I will have it for you on Monday."

"Sank you very mach."

29

Turbans and Walking Cities

That Monday, I set out early for my first day at work so that I would have time to visit the butcher beforehand. Good as his word, Mr Cowles supplied me with two fresh ovaries for a ha'penny the pair, and promised to have the same every day, and four on a Saturday so that I might have a pair for Sundays when he was closed.

It was not a long walk from there to Creamers and I needed no directions because the smell as one got within half a mile of the factory was its own delicious signpost. I would describe it as the aroma of gingerbread, and not gingerbread as it smells under your nose when you eat it, but as it smells just out of the oven, when the air is sighing with ginger syrup.

Just as Mr Ardea promised, they were expecting me. My details were taken, and I was told that I would start at ten shillings a week. That was four shillings more than I made at Ardea's, and it meant I would definitely be able to keep the room in Grange Road.

I was then given a pinafore and led to a locker. I hung my coat inside and then, rather self-consciously, pushed in my bag, with the parcel of ovaries concealed inside. I would just have to hope they would last the day there, for I would have no chance to eat them until I got home in the evening.

I was then taken through the factory to my station, and what a startling journey it was – I had never seen such a modern place, full of the most impossible machinery – steam-driven conveyors and pulleys, and great

165

stamping things which were being fed biscuit dough by teams of men. There was something delightfully incongruous about the homely smell of baking set against the rattle and bash of the machines.

My post was next to the baking rooms where the cooled biscuits were packed into tins by teams of girls. The supervisor was Mr Walker – he was a squat, middle-aged man who wrinkled his nose as if trying to grip his spectacles in the wrinkles. He took me to a large table and introduced me to my team:

First was Prudence. She was tall and stiff, with carved cheekbones, and pale, faintly grey skin. She was dark around the eyes, but it made her look more severe than tired. She certainly looked a no-nonsense sort, and although she nodded in a friendly way, I sensed that the friendliness was at least partly conditional upon my hard work.

Next was Mercy. She was young, perhaps my age, but her expression had a woeful droop to it, as if someone was pulling down on her cheeks.

Finally came Lily. She was very pretty, with a face like a happy apple – all rosy cheeks and a smile that made little half-moons of her eyes.

"I'm very pleased to meet you, Emmeline," she said, in a voice as sweet as her face, but with a cockney twang.

"Likewise, I'm sure," I said.

"Let's get back to work then, girls," said Prudence, nicely, but with a motherly insistence. "Emmeline, you come to my side of the table and I'll show you what to do."

My job was a simple matter of taking biscuits from the baking trays, arranging them neatly in the tins in prescribed quantities and patterns, and then putting the lid on the tin.

Prudence's hands were amazingly dexterous, and she distributed biscuits in perfect symmetrical layers with the speed and precision of a card sharp.

"Don't worry," she said. "You'll soon have the hang of it."

"I haven't the hang of it," said Mercy, her face a picture of disappointment. "And I've been here a whole year."

"You're doing just fine, Mercy," said Lily with an encouraging smile. "Look at me – I'm hardly any faster than you."

"I suppose," said Mercy.

"She's a good girl, Mercy," said Prudence to me. "Not so fast as others, but she does her best and who can expect more than that from her?"

"I does me best," added Mercy and smiled at last. It was the sort of smile that has the corners of its mouth turned down instead of up, but it quite broke through the gloom of her face.

This was already a completely different experience to working in the offal rooms. They were so immediately friendly and conversational. Even the hardness of Prudence had a kindness about it.

What superior creatures women are to men, I thought, and then it struck me that I really was living this moment – a woman, amongst other women. I felt warm to the very centre of myself as if I had just been baked to perfection in one of the big ovens.

"I do hope we shall be good friends," I said to them all with a big smile that was returned, and I had to cough a little to explain the slightly tearful sound that had come out of my mouth upon the word 'friends'.

* * *

So this was my new life. I worked hard and saved as much as I could, and with the remainder I bought clothes and books. Not many of either – but enough clothes to look decent, and enough books to feed my curiosity.

In truth, I bought a few more clothes than I needed, but you must understand that I was so endlessly delighted by their fitting me – I would always look at a dress and think surely I will look terrible in that, not being quite a normal girl, but then I would try it on, and it would hang just so, and the dress would say to me: 'You see, you are a girl, and now you should buy me as the proof of it'.

But whilst my days were light, my nights were still very dark – haunted by the word 'Pollard' and the knowledge that he was out there somewhere, looking for me. The pattern was usually the same – upon retiring to bed, I would inspect and thoroughly test the lock on my door several times, and then, somewhat reassured, I would fall asleep. But an hour or so later, I would always awake in terror, with visions of Uncle Walter or Mason or, on the worst nights, both of them working together in a brutal conspiracy of rape and murder.

I would then usually sit up for a while and read something distracting, or sit at the window to watch the cats and foxes out-stare each other in Grange Road.

Later I would try again to sleep, and with a bit of luck I would make it through until dawn. But on other nights, especially when the weather tapped at the window, I might have several more terrors before the sun came up with another happy day.

* * *

"What are you smiling about, Lil?" I said.

I had been at Creamers a while now and was fitting in well enough with the other women that we had moved to the abbreviated versions of our names.

"I know what she's thinking about," said Mercy.

"Don't be vulgar, Mercy," said Pru.

"Don't you have a beau, Em?" asked Lily. "You're so pretty, I dare say the gentlemen fall at your feet."

"No, I... I um... as it happens, I'm completely unlovable." I laughed and then glanced at Pru because she would be the first to notice that my voice had cracked a little and there were tears in my eyes.

Lil, looked very softly at me.

"Oh, I'm sure he is out there, Em – I truly believe that we all have the perfect mate somewhere, if we can but find him." She closed her eyes and smiled as if she were reclining into a hay stack on a summer's afternoon.

"I take it that you have found your perfect mate?" I said, relieved that the conversation had turned back to her.

"I do believe I have," she said, suddenly animated.

"His name's George," said Pru.

"George Edward Frederick Simms," said Lil, announcing his name like a bride. "He's a clerk, and he has promised that one day he will take me away from all this."

Pru stopped sorting and looked very cross.

"There's plenty of unfortunate souls who'd give anything to have your job, young lady. If they had anything to give,"

"I don't mean to sound ungrateful, it's just that... ooh, Neapolitans." She was looking at the next batch of baking trays.

"Ah – see? I told you they'd be back," said Pru, who then looked at me and continued, "Neapolitans – I always rated them one of our best. I said all along they'd be back, and by public outcry if not by common sense."

"I don't like 'em," said Mercy.

"You don't like any biscuits."

"Well, I get sick of the sight of them, day in, day out."

I looked at the picture on the tin lid. "Napoli," I said, before adding, "Oh, but the picture is wrong."

Pru looked over my shoulder "How so?"

"Well you see the volcano? That is supposed to be Mount Vesuvius."

"Is it indeed?"

"Yes, and the artist has depicted the smaller peak on the wrong side."

Pru looked sceptical. "And how would you know that?"

"I have been there, but you can verify as much in any geography book."

She shook her head. "There you go again with all this bookishness – it's just not ladylike, Emmeline, and I won't support it. You should keep it to yourself rather than fill the minds of Mercy and Lil with things that will make them yearn for what they can never have."

"But what's Naples got to do with Neapolitans?" asked Mercy.

Pru looked at her severely. "I don't know; I don't need to know, and nor do you."

"Neapolitan is what you call a thing from Naples," I said.

"Why not Naplesish?"

"It's because Naples was once a Greek city named Neapolis".

"Well now you are talking nonsense," said Pru. "I don't see that anyone would or could move a whole city from Greece to Italy."

"No, no, they…"

Lily grabbed my arm. "What do the ladies wear in Naplish, Em? Is it terribly exotic – turbans and the like?"

"Enough now," said Pru, sharply. "I don't wish to be harsh Emmeline, but if you will fill your mind with such fanciful notions as turbans and walking cities, then it can hardly be a surprise that you have not found your match." She pointed a Neapolitan biscuit at me. "If you're not careful, young lady, you'll be mingling with suffragists before you know it, and then where will you be?"

V

A Woman Like Me

30

Florence

It was still my habit to go for a walk on Sunday afternoons, and this June Sunday found me somewhere just North of Oxford Street. The weather was more February than June, but the freshness was a welcome relief from a recent hot spell.

As I walked along a narrow pavement, a group of women were coming towards me – five of them. They were thickly engrossed in conversation and did not notice I was in their way until the last moment.

As we met, the lady on the inside stepped back to make space for me, and I squeezed through the gap between her and the shop windows. I glanced at her to smile a thank you, and there, to my absolute amazement, was Miss Bright.

She didn't see me, she was still frowning over the conversation, and the moment I saw her, I looked away. I don't quite know why I looked away, because I wanted very much to look at her - perhaps it was because I didn't want to be caught wanting to look at her.

I continued on my way for several yards without looking back, and when I finally did look back, it was just in time to see them disappear into a building – a public hall of some sort.

I kept on for a little while, then stopped at a bench.

I could have spoken to her, I thought – I could have simply stopped her in her tracks and said, 'Miss Bright, I believe?'

And then I would have said something funny like… well, I don't know what exactly, but she would have laughed and somehow or another, she would have invited me to join them and… no, I would have invited her to join me – 'Would you care to take a turn in Hyde Park, Miss Bright? It's such a pleasant day.'

'Why yes, Miss Stanton,' and she would take my arm and off we would go together for a perfect afternoon.

I smiled to myself, and wondered if I should take that walk in Hyde Park, just to imagine the route we would have taken, and the things we would have talked about, but the more vividly I imagined her company, the less I could be satisfied with imagination alone, so I stood back up and headed for the hall she had entered. I wasn't actually going to speak to her, of course – I just wanted to see her again – to admire her, if only from a distance.

Outside the hall was a sign proclaiming:

The Proper Place of Women.
A speech against the danger and delusion of Women's suffrage by Lady Parkes.
Sunday at three.

So, Miss Bright was against women being able to vote – what an utter disappointment. I felt immediately quite angry about it, as if a good friend had let me down. And I could not understand it at all – how could such a lovely appearance disguise such self-defeating ideas? But then again, how silly of me to feel disappointed by a complete stranger.

I decided to enter the hall anyway, and in the back of my mind was a fantasy about telling her how difficult it is to be an impoverished woman on the streets of London, and how she might struggle to understand such a thing given the obvious quality of her perfectly-fitting dress.

"Then educate girls as you do boys," was the cry as I entered, but I had missed the remark that provoked it.

There were perhaps fifty people seated, and I took a chair at the back of them. I could not see Miss Bright anywhere, and wondered if perhaps she had left already. Just as well, I thought, and it seemed a sensible moment for me to leave too, but I was afraid that it might look a bit silly to walk out just as I had walked in.

On the stage, a portly, well-to-do lady that I took to be Lady Parkes, was holding forth at the lectern. She was flanked on either side by two more ladies of a similar demeanour who were spearing a certain section of the audience with their facial expressions.

"And who is to pay for such a thing?" asked Lady Parkes, in answer to the question about educating girls. Her friends nodded their firm accord.

"The money could be found," came the reply.

"Even if that were the case, and it is not, you would only be wasting it on trying to teach girls things that they are simply not able to understand. And I do our sex no disservice in saying that, for there are a great many things that *only* women can understand. However, politics is not one of them, and to fill the head of a woman with such things can only be to the detriment of the things that she should know instead."

I felt instantly certain that this was nonsense... though I could not immediately work out why.

"A mind can only hold so much," she continued, "and for every fact that a woman might retain on politics, another is lost from the care of children, or from the proper running of the home. Ladies, it is our place to make the home, it is the man's place to make the country in which that home is safe."

There was a round of applause from the ladies on stage as well as from many in the audience, but opposing it were boos from a smaller group – the same ones who had been on the receiving end of the spiky glances from the stage. I felt myself quite definitely on the boo side of the debate, though I didn't actually make any boos myself.

"Please," continued Lady Parkes, pleading for order from the booers. "Would you seek to displace men from all their positions in society? Firstly, there are already not enough jobs to go round, and secondly, women are in no way suited to the work of men – who amongst you, for example, would trust your life to a female train driver?

I would, I thought to myself. Then a woman from the boo group stood up.

"I would," she said, echoing my thoughts exactly and adding, "What is there to it after all, but the coordination of a few valves and levers. Any woman could manage such a task given no more instruction than a man."

What a brilliant point, I thought, and what a very... and I then I saw her – Miss Bright – all lit up in the gap the woman had made by standing up. She was with the booers – right in the thick of them. She was on my side, and she was absolutely beautiful.

"She would be incompetent" continued Lady Parkes. "Women are not mechanically minded. And where will you stop?"

I wanted her to see me...

"Do you propose to take on the men at cricket?"

I wanted her to know that I was like her...

"Or perhaps you envisage female members of parliament."

That I was one of her...

"Or even a female Prime Minister."

And then, beyond all sense, I stood up... and I said:

"Well, if it comes to that, um... how about... um... how about a female monarch?"

My reply provoked some laughter. I glanced at Miss Bright, and she glanced at me, and I am sure she smiled.

"That is not the same thing at all," said Lady Parkes, as two men in the front row turned round to look at me as if I had broken wind.

"W... why not?" I asked, hoping for a second smile from Miss Bright.

"The Queen rules by divine right – she is therefore a special case and it will not do to draw general conclusions from special cases."

Miss Bright's smile displaced all memory of the question I had just been asked, so I stood there, mortified in a mental gap, with no idea what to say.

A middle-aged woman now stood up amongst the booers. She said nothing at first, but utterly filled the silence with her presence. She indicated for me to sit down. I did so with some relief. There was something quite volcanic about her – it was not only that her hair emerged from her head in untidy fumaroles of grey, but that one sensed they betrayed a barely retained storm of fire within her. Her posture too, was one of retention, her arms clasped tightly at her sides to hold them together and her head tucked into her neck like a volcanic plug.

When she finally spoke it was in a measured and sharp voice that gave vent to her thoughts in small hot bursts, a few words at a time.

"Lady Parkes," she said, "I am sure my new friend," she nodded towards me, "and indeed all present, would agree that men and women are not the same in some details of anatomy. And men certainly have a brute physical strength beyond women, as many of us have learnt to our cost."

She paused and looked about the room for men to aim that remark at… and found them.

"But it does not require brute strength to sign a ballot paper and place it in a box – it requires only an ability to apprehend the issue in question, and to have an opinion upon it. And there is nothing in politics that is beyond the understanding or opinion of a bright woman."

"Even if that were the case, and it is not…" said Lady Parkes.

"You will allow me to finish, Madam," said the volcanic lady. "Now then, with apologies to my young friend," she indicated me again and I sank a little deeper into my seat. "I will concede that the queen is an exceptional case from whom general conclusions cannot be drawn. But you, Lady Parkes, are not the queen, and if you maintain that women are unable to understand politics, then one can only wonder why you – a woman – are here discussing them. Indeed, if we are to accept your thesis as presented, then we must conclude either that your children have been neglected, or that you do not know what you are talking about. Which is it to be?"

"How dare you, madam. I have never been so… well I…"

The debate was now interrupted by a cough from the side of the stage, which came out of a man whom I had already noticed wringing his hands pleadingly towards Lady Parkes during her previous statement.

Taking advantage of the pause he had created, with his cough, he tiptoed onto the stage as if he were creeping into his house late at night and trying not to wake his wife.

"Ladies and gentlemen. I am so very sorry, but this meeting has already overrun by ten minutes and there is another party awaiting use of the hall.

May I humbly implore you to vacate the facility now? Thank you, thank you so much."

I couldn't help thinking that Lady Parkes looked relieved to be offered an escape from her opponent. She politely complied, and thanked the attendees for their attention.

* * *

As I was at the back of the room, I was caught up with the people leaving first, which also meant that I left well ahead of Miss Bright.

I wanted to wait outside for a glimpse of her, so I walked to the kerb and tried to justify my standing there by looking as if I were waiting to hail a cab, whilst at the same time trying not to look so much like a cab-hailer that I would actually stop one.

The volcanic woman was the first of the suffragists to emerge. She spotted me right away and approached.

I held my breath as if a great wall were about to fall on me.

"Well, young lady, I think you did rather well in there."

Her voice was a little more relaxed than it had been inside.

"Oh... thank you," I said.

"May I introduce myself?" she said, "I am Agnes Grendle of the WLSC – the West London Suffragist Committee."

As she was speaking, I sensed the arrival of her colleagues, but having hoped so much to see Miss Bright amongst them, I was now afraid to look.

"And these are my colleagues: Miss Daphne Cole, Miss Clara Cardwell, Mrs Peterson, and this is Miss Florence Bright, whose name is no doubt familiar."

At last I looked, and there she was – Miss Bright, Miss *Florence* Bright – she was smiling at me... and we had just been introduced.

I had no idea at what to do with her smile, so I looked away from it and at the other ladies instead, giving them all a little nod of acknowledgement:

"Pleased to m... meet you," I said.

"May we know your name?" asked Agnes.

"I'm… I… I do apologise. My name is Emmeline Stanton."

"Well, Miss Stanton, it would be our good fortune if we were to persuade you to join our committee. Are you game?"

"Me?"

"You."

"Well, I'm not sure I'm…" I glimpsed Florence again, "Well I… I don't really see why I shouldn't."

"Good," said Agnes. "Here's my card. Mrs Peterson, would you be so kind as to take down Miss Stanton's address?"

Mrs Peterson seemed a very serious woman indeed – dark hair, dark clothes, dark frown, deep thoughts. She took a pencil and a large notebook from her bag, gave the pencil a stern lick and awaited my instructions:

"Two hundred and four, Grange Road, Bermondsey," I said.

"And what do you do there, Miss Stanton?" asked Agnes.

I felt a quiet a panic at this question, as I was clearly not amongst factory ladies, but I answered honestly. "I… I work in a biscuit factory… packing."

They all looked at each other, surprised I think.

"There you see?" said Agnes. "Only a factory girl, and yet who could question her capacity to form an opinion on politics? Well then, Miss Stanton, I shall write to let you know of our next meeting. We would be very happy to have you attend."

As they left, Miss Bright – Florence – seemed to hesitate for a moment, then just as she was about to follow her friends, she turned to me, and with the briefest glance into my eyes, she said, "I thought you were wonderful." And then, for a fraction of a second, a tiny tangle of anxiety played across her forehead.

"Thank you… I um…"

I didn't know what else to say, and she didn't seem to either, but before the silence had a chance to become too painful, we were rescued by the reappearance of Agnes.

"Miss Stanton, it occurs to me – we are all going to take tea at the Stanhope."

"In Piccadilly?" I said.

"The very one, and I don't see why you shouldn't join us. Don't you think so, Florence?"

"Oh, I… why… yes…" Her hesitation seemed to frustrate her, and as if to correct it, she continued very assuredly with: "You really must, Miss Stanton – they have the most outrageous strawberry cake."

I could remember my previous visit to the Stanhope so deliciously well – that first wonderful day as myself, when all was possible – even happiness, and as I glanced at Florence's lips, I could even taste the strawberries again.

"I would be delighted – thank you," I said.

"Well then, we're taking Florence's brougham carriage," said Agnes. "I'm sure we can fit you in."

31

Tea and Perspiration

Somehow, I found myself sitting in the opposite corner of the carriage to Florence making conversation between us impossible, and I did not contribute to the general discussion, as I felt completely overawed.

Florence did look at me at one point with an encouraging smile, which seemed, at the same time, a slightly nervous smile. I returned it, but I did not have the nerve to look at her again for the rest of the journey, and watched the others instead.

Agnes led the debates and was the most vocal, whilst Mrs Peterson said nothing at all. She sat next to Agnes and seemed almost her shadow. Every so often, out would come her black notebook, into which she would scratch something, and twice Agnes tapped at a word to indicate for her to move it, or cross it out. Mrs Peterson would do so without question, and I had the impression that they spent so much time together, that their communication had finely-tuned itself to a few silent gestures.

Daphne Cole's distinguishing features were a large nose, and a half-smile of mock-disapproval – it was the expression of someone to whom you had just made a facetious remark, but one that she was taking in good humour. This expression had a sort of disarming effect in the debates, but it was difficult to know for sure what it meant, because she actually said very little.

Clara Cardwell was very different to Daphne – she was petite and pretty, with black, curly hair, and a faint moustache towards the corners of her mouth. She had a shrill voice, and unlike Daphne, she also had a lot to say. There was a restless intensity about her – the air of someone who was late for something, and was in a hurry to finish the conversation. Not that she did reach her conclusions in a hurry, it was just that she spoke as if she needed to.

* * *

"Why don't you sit there next to Miss Stanton, Florence, and I'll sit here opposite Agnes," said Clara as we took our seats at the Stanhope.

Clara stood back to let her pass.

I felt myself blushing, and to distract everyone's attention from my cheeks, I jiggled my chair sideways as if I were somehow helping to make space.

"Sorry, Miss Stanton," said Florence, raising her shoulders a little as if expecting a bang, "do you mind if I sit here?"

"Not at all, Miss Bright," I said, the fire in my cheeks spreading to my ears and chest.

"Please, call me Florence… if you like."

"Thank you… Florence. Oh, and please call me Emmeline."

A waiter arrived to warn us that the Stanhope would be closing in half an hour and for the next five minutes, we were all distracted by the ordering and arrival of tea and cakes.

After that, Agnes and Clara started a lively discussion on the funding of women's education, closely observed by Daphne and Mrs Peterson.

I made a deep frown, and it must have looked as if I were paying earnest attention to the discussion, but actually, the frown was more for myself – for what on earth was I doing here? I mean, how does a solitary afternoon stroll turn into tea and cakes with five such extraordinary women? It was quite impossible.

Florence and I were sitting slightly outside the main circle of discussion. This made it feel as if we were not obliged to join in directly, and that in turn, made for a perfect opportunity to talk to each other instead.

All I needed was a subject and a little courage.

"They do make a lovely cup of tea here, don't you think?" I said, and was immediately mortified by the banality of my question.

"Oh yes," she replied, and then we had a moment of stiff sipping together.

Rallying my courage once more, I continued in a similarly uninteresting vein with, "Isn't it funny how a hot cup of tea is refreshing, even on a warm summer's day?" This was not only uninteresting, but it wasn't even very warm today.

"Yes it is... I... I wonder why that would be."

"Perhaps it encourages perspiration," I suggested. "And that of course, would have a cooling effect on... um..." I could hardly believe that I was now talking about sweat.

"Yes," she said, with a generously earnest expression. "It must, on balance, cool more than it warms."

I felt horrible – how absolutely hopeless I was at conversation, and I thought I should try to make amends rather than just leave it sitting there:

"I do apologise, Florence, I seem to have chosen a rather inappropriate subject."

She seemed to jump at this, almost as if to catch a falling child. "No, not at all," she said, "You raise a very valid point, and well... frankly... how refreshing – like the tea." Then she smiled – beautifully – and the beauty of it made me momentarily reckless enough to say:

"You know, I think I might have seen you before."

"Really?" She stopped still, but now looked at my plate rather than me.

"Yes, it would be about three years ago and not far from here – Brinkley's Photographic Studio. I was in the waiting room when you arrived to collect some photographs and I..." What on earth was I saying? This was surely a terribly bizarre confession. "Well, it probably wasn't you, of course," I continued, "it's just a vague... um... a memory – a vague one."

"Brinkley's?" Florence turned to her own plate and frowned at her cake. Either she was trying to remember, or she was trying not to look alarmed at being sat next to such a peculiar creature. "Yes, I... I have been there – I'm just trying to remember the circumstances."

My mind was now screaming ways to change the subject, but then I suddenly thought of a way to justify my remembering her:

"Yes... it's just that you took a big dusty hammer out of your bag." Once the sentence was out, I decided that I had probably now made things even worse.

"Oh... did I? That must have looked rather queer." Her shoulders seemed to rise a little and I'm sure she winced. "I have an... um..." Then she took a deep breath. "It would have been a geology hammer – I have an abiding interest in fossils, you see. It's rather a strange hobby, I know, but I... are you at all interested in fossils?"

"Well, I..." I wanted to say 'of course' because why wouldn't someone be interested in something so interesting, even if I had not yet really happened much upon the subject myself, at least not yet. But just as I was hesitating over how emphatically I should say 'of course', Agnes interrupted us.

"Florence?" she said.

Florence jumped. "Sorry, Agnes, you were saying?"

"I was asking if you agreed – the costs of educating women?"

"Oh – I think I might have missed what you said."

"That the costs would be more than repaid."

"Well of course, you know my opinion on that," she said. "An educated woman is always worth more than the cost of her education."

Agnes now looked at me with a hint of disapproval. "Do you agree, Miss Stanton?"

"Oh, very much," I said. "I mean, I hadn't really considered it before, but... but yes... yes of course."

She now nodded a very small approval at my answer, just as the waiter returned.

"I'm very sorry to hurry you, ladies," he said, "but two more minutes, if it is not inconvenient."

"It is inconvenient," said Agnes. The young man looked rather frightened, and Agnes held him in place for a moment with a raised eyebrow before saying, "Why don't you bring us the bill then, young man, the sooner we pay, the sooner you can have your evening."

The bill arrived and I got my purse out, but Florence smiled and said, "No, that's quite all right, Emmeline, I'll pay." And she did, and it was interesting that none of the other ladies even attempted to contribute. I thanked her very much.

* * *

Outside the Stanhope, we waited for the brougham carriage to be brought round. Florence stood next to me and I tried to continue our conversation:

"To answer your question – yes I am," I said. "I mean fossils. I mean... I... I'm very interested in them." I shook my head as if doing so might dislodge my stutter, but Florence smiled at me again, and I started my next sentence feeling reassured that I might be able to get to the end of it: "And I..."

"Bermondsey is rather out of our way, Miss Stanton," said Agnes, chopping me off before my third word. "Perhaps you should take a cab."

"I can walk from here, it is no problem at all."

"All the way to Bermondsey?" she said.

"I really am quite used to it."

Agnes ignored my answer and beckoned a cab. It was unable to pull into the curb so I mounted it in traffic. I could not afford a cab to Bermondsey, but I thought I could simply get out around the corner. However, Florence went straight to the cabbie and paid him in advance.

"Please no, Florence, I can pay."

"It is already done, Emmeline," she said with a big smile. "And I... it was very nice to meet you."

"If you please, ladies," shouted the driver of an omnibus, stuck behind my cab.

My driver had no choice but to pull away and I barely had a moment to wave a goodbye to them all.

32

What, Pray Tell, Are These?

I know I must have slept at least a little that night, for there are parts of it that I don't remember, but I do remember Florence in the bedroom with me, as if her face had been so bright in the day, that it had left its photograph inside my eyes.

The first half of the night was remembering what she had said, and how she had said it, and how she had moved as she said it, and blinked and smiled and breathed.

The second half was imagining – imagining other things she might say to me one day, and how she might say them – close to me, her big, glorious eyes and her soft lips...

When dawn came, I should have been exhausted, but I had never in my life felt so full of energy.

* * *

"Somethin' on yer mind, Em?" said Pru, that morning shift.

I didn't answer.

"Mind you don't mis-pack."

"Sorry, Pru... you were saying?"

"You've crossed your Neapolitans wrong – do that layer again."

"So I have. Sorry, Pru."

Why should I have known Florence's name? That was the question distracting me from biscuits, for Agnes had said, 'Miss Florence Bright, whose name is no doubt familiar.' And then there was the assistant at Brinkley's who said that she was quite famous.

Was it perhaps that she was a famous suffragist, and that Agnes thought that I, as a woman with suffragist tendencies, would have heard of her?

"Did you have a nice Sunday, Em?" said Lily.

"Oh… just the usual."

Perhaps she has written pamphlets, I thought, perhaps even a book, or made a famous speech. No, she seems so shy, I could not see her making a speech at all.

"Pru," I said, "what do you really think of suffragists?"

"You can keep 'em."

"But do you not think it unfair that women cannot vote?"

"It is not a question of fairness, it is a question of a woman's place, and that's in the home."

"But you're at work," I said.

"Yes, some women must work, but even at work we don't do the same jobs as the men."

"We could though."

"Then I should like to see you unload a cart of those two-hundred-and-eighty-pound sacks of flour."

"Well not the really heavy jobs, but we could work the machines – it only needs us to be shown how."

"My cousin Minnie could lift them sacks," said Mercy. "She's as strong as a cart horse."

"And what will the men do then?" continued Pru, answering me, and ignoring Mercy. "Can't you be grateful for the work you have, before you try to take a man's livelihood away from him? I don't mean to be stern, Emmeline, but I for one, don't want the world meddled with when it works just fine as it is, and I'm sure there's most women as agree with me on the matter. And anyway, what would a girl like Mercy do with the vote? She'd be frightened half-to-death at the prospect."

Mercy frowned and we continued to pack in silence.

Fossils – how absolutely fascinating, I thought. I could feel a deep interest in the subject growing inside me. Perhaps we could go fossil hunting together – Florence and I, hand in hand...

"You're doing it again, Em. Left to right, now pay attention or they'll dock your wages for finishing short."

"Yes, sorry, I..." And then I thought of something: "Oh, I know what Mercy would do with a vote – Mercy, if it was put to the vote whether a woman should be paid the same as a man for the same work, would you vote for it or against it?"

"I would vote for it."

"There, you see, Pru, even Mercy can vote if it's explained to her."

"Politics isn't all a matter of simple questions of the sort that Mercy can apprehend. And it wouldn't matter if it was, for it is not our place to vote – it's not our job is what I'm saying. And anyway..."

"STANTON."

I jumped.

It was the supervisor – Mr Walker. We all stopped.

"Yes you, Emmeline Stanton," he said as he held out a familiar wax-paper parcel. It was open.

"And what, pray tell, are these?" he said.

He had my ovaries in his hand.

I could not speak, I could not even breathe in.

"That's why we do locker inspections, young lady."

I stared at them, as if looking into the twin barrels of a shotgun.

"Well? What have you got to say for yourself?"

"I... I... they're just... I don't..." I filled with tears. Lily put her hand on my arm.

"You do not store food in the lockers, Emmeline," said Mr Walker, a little more softly. It attracts rats, and where will Creamers be if we send out a tin of biscuits with a rat in it? We don't make these rules for our entertainment, you know."

"Sorry," I said, except it was just the shape of sorry – no actual sound came out of my mouth.

"If you do it again, young lady, I'll have you on report."

When he left, my legs almost buckled.

Lily, rubbed my arm. "Don't worry about Walker, Em. He's all right."

"Thank you, Lil," I said, finding my voice again and wiping my eyes.

"Funny looking things though – what were they?"

"Oh, they're... the round things? It's um... it's just some giblets the butcher let me have cheap, I was going to give them to my landlady – she's... she's making a stew tomorrow."

"Well, I'm sure we'd all like to stand around talking about tomorrow's supper," said Pru. "Come along now, all of you, and pay attention this time, Em – we've got trays backed up, look."

* * *

It was clear that I could not take my ovaries to work any more, so I would need to eat them before I got there. The next day, I arrived at the butcher's ten minutes early to give myself time to find a quiet corner of a park or alleyway, where I could hide for the minute or two it took to cut them up and swallow them.

"Good mornink, Mr bootcher," I said in my now well-practised exotic accent.

"Oh, you're early this morning, Miss," he said.

"What you mean? You not haff my ovaries?"

"Yer cow eggs? Of course, Miss, but there was this gentleman here – he was looking for a particular young lady.

My heart stopped and I looked at the door.

"What sort of man?"

"A gentleman. Well he got out this photograph, you see, said he was looking for the sister of the lad in the picture."

"And did he look like me?"

"The absolute spit, Miss – a close relative of yours for a certainty, but if you'll wait he'll be back shortly, 'cos I mentioned that..."

"Which way did he go?" I barked, loud and English. "Which way? Quickly."

"Out the door and turned left, Miss, but if you'll…"

I burst out of the door, turned right, and ran as hard and as fast as I could. When I could run no more, I slowed to a pace just short of a run.

It must have been Uncle Walter – it must. What other person who can pass for a gentleman would be looking for me? And to think he had Mother's picture of me to help him.

Well, I knew he would come for me in the end, but he was already so very close – not a twenty minute walk from my home.

How though? How was he finding me? What clue had I left?

* * *

Packing biscuits that morning seemed incongruously normal when set against the terrible threat that lay outside, but I played along with it, hiding any hint from my colleagues that this was not an ordinary day.

After work, I took a very circuitous route home, looking out for the police and my uncle along the way. I decided not to enter the house by the front door, and walked an extra half-mile to reach the alley behind the house so that I could enter through the back door.

* * *

The next day, I also left by the back door, and at five in the morning too, because it seemed at least an hour earlier than Uncle Walter could reasonably be expected to be out looking for me. It also gave me time to search for a new butcher.

I decided that it would be safer to go well out of my neighbourhood for the ovaries, and I eventually found a butcher near the Elephant and Castle.

"Cow eggs?" said the butcher – a red-faced man with a disgusted curl to his lip. He walked slowly out to the back of the shop, but shaking his head as he went. When he reappeared a few minutes later, he placed a pair of ovaries on the counter, then stood with his hands on his hips.

"You mean these?"

"Yes," I said, maintaining my exotic accent.

He shook his head very faintly and said,

"A penny the pair."

After taking my money and handing them over he said, "Now get out of my shop, and don't come back."

"But why?"

"It's not natural, eating a thing like that – it's not Christian."

"But in my kantry…"

"Look, I don't know where this so-called land of ice is supposed to be, but I'll not supply unnatural foods to heathens. Now, clear off."

My focus at that moment was so much upon getting them inside me that I ignored his rudeness and hurried to a park bench in West Square.

Eating them was not as difficult as I had feared, and the wax paper rose naturally either side of the ovaries to hide them as I cut them up. I think I looked like nothing more than a factory girl having a little something to eat before work, and indeed I was, but West Park is also only a stone's throw from the Bedlam asylum, and there was I, eating raw cow ovaries and all but inviting them to drag me inside.

* * *

As I hurried home from work that evening by another circuitous route, it began to dawn on me how strange it was for the butcher to refuse my custom. After all, butchery is probably not such a lucrative business that you can turn money away, unless… unless by turning it away you can make more money? Yes, I could smell my uncle in this too – indeed, he might have a tentacle in every butcher's shop in South London by now.

Even my back-door route into the house seemed too precarious that night, and I hid for some time in the alley outside, listening for a footstep, a rustle, or even a breath, before risking a sprint to the door.

191

* * *

As I entered my room, and before I could even sigh my relief, I noticed a letter on the chest of drawers and jumped as if the person who wrote it was standing there.

I drew close, but without touching it.

It was addressed to me, but I didn't recognise the handwriting. It certainly wasn't Uncle Walter's, but that didn't mean much, for he would be quite capable of mangling his writing to disguise himself.

But why write? If he knew where I lived, then why not keep it secret? He could then lurk nearby, and drag me into an alley when I was least expecting it.

Perhaps then, he means to blackmail me, I thought. No, it would be futile to blackmail someone on factory wages. More likely, he wants to tell me what he plans to do to me, so that I might have some time to dread it first, and he might have time to enjoy my dread. Yes, that would be my uncle.

Unless… unless the letter is not from him. Yes, it could be from Creamers – telling me that I am to be let-go for keeping food in my locker. No, they would tell me at work and save the stamp.

Oh, but what about Agnes? Yes, for she has already promised to let me know of their next meeting – she even had Mrs Peterson take down my address for that very purpose. Yes, of course – it's from Agnes.

I finally let a sigh of relief out, picked up the letter, and sat on the bed to open it.

I took a quick glance at the final signature first, just to be sure, but it wasn't from Agnes – it was from Florence.

I stood up again and tried to read from the beginning, but the words 'it's from Florence' were so loud in my head, that for a moment I could take in nothing of the letter itself.

I sat down again, took a deep breath to calm myself, and here is what it said:

* * *

June the 9th, 1887.

Dear Miss Stanton,

It was such a pleasure to make your acquaintance this Sunday last, and I hope your journey home to Bermondsey was pleasantly uneventful.

I am writing to let you know that there is to be no meeting of the WLSC this coming Sunday, for Agnes has a prior engagement.

(I sank at this, and may have pouted too.)

However, I am planning to make good use of the day with a visit to the Japanese Village exhibition in Knightsbridge.

(Now, I made an envious sigh, and that certainly did end on a pout.)

I am sure you have already been to it...

(I had not even heard of it.)

...However, if by some chance you have not been, and are available to go, and would like to go, then you would be very welcome to accompany me.

* * *

I stood up and re-read that paragraph almost a letter at a time to be absolutely sure that she really had just invited me to go with her – with Florence Bright – to a Japanese exhibition.

Almost immediately I set about a reply – I wanted to write it now whilst the invitation still seemed believable. I tried to be as formal as she had been, saying that I would be delighted to accompany her and suggesting we meet at Hyde Park Corner at midday.

I could not post my reply right away – it was too dangerous to go outside, so I slept badly, with her letter and my reply on my bedside table, waiting for dawn.

33

Hippopotamus Tails

The following morning was a Saturday. I left the house at five again, and I ran up the alley and along two further streets before I allowed myself to slow to brisk walking.

When I found a letter box, I stood for a moment, reading through Florence's name and address very carefully, just to be sure I hadn't misspelled anything or been untidy in my writing, then I took a breath and posted it. I now had precisely thirty-one hours to wait until my appointment with her.

Only a few yards later, I was furious with myself for choosing to meet her at Hyde Park Corner – this was so close to the exhibition, that it meant I would only get to have a short carriage ride with her. Not only that, but how silly I must have seemed – asking to be picked up when I had already travelled nine-tenths of the way there.

* * *

As for my ovaries, I could no longer risk anywhere in or around South London, so with an hour in hand before work, I took an omnibus towards Soho. The journey was frustrated by traffic and by the time I arrived, I really only had ten spare minutes left. I walked into the very first butcher's I saw. It was busy and I was cringing at the prospect of being overheard.

As I reached the front of the queue, there were five hurried women waiting behind me and within ear shot. I went into character, but as quietly as I could.

"Good mornink, Mr bootcher."

"Good morning, Miss."

"You will exkoos an unusual requess?"

"Beg pardon, Miss?"

I cleared my throat, and beneath the general conversation around me, I heard a tut.

"You will exkoos an unusual requess, please?"

"A what, Miss?"

I decided to go straight to the next part of my act: "I am from Iceland. We haff special dish we call ovumpioff. We haff for breakfast every day. For ovumpioff we need, um, ovary of cow. Can you supply?"

"You eat ovaries?" The room went silent, and the silence sat right on top of me.

"Yes," I whispered.

He shrugged and shouted towards the back-room.

"Mr Connors, there's a foreign lady here wants to eat ovaries."

Connors stepped into the doorway wiping his hands with a cloth. He had an expression of mild disgust that I assumed was for me rather than for whatever was on his hands.

"Pig? Goat? What sort?" he asked.

"Cow, I um, any will do."

"That's a new one." He shrugged. "But we don't do 'em – we don't gut here. Try Percy's on Beak Street."

"But could you do them?"

The first server I had spoken to now gave a dismissive shake of the head, and began to deal with the next person in the queue. She knocked me aside a little in taking her position to make me know I was in her way.

"Two lamb chops, please," she said, in smug normality.

"Are you sure you don't want some hippopotamus tails instead?" laughed the butcher, as he wrapped them for her. The other customers laughed.

I left, head down, and as I waited for the omnibus back to Bermondsey, I cried a little and had to pretend that I had something in my eye. It was becoming clear that my original butcher, Mr Cowles, was rather special – willing to accommodate my unusual needs without question, and I damned Uncle Walter for taking him away from me.

Perhaps this new embarrassment was also my uncle's work – perhaps he has not just contacted every butcher in Bermondsey, but every butcher in London, telling them not to serve ovaries to anyone who looks like me. Yes, that was probably it – he was both torturing me and searching for me at the same time.

There was nothing I could do now until Monday, except hope that my physical femininity would endure, and that Uncle Walter would get no closer.

34

The Japanese Village in Knightsbridge

On the Sunday morning, I took my usual precaution of leaving at five, and walked very briskly out of Bermondsey with my head down. Once I was a safe distance from home, my uncle-terror rearranged itself in my stomach to become anxiety about meeting Florence.

I started by worrying that we wouldn't find anything to talk about, but as I got closer to Hyde Park, I began to worry mostly about how I looked, so I kept stopping to look at my reflection in shop windows, checking that I could still see a woman, and rehearsing facial expressions that might seem likeable, or even pretty.

When I finally arrived at Hyde Park Corner, I realised that it was probably about the densest confluence of people in the whole country, and therefore the ideal place for a murderer to look for me, so rather than stand out by stopping still, I paced up and down with the crowds, while I waited. Fortunately, I didn't have to wait long – Florence's carriage arrived right on time and as I walked towards it, I tried not to let it show that an entire firework display had just erupted in my chest.

"Emmeline," said Florence, whispering aloud to me from the window. The driver opened the door and Florence bounced down the step in a pale violet, silk dress, and for that moment, my fears, my secrets, my uncle, and everything in the world but her, disappeared.

"Florence, you look absolutely b…" I wanted to say 'beautiful' but it seemed too forward. "You look... what a lovely dress."

"Oh, thank you very much." I watched her cheeks pinken. "It's new." She held out the skirt with her hands and I could see that she was trembling a little, perhaps because it was chilly today.

There was a short silence during which I also went pink, then the driver opened the door again, and we both climbed in.

"But you look lovely too, Emmeline," she said, as if she were correcting herself. "You really do." She scratched her nose but her hand was still trembling and she placed it firmly on her lap with the other one on top of it to hold it still.

I did not look lovely – how could I when I was in such beautiful and expensively dressed company? But the small nicety of her saying it to me, was so exciting that I got my next words all tangled up:

"Me? I... Well, not really I... um..." I sighed and rolled my eyes. "I think I've forgotten how to talk today." We both laughed at that, and it was a relief to laugh.

The driver pulled away into the traffic, and I looked out of the back window to check we weren't being followed, but I tried to cover my doing so by saying, "What a lot of people."

"Yes," she said, as I sat back down.

Another short silence was then broken by Florence:

"I have been to the exhibition before," she said, very politely, as if I were the queen, "and it was the most fascinating place, but I was alone and it is so nice to have someone to share it with... I have a love for all things Japanese, you see."

What a perfectly exciting revelation that was.

"Well that is a love we have in common," I said. "I have had a passion for everything Japanese since I was very little."

"Really?" she said, leaning forwards a little.

"Yes, I think it started with a painting we had at home called The Stray Shuttlecock – it was a Japanese scene, and I always imagined myself the little girl in it. Oh, and I can even say 'thank you' in Japanese – 'arigato'."

"Arigato. Well, you can try it out at the village."

We now had another silent moment, but a more comfortable one than the last, and then I thought of a good question:

"Florence, when Agnes introduced you last Sunday, she said: 'Miss Florence Bright, who's name is no doubt familiar,' and since then I have wondered what she meant."

"Oh, it's nothing – I have written a few books."

"Really? You mean as a hobby?"

"No, it is my profession, but they are only children's books – I like to draw and paint you see, and I have written some stories around the pictures. It's nothing really."

"But that is wonderful. Are they about prehistoric beasts?"

"No, actually they are about a cat called Pippin, but they are really not at all good."

"Are they popular?"

"Um… well yes, they are quite." She laughed a little.

"Then it is my first intention to read them all, and I will purchase them as soon as I have a chance to get to a book shop."

"Oh, you needn't buy them – I have so many copies at home, I'll send some to you, and you will be very welcome to them."

"I would be delighted – thank you."

She smiled again, then stretched her legs.

How wonderful she was – a writer no less. And what a neat explanation for her being both shy and famous at the same time.

* * *

"Humphrey's Hall, Miss," shouted the driver, pulling up to the kerb.

"Thank you, Jenkins."

I looked out of the back and both sides of the carriage before getting out, on the pretence of wondering where exactly the hall was, but I think I only made myself look strange. The way was clear though, so when Jenkins opened the door for us, I was able to step out like a person who wasn't being pursued by a murderer.

The exhibition itself was absolutely extraordinary – an actual Japanese village, with real Japanese houses, and real Japanese people speaking Japanese and making Japanese things, and yet the whole village improbably contained within Humphrey's Hall.

"Isn't it wonderful, Florence."

A main street rose from the entrance, thick with tourists, and lined either side with houses and workshops in perfect imitation of their counterparts in Japan. The people inside the buildings were all engaged in craft-work of one kind or another – we watched umbrellas being made in one workshop, whilst in another we saw the finest cloisonné being cast on copper; there was a maker of hairpins, a lantern maker and a fan maker, but Florence's favourite was an artist who painted vivid depictions of Mount Fuji with a brush in either hand.

We spent perhaps a whole hour making our fascinated way along the main thoroughfare, trying to absorb every amazement until we reached the end of the street, where stood a grand wooden teahouse. We looked at each other, then right away took a table and ordered two teas.

The waitress was just about as pretty as she could possibly be, and wore an immaculate, jade green kimono, with a pink flower in her hair. She placed before us a black lacquered tray upon which sat a flat metal teapot and two small, handleless teacups that were more like sugar bowls. Then she said, "Sixpence please." And she not only said it in the tiniest voice with the deepest accent, but she wrinkled her nose and blinked at the same time as if she had been very slightly frightened by a noise.

Florence opened her purse.

"Florence I… could I pay for this? You have already paid my entrance. She smiled and I gave the sixpence to the waitress who then touched the teapot before pulling her hand away quickly with a mock gasp.

"Hot. Please be careful."

To thank her, I decided to attempt my only Japanese word:

"Arigato."

She looked very surprised, then smiled at me and said, "Perfect." Then she bowed and walked away in tiny steps.

"Wasn't she absolutely charming?" I whispered.

"Yes," said Florence, leaning forwards, "and how very beautiful."

We both looked at her again as she served a nearby table.

Florence poured the tea. It was a vivid green and it had a sort of grassy note to it, as if it were actually a mixture of tea and fresh hay. There was also a tray of little sweets – cubes of jelly dusted in green powder, and other soft confections in the shapes and colours of flowers, all arranged with extraordinary beauty and precision.

"Everything is simply perfect," I said, "and I think that after today, it will take very little imagination to believe that I have truly been to Japan." Then I stuffed a whole flower-sweet in my mouth.

Florence put her tea down and seized upon the subject of travel.

"Have you ever been abroad, Emmeline?"

I swallowed. "Um... yes, I have, I... I lived in Italy for a few months... last year – in Naples."

"That must have been very exciting."

I winced a little.

"The city itself is exciting – a very wild place, full of passion and... and full of danger." I shook my head – I didn't want to think of my uncle in case my thoughts somehow summoned him.

"They do have some wonderful food though," I said, trying to steer in a happier direction, but I was already studying the room for uncles and policemen. "I um... I had the most delicious flat bread thing with tomatoes on it called a pizza".

I looked behind me. I was being strange again, but once I had established that no one was watching us, I turned back to her with one of the light smiles I had practised in the shop windows.

"Pizza – that is a good word," said Florence. "I think I should like to try pizza. But tell me how you came to be in Naples."

"Well, I... I was staying with my..." I picked at my fingernails for a moment, as if by confining my attention to one tiny thing, I could somehow forget the big monster in my head. "I stayed with a relative."

"That's nice," she said, but in a tone that seemed to acknowledge my discomfort.

How I wished I could tell her everything – to have another human being know me – I mean to like me, and to like me despite knowing my horrible secrets. But I could not – not ever, for if the truth about me was so terrible that it could tear the love of my own mother out by the roots, how much more easily it would snap the weaker branch of a mere friendship.

Florence smiled. "I know," she said brightly. "I should tell you how I came to join the West London Suffragist Committee."

"Oh yes, please do."

"Well, by chance, I saw Agnes make a speech in Hyde Park, and at the end of it, Clara came right up to me, bold as you please, and asked if I had a position on the matter. I said that I was very much in agreement and the next I knew, I found myself talking with the whole committee."

How perfect she was, and how I envied her life – a normal woman, writing books and enjoying the company of her clever friends. But then she added:

"In truth, it was more frightening than anything. I am quite a solitary creature at heart, you see – not the sociable type at all."

I had not imagined that for a moment – I had seen her amongst her friends and had assumed she was completely at ease with them. It seemed we were more and more alike.

"But they are only a small group," she continued, "and as I spend so much time alone, I am convinced that it is good for me to be sociable at least once a week, otherwise I might lose the knack of human company altogether." She smiled, but then suddenly she looked rather distressed. "Oh, but please don't misunderstand me – it is groups of people that I struggle with – to sit here with you, just the two of us, is a different matter altogether, and one that I am enjoying very much." She gave me a little worried smile.

"But we are very much alike in this," I said. "I am usually terrible with people, but this... well I am enjoying it too – very much."

We both took a sip of tea.

"Agnes seems a remarkably strong character," I said. "She makes me quite nervous."

"Yes, people are often afraid of her."

I laughed. "The moment she looked at me during the anti-suffrage meeting and signalled for me to sit down, I felt very much inclined to do as I was told."

Florence laughed too. "She does have a tendency to go a bit far, and she can be quite infuriating, but you mustn't let her frighten you too much." Florence now leaned forwards and whispered, "You know, she is rumoured to carry a loaded revolver."

"I don't believe it," I said, but really it was that I couldn't believe how well our conversation was going. We were talking, like friends – like proper friends, as I had seen people do, and it was a lovely, happy feeling – not the normal, mildly pleasant sort of happy, but a profoundly deeper one that the word 'happy' didn't quite do justice to.

"Nor I," she said. "It was a story that Mrs Peterson started – saying that if ever a man tries to lay a hand on Agnes, she will shoot him dead on the spot."

"She must be speaking metaphorically."

"Yes, I think so," said Florence, then she leaned even closer and whispered again, "I fell out with her quite badly once."

"Over politics?" I asked, reciprocating both her lean and her whisper. This was the closest I had been to her face. Given a moment longer, I might have counted her eyelashes.

"No, it was a personal matter... it is difficult to explain. Don't mention it to anyone – I know you wouldn't, but..."

"Of course not," I said. "I keep secrets very well."

She is confiding in me, I thought. Friends confide – what if I were to confide in her after all?

"She was very angry about my reaction," she continued, "and berated me for misrepresenting an entirely innocent expression of affection."

"Affection?"

Florence nodded, but looked rather alarmed at herself for having said it.

I had no idea at all what she could mean, but I didn't like to add to her distress by asking her to explain so I jumped straight to, "Was the matter resolved?"

"Oh yes, it's all quite forgotten now." Then she took a sip of tea and looked a little sad. "Except that in truth, I don't really forget, and I am always wary of a person having once fallen out with them... it spoils things a little, if you know what I mean, because there's always that fear of it happening again."

Then perhaps friendship is weak, I thought, in which case, I should not confide in her – I should keep my secrets to myself – all of them. How empty it felt – to be so full of secrets.

Her sad expression lingered, and beyond all common sense, I actually reached out to comfort her by placing my hand upon hers.

Almost instantly, I pulled it away, as if her hand were as hot as the teapot.

I had not expected to feel such an intense urge to keep a hold of it, and to hold it tightly rather than touch it reassuringly, and it was the intensity of the urge to hold on that made me let go so suddenly.

She immediately looked uncomfortable and hunched her shoulders. What a silly spectacle I had made – holding her hand, then pulling it away so quickly. This would probably be the end of my good first impression, and the first step towards her inevitable dislike of me.

"I do apologise, Florence... I'm always... it's just that sometimes people are very uncomfortable to be... to be touched by strangers and... and I shouldn't like to make you uncomfortable."

"You didn't," she said, with the warmest and most beautiful smile in the world. "Not at all. Here, look..." She reached forwards, hovered for a moment, then placed her hand upon my wrist, and my whole arm burst into a cloud of starlings.

* * *

"You paid sixpence for a cup of tea?" said Pru, the following Monday at work.

"It was a special treat."

"Why didn't your rich friend pay?"

"Because I insisted."

"Well, you're a foolish girl to part with sixpence of factory wages for a cup of tea when you might have done otherwise."

"I didn't mind."

"Well, she mightn't be quite so friendly when she finds out you're a biscuit girl."

"She already knows, and doesn't care a jot," I said, and smiled a floating-away sort of a smile.

Pru narrowed her eyes. "It's not right... I mean it's not right for two women... look here, Emmeline, it's not right for the classes to mix like that – if we seek to... to ape our betters, we only make monkeys of ourselves."

"Dear Pru, must you disapprove of every single thing I do?"

"I am trying to protect you from your own folly is all – nothing good can come of this, Emmeline, not for either of you."

35

The Rambles of Pippin

London was clearly no longer a good place to get ovaries given that Uncle Walter seemed to have forewarned every London butcher against me, so I decided that my best option lay in getting up early enough to travel outside the city – perhaps to a town, or village that I could reach by train. There I might find a small friendly butcher who is beyond the reach of my uncle and also in need of any business he can find.

Every compass direction offered possibilities, but then I realised that I already knew not only the place, but the very man – the butcher of Otford. Yes – that day, that first happy day as myself, when the train broke down at Otford station, and the butcher and I had stood together watching the sunlight on the pond.

I remembered him as a quiet man – unassuming, and a man who saw the good in a beautiful day. Yes, I would go to him – he would help me.

According to Mrs Stanton's copy of Bradshaw's, there was a five thirty-five train from Victoria that stopped at Otford at six twenty-nine. Victoria station was about an hour's walk from Grange Road so I could rise at perhaps three-thirty and be there in plenty of time.

Once in Otford, I would have eighteen minutes to buy the ovaries before the return train, which would get me back to Victoria by seven forty-one. At a brisk walking-pace, I was fairly sure I could then make it to Creamers for the start of my shift at nine.

* * *

The following morning, I set my plan in motion. The first light of dawn was on the horizon when I left, but the streets were still quite empty and dark. In a sense, that made them more dangerous than normal, but they actually seemed safer to me than they normally do, because I was sure that my uncle would not think to look for me so early in the day.

It took me an hour and ten minutes to reach Victoria – a little longer than I had anticipated given my fast pace, but there were not many other travellers at the station yet, so I had no trouble in buying my ticket in good time. Forty nine minutes later, I arrived in Otford.

The butcher's shop had not actually opened yet, but the butcher was already there preparing for the day and was happy to let me in for some early business.

I decided not to attempt my foreign accent this time, having learnt that some people do not take kindly to foreigners, but I had devised a variation on the theme.

"I have an unusual request," I said.

"Go on, Miss, I'll be happy to oblige if I can." He still seemed a nice man – it was in his face – something quiet about it, as if he were listening to a bird singing in the distance.

"I work at the Icelandic embassy in London."

"Well now," he said, as if I had come from Buckingham Palace. I did not want him to think me grand – not that that I thought he would in my working clothes, but just to put him at ease, I said:

"I work in the kitchen you see. I have been sent to make a small order, but… but it's a somewhat unusual one."

"Go on."

"Um… ovaries – cow ovaries." It never sounded good out loud, and I could feel my pulse rise.

"That is an unusual request, Miss."

"They eat them you see – for breakfast," I said, then blurted right through the next section at speed: "We need a pair a day, and I will come to collect them at this time, Monday to Saturday, and perhaps you can supply four on the Saturday to take them through Sunday."

"No problem at all," he said, shrugging off the peculiarity with a smile. "I'll have them tomorrow. Shall we say a penny each? Tuppence the pair?"

"Yes," I said, "of course – that will be fine." It was very expensive, but I was so relieved at his saying yes, that I dived straight at it without thinking to haggle.

"Long way to come for 'em, Miss."

"Yes, well um… well they won't touch city butchers, you see? They don't like them."

"Very wise too. Well then, I will see you tomorrow morning, Miss."

"Thank you. Oh but…"

"Miss?"

"I'm sure they would appreciate your discretion."

"Won't mention it to a soul. If anyone asks, I'll tell them it's for my Otford sausages – people certainly do travel for those."

I smiled, he smiled, and I left.

* * *

The next morning, after almost an entire week without female emanations, I finally had my ovaries. I ate them on the train back, and I was so pleased to have them that I almost enjoyed the taste.

The rest of that day was spent paying the price for two very early mornings and all the running to and fro, and by mid- afternoon, I could barely keep my eyes open. I ploughed on though, and did a good enough job that I managed to get through the whole shift without being told off by Pru.

By the time I got home, I was almost asleep on my feet, but a parcel sitting on my bed woke me faster than a bucket of cold water. I even made a small sound about it – a little cry of alarm, as if someone had leapt out of a corner at me.

It's him, I thought – this time it must be Uncle Walter. It's probably a bomb, or at least something dead – something strangled or stamped upon.

For a minute or two I couldn't move at all, then I inched a little towards it, stopped again, inched a little more, until at last I could see the writing on the label. It was from Florence.

Relief came as quickly and as completely as the initial shock had done. I sat upon the bed next to the parcel and put my hand on it.

"Dear Florence," I said, "you almost frightened me stupid." And I laughed a little.

I unwrapped the brown paper very carefully. Normally I was one to rip paper off a parcel, but a parcel from Florence was something more precious.

Beneath the brown was another layer – this time a beautiful oriental wrapping paper with a bamboo print. Within that were seven books, all tied together – Florence's books, and there was a letter attached:

* * *

June the 16th, 1887.

Dear Emmeline,

Thank you so very much for your company on Sunday, I had such a nice day.

Please find enclosed, as promised, copies of all my little books. I hope you will enjoy them, and that your expectations are not too high.

With regards to this coming Sunday, Agnes insists that we conduct the meeting in the brougham carriage whilst driving about London, but rather mysteriously, she refuses to give a reason until we are all in it.

We're going to gather at the Stanhope. Could you be there at ten perhaps?

I very much look forward to seeing you again,

Your friend,

Florence Bright.

* * *

There you see? – 'Your friend' – we are definitely friends, I thought. And not only that, but she 'looks forward' to seeing me again. Imagine if that is not mere politeness – imagine if she is thinking of me right now, anticipating me – how absolutely lovely that would be.

I picked up the first book as if it were her hand. "The Rambles of Pippin" it was called, "Written and Illustrated by Miss Florence Bright".

On the first page was an exquisite drawing of a cat. He was a determined-looking fellow – courageous, resolute, but with a naughty grin. He was striding towards me with a carpet bag in his paw (this endeared him to me immediately, of course) and he was looking into the distance – towards his adventure.

Suddenly I felt young again. Well, I was young really – only seventeen, but the events of my life had seemed to make me feel so much older than that. Now though, just for now, I was young, and being young made me feel safe, and I curled up in my bed with my little part of Florence.

Not just Florence though, for Pippin made me think of Geronimo, and if I am young again then he is here with me and I don't have to miss him so much. Geronimo and Florence, past and present, together in a warm bed.

I fell asleep within the first page of Pippin's rambles, and for the first time in such a long time, I slept well, and right through to my three-thirty start.

36

Save One Perhaps

On the Sunday morning, I left the house at five, ready for my meeting with Florence and the suffragists.

Once well out of Bermondsey, I sat on a bench, and took out my notebook to calculate my incomings and outgoings – a task I had been dreading. I already knew that the cost of my ovaries and train tickets must be at least at the edge of what I could afford, but after doing my calculations three times to be sure, it was absolutely clear that my outgoings far exceeded my income. I would only manage a few weeks like this before I ran out of money altogether.

I had no idea what to do other than worry about it for the next few hours until I met Florence at the Stanhope.

* * *

When I finally walked in, Florence was there alone. She waved to me across the room, and shook my hand very gently. She was trembling again. I didn't quite grip her hand back – I wasn't sure whether I should or not, so my hand must have seemed incongruously limp.

As soon as she let go, I felt certain that the limpness must have seemed to express some indifference to her, so I tried to compensate with an overly broad smile.

How stupid I was – we had left on such good terms last Sunday, and now I had introduced a note of awkwardness that might take us right back to the beginning.

"Thank you so much for the books, Florence. I like them very much indeed."

"Oh... the books. Well, I hope you weren't too disappointed." She seemed to cringe a little.

"Not in the least," I said, trying to work out exactly what it was I needed to do to the tone of my voice so that I sounded sincere and not patronising. "I have read the first one – The Rambles of Pippin, and I enjoyed it immensely."

In fact I had loved it, but I thought 'loved' might sound falsely enthusiastic.

"Well it was my first, you see," she said, dismissively, "and it takes a little while to get the hang of it."

"But really, Florence, I really did enjoy it – I like Pippin very much."

She half opened her mouth, but didn't seem to know quite what to say.

"He's an adventurer, you see," I continued. "I have always loved geography and tales of exotic places, and here's little Pippin, with his carpet bag – I have one just like it – and off he goes in search of adventure, meeting every contradiction with courage... and he always does the right thing in the end. Yes, I... I like him very much."

"Well, thank you," she said, then she stretched a little in her seat and tilted her head to one side, smiling as if she was thinking something nice about me.

I should perhaps have stopped there, but her smile was so encouraging that I went on:

"And the illustrations are exquisite. I believe you have a true gift for illustration, I really do."

Now she blushed, and I blushed back, so I attempted a half-change of subject:

"You know, my dearest childhood friend was a cat."

"Really?" She smiled again, but an amused sort of a smile.

"Geronimo," I said. "I mean that was his name – 'Geronimo' – he was... a cat, and from the Far East – my father brought him over on a ship."

She leant forwards a little. "A cat from the Far East? That's extraordinary. I have a cat too – his name is Ming, but despite his name, he's quite definitely British."

I laughed.

"And was he the inspiration for Pippin?"

Now she laughed.

"Yes and no, by which I mean, he is the exact opposite of Pippin, being fat and lazy, and lacking all signs of motivation. I think Pippin is the product of my disappointment in Ming."

We laughed together now, just as we had done at the Japanese Village Exhibition. What a truly lovely day that had been, and I was just about giddy enough to say so.

"Florence, I cannot describe how delightful it was to visit the Japanese village with you. I struggle to remember if I have ever had a more enjoyable day – save one perhaps."

Those last three words were out before I had a chance to catch them. I could not believe that I had been rude enough to demote my day with her to only second best position.

"What I mean is..."

"Oh... you two here already?" It was Clara – Daphne was with her. "I thought we said eleven."

"No, I think it was ten," I said, looking to Florence for confirmation, but she now seemed rather uncomfortable, and I knew it must be my fault for being rude to her.

"Well, we're early anyway," said Clara. "Thought we'd try to sneak a cup of tea before Agnes arrived."

They joined us and we talked politely for the next half an hour on all manner of things – the new Hammersmith Bridge, the Jubilee, even women's suffrage, but all I wanted to do was to find some way to apologise to Florence. I mean, even if my first day as Emmeline was indeed my happiest day, I could at least have lied to her for the sake of politeness. I hadn't even thought it through enough to know which day actually was the happiest – they were so completely different, and had entirely different sorts of wonderfulness about them.

Agnes now arrived with Mrs Peterson.

"Good morning, Ladies," she said, then she looked at the tea cups – first Daphne's and Clara's which were still half-full, then mine and Florence's which were now quite empty. "You seem to have been here quite some time," she said, specifically to Florence and I.

"Since ten," I said.

"Why?" she asked.

I looked at Florence. "It was ten wasn't it?"

"I thought so," said Florence, but looked neither of us in the eye as she said it.

"It was eleven," said Agnes, looking from Florence to me and back again. "As well you know, Florence, given that you sent out the letters."

"Yes, I thought it was eleven too," said Clara.

Florence opened her mouth but was quite mute. Now was my chance to make up for my rudeness and rescue her, but I didn't know how to do it, and Clara spoke first:

"Well, we're all here now." Then she looked up at Agnes. "Would you and Mrs Peterson like a cup of tea first?"

"There's no time for tea," said Agnes, firmly. "Come along now, all of you."

37

Albert

Wclimbed into the brougham and took our usual positions. This was immensely frustrating of course, because it put Florence in the opposite corner to me and well beyond private conversation.

"Now then, ladies," said Agnes, as we pulled out into the traffic, "we are having our meeting here because I felt it best to discuss my plan beyond the possibility of prying ears."

"This sounds very intriguing," said Clara.

"I have decided that it is now time to move from talk to action, and I propose that we do so by the carrying of placards to the Houses of Parliament – a march in support of votes for women, taken by women, to the very heart of democracy. We should all..." at the word 'all' she looked rather cuttingly at Florence, "...march together, wielding placards, and indeed our bodies in lieu of ballot papers."

"That sounds like fun," I said, but then glanced at Florence whose face was a thundercloud. I now seemed to have removed myself even further from her good opinion.

"Fun?" said Agnes, as if it were a swear word. "Do grow up, Emmeline." Then she shouted at the driver, "Jenkins, make for Charing Cross, would you?"

"Right you are, ma'am,"

"We're not marching now are we?" laughed Clara.

"No, but I am going to show you the route I have planned. The most conspicuous course is from Charing Cross along Whitehall – that way, we march on Parliament in full view of the largest number of people."

Florence sat forwards and frowned in the direction of Agnes but not quite at her. "We have discussed this before, Agnes, and you know that I cannot be involved in a march. I have no objection in principle to marching with placards, and I am still all for the cause, but you also know that my publishers are very conservative and would not react favourably if they found out."

"It is a question of priorities," said Agnes, sharply.

"Yes it is," said Florence, now looking directly at her, and revealing a firmness of character that took me completely by surprise. "I am happy to pay for the placards and sundries," she continued, "and you may of course use the brougham to take you about, but…"

There was a deep, cluttering thump outside and the carriage lurched to a halt.

Jenkins scrambled down from his seat. "Oh, Peggy, oh dear, oh dear, Peggy."

We all climbed out of the carriage. The horse was on her belly, her head up, almost as if she were resting in a field, but her eyes were wrong – unfocussed, confused. She jerked her head back as if she were about to get up, but her body made no reply.

"Oh my dear old girl, Peggy." Jenkins was close to tears and stood with one hand on Peggy's nose, the other on his hip, and no idea at all what to do.

"What's the matter with the thing?" asked Agnes.

"Just seemed to lose her legs. Dear oh dear, Peggy."

I couldn't bear it.

"Let's unharness her, Jenkins," I said.

"Yes," said Florence, and she touched my arm. "We'll see if she can stand without the encumbrance."

Jenkins, Florence and I began to unbuckle Peggy. Florence caught my eye and gave me a reassuring nod. I did not know if it was to reassure me about the horse, or about my clumsy comments, or even to approve of my present actions, but whichever it was, I was relieved to have it.

Jenkins now took Peggy by the cheek piece and encouraged her up. She scrambled and flapped for a moment, but finally made it back onto four legs.

"Oh well done, Peggy old girl, well done," said Jenkins. "Nothing broken I think, Miss, just seemed to lose her legs."

"She slipped or tripped perhaps," said Florence.

"Not sure, Miss. Very odd. Very fond of Peggy, Miss."

"Well, can you walk her back from here?"

"Certainly, Miss. It's a mile perhaps, but I can take her good and slow. What about you and the ladies, Miss?"

"We'll take cabs – it's no problem. Now off you go, take her gently and let me know what you need."

"Thank you, Miss, thank you very much. I'll be back for the brougham when I've seen her safe." And off they went gently together, like an old married couple.

"There is always something rather shocking about a downed horse, isn't there," I said.

"Yes, there is," said Florence, looking me right in the eye.

"Sentimentality," said Agnes. "You have every compassion for the horse, but none for the cattle that were killed to make the leather seats of the carriage. It is not only sentimentality, but hypocrisy."

We were all silent for a moment, as Agnes' logic seemed inescapable… except, "Surely," I said, "better one inconsistent moment of compassion, than a consistent absence of compassion."

"Oh, well put, Emmeline," said Florence, and I felt as if I could have floated right off the ground.

"Semantics," said Agnes, as she hailed a cab. Two pulled up. "We can squeeze three in each. Florence, why don't you join Mrs Peterson and I in this one?"

"Oh, I don't like to squeeze," said Florence. "You and Mrs Peterson take the first, then Daphne and Clara, you take the second. Emmeline and I will take the next that comes by."

I held my breath.

"You live in completely opposite directions," said Agnes, sarcastically.

After an almost endless pause, Florence said, "Nevertheless."

Agnes rolled her eyes and without looking at me or Florence said, "I will write to you all with further details and arrangements during the week. Next Sunday, we march."

* * *

Another cab came along almost immediately, and we both got in.

"Silly taking two cabs," said Florence. "We'll drop you off in Bermondsey first, and then I'll take it back to mine."

The illogic of the plan sat with us in the cab for a couple of minutes – she may have simply done it to defy Agnes, but I could not have been more delighted, and I tried to think of something to talk about.

"Poor old Peggy," I said. "Not pleasant to see a horse down. Oh, I said that didn't I?"

"Yes you did, but it is still true." She smiled.

"And your publisher…" I said.

"Purdey's."

"They sound very stern."

"Yes, and there is much restriction upon what I write. The funny thing, Emmeline, is that my success is based almost entirely upon a chance remark by the Princess Helena."

"Good heavens – you know a Princess?" I said.

"Oh, goodness no," she laughed. "There was an article in The Times, covering the moral education of children in the home which mentioned that the Princess and her husband very much approved of the works of Miss Florence Bright, claiming that they 'always have a solid moral foundation'. I began to sell rather well after that – I think the middle classes rather like the idea of their children reading the same books as the prince and princesses.

But that is also why I am afraid to be seen causing a stir."

"After the way you dealt with Agnes, I am surprised that you are afraid of anything."

Florence laughed again. "Well, she was being very rude to me, which I find quite distressing, especially in company – I wonder if perhaps I am quite a wild creature when trapped in a corner like that."

She continued to smile – she seemed to have forgotten, or perhaps even forgiven the clumsy remark about my happiest day, and we were now talking like proper friends again.

This is how friendship grows, I thought – we talk to each other, we visit exhibitions, we have little adventures with fallen horses, and measure by measure we become... inseparable.

"Agnes thinks I am simply too greedy for the income to jeopardise it for the cause," she said, "but as you know yourself, it's so difficult to make a living as a single woman and I'm constantly afraid that I might lose it all. Especially when in truth, my success is based upon no great talent."

"But your drawings are exquisite," I said, "they really are."

"Thank you," she said, with an expression a little like relief. "I can draw a little, but I'm no writer. It was all really just an experiment started by my fiancé, Albert. I had made a few sketches of a cat that he thought were quite good you see, so he persuaded me to pen a little tale to accompany the pictures."

She had a fiancé.

What absolutely appalling news.

Florence was in love... with a man.

I knew immediately what I had been doing – daring myself to imagine that she was one of the women who loves women, and that we might somehow... well... how foolish of me, how very foolish, and how immediately and completely I hated Albert.

"This became The Rambles of Pippin" she continued, "and with Albert being a good friend of the Purdey brothers, I was published without any of the usual difficulties."

The more I thought of him, the more I hated him. I could see him too –

he would be tall, broad-shouldered, an heroic face, his hair dark and wavy, his eyes a confident blue…

…and she loved him. She loved him so much that she meant to marry him. I felt utterly wretched.

I looked out of the window. "Oh look, here already," I said. "This is the best place for me – I am a short walk from home and have a small errand to run on the way."

The cabbie pulled over.

"Well," said Florence. "I… I um… well thank you, Emmeline – thank you for your help with Peggy… and… and for your company."

She smiled her lovely smile and I wanted to cry. "No – thank you," I said. "It has been another lovely day." And then I left before my disappointment had a chance to run down my cheeks.

*　*　*

Once home, I went to my room, cried for half an hour, and then sulked for another two. At the end of that, I decided I must, for the sake of my sanity, try to rationalise the situation and find a more positive way to look at it. We were at the beginning of a wonderful friendship after all, so why shouldn't that be enough? I mean Albert clearly hadn't hindered our friendship so far, and there was no reason to think that he would do so now just because I knew he existed.

Anyway, I thought, what is it that we would have done if we were something more than friends? I mean, my body is my darkest secret – if she knew how I was constructed below, she would be disgusted. You could even argue that I had gained something in finding out about Albert, for by abandoning hope of anything more than friendship, it left me free to pursue that friendship honestly and innocently.

Yes, a deep friendship which might now grow even deeper for my having left the notion of romance behind.

When I had finished rationalising, I went back to crying.

38

Calm Yourself, Emmeline

As the working week progressed, I began to sink into the exhaustion of my ovary expeditions, and by Thursday, I was completely drowning in fatigue.

"For goodness sake, Emmeline," barked Pru. "I do believe you are actually asleep standing up."

"Sorry, I…"

"You keep saying you're not ill, but frankly, you look a fright."

"I'm not ill, Pru. I am just…"

"Stanton." It was Mr Walker, the supervisor again. "Had three bad tins from you yesterday. It won't do. Buck your ideas up."

"Those were my fault, Mr Walker," said Pru, lying for me. "I forgot I hadn't showed her the gingerbread stacking before – she didn't know what she was about. It won't happen again."

"See that it doesn't." He looked at me and frowned. "You all right, Emmeline?"

"Fine," I said.

"If you're not well, you can take a day off – we treat our ladies decently here, you know."

"Thank you, Mr Walker, I'm quite well – really."

He looked sceptical, but left us to our work.

"Thank you, Pru. You didn't have to do that."

"Just buck up, Emmeline, and if you're not well, for goodness sake take a day off – we don't want you passing it around, whatever it is."

* * *

On Sunday, it was the day of the march on Parliament. I was able to have extra hour's sleep that morning, but it was not enough to counter my exhaustion, and it only brought me back to the mildly lesser exhaustion of two days ago. Never-the-less, I slapped my face a few times, and the excitement of the march kept me going all the way to our meeting point outside the Stanhope.

And there she was, as pretty as the sunrise – Albert's fiancée, beaming at me through the brougham window.

I climbed in.

"Good morning, Florence... Ladies," I said.

I glanced at her as I took my seat, but worry-clouds obscured her smile as she looked at me. I must have looked awful, so I tried to counter any apparent exhaustion by following the conversation in as animated a fashion as I could.

We stopped as planned at Charing Cross. All but Florence got out of the carriage, and as I climbed down she said, "Emmeline, you look a little... well... a little weary. I mean, you look lovely, but are you tired perhaps? Or not quite well?" I was about to answer but she continued, "You don't have to go if you don't want to, you can stay in the carriage with me."

"Come along, Emmeline," shouted Agnes.

"I had better go," I said quietly to Florence. "I did promise."

"Good for you," she said, and smiled again.

This is how their mornings will be, I thought – Florence staying behind, and Albert off to work, taking her sunrise smile with him. Suddenly I felt even more exhausted than I had the night before.

* * *

As we arranged ourselves outside, Agnes handed us each a placard proclaiming 'Votes For Women', but all my enthusiasm for the march had left me now. A couple of young men who were leaning on each other nearby, laughed at us while a middle-aged lady looked disgusted, and all I could think was how much more hilarious and disgusting I would seem to them if they knew the truth about me.

"Now then, ladies," said Agnes, very loudly to maintain the attention of the gathering crowd. "Let us remember our noble purpose, and march with dignity on Parliament."

Now I felt embarrassed too – all these people looking at me, and then I felt ashamed of my embarrassment, and then I realised I was about to march through central London advertising myself with a placard when a resourceful murderer is looking for me. This was surely madness.

* * *

We walked in single file, the pavement being very busy on a Sunday afternoon, and several times I had to stand aside to let people through.

It was not quite what I had imagined – I thought we would stride forth, stern and resolute, and that there might even be the occasional cheer or round of applause, but in fact, we were continually separated from each other as we picked our way through crowds who, for the most part, did not even notice the placards.

And it got worse when Agnes decided to rally us all with a full-throated cry of, "VOTES FOR WOMEN."

She looked back at us and gave a nod to indicate that we should join in. Clara did so with some energy, but I was so conscious of drawing attention to myself that I could only bring myself to mumble it.

Moments later, a small gap opened in the throng, and a man, his arms outstretched in a crucifix, held back a group of pedestrians to let us through.

It was Albert, it had to be – he was tall, broad-shouldered, an heroic face, blue eyes, dark wavy hair, and as he caught my eye he gave me a firm nod of approval.

He was exactly as I had imagined, and to see his face was to see him and Florence together, arm in arm, in love, kissing and… and I hated him.

"Votes for women," I snarled at the ground.

I could not compete with Albert. Well, I knew that anyway, but despite my attempted arguments in favour of platonic friendship with Florence, I wanted her, and the impossibility of my ever having her, set against his actually having her, was unbearable.

"Votes for women," I snarled again.

"I think not, ladies."

A man – a policeman, grabbed me very firmly by the upper arm. Another snatched the placard from me. There were a few moments of confusion and pulling, and the next thing I knew, we were all being lifted into a black police carriage and pushed into its tiny, separate cells.

Incarceration – prison.

Would I go to prison?

I couldn't. I couldn't be caged, I couldn't bear it.

Uncle Walter flashed into my cell, holding me down, suffocating me.

I shook my head, but I couldn't breathe.

"PLEASE," I screamed, "I HAVE TO GET OUT, I HAVE TO GET OUT."

"Calm yourself, Emmeline," shouted Agnes. "It's only as far as King Street Station. We're almost there."

I spent the rest of the short journey shaking and muttering, "No, no, no, no," to visions of my uncle.

* * *

When I was finally released from the van, I gulped in the air and the sunlight as if I had escaped from a week in a collapsed mine.

"For goodness sake, Emmeline," said Agnes. "They will lock you up for a lunatic if you don't calm down."

Once inside the police station the desk sergeant was very stern.

"Marching on Parliament, ladies, is an extremely serious offence – it might even be treason, and that carries the death penalty."

I had no idea that we could be in so much trouble and I staggered faintly. A constable held me upright and the sergeant answered my swoon with:

"All right, all right, I dare say you're not going to hang for it, not this time at least, but really ladies, it is very irresponsible and very childish. Not to mention that you have brought four police officers away from their duties."

Agnes was silent.

"I shall take a note of all your names before we let you go, and make no mistake – if I catch any of you at this sort of nonsense again…" He let us finish the sentence in our heads.

"Now then…" he dipped his pen and looked at me. "Name?"

"Um, Eme… Stanton, Emmeline Stanton."

"Stanton, is it?" He frowned and paused before scratching it into his ledger. "Stanton, Stanton, Stanton," he mumbled, then he frowned to the side for a moment to think. Nothing came of it, so he said, "Address?"

I also couldn't think for a moment.

"Um, Bermondsey, Grange Road – two hundred and four, Grange Road, Bermondsey… Sir."

He took it down, mumbling it to himself.

"Age?"

"Seventeen."

After the full stop, he frowned again, then looked at one of his constables.

"Aren't we supposed to be looking out for a Stanton?"

"Yes, Sir, but not a woman, Sir – a Thomas I think."

I felt all the blood drain out of me.

"Do you know a Thomas Stanton, young lady?"

I shook my head but could make no sound, and then I staggered again.

The constable held me up by the arms, I wanted to fight him, to run, but I was trapped, and would stay trapped if I did not stay calm.

"Well, give her a seat then, before she passes out."

I sat down, and tried to compose myself. There was no doubt about it – my uncle has the entire London police force looking for me, and I am sitting in a police station.

Clara, Daphne and Mrs Peterson gave their details in turn, and then he reached Agnes.

"Name?"

"Tell me," she said, very calmly, "do you think it appropriate that this specimen of a constable saw fit to grab my arm so forcefully, when we were marching so peacefully?"

"Madam, if you will march on Parliament, you must expect to find yourself forcibly detained."

"How very male of you."

One of the constables stifled a laugh, and the Sergeant raised a finger of disapproval whilst trying not to smile. "I do indeed have that privilege, Madam. Now then, what name was it?"

"A privilege, derived from a penis – how very ridiculous."

The mood immediately darkened and the constable grabbed both her arms from behind.

"No, Madam, that I will not tolerate," said the sergeant. "Take her away."

"No, please," I said, wondering where my voice had come from. They paused and I stood up. "She doesn't mean to be... we are very sorry, Sir... Agnes, please – please just give him your details."

The sergeant looked at her expectantly and she very smugly complied, reciting her name and address in a slow, deliberate staccato, as if she were sentencing herself in court.

The Sergeant then looked at us all, his face a dark bruise of disapproval.

"Go on – all of you, and I don't want to see any of you again."

* * *

We left the station in silence, and to be outside, free again – free of Uncle Walter's grasp (at least for now), quite overwhelmed me. And then I saw Florence – she had been waiting nearby, and must have followed our progress from a distance. I began to cry and she hurried forwards to take my hand.

"Emmeline, you poor thing." Her hand was warm and soft – this is what Albert would feel when he held it. "Are there to be charges, Agnes?"

"Of course not," said Agnes with a scoff. "For the last time, Emmeline, pull yourself together, you're not going to hang for treason for goodness sake – don't dignify their childish attempt to frighten you with tears."

Florence put her hand around my waist and pulled me away from Agnes' comments.

I could feel her hand on Albert – this is how it felt for him.

"The brougham is parked around the corner," she said.

Agnes, Daphne, Clara and Mrs Peterson all climbed aboard, but Florence did not. "You four go ahead. I will put Emmeline on a cab, and then I have a meeting with my editor."

"On a Sunday?" asked Agnes, sarcastically.

"Yes," she replied. Agnes looked extremely irritated as they pulled away.

As soon as they were out of sight, Florence smiled at me and said, "Let's get you home, Emmeline. I think you will feel better for a cup of tea and something to eat."

Two weeks ago, the thought of another journey with Florence was about the most wonderful thing that I could possibly imagine, but now we would be sharing the carriage with Albert and Uncle Walter.

As we climbed into a cab, Florence said, "Brompton Square, driver – thank you."

"Your house?" I said, feeling confused, and something else – just a glimpse of excitement through the darkness of my mood.

"Oh," said Florence, with a slight panic in her eyes. "Well, not at all… would you… would you rather go straight to Grange Road?"

"No it's fine, I'd be very happy to come."

"It's only that I thought it would be good for you to relax for a little while, after such an ordeal, and… and you don't seem quite well, Emmeline."

"Oh, I'm just a little tired – long hours at work this week, and sometimes I don't sleep very well."

"Are you hungry too?"

"I am quite."

"Good. We can have some sandwiches, and you can have a very quiet hour or two with me."

I smiled. How lovely she was, and she will still be lovely when she is married, I thought, and she will still be my friend, if only I can find a way to bear Albert and survive Walter.

39

In the Snuggle of the Curve

Brompton Square was off the Brompton Road – a pleasant, narrow 'U' with a thin but happy park in the middle. It was remarkably quiet considering its proximity to the Brompton Road bustle, and Florence lived at the deep end of it, in the snuggle of the curve.

She rang the bell, and I was almost floating with anticipation. A young maid answered.

"Thank you, Nellie," said Florence. I followed her in, and Nellie shut the door behind us. "This is my good friend, Miss Emmeline Stanton." Nellie gave me a little curtsey, which seemed so funny to me as a biscuit girl, but I didn't let it show.

The hallway was quite grand – black and white chequerboard flooring, but blotched with oranges, yellows and greens from the sunlight coming through the stained glass of the door.

Facing me from atop a marble plinth, a very ancient, and very gentle ceramic Buddha head smiled a welcome to me.

"Nellie, ask Mrs Dockerill to make us tea with plenty of sandwiches. Something very wholesome and filling if she can."

Nellie left us and Florence took me into the drawing room.

"Florence, your house is absolutely... it's lovely – it really is."

"Thank you," she said, and I think she blushed a little. "It's quite modest really, and I must confess, it has been quite a mortgage, but it seemed sensible to invest my earnings in property."

I took a deep breath as if trying to take in my surroundings, but really it was because I could smell her – she had a delicious scent of warm pineapple about her. I had noticed it before, but now, in her own home, the scent was edibly deeper.

I then felt rather self-conscious about breathing her in so deeply, so I turned to the room and said, "Yes, I should think property is a very good investment."

A few minutes later, the tea and sandwiches came in.

"Just leave it all there, Nellie."

"Very good, Miss."

Florence began to set out the tea cups. "Do just eat as much as you want, Emmeline."

I really was very hungry and had to restrain myself to eat politely.

Three sandwiches later, I felt I was neglecting Florence, so I swallowed a final mouthful to make way for conversation.

"I'm glad to see you eat so well," she said. "I am sure you will feel better for it."

"Thank you," I replied, and then I imagined her saying the very same thing to Albert, perhaps with him sitting in this very chair. And then they would talk, and I wondered what they talked about. Perhaps he is a palaeontologist too, I thought – yes, they must have the most fascinating conversations about prehistoric beasts.

"Tell me something interesting about dinosaurs, Florence."

It sounded a little tangential out loud, but she put her tea down, and her face was all of a sparkle.

"Well, let me see… it is difficult to think of something just like that but… um… well did you know that until quite recently, the iguanadon was assumed to have a horn on its nose like a rhinoceros?"

"I did not."

"Yes, you see they found the horns amongst their bones, and indeed, if you go to Crystal Palace gardens, you can see a re-creation of the creature much like a rhinoceros. However, on closer inspection, it now turns out, the horn is actually a thumb."

"A thumb horn? How extraordinary."

"Not only that, but the Crystal Palace beast is depicted on all fours whilst we now know iguanadon to have been bipedal."

She took a sip of tea.

"And that is not the only time such a mistake has been made – even the very first dinosaur discovered, megalosaurus, was originally assigned a quadrupedal attitude when now we know it to have been two-legged.

"Fascinating – truly," I said.

"I really will talk all day if it is upon one of my subjects," she laughed. "But what of you, Emmeline, what are your interests?"

"Me? I think anatomy is probably my deepest subject."

"Well that quite overlaps with palaeontology."

"Yes, in fact, when you mentioned the iguanadon's horn, I wondered if, like the rhinoceros, it would have been made of keratin, this being the same substance that our hair and fingernails are made of."

"A very interesting suggestion."

We smiled at each other, and it was almost as if, in that brief exchange on subjects so unusual for women, that we knew we really were friends, almost as if we had never needed to *become* friends, because we were too alike not to be friends. Indeed, I had never felt closer to any human being than I did at that moment.

"May I show you my living room, Emmeline?"

"I'd love to see it," I said.

She jumped up, and led me out of the drawing room by the hand and along the hallway, until we reached the living room door.

"Wait here a moment," she said, before going inside.

I heard a clockwork key being turned, and then music from a music box with an oriental melody. Then she opened the door and stood aside to let me in.

The first thing to announce itself as I entered was a huge Chinese lantern hanging in the middle of the room – it was a grand, red fretwork box, with painted glass panels, and long red tassels hanging from each corner.

There were oriental paintings upon the walls, and the walls themselves were dressed in a pink wallpaper with a beautiful blue bamboo print upon it. There were bamboo chests to answer the wallpaper, Persian carpets to contradict it, and in three corners of the room, tall, frondly, pot palms stood like exotic waiters.

Across the fourth corner was a large, golden screen that was painted with exotic birds and landscapes, and in front of the screen was a scarlet sofa upon which cushions of tropical brocades reclined like princes.

"Florence, it's like a harem."

"Do you like it? I thought you might appreciate the exotic touches."

"I adore it – I feel as if I have travelled to a strange and wonderful land, and the strangest part is how much at home I feel."

There was a table beside the sofa, and on it sat a collection of strange ornaments. They seemed to be rocks at first glance, but upon closer inspection I saw that they were fossils – beautiful spirals of shell, shark's teeth and skeletal fish, shining against a matrix of grey rock. But one rock amongst them was incongruous – it was orange – a translucent orange.

Florence moved in close beside me and I felt the blood rush to that side of my body to meet her. "What do you think it is?" she asked.

"It looks like a boiled sweet," I said.

She held it up to the window, and the sun shone through it to reveal a large black ant trapped inside.

"And now what do you think?" she said triumphantly.

"An ant – in amber?"

"Yes, trapped in the resin of an ancient pine tree, perhaps a million years ago."

She put it into my hands.

"It is absolutely beautiful," I said. "How extraordinary, that a tiny drama of a few seconds might be preserved for a million years. And he's perfect, I even see the minuscule hairs on his legs. And look at his jaws, wide open and gulping in the amber as if he were trying to escape by devouring his own murderer."

"What a singular thought," said Florence, her cheek now almost touching mine. "I think you are a very singular person, Emmeline."

I smiled, and I wanted to turn my face towards her, but I could not, because at this distance, my lips would have brushed her cheek.

"No one has called me that for a long time," I said.

There was movement amongst the cushions on the sofa, and I jumped as if I'd been caught out.

It was a cat.

"Well I know who this must be," I said with a cough to clear the awkwardness away.

"Yes, this is Ming," said Florence.

He was quite fat – about the size and shape of a cushion and with a similar air of lazy opulence. And his face was flat, as if someone had been sitting on it.

I sat down on the sofa, lifted him onto my lap and buried my fingers into his deep coat.

"I think you have made a friend," said Florence.

"He's so lovely – what a grumpy little face," I said, rolling his cheek fur around my fingers.

Florence sat down too and leaned back a little to look at me.

"How funny that you are in my living room, Emmeline – you're all out of context." We laughed. "And you know, I let very few people in here. The WLSC ladies have never seen it – I only entertain them in the dining room."

"Well, I think it's like heaven," I said.

I fussed Ming for a few minutes more – I felt so profoundly at home to have a cat in my lap again, and as I muttered all sorts of nonsense to him, I began to feel more and more sleepy.

Eventually, he plopped himself onto the floor and wandered away.

I sighed.

"I'm so very tired, Florence."

"Then why don't you rest a while? It's a very comfortable sofa. Here look..." She put the cushions on the floor, except the largest and softest one which she put at the end. "And it isn't late, so I'm sure you have time for a nap."

I sank my head into the cushion as Florence walked to the door, and I smiled a thank you as she turned to close it.

Once alone, I started to cry – not a sobbing cry, it was a quiet cry. I was not even sure which of my myriad emotions was the cause of the tears – whether they were happy or sad or frightened or hopeful, and I was asleep before I could decide.

* * *

When I awoke, it was dark. I did not know what the time was, but the depth of the silence convinced me that it must be the small hours of the morning.

"Emmeline?" It was Florence. She was sitting in a chair near my head. She was awake, but her body was in the position of someone who was asleep.

"Florence, I'm so sorry, I only meant to have a little nap."

"No, don't apologise," she said, sitting up. "I am glad you slept – I think it will do you good."

She was so close, and so quiet that I could hear her breathe.

"You were right about the sofa," I said, "I'm not sure I have ever been more deliriously comfortable than I am right at this moment." And I closed my eyes to savour the sensation.

She smiled. I didn't see it, but I heard it in a little puff of air from her nose.

"Tell me of your one happier day, Emmeline. The day you said was even better than our day at the Japanese village."

I should have felt a panic at this, but all I felt was warmth and calm and companionship.

"Well," I said, my eyes still closed. "A superficial description is simply that it was a day spent wandering about London on my own – the first time I had ever done so. That does not sound much of a thing to be so ecstatic about, does it? But you see…"

Only now did a small itch of hesitation falter me and I opened my eyes. I decided that perhaps I could tell her just enough without alluding to the brutal facts.

"...throughout my childhood, I felt somehow trapped within myself, as if I were invisible to the world, and on that day, for the first time in my life, I felt that I had somehow come to exist. I walked along Piccadilly and there I was, and everyone could know it."

No, that is too much, I thought. I grimaced slightly and tried to deviate a little:

"But it is rather difficult to explain, and... and sounds... foolish out loud. I think perhaps the happiness of it stands out partly by contrast to the unhappiness that followed, for it was on the evening of that same day that my mother took against me, and a few days later I was dispatched to Naples for a very unhappy time." Uncle Walter appeared in my head and I sat up.

She touched my arm and sent a warm breeze of shivers down my back. Walter disappeared and there was a peace again.

"I am sorry to have made you think of it," she said.

Her wedding day, I thought, will be her happiest day, and now I could see her and Albert hand in hand – man and wife. I tried to displace the image, but it was immediately replaced by Uncle Walter again, and then Mason too, and all my alarms began to ring at once – the police, money, my ovaries, yes, my ovaries – it's Monday – I must get to Otford.

"Florence, what time is it?" She turned towards the mantelpiece clock and moved her head like an owl to catch a little light from the window against the hands.

"It's only a quarter to four."

"I shall be late." I stood up. "I must go."

"To work? What time do you start?"

"Oh, I... very early, I have to get to Victo... no, Bermondsey... I mean... I must go, Florence, I really must."

I walked to the front door and she followed me.

"Well, thank you so much for letting me sleep," I said, standing on the chilly doorstep. "I um..." I had no idea how to say goodbye.

"But how will you find a cab?"

"Oh... they do run at this hour – I'll pick one up as soon as I'm on the Brompton Road." I took a few steps up the path but stopped to look back at her. She looked worried. I smiled.

"It's fine, Florence, really – the city is just waking up – milkmen, postmen – it's really quite safe."

* * *

How horrible it was to step out of the sensuous, pineapple warmth of Florence, and back into the cold, fraught exhaustion of my daily life.

I should at least have felt better for the extra sleep, but there was now an aching in my back and down my legs, and a different sort of tiredness – not just a lack of energy, but a lack of strength, as if I was coming down with something.

I could not afford to be ill. It was not just that I couldn't afford time from work, or time without ovaries, but I could not afford to be an invalid when Uncle Walter has every policeman in London looking for me.

40

The Tunnel

"I have an announcement to make," said Lily, that morning at work.

We all stopped packing for a moment, and it was a relief to stop because I could lean my illness on the table for a moment.

"Well," she said, smiling so broadly that her rosy-apple cheeks looked as if they had been polished with wax. "George Edward Frederick Simms and I are to be wed – it's official. Father has given his blessing, and we have set a date for next spring. I am going to be Mrs George Simms."

"Congratulations, Lily," said Pru. "It's not unexpected, but it is welcome news none-the-less. I hope you will be very happy together."

"So do I," I said, whilst trying to smile through an agonising vision of Florence and Albert kissing at the altar.

"Oh, it's too lovely – just think, Em, I shall be a wife, living with the love of my life, and we will have a house and everything – it's too wonderful to be true."

"Well, you deserve it – you really do."

"Thank you, Em," she said, but then perhaps something in my expression gave me away, for she made a slightly sad smile and said, "I am absolutely sure that one day you will meet someone and fall in love too, Em, I mean look how pretty you are."

I smiled, but it was no good – tears came to my eyes so quickly that I even made a small 'Oh' of surprise.

"Em, please don't cry."

"Don't spoil the happy news, Emmeline," said Pru.

"No, no, no, these are happy tears," I said. "I'm a romantic – that's all, and doesn't everyone like a love story with a happy ending?"

Lily seemed satisfied by this but I could feel Pru's eyes narrowing a little.

There was more well-wishing, which spread to the ladies on neighbouring teams, and there was even one other girl in tears to make my own seem more appropriate.

All I could think was that I would never marry Florence, and how much more bitter it tasted having spent last night together, waking up in the beautiful dark, side by side, breaths and whispers – that will be Albert's world for as long they both shall live, and whatever energy I had left was used up in not crying about it.

I should have just endured life as a man, I thought. Then it would have been different – Florence and I would have gotten along just as well, but she could have looked at me in a different way – in a romantic way, and I would have stolen her away from Albert. Not only that, but I would still have my family, and Geronimo, and no one would want to murder me.

But then again, I'd had a family and safety and normality before, and none of it was enough to counter the pain of being trapped as a boy – even Florence could not have saved me from that, so perhaps I was always doomed.

And besides, how could I have looked into her eyes, knowing that she in turn was looking into the eyes of an imposter – a woman masquerading as a man. It would have been a marriage based on deceit, and I think I would have hated my existence more than ever.

* * *

As the day wore on, my illness got worse and worse – one minute hot and sweating, and the next shivering in the cold of the sweat, and then, sometime in the afternoon, not long after lunch, I found myself on the floor, looking at the factory ceiling. I had never really noticed it before, and I couldn't understand why it was glittering.

A slap.

"Emmeline, look at me." Another slap. It was Mr Walker.

I covered my cheek. "How dare you?"

"You fainted, Emmeline."

"Did I?" Pru was standing behind him, hands on hips, looking very cross…
or perhaps concerned – it was always difficult to tell.

The next I knew, I was being lifted from the floor.

"You're going home, my girl," said Mr Walker. "And I don't want to see
you before Monday at the earliest – later if you aren't better. Do you hear
me?"

"Yes, Mr Walker."

I sat quietly for half an hour in his office with a cup of brandy-laced tea,
which was revolting, but strangely restorative, and then they put me in a
cab home.

I had the driver take me to the alleyway behind the house so that I could
use my safe route, and once in, I went straight to bed.

* * *

By the evening, I was aching, deep into my bones, and my skin tingled as if
I was covered in ants. I drifted in and out of a wet sleep for an hour or two
until a great thumping on the front door shocked me right out of my bed.

I shuffled weakly to the window in my blankets.

There were two policemen outside.

I stepped back and stood in the middle of the room looking from window
to door and back again. There was no way out, not unless I could get out of
the back door before Mrs Stanton answered the front one.

"All right, all right," She shouted down the hallway, "there's no need to
break your knuckles."

I was too late, she was going to let them in.

"Emmeline Stanton, where is she?" The policeman's voice was hard and
pointed.

"Emmeline? She'll be at work still. What's this all about?"

There was hope – she didn't know I was home.

I began to whisper 'please' to myself, over and over again.

"And where does she work?" Asked the policeman.

"Creamers – she's a biscuit girl. What on earth has she done? I'm her landlady – I have a right to know."

"When do you expect her back?"

"Not before ten usually. What has she done for goodness sake?"

"Then we'll return at ten. And don't you be tipping her off either," he added. "You don't want to make yourself an accessory now, do you?"

"I beg your pardon? This is a very respectable household."

The door closed and I heard the policemen's footsteps recede up the road.

I had to get out, but how, when Mrs Stanton was between me and the door?

I could hear her clattering about downstairs – it sounded like she was putting on her boots. A few moments later the front door opened and slammed, and I heard the stiff clop of her footsteps as she walked up the road – perhaps off to tell her sister, a few doors along, what had happened.

I dressed as quickly as I could, stuffed a few things into my carpet bag, then ran down the stairs and flew out of the back door as if I had been thrown.

It was too much for my legs and I crumpled face-first onto the path.

I got back up and tried to run again. I couldn't – there was just no strength in my legs, but I could walk, and I made my unsteady way along the alley behind the house.

I hid in some bushes at the end, waiting for a cab to pass by on the main road, and I did not have to wait long.

"Where to, Miss?"

"Anywhere, um North – North of the river." I am not sure why I said North – perhaps it was only that I lived South of it, and that North therefore sounded the furthest away that I could go. The cabbie shrugged and headed off.

The motion of the cab made me deeply nauseous, and a few minutes later, as we crossed London Bridge, I had a moment of spinning, exactly as if I had stepped off a roundabout. I closed my eyes and tried to wish it away.

"North Bank," said the driver as we came down from the bridge.

This was no good – I needed to find a lodging house and the best place for that was Chelsea – we should have gone West.

"Um… West, towards Chelsea," I said

The cabbie set of again but the turn to the left made my nausea worse so I closed my eyes again, thinking that if I couldn't see the world move, it couldn't make me feel sick about it but before I could even put my hand to my mouth, I vomited over my skirt and the floor of the cab.

"Agh, you filthy bitch. Get out of my cab."

I dragged myself out and the driver climbed down.

"Damn you, look," he said, grabbing me by the front of my coat. "That's criminal damage that is – you'll pay for it."

"I'm so sorry, please. Here…" I pulled out my purse. "How much do you want?"

"Two shillings the fare and… and three more for the damage."

"But five shillings?"

He tightened his grip. "Pay it, or I'll fetch a constable."

I handed him the money, and he stuffed it in his pocket whilst looking at the pool of vomit.

"You really are a filthy little bitch, aren't you." Then he shook his head, climbed aboard, and pulled away into the traffic.

* * *

I staggered to a bench to sit for a few minutes and gather my strength. I had sat on this bench before. In fact I had slept on it several times – I was at the embankment, amongst the homeless again.

My London adventure had come full circle. I had a few shillings left, but as both the police and consequently my uncle now knew that I worked at Creamers, I could not return there and my income was lost. Along with the income I had lost my ovaries, my friends, and I had lost my home.

All I could do was wonder what sort of a useless person can lose everything twice before they are even eighteen?

No, not everything – I still had a friend – I still had Florence.

I could think of a million reasons not to go – the fear of imposing on her, of burdening her, and more than anything, the fear of disappointing her by showing myself to be a such failure. But all of that was superseded by the need for her – the need to reach for the only hand that might reach back.

* * *

My mind was as dark as the Thames as I walked alongside it – I could manage no thoughts beyond the concentration of walking itself, as if the weakness in my legs could only be overcome by the application of every last atom of my mental will.

At times I thought perhaps I was still asleep, for there was something wrong with the sounds I could hear – they were muffled and they echoed, as if I were following myself from a distance, and through a long tunnel.

The sights too, were wrong – stretched out, like a view through the same tunnel – everything concentrated in miniature and at a small point in the distance.

I know that I was sick several times, and I remember both Hyde Park Corner and the corner of Brompton square, and then I think I saw Nellie's face, but beyond that, my journey is black.

VI

I Love Her

41

It's Warm, and the Sun is Shining

The next day was a vague thing – there was a doctor, and there was more vomiting, and I remember a period of indeterminate time where I voiced every breath with a monotone hum. I remember thinking that it was my purr.

And there was Florence – her face soft, concerned, and I think she stroked my head.

* * *

The next time I awoke, I felt a tiny bit better. My mind was clear enough to know I was in Florence's house because Ming was sleeping a few inches from my face.

I lay there for a moment, drowsing in the smell of clean cotton, then I rolled over and found Florence sitting in a chair next to the bed.

She smiled. "Well now, how much better you look." Then she stroked my hair to the side of my forehead.

"Is it Saturday?" I mumbled.

"Yes – Saturday morning."

"It looks a lovely day."

She smiled again. "Yes, it's warm, and the sun is shining."

I smiled too, then drifted back to sleep.

* * *

There was a knock… the police… they have found me again.

I sat up in bed and pushed myself back against the headboard.

The door opened and I cried out.

"Emmeline, it's me – it's Florence."

"Am I safe?" I said.

She hurried over to the bed. She had a tray in her hands and all but threw it on to the bedside table before sitting beside me and grabbing my hand.

"Emmeline, everything's fine – I promise you."

"But who did you tell? I mean, who knows I am here? My landlady? Creamers?"

"None of them."

"So I am safe."

"Yes," said Florence, "you are safe."

I sighed and sank back into the pillows.

She squeezed my hand before letting it go, then reached over to the tray and placed it in front of me.

"It's vegetable soup – Mrs Dockerill made it specially for your recovery. I seem to have spilled rather a lot of it, but there is still a stockpot full in the kitchen." She wiped the spoon handle with a serviette and handed it to me. "Eat what you can, but the more the better I think."

It smelt wonderful, and although I wasn't very hungry, I did think I could manage at least what was left in the bowl.

I leaned forwards to eat, but then I realised that I was in my undergarments, and the alarm went straight to my face.

"What is it now, Emmeline?"

"Did you? Florence, did you…"

"Did I what?"

"Did you undress me?"

"Well… um… we got your dress and corset off, but then you became quite severely agitated and we had to leave you in your underwear. But I have some fresh for you – on the chair look." She smiled and pointed to it.

I tried to look grateful instead of relieved. "That's very kind, Florence. Thank you."

"The dress was ruined, I'm afraid, but don't worry, I've gotten you a better one."

"You didn't need to do that – really you didn't."

"Well… unless you want to go about in your undergarments." We both laughed, and a church bell rang.

"Sunday… is there a suffragist meeting today?" I said.

"No, I cancelled it," said Florence.

"Did you tell them I was unwell?"

"No, that is none of their business, and I didn't tell them you were here either, but I… but I did tell them that you might be coming to stay with me."

"Well, I think I should be well enough to leave in a few days, if you can bear me that long."

Florence scratched her nose and then stretched a little.

"I think you should stay longer than that – for as long as you like really. I have plenty of space and I… well, why not?"

I thought for a moment that perhaps my illness had done for me and that I was now being admitted to heaven.

"But why would you do that for me?"

"Because you are my friend… and I know that you are in trouble."

I sighed and covered my eyes.

"You can tell me all about it," she said. "I will help in whatever way I can."

"My life is impossible, Florence. I would dearly love to tell you everything – everything that brought me to your door in the night, but I can't – I just can't."

"But if you won't tell me, how can I help you?"

I shook my head slightly and tried to hide my frown behind my fingers.

"I don't know what to say, except that… except that I did nothing wrong – I promise you with all my heart that I did nothing wrong."

Florence put her hand behind my shoulder and lifted me towards the soup. "Come on now, eat up."

I stared at the bowl, trying to find my appetite. If only it was ovary soup,

I thought. I mean, even if I am safe for the moment from my uncle and the police, I am never safe from my secret, and the longer I am without ovaries, the greater the chance that it will be revealed through my diminishing femininity. But what could I do without any money?

I winced, and put the spoon down.

"Florence, I... um... you see there is a way you could... um... Florence, could you? I mean would it be possible to borrow... I will pay you back, I promise – every penny."

"You need some money?"

"Just a little, just until I find a position."

"Emmeline, that is not a problem, but you really won't need any money staying with me – I am not going to charge you board, you silly girl."

"No, but you see..." I hid my face behind my hand again. "There is something I have to do every day. Well, except Sundays – somewhere I have to go, and I have no money for the train, nor for the thing I have to do when I get there. I mean, it only takes a couple of hours, but it's something I simply have to do."

Florence put her hand gently on my shoulder.

"Is it opium, Emmeline?"

I laughed, nervously, "No, no, nothing like that – it's... I just can't tell you what it is, Florence – I just can't."

She sighed. "I will still help you, Emmeline – of course I will, but I hope that in time, you will come to trust me."

"No, no, it's not trust, it's nothing to do with trust." I grabbed her hand and looked her right in the eye. "I trust you absolutely, and without question."

She tilted her head to one side, and gave me little frown that sat somewhere between compassion and exasperation.

"How much do you need?" she said.

"Perhaps... um... perhaps two shillings a day?"

She looked surprised, and then she laughed.

"But, Emmeline, that is no money at all."

42

Bloody Bastard

That Thursday, I finally made the journey back to Otford for my ovaries. I ate them on the train and as I swallowed the last mouthful, I closed my eyes to feel the electrical emanations radiating through my body, curing me, making me myself again.

Florence had insisted that I take a cab to and from Victoria, and that made my journey so much safer, but on the return journey, I still made the cabbie take several detours and watched out of the back window for policemen or stocky men who might be following me back to the one place I could hide from them.

Aside from my ovary trips, Florence and I spent every day at home together – reading aloud to each other, playing with Ming, and talking of foreign travel and dinosaurs.

I did my best to enjoy every moment, but I was in constant dread of a knock at the door. And it wasn't just a visit from the police that I dreaded – it was Albert too. He cast a shadow over everything – if she smiled at me, I thought of him, if she touched me, I thought of him, and if my life were to follow its usual disastrous trajectory, then when he finally did come to the door, I felt fairly sure he would turn out to be a policeman as well.

* * *

On the Saturday evening we watched a pink sky through the French windows in the living room. I liked the living room windows because the back of the house was not overlooked and I could see the outside without fear of being seen myself.

"Should be another lovely day tomorrow," said Florence.

"Yes," I said.

"And it's a Sunday."

"Yes it is," I said.

"And you don't make your secret journey on Sundays."

There was silence for a moment.

"You know," she continued, "we could go for a walk tomorrow – to Hyde Park perhaps."

My heart did a somersault. "But… but I can't, Florence, I can't."

She sighed. "Emmeline, I can't bear to see you frightened all the time."

"I can't bear to *be* frightened all the time."

"Well, I don't know who it is that you think is looking for you, because you won't tell me, but really, Emmeline," She held my hand, "London is a city of millions – we are tiny specks in it. What chance do they really have of finding you amongst everyone else?"

What a burden I was – confining her to the house, making her life dull despite all that she had done for me. It would only be a matter of time before she ended up resenting my existence as much as everyone else did. No, it wouldn't do.

I took a deep breath.

"You're right," I said. "I mean… I mean logically… I'm probably in more danger of being hit by an omnibus."

"That's right," she said.

"So…" I took another deep breath. "Let's do it – let's walk in Hyde Park tomorrow and I will put my faith in logic."

* * *

Logic got me as far as the park gate, and then I had to pause for a minute to give my rising panic time to dissipate.

"Are you sure you want to go ahead with this, Emmeline?" said Florence.

"Yes," I said. "Quite sure – quite terrified," I laughed. "But quite sure."

The park was, as expected, full of people, and there were twice as many eyes as people. I felt exactly as I would have done if every person in the park was pointing a gun at me. I think the first thing Florence said was, "It is a lovely day, isn't it?" but I'm not sure, for at that moment, I saw a man in uniform in the distance and he required my full attention.

Rather than pass him, I turned onto a different path and Florence followed. This path looked clear of uniforms but had more people on it. We followed it for a minute or two but then I saw a stocky man in a suit up ahead – he was uncle shaped and looking about for someone, so I turned again and onto another path.

"Tell me, Emmeline," said Florence. "Why do you think the ichthyosaur had such large eyes?"

"The what?"

"The ichthyosaur – an ancient sea reptile. It was very similar in size and shape to a dolphin but it had enormous eyes."

"Well," I said, "I... I um..." A particularly dense group of people appeared.

"Ignore them, Emmeline – it's just the two of us here, walking through the park and talking about dinosaurs. Now, what do you say about those enormous eyes?"

"Like... like the giant squid?"

"That's right."

"An um... an adaptation to the dark I should think. Did it hunt in the depths?"

"That is the speculation, but consider this – the sperm whale also hunts in the depths but has very small eyes. How do you account for that."

I stopped walking for a moment. "Hmm, that's a very good question."

It was working, I was beginning to relax a little.

"Well, two things occur to me," I said, starting to walk again, but more slowly now. "The first is that perhaps the ick..."

"Ichthyosaur."

"Perhaps it hunted deep enough that the light is only dim, making large eyes an asset, while the sperm whale hunts so deep that there is no light at all, making eyes redundant."

"That was my conclusion too."

"But conversely…" I glanced behind me. I could see the man in a uniform again – a black uniform. Maybe the same man, maybe another – I couldn't tell. A narrow pathway, shaded by trees, opened to our left. I pulled Florence in by the arm.

"It looks very nice along here, don't you think?" I said.

There was a secluded bench halfway along, set back from the path. We sat down together and I felt safe enough to sigh some relief.

"I think you are doing very well," said Florence.

"Sorry to make such a fuss," I said.

Florence smiled and we sat quietly for a minute. Then she said, "But it's dark half of every day."

"What do you mean?"

The ichthyosaur – I mean all sea creatures spend at least half their lives in the dark because of the night. Where does that leave the question of eye size?"

"Well, that is an excellent obser…"

"Well then, Ladies. What a fine looking sight."

Two men appeared from behind us – soldiers – drunk. They came either side of the bench and circled into position in front of us.

I froze.

Not police, I thought; not my uncle's men – don't let them be my uncle's men.

"May we introduce ourselves? I am Private Peter Pratt and this is my brother in arms, Private Nathaniel Burke." The words themselves were polite, but he pushed them on to us with a lean. "Now why don't you two lovely ladies come walk with us a while, eh? And we'll show you a very good time."

I could not speak.

Florence ignored them and looked down at my lap. I didn't look directly at them either, but watched them intently with the edge of my vision for any sign that they were going to attack.

"Shall we go?" whispered Florence, and we stood up together.

"Now, now, now," said Pratt blocking us in from one side, while Burke blocked us in from the other. "That ain't very polite is it?"

"Come on, girls – we just wants a bit of fun," added Burke.

"We are not interested, sirs," said Florence. "We prefer to be alone."

I was desperate to run, but even more desperate to stay with Florence.

"Yes, and we prefer company," said Pratt – his tone had darkened and he looked either side to see if anyone was near.

No one was.

"Nevertheless, we decline your company and have every right to do so," said Florence.

"Well, rights don't stand for a great deal in such a secluded spot as this now, do they?"

This had to be my uncle's work, it had to be – he had sent soldiers after me.

"Do you threaten us, Sir?" Florence sounded frightened now.

"Only with a kiss," said Burke.

They were going to attack.

"Don't be disgusting," said Florence.

"Think you're too good for us, is it?" said Pratt. "Think we're not posh enough for you, eh? Well I can do posh all right – 'ere look." He leaned towards me. "Oh I say, jolly good, splendid."

That word – 'splendid' – it was Uncle Walter's word, and I could hear his voice in it. Then the puff of breath hit me – whisky – Uncle Walter's smell, and those two Walterisms conspired together like an evil spell to summon him before me, as real as day, his hands about my neck and the world disappearing in a choking fog, and this time Mason is at his side.

"No, no, no, no," I whispered, trying to shake the vision out of my head, then I looked directly at Uncle Walter or Pratt, or whatever monster had grown out of their marriage. "If you... if you don't... I..."

Pratt turned to Burke, amused at my frightened stutter and then, very suddenly, turned back with a 'boo!'

I screamed at him.

"GO AWAY, YOU BLOODY BASTARD."

And then, without any thinking at all, I pushed him, with all the strength that I had.

He fell backwards and landed on his bottom.

Florence reached across my chest and held me back.

"No, Emmeline."

Pratt leaped back to his feet, his hand already in a fist, but Burke grabbed him and pulled him away from me.

"Come on, mate, don't waste your energy – we'll go and get ourselves some factory girls."

"Bitch," spat Pratt, just as three more soldiers walked past the entrance to the path with their lady friends – higher ranking types though – officers. They didn't see us, but Pratt saw them and immediately he and Burke walked away.

I was blank.

Florence turned me towards her and wrapped her arms right around me. I began to tremble.

"It's all right, Emmeline, it's all right – you're safe now." I buried my face in her warm, shoulder and began to sob like a baby.

"I'm so sorry, Florence, I'm so sorry."

"There is nothing to be sorry for," she said, lifting my face from her shoulder and wiping my tears with the sides of her thumbs.

"It was my uncle you see," I said. "He tried to murder me, Florence, he really did – he strangled me and beat me and left me all for dead. And… and sometimes I see him – he comes back – it's so very clear. And there was Mason, at the abattoir – he tried to… I can't say it. He had a knife, and they all held me down, and I see them staring at me, dead eyes. I see them, Florence, I see them…"

I was breathing so quickly by now that I was ready to faint.

Florence held my face firmly between her palms and made me look into her eyes.

"Listen to me, Emmeline. These are phantoms – what you see are memories, and they cannot hurt you. Do you hear me? They cannot hurt you."

I nodded and dropped my head.

"Look at me."

I did so.

"Let the memories run their course – if you resist them, or try to block them out, they will grow stronger, but if you let them pass, knowing that they are mere recollections, they will eventually evaporate and all will be well. I promise you, Emmeline, trust me."

At last I began to calm down.

I wiped my eyes firmly with the back of my hand, just as a tear rolled down Florence's cheek.

"They failed though didn't they," I said, "both of them – Uncle Walter didn't kill me, Mason didn't rape me. I defied them both didn't I? Because I am singular. I really am singular, Florence, even my mother said so."

"Of course you are – my own singular Emmeline."

We stood for a minute drying our faces with handkerchiefs until Florence said, "Let's get you home."

"No, no – not yet," I said. "Let's..." I took a deep breath, "...Let's sit for a bit longer on the bench, otherwise we won't be defying them."

Florence smiled.

We didn't speak for a while. So much seemed to have happened in not five minutes of our lives, that it almost felt as if we needed a few minutes of silence to make space for it all to sit in.

At the end of the silence, Florence said, "Was it visions of your Uncle that you were fleeing when you arrived in the night?"

"No – not visions. He really is trying to find me."

"And you know that for certain?"

"Yes – he is a very persistent man. He has the police after me."

"But is this something you know, or something you feel or suspect?"

"No, he really is looking for me, Florence. He's a murderer – he killed a boy. I still have the boy's necklace – I can show it you. And Mr Grimaldi –

Uncle followed him all the way to Marseilles and killed him. He uses the police you see – he can do that – he's with the foreign office – a consul. And when we were arrested during the suffragist march, the desk sergeant noted my name and said they were looking out for a Stanton. But they... well, for various reasons, they didn't think I was the particular Stanton they wanted. But then, just a few days later, they came to my door, having worked out that it was me after all. That's when I ran away."

"I see." She thought for a moment. "But have you actually seen your uncle, with your own eyes. I mean, do you actually know him to be in London?"

"Well no, in truth, I don't. I know he was at my Mother's house briefly a couple of years ago looking for me, but I haven't actually seen him myself, other than in my horrible visions. I feel him though, Florence, nearby – I feel him."

"But he lives in Naples, yes?"

"Yes."

"And he is a diplomat – he has important work there."

"Yes, but..."

"I do not dismiss your fears, Emmeline, but on balance, is it not more likely that he is a thousand miles away working in Naples, rather than here in London, chasing his niece at the cost of his career?"

"It's a rational point, Florence, but Uncle Walter is not a rational man – he is quite insane. I told you – he followed Mr Grimaldi all the way to Marseilles, and that was just over a small debt."

Florence didn't press me further on it and we were silent again for a little while.

Then she frowned and smiled at the same time and said, "How on earth did you come to be in an abattoir?"

I cringed a little. "That was my previous employment, before Creamers – I sorted offal."

"Oh, Emmeline, what an extraordinary time you have had."

256

43

To Be True To My Nature

That evening had a strange atmosphere – disconcerting, as if everything in our lives had been rearranged, then put back in place so that it all looked the same whilst feeling different. But it was a kind strangeness – something that didn't hurt, and I felt as if I had let a little bit of my pain out to sit apart from me, where someone else could see it too.

"Florence."

"Emmeline," she said, in playful imitation of my sincere tone.

"Florence, please promise me that your being married will take nothing away from our friendship. I can hardly bear to share you at all."

"Oh, Emmeline," She seemed suddenly quite distressed. "I'm so stupid – I should have told you the whole story, not half of it. Albert is dead – long dead."

"But…"

"Our engagement was six years ago. He passed away with influenza before we could even set a date. I am so sorry, I should have explained – it's just that I try not to think about him too much and always end up changing the subject."

I had never before felt ashamed for feeling relief.

"I see… then… then I am very sorry for your loss."

"Thank you," she said.

I kept repeating it in my head – 'Albert is dead', 'Albert is dead' and I wanted to say it out loud too, as if to reassure myself I had actually heard it, but I convoluted the urge into asking about him instead:

"What... what was he like? If you don't mind me asking. Terribly handsome I imagine."

"No, not at all." She smiled. "He was rather a delicate creature – very thin, very short, but studious and bright, and altogether an exceptionally kind and gentle man. I had known him for years but..." she leaned in and spoke quietly, "the funny thing is that we were never in love – I seem to be quite immune to the charms of the male sex, and he was similar, having never fallen for a woman, but we did get on awfully well."

Albert is dead, I thought, and she never even loved him.

"I do think we would probably have made quite a successful partnership though," she continued. "He made no demands upon me, and offered far more than I could in return. It was his plan to give me a home, companionship, an income, and my freedom, only in return for a respectable marriage that would satisfy his family. In the end he did give me the income and the freedom, having set up the publishing of my first book. The part I struggle to accept is that he did not live long enough for me to fulfil my part of the bargain."

She looked away.

"You can't blame yourself for that," I said, and grabbed her hand.

"No, but it hurts anyway."

The sadness in her eyes now became deeper – deep enough to drown my tasteless relief. But I didn't know what to say about it, so I just held her hand a little tighter.

"I promised myself at the time," she said, "that I would find a way to make some good come of his passing, and I resolved to live my life fully – to not waste it. In particular I resolved to be true to my nature, and embrace whatever happiness I could find, but in truth, I cannot really claim to have achieved anything of the sort."

I pulled on her hand to make her turn more towards me. "Florence, this may sound terribly conceited, but it is not an unjustified boast to say that I know what it is to be true to oneself. Perhaps I am the very person to help you towards the fulfilment of that promise."

She smiled, and I think she thought nice things about me.

After a moment or two, she laughed.

"What's funny?" I said.

"The way you spoke to the horrible soldiers, Emmeline. It must be very satisfying to swear like that."

"Oh it is," I said. "Why don't you try it?"

"I couldn't."

"Of course you could."

"Emmeline, really, I couldn't possibly."

"But they are only two little words. And from a scientific point of view, one is merely a description for something that is covered in blood, whilst the other is a term for illegitimacy."

Florence looked about her as if to check we were alone. "Blo... blo... I can't, Emmeline, I really can't." Then she looked directly into my eyes. "You say it."

I leaned towards her face. "Bloody bastard."

She didn't laugh, but held my gaze. "How silly," she whispered.

"What is?"

"That swearing could be so exhilarating."

44

What If?

That Sunday, was our first meeting with the WLSC ladies in three weeks. Florence had decided to hold it in the dining room at home this time as she didn't want me going out again just yet.

Daphne arrived on the dot of midday, and Clara a few minutes later. Agnes and Mrs Peterson then arrived together as they always did.

"Good afternoon, Ladies," said Agnes. "Ah, and here's Emmeline, snug in her new home. This is no progress for you, young lady – I think you better served your sex when living independently."

I did not know how to answer, but Florence did it for me:

"Well, she is no longer working at the biscuit factory, so at least she is not serving male factory owners."

I tried not to smile.

"You deliberately miss my point," replied Agnes, with the indifference of a Duchess handing her hat to a maid. "I only hope that soft living does not take the fight out of her." She looked at me. "I dare say it will though – young and impressionable as you are."

I hardly heard her – I was too warmly muffled by Florence defending me.

We all took our seats around the dining room table, except for Agnes who remained standing to address the meeting. Mrs Peterson handed her some papers, then laid out her black notebook and licked her pencil as if she was sticking her tongue out at the notebook when the pencil got in the way.

Agnes glanced through the papers and cleared her throat.

"Ladies, we have talked a great deal of the rights of women, and despite my full intention that this year would see us turn those words into deeds, here we are with half the year gone, having managed one ineffectual march, and a handful of meetings – meetings during which, I might add, you all waste far too much time on vacuous conversation and tea-drinking."

"Well, hardly vacuous."

"Calm yourself, Clara. How can we make a change in the world if we cannot talk directly to each other? And if talk of action leads not to action, then that talk is by definition vacuous."

Clara shrugged an agreement, suggesting that she thought it a fair point.

"Now then," continued Agnes, "why was our march ineffectual? I will tell you – it is because five women..." she glanced rather rudely at Florence, "... merely walking along the street with placards, are too weak, and too quaint a proposition to shake the foundations of government.

"I intend to remedy this situation with another march," she continued, "but one that will end with a direct action worthy of a newspaper column or two. Ladies, our oppressor is not lazy – a man does not hesitate to meet a quarrel, to declare war, to kill his enemy, or even to rape a defenceless woman."

"Agnes, please."

"Don't be weak, Florence – this is exactly the problem, this weak hesitation, this retreat into so-called 'feminine' sensitivities. This is not what women are, this is only what men have made you."

"But there are also reasonable men," said Daphne in a rare interjection. "My brother is one."

I thought of Uncle Walter and Mason, the lecherous man on the embankment – even the soldiers in the park, and I wanted to agree with Agnes, but I knew that they were not the whole truth of men.

"I have to agree with Daphne," I said. "For although I have seen more than my share of unpleasant men, I have also met good men – I really have. In fact, my position at the biscuit factory was owed purely to the kindness of a man who chose to help me when I was in... well... in distressed circumstances."

"He offered you a job?" said Agnes.

"He spoke on my behalf to Mr Crean who happened to be a friend of his."

"And what did you do at the factory?"

"You know perfectly well, Agnes, I packed biscuits into tins."

"And you gave your services freely, or you were paid?"

"I was paid – of course I was paid."

"Yes – you were paid a pittance, and you worked hard for it. You therefore owe him nothing. This is the insidious way that men work – they exploit you, and make you grateful for it. Open your eyes, ladies, please."

There was something wrong buried in her statement, but I had the feeling that it would take some time to dig it out, so I only offered a frown as my answer.

"We are at war," she continued, "and war necessitates direct action. And even if an innocent man were to be hurt as a consequence of our actions, the blame would not lie with us – the true fault lies with all those men who have, for millennia, deprived us of our fundamental needs. Ladies, I am not suggesting we commit murder… even if there are plenty of men that deserve it…"

"Agnes," said Florence.

"An uncomfortable truth is still a truth, Florence, but if you were paying attention, you would have heard me say that I am *not* suggesting murder."

Her sarcastic tone was completely unwarranted, and I could feel the anger rising in my chest.

"But we must be more forceful," continued Agnes, "otherwise our message will be lost in the general commotion of London." She glanced at Florence again. "Especially given that we are so few in number."

It wasn't just that she glanced at her, or that she glanced rudely – it was the spite in her eyes. I began to clench my fists.

"I cannot take part, Agnes, you know that," said Florence.

"So you claim, Florence, but I still think it is a great pity that you continue to value your minor reputation amongst male publishers so far above the betterment of all womankind."

That was enough.

"How dare you?" I said, standing up to meet her eye to eye. "Your campaign would not... would never... you would not even have a campaign if Florence did not fund it for you, and let you use her carriage, and..."

Florence put her hand on my arm.

Agnes seemed to rumble for a moment, and then spat her reply at me:

"Emmeline Stanton, You are practically a child – you have not yet learned, and I suspect, never will learn, to rise above the feminine weaknesses that patriarchal society has imposed upon you. Nor do you have the strength of character to take decisive action when it is needed. So my suggestion is that you keep your remarks to yourself, and learn something from your elders and betters."

"You know nothing about me, Agnes. You know nothing of my struggles."

Florence now pulled me back into my chair, as Agnes continued:

"Firstly, that you take offence at all only shows your weakness. Secondly, you have, to my knowledge, had one position of employment, and that was, by your own admission, given to you, and was hardly difficult. And now you live a life of middling comfort in a very nice house, simply because Florence is unable to control herself in the presence of a pretty face."

"Agnes," said Florence, jumping to her feet. "I am closing this meeting right now. I won't have it, I really won't have it. You do not know the first thing about Emmeline, and I will not have her bullied in my house."

"Calm yourself, Florence." Agnes was clearly taken aback.

"No, Agnes, you are quite unbearable today. We will convene again next Sunday when you are in a better mood."

There was a pause, and then, instead of exploding, Agnes gave a little dismissive shake of the head as if a tiny child had thrown a snowball at her.

"As you wish," she said. "You are being very childish, but I'm sure we can find somewhere else to continue today's meeting." She looked at the others. "Ladies?" And they all stood up.

* * *

After they had gone, Florence put her head on my shoulder, and before I even thought to hesitate, I was stroking her pineapple hair.

"I think you handle her marvellously well," I said, trying my best not to sound excited by the closeness of her. "Agnes, I mean. Much better than I do. Sometimes, when she fixes me in her gaze, I cannot seem to hold a train of thought long enough to defend myself with it."

"Ah, but I have also seen a weaker side to her," said Florence, "which makes her seem a little less formidable to me perhaps. Still, that doesn't mean I have no fear of her. Or rather, it's not so much a fear of her, as a fear of what she might do next. I mean sometimes she seems… well, really quite dangerous."

Florence now slid her hand down into the space between our thighs as if to keep it warm.

"Yes," I said, trying not to concentrate on her hand, "at the… at the um… at the police station, she quite terrified me… she um… I mean… it wasn't only her… her complete lack of fear, it was… it was the way she deliberately antagonised them – trying to draw them into a fight that she knew she couldn't possibly win."

My mind leapt straight from the police station to Uncle Walter. Why did I have to think of him now? I tried instead to think my way back to the park last Sunday – to remember what Florence had said about it being unlikely he would bother to find me, but all I could see in my mind was his hand in her hair instead of mine, not stroking, but grasping and tearing at her.

"Yes, that's Agnes," said Florence, "and as much as I admire her courage, when you weigh the rudeness and the danger together, I wonder if perhaps we should consider leaving the committee altogether. What do you think about that?… Emmeline?"

"About what? Sorry, I was thinking about… um… sorry, Florence, what was your question?"

"That we should consider leaving the committee – Agnes being both rude and dangerous."

What if he comes for her, I thought. What if he comes for my Florence. I shook my head and attempted to answer:

"Difficult… it um… the cause is so right, but… but she does always steer for trouble."

"Well, today might have given her pause for thought. We'll see how things go next week. Who knows – she might even apologise."

I made no answer.

Florence lifted her head from my shoulder and read my thoughts as if they were printed on on my face.

"Emmeline, I still do not believe he would come for you, or that he could find you if he did. I think it's just that you have been so frightened for such a long time, that you see him around every corner."

45

Plum Juice

"Ming was stuck in the plum tree… again," I said, carrying him into the kitchen that following Sunday. "He was making that mournful little mew, but there was no reasoning with him today so I had to climb up and give him a prod. I really don't think he gets stuck at all, he just tries to draw us into humiliating ourselves. Look – I've got a moss stain on my skirt from the tree. I hope it will come out."

"Oh, Emmeline, I do wish I had seen you climb the tree," said Florence, laughing. "You really are such a boy at times."

"What do you mean? I am not a boy. Do you think I look like a boy?"

Florence laughed again. "My goodness me no, you silly girl."

"But does tree climbing make me boyish? I mean, surely we would both agree that many women would do things like that if there were not such a weight of expectation upon us to behave more delicately… wouldn't we?"

Florence looked a little taken aback.

"Of course," she said. "And I admire boyishness, Emmeline – it really is a most appealing quality in a girl."

"But it is not boyishness – it really isn't." I clung on to Ming – I wanted to hide my body behind his fat fluffiness. "It is simply that I happen to have the nerve to do something that only boys are normally expected to do. Do you see?"

"I do see, and I agree with you – we are both suffragists after all."

"Yes," I said, speaking to myself for a moment, "I mean that the behaviour is not intrinsically male, and I, therefore, am not boyish, I am merely... um... unbound."

"I agree – unbound."

"And you are sure that I don't look like a boy?"

"Quite sure." She smiled, and as she placed her hand on my arm, Ming went from being a shield to being an obstacle so I let him onto to the floor.

But what did I mean? Was I saying that there was no difference between the mind of a man and the mind of a woman? If that were the case, then how could I feel that I was a girl? But if there was a difference, then why was I behaving like a boy?

"I don't know, Florence," I said. "Perhaps it is odd for a woman to climb a tree. I hope I am not too odd, I hope I am still feminine. I don't feel boyish, I really don't – I feel quite a normal girl."

Florence tightened her grip on my arm. "Come on," she said, pulling me out of the kitchen door, into the garden. "I want you to show me how to climb, Emmeline, I want to be unbound."

"Well I... are you sure?"

"Of course."

"Well it's not so difficult – this is a very accommodating tree. Here look, put your foot in the crook and take a firm hold of this branch, no, with your left hand. That's the idea. Now tug yourself forwards and grab that thinner branch with your right. Nearly. Try again. That's it. Now, stick the toe of your left boot in there."

"Here?"

"That's right, and step up. Now we are going to do almost the same but on the opposite side, so reach up with your right hand to that branch. That's it, and tug forwards again."

"I think I'm stuck."

"You need to put your right foot up into that fork."

"In a corset?"

"It can be done – I've done it."

She struggled for a moment but then pulled herself up quite easily.

"My goodness me, I am in the plum tree. It's really not difficult at all, is it?"

"Not at all," I said. "Can you get up into the fork on the right?"

She did so and was now perhaps ten feet above the ground. I then climbed up to join her and sat in the opposite fork.

"Oh, Emmeline, isn't it wonderful?"

And it was – this secret dappled world of mossy perches, and there was enough wind today to allow the leaves to whisper their surprise at us for being there.

"The view of the house is so entirely different from here," she said, "and the garden... and look at the neighbour's gardens – it's quite literally the bird's-eye's view."

"Yes – isn't it amazing how gaining only a little height makes everything below seem so disproportionately small. I think we must look very insignificant creatures to birds."

The wind picked up a little and we laughed as the tree rocked sideways. When it settled again, Florence looked right into me. She was sitting perhaps five feet away, but her eyes were so vivid that I felt we were almost nose to nose.

"It's very... um... uh..." I stuttered, but then I saw a plum, and it gave my mouth its momentum back. "Well, now that we are in a plum tree, it seems only sensible that we should eat plums. There's a big pink one just behind your head."

She reached behind and plucked it off, while I picked my own rather less pink one from the branch above me. I took a bite. It was sour and I winced.

"Emmeline, this one is sinfully delicious." Her lips were a wet pout of plum juice, as if she had kissed the inside of the plum rather than bitten into it. "Here, you must have the other half."

I stretched across the gap between us as far as I could. "I don't think I can lean any further forwards than this," I said.

"Stay there, I can reach you."

She pulled the stone out very gently from the wet flesh of the half-plum with her teeth, took hold of a branch, stepped forwards into a crook, and

268

with the most graceful lean, she crossed the gap and pushed the plum into my mouth.

It was ecstatically sweet and wet, and still warm from the late summer sunshine. As I closed my lips around it I briefly caught her fingertip between them.

A dribble of nectar ran down my chin – she pushed it back up to my lips with another finger, and I tasted that one too. It was salty, very slightly, and the salt seemed to make the plum juice sweeter.

"What in heaven's name do you think you are doing?" It was Agnes. She was standing at the bottom of the tree with Clara, Daphne and Mrs Peterson.

We both jumped and leaned straight back into our respective forks.

"Oh, Agnes, is it five already?" said Florence. "We quite lost track of the time."

"You have not answered my question." She looked remarkably angry.

"We are reclaiming tree-climbing for women," I said, and almost giggled, for she was so diminished by both her distance below me and the foreshortening of the angle, that her grumpy face couldn't quite make me nervous.

"Whilst I appreciate that a woman might climb a tree just as easily as a man, I am also quite sure that it is not dignified for her to do so," she said.

"But why not?" said Florence, also not quite giggling.

"Because, whilst women are the superiors of men, Florence, it does not serve the suffragist cause for women to lower themselves to the behaviour of children."

"Oh, but we did not lower ourselves, Agnes," I said. "Climbing a tree can surely only raise a woman above her previous position."

Now we both laughed.

"We will wait for you in the house," said Agnes with open disgust, and she took the other ladies back up the garden.

46

Happiness Matters

Florence and I climbed down from the tree and walked up the garden together. We were still giggling, and I don't know if it was the change in altitude or the intoxicating effect of Florence's plum juice and salty fingers, but I felt quite blissfully delirious.

As we entered through the back door, there was a knock at the front door. Agnes answered it to three women, none of whom we knew.

"Florence, Emmeline, I want you to meet our new members. Miss McClaine, Miss Dalrymple and Mrs Trevelyan."

"How do you do," we said, together.

They were a stern-looking trio, very much in the mould of Mrs Peterson – dark clothes and earnest expressions.

Florence was clearly taken aback. "Agnes, I…" she said, but then she turned to the ladies and said, "Do please come in, you are very welcome." Florence then showed everyone through to the dining room as Agnes took the floor:

"May I first welcome our three new members to this, their first WLSC meeting. I am happy to describe them as women of the utmost determination, unwavering in our cause, and I'm sure that you will all find them more than equal to my description."

I glanced at Florence. Sticky plum juice still glistened on her chin and I wanted to lick it.

Florence glanced back at me, and made me a secret smile with her eyes.

Agnes meanwhile looked from Florence to me and back again, as if there were a line of words between us that she was trying to read.

Whatever it was she saw seemed to bruise her expression very darkly. She made a dismissive shake of her head and looked down at her notes.

"Ladies, why are we here? Is it only to fill our spare time? An amusement? A distraction? No, we are here for all the women of England – perhaps even, for all the women of the British Empire."

"Hear, hear," said one of the new ladies, but I had now forgotten which was which.

"And why do those women need us? They need us because they are weak. Yes – that is correct, ladies – the women of the British Empire are weak."

I licked my lips – they were still sweet around the edges and in the corners.

"They are weak, not because of their bodies," continued Agnes, "for although a woman cannot wrestle a man, she can endure longer."

I licked again, I wanted to find her finger salt, but it was all gone.

"They are weak, not for lack of fighting spirit, for a woman is the equal of a lioness when protecting her young."

Only a few minutes ago, one of Florence's fingers had been a little bit inside me. I took a breath.

"Women are weak in one sense only," said Agnes, "and that is in the sense that we have no influence. And why do we have no influence?"

"Because men have stolen it from us," said Clara.

"Precisely, Clara," said Agnes. "So then, our purpose as suffragists is to take it back and we can only do so, as I keep telling you..." she paused for effect, "...by force."

Florence shook her head, and her hair scattered the sunlight.

"You may shake your head, Florence," said Agnes, "but if some brigand were to steal your purse, what good would it do to ask him politely to return it?"

There were chuckles. I didn't like it – they were laughing at Florence.

"But now imagine that you were armed with a revolver," Agnes continued, "and you told the fellow, in no uncertain terms, that his life depended upon the immediate return of the article?"

How dare they laugh at my Florence, I thought, when it is she who finances their little meetings.

"No," said Florence, "I prefer to build a world in which the young man is better educated and better employed so that he need not resort to such desperate behaviour, and it is surely preferable to build such a world through civilised discourse rather than through threats of violence."

She was wonderful.

Agnes slammed the book shut. "That is not how men negotiate," she said, her voice considerably raised. "They take by force; they keep what they take, and they defend it with violence. That is the way of men, and if we are to defeat them, then we must play them at their own game, and be better at it."

"Which only reduces us to their level," said Florence. "and... and if your answer to male oppression is to be oppressive... why then you... you abandon all that is best about women – indeed you re-make the world entirely out of maleness."

Agnes slapped her own forehead. "How can you possibly be so stupid? Of all people, how can you be so stupid?" She was shouting now. "Femininity is a male invention, imposed upon us by their brutal manipulations – wake up for goodness' sake."

"No," I said, trying to draw her aim away from Florence.

"Well now," said Agnes, with clear disgust, "it seems that Florence's pretty little muse is about to enlighten us all with her great wisdom."

"Agnes," said Florence, her voice now also raised almost to a shout. "I won't have it."

Agnes' shoulders rose a little with Florence's voice, but she carried on regardless.

"The question before us is not whether to use force – that is a given – but where and how that force might be applied to the most devastating effect. This too is simple to answer – men wield their power above all through property, so let us damage their property, let us smash their windows, let us set fire to their living rooms, and may both stand as a warning of worse to come should they ignore our demands."

"Hear, hear," said the new ladies – one first, and the other two in chorus directly after her.

"Well, I'm all for it," said Clara, "let's really do something this time."

"Stop it, all of you," said Florence.

"Agnes is right," said Clara, "violence is the only thing that can work against men."

"No," said Florence. "Women are different to men, innately different, and we..."

"So says the woman who was climbing a tree like a schoolboy not half and hour ago," said Agnes.

"No," said Florence. "Don't mistake what I do for what I am. We are the gentler sex, even when climbing trees, and we make a superior argument for women's suffrage by peaceful means."

"And where has that gotten us?" said Agnes. "I bring you back to our brigand in the street..." she banged the table with her fist. "Will you ask for your purse back and expect to get it?"

"And I still say that he only wants for a better life."

Agnes now leaned right over the table at Florence. "You are a very stupid, and very weak woman."

It was too much. I stood up, knocking my chair over, "Don't you bloody dare speak to her like that."

"I will dare," she shouted back. "Because I know what men are – I know better than all of you what men are. And I will tell you this..." she looked at us all in quick succession. "If ever a man lays his hands upon you, forcing himself upon you without your consent, even if that man is your own father... then you shoot the bastard dead."

She pulled a cold black revolver out of her bag and held it aloft.

We gasped.

"My own mother taught me that... and she taught by example."

Silence.

Florence glanced at me and I nodded my agreement. "Agnes, you have my sincerest sympathy for whatever terrible tale lies behind that gun – I think you know that, and I think you know that I am all for the cause of women's suffrage, but this is too much. Emmeline and I are leaving the committee forthwith. Ladies we must ask you all to leave and conduct your meeting elsewhere."

Agnes put her gun back in her bag.

"Does this mean that you also withdraw funding?"

"Yes, yes it does. I can no longer play any part in this committee."

Agnes opened her mouth to speak but was momentarily dumb and closed it firmly. I had never seen her short of an answer before. Her eyes remained fixed upon Florence, her lips pressed together in the expression of a butcher cutting a sinew.

Finally she spoke:

"Will you fund it if I take measures to ensure that your name is never associated with us?"

"No," said Florence, "I can't, because I am opposed in principle to your methods."

"Very well. Ladies, let us leave these wretched disappointments to their life of cakes and romantic frivolity, for we have work to do."

They all filed out of the room and Agnes left us with, "One day I will accept not only an apology from you both, but also your humble thanks for the risks I was willing to take to improve your pointless little lives."

* * *

When they had gone, we sat on the living room sofa trying to calm down.

"I really think it was for the best," I said.

"I hope so," said Florence. "But somehow I feel a bit as if I've let them all down."

I put my hand on her shoulder.

"Florence, Agnes has a gun in her bag."

She sighed. "Yes, I suppose that does rather settle the matter, doesn't it."

"Of course it does. I mean, I feel sympathy for her too, but she is dangerous, Florence, too dangerous – just as you said she was. And anyway, marches and violent disorder, and getting ourselves locked up in tiny cells, can't be the only ways to make the world a better place for women."

Florence smiled, and placed her hand on top of mine.

"I just want to be happy," I said. "Isn't that what everyone wants really? And we have it here, don't we?"

Uncle Walter appeared in my head, laughing at me.

"Of course we do," said Florence.

"We… we must protect it, Florence, because it matters – happiness matters… it really…" Walter laughed again and I shook my head. "I mean, that is all we were trying to do with the committee isn't it? To make women happier?" He laughed again, harder this time and I slumped into my seat.

"Your uncle again?"

"I know he is coming for me, Florence, I feel it, and even if he can't yet put his hands upon my body, he has already stolen my peace of mind and left my happiness so soiled with his dirty fingerprints that I can't quite see it. And what if… what if he hurts you?"

"Emmeline, I…"

"This is what I am learning about lov… about happiness… I… I mean happiness…" I felt my cheeks go crimson. "It's so precious that… that when you have it, you worry so much about losing it that you don't have it any more. Do you see?"

"Of course I do. But… but I would advise someone who was happy, or even… or even in love, to not think so much about the future and to try instead to enjoy the present."

We sat quietly for a few minutes and I waited for the colour to leave my cheeks.

Florence smiled distantly and sighed.

"May I lean on your shoulder, Emmeline?"

She did not lean on my shoulder, but instead lay her head in my lap and wrapped her arm over my thighs. How achingly wonderful it was to have her in my lap, and yet how close she now was to the repulsive secret between my legs that might one day ruin everything.

"It was wonderful to climb the tree," she said.

"Yes it was," I said, daring to slide my finger into her curls again and coiling them in little circles. She sighed and closed her eyes.

"And what a delicious plum it was, Emmeline. My mouth is watering just to think of it."

47

Obis and Rouge

The following morning there were plums on the breakfast table – a bowl of them. I looked at them, Florence looked at them, and then she looked at me.

"They're from our tree," she said, holding my gaze and smiling at me. She was probably just smiling because of the jokes we had made when Agnes arrived under the tree, and I smiled back to remember the joke with her, but I wondered what she would think of me, had she any inkling of the erotic excitement I had felt when she pushed the plum in my mouth.

"Have you heard of the Ragged School Society?" said Florence, politely, as if the plums needed a more civilised counterpoint.

"I have certainly heard of the ragged schools – for orphans and the like."

"It's a charity," she said. "I patronise them – I think they do such important work. Every year, they hold a charity ball – patrons attend and we give some money."

I stopped eating.

"Don't worry, Emmeline – we don't have to go at all if you don't want to. Personally, I hate them – horrible stuffy things, but I go because... well I suppose it's a sort of personal approval of their work or something, but also, I think it is healthy to spend at least a little time amongst other people occasionally, even if it is uncomfortable."

"You're right," I said, and took a deep breath. "We... we should go. After all, a charity ball is the last place on Earth you would find my uncle." And we laughed.

At the end of breakfast, Nellie came in and whispered something to Florence. She listened with a straight face, but as soon as Nellie left the room, she beamed at me, stood up and said, "Come on."

"But where are we going?"

"Come on," she said again, holding out her hand. I took it, and she led me out of the room and along the hall.

"The living room?" I said.

She opened the door, "Go in."

I could see nothing new or out of place.

"What am I looking for?" I said, but then I noticed two piles of fabric on the sofa. "These? What are they, Florence?"

"I bought them – they are genuine Japanese kimonos from Liberty. Well, not the fancy ones, but never-the-less, they are quite genuine.

"Oh my – I don't know what to say."

"Here, this one is for you."

It was beautiful – a pale, apple-green, printed with darker green leaves, and between them, vivid crimson chrysanthemums. Florence's was a soft, lilac-pink, with enormous, cream and burgundy lilies.

"It's so beautiful, Florence." I held it up. "Will it suit me, do you think?"

"Oh yes, very well – I knew it would."

There was a moment's silence.

"Should we, um… should we try them on?" I said.

"Well, given that in less that an hour, a certain Piccadilly photographer by the name of Mr Robert Brinkley will be here to capture our image in them, I should think that would be a very good idea." She beamed at me again.

"Oh but not Brinkley, Florence, I… I mean thank you – it's the loveliest idea I've ever heard but… but I can't."

"Why ever not?"

"He um… oh dear… the thing is, Florence, Mr Brinkley thinks I'm dead."

She laughed. "Dead?"

"It's a bit of a long story," I said, then I paused to think how much I could safely reveal. "I um… I lost my ticket you see, for my photograph, and I got someone to pick it up for me…" Now I felt horrible – I was lying to her. "But… well, she… um… he had to pretend that he was my brother and I was his deceased sister, so that they would give him the picture without the ticket." No, it wasn't quite a lie, more a mislaying of one particular fact, but it still felt wrong somehow.

"But when was this, Emmeline? About the time you saw me in the waiting room? That's at least three years ago isn't it?"

"That's true," I said, lying again, for although it was three years since he had seen me as Emmeline, it was only a year and a half since he had seen me as Thomas. But then it occurred to me – if he didn't recognise Thomas as Emmeline then, why should he now recognise Emmeline as Thomas?

"You're right," I said, laughing a little. "I'm such a worrier aren't I?"

There was silence again.

The obvious thing to do, would have been for one of us to go behind the screen to change. She was closer to the screen than me, but she just stood there, with a little smile, almost as if she were daring me to undress in front of her.

Of course it was impossible, even if she really had wanted me to, but it felt so exciting to spend a moment or two imagining that I could.

When I could bear the excitement no longer I stepped towards the screen to break the impasse, but she reached for me with one hand and popped open the top button of my dress.

I couldn't breathe.

The next button followed.

Then she moved down to the third. This one was stiff and reluctant. She tried both hands and then I tried to help too, but my hands were shaking too much to be of any use.

She clasped her hands over mine to hold them steady and gave me a gentle smile. "It's all right, Emmeline – you carry on with your buttons here and I will change behind the screen.

As she stepped out of view I wanted to cry with relief and disappointment at the same time. Perhaps I was also a little embarrassed that my trembling might have given too much away.

"Do we take our corsets off?" I said, trying to sound as light and carefree as I possibly could.

"Oh yes, the Japanese ladies favour a broad waist – we should strip right down to our combinations."

A few moments later, we were standing together in our underwear, a foot apart, and separated only by a screen so thin that I could feel her heat through it.

She moved and the screen wobbled.

I wrapped my kimono around me quickly to hide my body, or perhaps my thoughts, and Florence stepped out from the screen.

"Florence, you are so pretty I could almost cry about it."

"Arigato," she said, with a little bow. "But if you really want to see pretty, you should look in the mirror – didn't I say it would suit you?" She looked me up and down then paused a little on my eyes before saying, "Let's try the sashes. The golden one is yours, mine is the green."

We wrapped them around our middles, and I tied Florence's in a huge bow behind her.

"It's beautiful, Florence – it looks like a giant green butterfly has settled on your flowers."

"Let me do yours," she said, and I turned my back towards her. She tugged a little on the sash. "The ends are not quite level. Here…" As she reached right around me to adjust it, her face touched the back of my neck and an avalanche of goosebumps tumbled down my back.

"Perfect," she said, then she paused for a moment and gave me a smile that was both mysterious and mischievous.

"What is it?" I said.

She didn't answer, but led me to the small table in the corner of the room. She opened a draw and removed a small, round jar.

"This is the finishing touch… but only if we have the nerve for it," she whispered.

"What on earth is it?"

She opened it as gently as if it contained gunpowder.

"It's lip rouge," she said.

After we glimpsed inside, she held the lid over the pot to hide it again. "It's just that I have seen pictures of geishas wearing it and I thought we... do you...? Do you think it's too much?"

"No, I don't think so. I had no idea whether or not it was too much, but this already felt like a day for daring things.

"Shall I go first then?"

She placed her middle finger into the shiny crimson paste and made a small circular motion, then she pouted, placing the finger gently on her lips and repeated the soft rotation. She watched my eyes as she did it.

"How does it look?"

It made her lips the same deep red as the plum she had pushed into my mouth, and all I could think was how much I wanted to taste it again.

"Florence, I... I think it looks lovely. You have such b... beautiful lips... you really do."

"Your turn."

I reached towards the pot.

"No... why don't I do it? I already have some on my finger. No need for us both to get our hands greasy."

She leaned very close to me and rubbed the paste gently into my open lips, more slowly and for much longer than she had rubbed it into her own.

As she finally pulled away, I briefly pursed my lips forwards to follow her finger, and when I pulled back, I made a little smacking sound as if I had kissed her finger tip... which perhaps I had.

That was certainly too much, I thought, and I turned my head to the side to make the kissing sound again, as if it were merely the sound of me testing the feel of the rouge upon my lips.

* * *

"My goodness me," boomed Mr Brinkley as he clattered into the room with his tripod and bluster. We both jumped. "But a moment ago I could have sworn to my being in Knightsbridge, and yet now I am quite sure that I find myself somewhere in the exotic East. And whom do I perceive before me but a pair of the most exquisite geishas. Ladies, I am charmed."

"Good morning, Mr Brinkley," we said in chorus, and rose to our feet. Florence cringed a little and pressed her lips together to hide the rouge. I could see no sign that he recognised me, but I let my rouge show as a sort of disguise.

"Rouge as well, a bold, and may I say, a very authentic choice, ladies."

Mr Brinkley's thin and tidy assistant from the shop now walked in carrying the large camera box. I hadn't accounted for him coming as well, and I felt a momentary panic.

"Now then, am I to assume from your wonderful attire that this is not to be a simple portrait?" asked Brinkley.

"Yes, we want to capture an exotic tableau," said Florence.

"Oh but the light is very poor," he said, looking about the room.

"Will it suffice?"

"Don't mind him, Miss," said the assistant. "A photographer never has the light he wants."

"True enough, true enough," said Brinkley, taking a seat as the assistant began to assemble the camera. "Do you mind if I sit? Now then, ladies, I am given to believe that I have had the pleasure of capturing you both before."

"Yes," said Florence.

"No," I said. "I mean, yes – you photographed Florence, but not me."

"That's right," said Florence. "I um… it was just me, but you probably don't remember."

He leaned forwards conspiratorially.

"At this point, I am supposed to say that I never forget a face, but in truth I do – in fact I have a terrible memory for faces."

We laughed and so did he.

"Indeed, I thought I had a visitor this morning until I realised that I was looking at my own reflection in the shaving mirror."

We laughed again.

"Come on lad," said Brinkley, "we mustn't keep our geishas waiting – the Japanese are very particular on punctuality."

He winked at us with that last remark, his expression suggesting that he wanted us to know him as very knowledgeable about the world and its inhabitants.

With the camera in place, we tried several poses with Mr Brinkley choreographing us towards the best light. We even tried to recreate The Stray Shuttlecock, but nothing we did seemed quite worth a glass plate.

Eventually, he raised a finger and said, "I have an idea – let's take all these wonderful cushions, and strew them about the floor in front of the French windows."

We did so.

"Good. Now, we'll set up the camera in the garden so that we might have the best light falling upon your charming faces."

With a small struggle, Mr Brinkley and his assistant managed to clutter it through the doors without taking it off the tripod.

"There, now both of you sit on the floor amongst the cushions."

We did so, as he disappeared under the black hood of the camera.

"Oh yes, now we are on to something. Sit a little closer... a little closer..."

He emerged from the hood.

"Ladies, would you mind sitting right against each other? I do think it would make the sweetest photograph if you were cheek to cheek, and it would help steady you both for the exposure. Would you mind?"

He disappeared once more under the hood.

"Oh that is marvellous. Now then ladies, hold very still indeed..."

Florence's cheek was hot against mine and as soft as a cat. I could smell her breath, and her skin, and her pineapple hair, and I wished it was dark enough outside to prolong the exposure all night.

"And there we have it, ladies."

48

And There We Have It

The assistant, who's name we still didn't know, took the camera down as we made arrangements with Mr Brinkley for the number of copies we wanted.

"Also, Mr Brinkley," said Florence, "might it be possible to have a large copy tinted so as to display the true colours of our kimonos?"

"A service I am very able and happy to render."

He gave a little bow and walked to the door.

"Well thank you for your help, Mr Brinkley," I said.

"Good afternoon to you both, Ladies, the pleasure has been mine."

After they left, Nellie came in for a moment:

"Will you be needing me, Miss?"

Florence didn't answer the question directly, but instead said, "Nellie, is your mother still visiting your Aunt?"

"Yes, Miss Bright, she's down 'til Sunday night."

"Well then, why don't you take the rest of the afternoon off to see her."

"Thank you, Miss, I would be very grateful."

"Off you go then. We'll expect you for supper but you needn't be back before six."

She gave a little curtsey and hurried away.

Suddenly, we were very quietly alone.

Florence held my hand and we walked to the French windows together.

The warmth of the cheek-to-cheek moment still glowing from the cushions.

She fixed her gaze into mine, just as she had done when she rubbed the rouge into my lips.

The urge to kiss her at that moment, was almost as vital and desperate as the urge to breathe, and it rose and rose inside me until it reached my lips in the form of these careless words:

"You look so lovely, Florence, that I could... I could kiss you."

"Oh, Emmeline," she purred. "What an idea."

What had I said? I stepped back a little. "Yes, silly of me... Sorry Florence."

She suddenly spun on her heel, whipped the curtains shut, and spun back again.

"I don't think it silly," she said, "not really, I mean... what harm could there be in it?"

"Well I... none... none that I can think of."

"And wouldn't it be interesting? I mean, from a scientific perspective – female osculation."

"Yes I... perhaps it might." I didn't know what to do. "How... how would such an experiment?... um..."

"Well, the subjects would have to move closer to each other... like this..." She stepped forwards. Her face was not an inch away, and I could feel her warm breath fluttering over my lips. "And then they would put their arms about each other... if only for structural stability."

We embraced, gently at first. How wonderful her back felt beneath the silk kimono, how softly divine her breasts against mine.

"Emmeline..."

And then she kissed me...

I thought I might die – strawberries and cakes, sneeze shivers, and summer's evenings in a single, glorious swoon.

"It cannot be wrong, Emmeline," she whispered. I buried my fingers in her rich, pineapple hair and pulled her face on to me.

I had never kissed anyone before, and yet it seemed so easy to do.

She put her tongue into my mouth, not deep, just beyond my front teeth. I caressed it with the tip of my own.

It was now that some impulsive spirit that I had never met before, took control of me, and I watched myself reach around her waist, grab the ends of the obi and unravel her.

She, in turn, reached for my obi ends, but the moment she did so, the impulsive spirit evaporated, and I froze.

"No, Florence, I can't... I mean, I want to, but I... would it be all right if I kept mine on?"

She paused for a moment and looked into my eyes as if she were about to speak, but instead, she let go of my obi, slid her hands up my back, into my hair, and we sank, kissing into the cushions together.

She writhed out of her combinations, threw them cross the room and lay beside me, completely naked.

I had never seen a naked woman before, and I could hardly breathe with the amazement of her. Until this moment, the female body had been something seen from a distance, examined in a medical textbook, or simply imagined beneath layers of clothing, but now, here was this legendary creature in person, and I was overwhelmed by the reality of her – that every inch and part of her was of a natural and beautiful woman – not like me, no incongruous appendages, nothing male at all – she was complete.

I kissed her again and again, at first upon her lips, but as the impulsive spirit returned, and the passion overwhelmed me, my mouth opened wider, and my lips and tongue explored her cheeks and ears and neck.

I kissed down as far as her breasts, and as I did so she craned her body as if the cushions were too hot for her back.

My hand stroked in circles down her, rolling over the edge of her ribcage, across her soft, flat belly, and then between her legs.

How extraordinary that she had no penis, that my hand could slide over the soft slope of her pubic bone and meet no obstruction – how must this feel to her, right now, to inhabit this form so different to mine?

And then my fingers found their way into her hot body.

"Deeper," she sighed. "Please, Emmeline, my darling girl." She reached down to my wrist and angled it inwards so as to force my fingers inside.

"Say those words to me, Emmeline, those words again."

286

"What words?"

"The men, in the park, the naughty words."

"Do you mean 'bloody bastard'?"

"Oh, Emmeline, bloody bastard, bloody bastard, oh, it's so lovely – bloody, bloody, bloody, bloody. I love you, Emmeline Stanton, I bloody bastard love you…"

* * *

Some uncertain time later we lay together on the cushions, nose to nose and sleepy giggles.

"Has this ever happened to you before, Florence?"

"No, never."

"Did you even know that women could love women?"

"Oh yes, I did know that," she said. "I have known that for years."

"The Norwegian Consul-General to Naples, told me that women like us are called toms."

"The Norwegian Consul-General?"

"It's a long story, but have you heard the word before?"

"Oh yes," she said, "but I think it refers to a certain type – ladies who not only love women, but who have short hair and favour masculine attire."

"So we are not quite toms then are we?"

"I don't think so… what are you smiling at?"

"Do you know," I said, "on the day I was told that women could love women, I imagined myself kissing a certain Miss Bright – a beautiful lady with a dusty hammer, whom I had seen in Mr Brinkley's waiting room. Isn't that extraordinary?"

Florence smiled back and touched her nose against mine.

"We were surely destined for each other."

We embraced, and over her shoulder I noticed Ming. He was flopped on his side with his chin over the edge of the sofa, watching us.

"Oh dear, I think we might have corrupted the cat," I said.

Florence looked over at him too. "Ming, have you been there all along?"

He half closed his eyes. "There, you see?" she said. "Complete indifference."

"But can you imagine what people would think to see us like this?"

"Agnes would be jealous."

"You don't mean she is... like us?"

"Why do you think she is so horrible to you? She's insanely jealous of my feelings for you."

"No, I can't believe it." Then we laughed and rolled onto our backs.

"Mrs Peterson looks quite a tom doesn't she," I said.

"Oh, and don't think I haven't speculated about her and Agnes," said Florence.

"What a thought – can you imagine the two of them speaking tenderly to each other?"

"Not really." We laughed again.

There was a light thump as Ming tipped himself onto the floor and sat there, looking from us to the French windows and back again.

"And when you discovered that women could love women, did you immediately know that you were such a woman?" I said.

"Well, it was more of a confirmation than a revelation, but I was so afraid of it at first that I hardly dared think about it."

Ming now lumbered over to the French windows and looked at us expectantly.

"I wonder how your life would be now had Albert lived."

"I'm sure I would have been reasonably contented. He really was very sweet," she said.

"And do you think that in time you may have come to love him?"

"Well, he would always have been very dear to me, but he was a man, poor thing, and as such, it could never have been romantic love."

We were silent for a moment as I played with her hair, repeatedly tucking it behind her ear and un-tucking it again.

Ming patted the window to be let out and managed a tiny bleat of a meow.

"So you do not think that you could ever love a man," I said.

"After what has happened today, I think I can quite assuredly say no."

"But what if I were a man? Could you not even love a male me?"

"Well, I'm sure I would like you very much – indeed I'm sure we would be the very best of friends, but I could not love any man in the way I love you, Emmeline. No – you see it wouldn't be you."

VII

Converging Courses

49

The letter

August the 29th, 1887.

*M*y *Darling Florence,*

You must be wondering where I am, and why I have disappeared, leaving this letter for you.

Please do not be alarmed. I have something to tell you about myself – something rather strange, and something that you may need a little time to think about.

Let me come straight to the point, and tell you that when I was born, my mother named me 'Thomas'. It was not because of some eccentric whim – it was because I actually was born in the body of a boy.

Please, I beg you, do not draw any conclusions yet, but read on:

I do not know how to explain my knowing that I was really a girl despite my body, but I did know it – I was as certain of that as a person can be about anything.

There is so much to tell you of the events that lie between that day and this, and you must know from my current appearance that I was able to correct the accident of my birth with some degree of success. But, before you applaud my ingenuity, you should also know the brutal and repulsive truth – that I still retain one small, physical reminder of that body.

What I have is by no means the sort of thing you would see on a grown man, for I never gave it the chance to grow up, and how could such a small amount of flesh remove me entirely from the female category, and place me in the male one,

293

where you would find so many other characteristics that I do not possess?

Florence, if you love my face, or my voice, if you love my mind – me – the person that I am, then all such attributes continue as before, regardless of any extra part.

I thought it would be unfair to stand over you as you read this, so I have taken a room at the Bailey's Hotel in Gloucester Road. When you are ready, I hope, with all my heart, that you will come to claim me, and if you do not, I will understand.

I promise you, Florence, that I have not deceived you – I truly am a woman, and always have been, despite the lie that my body tells.

I wait for you, my dearest love,

Emmeline.

* * *

I felt very strange as I left the house – fear and hope combining themselves into an emotion that I have never experienced before, and for which I had no name.

I tried to think through the likely sequence of events – Florence would be home by four and would find the letter straight away because I have displayed it very clearly on the mantelpiece. She will read it and ponder its contents for a few minutes. I cannot know how she will react to my news, but she is too kind a person to prolong my agony, so I think she will take a cab straight here, and then, for better or worse, I will know if she can still love me. By that course, I thought I could probably expect her here at the hotel by about five.

I sat on my bed in the hotel room, and in order to fix my mind upon something other than dread, I decided to see if I could read every single word of every single article in yesterday's evening Standard, and hope that I would not run out of words before Florence knocked at the door.

I started with the personal notices:

* * *

'If PHILLIP MANNING ARTHUR, formerly of Barnet, will COMMUNICATE with his relatives, he will HEAR of SOMETHING to his ADVANTAGE.'

* * *

No – talk of relatives just made me think about my own, which made me think about rejection, and that was about the last thing I wanted to think about right now, so I abandoned my plan to read every word, and skipped to the travel advertisements instead:

* * *

'CHEAP RETURN TICKETS to the EAST – The PENINSULAR and ORIENTAL COMPANY are now issuing tickets at reduced fares, to INDIA, CHINA, and JAPAN – Full particulars can be obtained at the offices of the company.'

* * *

One day, perhaps Florence and I will take journeys like these together, I thought. We will see India and China on a grand tour to Japan, taking in the sights during the day, and sharing a bed at night – it will be perfect… if… if only she can still love me.

I shook my head. Even the travel section was not distracting enough, so I now tried to force my mind deeper into the paper itself, looking for grammatical errors and spelling mistakes - even examining the typeface for anomalies and imperfections.

And then, at the bottom of the foreign news section, I found this:

* * *

'FOUNDATION OF THE LONDON-NEAPOLITAN ASSOCIATION

'This new trade association, chaired by Lord Carstairs, seeks to consolidate trade relations between London and Naples to our mutual benefit. The first order

of business being to establish a cheaper route by steamer between our two great cities.

'Lord Carstairs will be assisted at his London offices by a select and bilingual staff with excellent connections to both cities, these including Mr P Loretti, Mr R F de Peters, Mr J J Carter and Mr W Pollard.'

* * *

'Mr W Pollard' – he was here – Uncle Walter was in London – there could be no doubt about it.

I threw the paper down as if he could see me through it, and by instinct I ran to the window. I'm not sure if I wanted to see if there was an easy route down the side of the building, or to check that there was no easy route up to my room, but the moment I touched the window frame, there was a knock at the door, and I leapt backwards, as if I had dropped a boiling kettle.

I hadn't even locked the room because I had wanted Florence to be able to come straight in.

I flung myself at the door and spun the key to lock it.

It could still be Florence though, couldn't it? I thought. Surely it must be her. After all, I am expecting her right now, and it would be far too great a coincidence for Uncle Walter to knock the door of my hotel room only a second after I read about him in yesterday's paper.

But... but what if it is him?

After a few moments there was another knock, but tentative, not an uncle knock.

I drew all my courage together.

"Who's there?" I whispered.

The voice that came back was young – it sounded like a boy.

"Message for Miss Stanton – from the hospital, Miss."

"From the hospital?"

"Yes, Miss."

"Are you alone?"

"Yes, Miss."

I lay down and looked under the door. I could only see one pair of feet, so holding my courage for a moment longer, I stood back up and opened the door to reveal a boy of perhaps twelve, holding out a note.

I looked up and down the hallway before taking the note. This is what it said:

Florence lies injured at St Mary Abbot's Hospital.
Come at once.

Uncle Walter had found her.

I was suddenly strangely calm – this was far too frightening to register within the normal range of human feeling, so my mind put the fear aside to be considered later.

"Have you come from the hospital?" I said.

"Yes, Miss."

"Do you know where Miss Bright is now? The room I mean."

"Yes, Miss – I can show you the way if you like."

"Can you run?"

"Swift as you like, Miss."

"Then let's run…"

* * *

At the door of Florence's room, fear returned to me in its full intensity and I couldn't breathe. Beyond this door may lie the worst of all possible things – Florence dead – an eventuality so completely insupportable that I knew I could not look upon it and live.

As I turned the handle, I took little short breaths, as if I were stepping into freezing water.

The light broke through the gap, and in an ecstasy of fear, I put my face into the room.

"Florence?"

"Emmeline."

As I ran to the bed, my legs collapsed, and I fell into her arms.

"I am fine, my darling girl, I am fine – just cuts and bruises."

"Was it my uncle, did he do this to you?"

"No, no, nothing like that – a silly accident."

I sobbed into her bosom and curled my fingertips into her clothes as she embraced me.

She let me cry for a minute or two, then she lifted my head, wiped my tears away with her thumbs, and fixed me very firmly in her enormous eyes.

"Your letter, Emmeline, I…"

"I am so sorry I did not tell you, Florence, but I am so afraid that you cannot love me."

"But listen to me, Emmeline - I don't care – I don't care at all."

"You don't think me a monster?"

"Of course not." She smiled. "And anyway, it wasn't quite as much of a secret as you assume. After all, you were ill and delirious in your underwear at my house for several days."

"Oh, how horrible. So you did undress me."

"Yes, I did, and then I dressed you again, because I knew you would be embarrassed. But don't worry, I didn't make a detailed examination, I just glimpsed something which made you a little different, that's all."

I could not speak, but I smiled hopefully and she smiled back.

"Emmeline, you are a girl, and you are my girl, and that is is the beginning and end of it."

50

Two Problems

"Now then, what's all this?"

"This is Miss Stanton, Doctor Kirkeby," said Florence. "She's my friend and…"

"And you are not to be disturbed," he said, looking very cross, but rather kind at the same time.

"Oh, but I…"

He cut me off with a raised finger. "Miss Stanton, I applaud your dedication to your friend, but above all things, Miss Bright needs rest. Now, she's not badly hurt, and if you will allow her a good night's sleep, I am sure she can return to her home in the morning. Perhaps you might come at seven with a carriage?"

"It's fine, Emmeline," said Florence. "I will see you tomorrow."

"Of course," I said, "I um… well good night, Florence."

* * *

My mood was now a complex tangle:

I felt profound relief that Florence was alive, and also profound relief that she didn't care about my problem, and that I would still see myself reflected in her eyes; but the echo of the terror of coming to find her was still resonating through my body, and even if her injuries were not the work of my uncle, he had never been closer, nor ever more dangerous than he was right now.

I did not want to go home – I could not quite escape the fear that I might meet him on the way, and besides, I didn't want to be too far from Florence, even if the doctor did say there was nothing to worry about, so I sent the messenger boy with a note to have Jenkins bring the brougham carriage at seven in the morning, then I settled into a chair in a corridor and spent one half of the night dozing, and the other half looking through a window at the hospital courtyard for Walter-shaped lurkers.

When the morning finally came, Doctor Kirkeby woke me to say that I should go down to the carriage to wait for the porters to bring Florence out. I looked out of the window – I could see Jenkins and the brougham, but no suspicious men, so down I went.

Right on time, Florence was wheeled through the front door in a bath chair, walking stick in lap, grimacing with embarrassment. She allowed the porters to help her stand, but then insisted they return to more important duties.

"Can you manage?" I said.

"Well, I managed to climb into the plum tree with two legs," said Florence, "so I am sure I can climb into a carriage with one. Perhaps if you get in first though and give me a hand up."

As the carriage pulled away, I looked out of all three windows, just to be sure we were not being followed, and then I kissed her – a kiss that began as a simple peck on the lips, but that extended for as long as it takes to draw a long slow breath... and exhale it again. And then I kissed her head to make it better.

"Perhaps I will kiss your ankle better too when we get home," I said, twinkling at her.

She smiled, and kissed me on the nose. "Well at least I will have an excuse not to dance at the Ragged School charity ball."

I lifted her hair away to examine her head injury more closely – there was a cut, near the hairline, and it lay across a small purple bump.

"I don't think I shall ever let you out of my sight again, Florence. I want you to tell me exactly what happened."

"Well, it's all very embarrassing," she said, "but a little while after I got home yesterday, before I even saw your letter, Agnes arrived."

"Agnes? My god, Florence, if she hurt you..."

"No, silly. Actually, she began with what might almost be construed as an apology about her recent behaviour – she said that *perhaps* she might have been a little stronger than necessary."

"What did you say to that?"

"I said that we had been very upset by the whole incident. She took immediate offence at that and replied, 'How very weak of you'. Then she accused us of not looking to the greater good again."

"Well, this is a timely reminder of why we left the committee."

"Yes, and at that point I asked her to leave."

"And did she go?"

"No, not at first, but it did bring her to the point of her visit, which was to ask me to reconsider funding the committee."

"You refused, of course."

"Yes, and I told her that she would have to work for her money. Well, at that point she was very rude about you, saying that I indulge a 'silly girl' in a life of frivolous leisure, whilst abandoning the rest of the female sex. This I refused to tolerate, and insisted, with a raised voice..."

"Good for you."

"...that she leave immediately. I then stamped out of the drawing room, and shut myself in the living room. That's when I found your letter."

"So were you injured on the way to claim me then?"

"Yes, you see I was in such a desperation to come right away, that I dashed out of the door without coat or hesitation, ran down the square, past Agnes, who had by now gotten as far as the corner, and then, with remarkable stupidity, I continued straight into the Brompton Road, intending not only to hail a cab, but to get myself right in front of one, so that I could stop it dead."

"You were knocked down?"

"Well, the horse took fright at my flapping arms, poor thing, and I am not entirely sure what happened next, other than my being helped into a seated position in the middle of the road with the most appalling pain in my ankle, and blood running down the side of my face."

I put my hand over my mouth.

"Beyond that, I vaguely remember a frantic cab ride, with Agnes beside me telling me not to make such a fuss, and a sticky, scarlet-soaked handkerchief pressed against my head."

I grabbed her hand.

"The thought of you being knocked down in the road, Florence – I can't bear it."

She squeezed my fingers and smiled apologetically.

"My head is fine – a small cut, despite all the blood, but my ankle is really quite sore and the doctor says it may take a while to mend."

"The disconcerting thing," I said, "is to find myself grateful to Agnes for helping you." Then I laughed. "It's quite an uncomfortable sensation."

"Oh, I wouldn't be too uncomfortable – she took good advantage of the situation, saying that she had saved my life – which actually she hadn't – and insisting, once again, that the least I could do in return was to fund her. Well, I said that no decent person would ever ask payment for such a thing. But…"

"But what?"

The carriage pulled up.

"Here look, we're home," she said.

* * *

As Florence settled on the sofa, Nellie brought in tea and sandwiches, and I arranged cushions and a pouffe to set Florence's ankle in a comfortable position.

Once we were alone, we both took a sip of tea, and then a deep breath, before placing the cups back down.

We both started to speak at the same time.

"No, please, you go ahead," she said.

"Well I… well you see… we um… I'm afraid we have a little problem."

"That's exactly what I was going to say."

"It can't be the same problem, surely," I said.

"Well, you tell me yours first and we'll see."

I took a moment to gather myself.

"It's my uncle, he… he's in London – there's no doubt about it now. He has taken up a position here – something called the London-Neapolitan Association."

"Are you sure?"

"I saw it in the paper – 'Mr W Pollard'."

"Could it be another W Pollard?"

"No, I don't think so – not with the Neapolitan connection."

She made a slightly sceptical wrinkle of the nose. "Well look, Emmeline, London is still a very big city. I mean, even if he is here, I still do not think he would be able to find you."

"You don't know him, Florence."

"Well, on the positive side, at least we know where he is, but…" she squeezed my hand, "let's not overestimate him."

"I'm not – I really am not – he is absolutely…" I sighed. "What is the other problem?"

She looked very earnestly at me. "It's your letter, Emmeline. I have lost it."

"Oh."

"I had it in my hand as I ran into the Brompton Road, and I think I must have dropped it when I was knocked down."

"And you're sure you didn't leave it in your room at the hospital?"

"Yes, I had the nurses search very thoroughly – it seems I arrived without it. I'm so sorry, Emmeline – I am heartbroken to have lost it at all, but more to the point, what if somebody finds it?"

"Well, in the first place, you never need apologise to me. And secondly, if, as is likely, you dropped it in the middle of the Brompton Road, then it would probably have been trodden into the dirt in the confusion and lay unnoticed as a piece of litter."

Florence was silent for a moment. "Unless…" She scratched her nose awkwardly, then sat forwards. "Unless Agnes has it."

"Why would you think that?"

"Well, she was there when I was knocked down, and then she was quite strange in the hospital, Emmeline. It's difficult to describe – quietly smug I suppose you could say. And when I asked her to leave, she said 'Leave now? But I was so looking forward to the arrival of Emmeline,' and she gave me a most peculiar smile."

My stomach tumbled over and I slumped into the sofa.

"Oh, but you mustn't worry, Emmeline," she said, quickly turning my face towards her with her hands. "I am only considering the possibility, but really, I'm sure you're right – I mean the confusion of the moment, a rearing horse, the noise, me lying in the road… I hardly think Agnes would have noticed something so trivial as a piece of paper in the midst of such a drama."

51

You, Sir, Are an Abomination

T hree days later found me standing at the French windows watching a torrential downpour, whilst Florence napped on the sofa.

My thoughts recoiled from my uncle to Agnes and back again, and I felt as if I were watching an expensive vase teeter over the edge of its pedestal – that hollow cringe of anticipation you feel after it falls, but before it breaks.

I looked round at Florence who was now awake, watching me.

"You're awake," I said.

She didn't reply for a while – just continued to look at me, softly. Then she smiled and said, "It would have been so funny to see you as a boy."

"That's the thing though, Florence, it's... it's difficult to explain because... well because I don't quite understand it myself, but to me, it feels as if I was never a boy at all, because I have never felt like one. The feeling is more that I was the female inhabitant of a boy's life – not the boy himself. So I don't know what it is like for a boy to be a boy. Indeed I cannot imagine it."

I shook my head. "Does that make any sense to you?" I said. "That a person can be one sex on the inside and another on the outside?"

"May I be completely honest with you, Emmeline?"

"Of course."

"Well, speaking for myself, I see you as a woman – it is obvious, and I don't question it, and your little physical anomaly is far too inconsequential to have any bearing on my perception of who you are. But that is one person's perception of another. When it comes to one's perception of oneself, I would have assumed that a woman feels herself to be a woman because she is one – physically I mean, so while you must obviously feel female now, looking as you do, it is difficult for me to understand how you could have felt female when you were still physically... um... a boy."

She smiled very gently.

"But that doesn't mean I don't believe you, It just means that I haven't understood it yet, and that's my shortcoming, not yours."

"Not at all, Florence – why shouldn't you find it difficult to understand something about me that I cannot understand myself?" I sighed and frowned at the floor.

"Isn't it ironic," said Florence, sitting up with her mischievous smile, "that you gave up the vote in changing sex, and now must be a suffragist to get it back again – some people might think that you want the best of both worlds."

I laughed. "Yes, perhaps I should put on trousers just for polling day. Perhaps all women should become men for that day."

"What an excellent idea – I think I'll..."

Three hard thumps rattled the front door.

I froze.

Florence limped into the hallway where she could see the front door through a side window.

"The police?" I whispered.

"No it's... it's Agnes."

"Don't let her in."

"We must, Emmeline – if she does have the letter, then we need to deal with this, one way or the other."

"But..."

"It'll be all right – trust me."

We took up position in the drawing room and held hands for a moment as Nellie went to the front door.

There was a small commotion, then Agnes stormed into the room, steam rising from her wet coat as if it had been draped over a stove.

An apologetic Nellie tumbled after her.

"It's Miss Grendle, Miss," said Nellie. "Sorry, Miss."

Agnes' eyes fixed on me as she came forwards. She halted perhaps five feet away, but her eyes continued to hold me for a few seconds like a pair of hot tongs.

Then she spoke:

"You, Sir, are an abomination."

The words had a physical weight to them, and as they hit me in the chest, all the mortification of the day I had been caught in Elizabeth's clothes was knocked awake.

"Not that you don't deserve some credit of course," she continued. "Your entrance into the committee for example, was executed with sublime deceit – I was certainly fooled."

"That'll be all, Nellie," said Florence, and Nellie left the room.

I remembered how I stood up to the Reverend Thomas on that horrible day, and it gave me the courage to answer.

"I am not a sir," I said it steady and staccato, and I looked her in the eye, if only for a moment.

"And then of course," she continued, "once you were ensconced, you manipulated everyone so very skilfully, particularly Florence. Not that you deserve any great credit there, for she has a decidedly weak nature."

"Don't you dare…" I said.

"And I must confess, that even to the point that you managed to tear the group apart, and terminate our funding, I did not quite see that you were doing it."

"That's enough, Agnes," said Florence.

"I wonder that you are foolish enough to defend him, Florence, given that he has gone to such great lengths to prevent your progress as a woman."

"Stop calling her him. She's not a man. It's very childish."

"Yes," I said, "don't be so childish."

"Childish?" said Agnes. "How typical of a man to patronise."

"Whatever I may be, I am absolutely not a man," I said.

Agnes snorted. "I think your mother might have something to say about that, and who could be better placed to pronounce on the matter than her, eh, Thomas?"

By invoking both my mother and my old name in one sentence, she managed to knot my stomach tight enough to hold my mouth shut.

"Clearly you have the letter, Agnes," said Florence, "so please get to the point and tell us what you want for it?"

Agnes ignored her and remained fixed upon me:

"And what is more, Mr Thomas Stanton, you are a rapist."

There was silence for several seconds.

"A rapist?" I said at last, whilst Florence gaped. "How on earth would I rape someone with that little thing?"

"Observe, Florence, how the male mind can conceive of rape only as the carnal act. You see, Thomas, the WLSC is something female, it is a group of women acting for women – it is a space into which men are neither invited, nor welcome. That you – a man – should penetrate our group; that you should insert your male body into our female space, despoiling, corrupting and finally destroying it, is, and could only be, rape."

Florence and I looked at each other, both gaping now.

"And the mere fact that we are even talking about your penis rather proves that you are a man, don't you think?"

"Emmeline is not a man, Agnes. She is obviously not a man."

"Really? Well you are the scientist, so I dare say you have some means of proving that to me."

"Well, in the first place, look at her. In the second, do you not simply feel it?"

"Feel it? I do not think that science progresses by feelings, Florence. What about you, Mr Stanton, would you care to lift your skirts and resolve the matter once and for all?"

"There is more to being a woman than one small detail of anatomy," I said.

"Yes indeed – there are larger details of anatomy, like wombs, and there is also the little detail of living one's entire life as a woman, and wanting for

308

all the privileges that males enjoy; of living your life with no control over its outcome; to be assumed stupid and incompetent, as you assumed the ladies of the WLSC to be when you violated us."

"This is ridiculous – what masculine privileges do I enjoy?" I was close to shouting now. "I came to the group as a woman, suffering the same injustices as other women, and I joined for exactly the same reasons as every other member…"

"And now you don't like it. Well, Mr Stanton. You can't have your cake and eat it too – if you will live as a woman, you should prepare to suffer as one."

"I thought that being a suffragist was about ending the suffering of women, not just living with it."

"A redundant point, given that you are a man."

"No, I am not a man, I have never been male – never. Even if I couldn't live the first part of my life as female… I have always *felt* female."

Agnes seemed completely untroubled by my ever-rising voice, but took a moment before answering:

"How do you know?"

"What do you mean, how do I know? Of course I know how I felt."

"Oh yes, you know how *you* felt, but how could you possibly know how a woman feels, given the obvious fact that you are not one?"

"I DON'T KNOW HOW I KNEW, I JUST DID."

"I see – some sort magical insight was it?" She was quite calm, and clearly enjoying herself.

"Well, she is a woman to me," said Florence, "and she is a woman to herself. That is enough."

"It is not enough, Florence – it is most certainly not enough, and by accepting him as a woman, you diminish all women, for you make us no better than castrated men."

Florence touched my arm. "Don't say anything else, Emmeline – she will get to the letter all the sooner if we give her nothing to argue with."

"Ah yes, the letter," said Agnes, still calm. "A tawdry little missive by any account."

"Let's not play games, Agnes," said Florence. "What are your terms?"

"My terms?" She scoffed. "Do you think that I am going to blackmail you? Or do you mean to bribe me?"

"We just want the letter back."

"Well, you can't have it back."

"Then I will take it back," I said, stepping forwards.

Agnes reached straight into her bag and pointed her gun at me from inside it.

"My God, Thomas Stanton, if you lay a hand on me, I will shoot you dead."

"STOP IT, BOTH OF YOU," screamed Florence, reaching across me and planting her walking stick as a fence to hold me back.

Agnes, with deep satisfaction, took her hand out of the bag.

"How very male of you," she sniffed, "to underestimate a woman to the extent that you think I would be stupid enough to bring the letter with me. Not that I really need to shoot you of course – I could simply summon a constable and have you arrested for outraging public decency."

"Then why are you here? What do you want from me?"

She smiled, smugly. "What do I want? I want you to know that I know."

"And what do you intend to do about knowing?"

"Well, we'll have to wait and see won't we?"

"If you ever attempt to publish the letter, Agnes," I said, "I will tell the police that you did so because we refused your attempt at blackmail."

"Will you indeed? And what credence do you think a judge would give to the shrill claims of a self-mutilating eunuch who dresses as a woman?"

She turned and walked towards the door.

"Agnes," said Florence, "if you will return the letter, I will fund you, I will double your funding, I will even sign to it."

"Oh, I don't need it – I have a new patron now, one who supports us most generously. Your wealth has no power any more."

And with that, she left.

* * *

Florence embraced me.

"Oh, Emmeline – that was awful. I'm so sorry I let her in. Will you please forgive me?"

"Goodness me, Florence, you will never ever owe me an apology."

We held on to each other for a moment then, almost by instinct, we went back to the safe comfort of the living room and sat on the sofa.

"What troubles me the most," I said, "is the part that she's right about."

"What part?"

"The part that we cannot understand either: how can I have known what it felt like to be a girl even when I was physically a boy? I mean perhaps she is right – perhaps I am simply insane."

"You think too much," she said, brushing my fringe softly to one side.

"Can one think too much? How is one to resolve a complex problem without thinking about it?"

"Sometimes, Emmeline, it is the thinking about it that causes the problem. And anyway, surely what matters is that you knew, not how you knew."

"Well… I… well that is a very good point, but… but it still does not tell us whether what I feel is the same as whatever it is other women feel… so the mystery remains."

"But no one knows what anyone else feels, and mystery or not, look at you." She leaned back to take me in. "I mean to say look at your figure and your face, listen to your voice – look at your chest for goodness' sake. I think it is safe to say, Emmeline, that pound for pound, you are far more woman than man, and if Agnes thinks otherwise, then she must have the most extraordinarily broad definition of 'man' whilst at the same time having the most extraordinarily narrow definition of 'woman.'"

"Well, that is an even better point."

We sat in silence for a few minutes, but despite Florence's good points, Agnes still had the letter, and the rain beating against the window held the tension in the room like an executioner's drum roll.

"So, what are we going to do?" I said.

"I don't know. Perhaps all we need do for now, is try not to anger her, and in a few days I will…"

I stood up and began to pace. "But who knows what will make a mad woman angry? And what if, in the meantime, she goes ahead and exposes me?"

"But she..."

I looked out of the window at the black clouds. "And then there is my murdering uncle, creeping his steady way towards me. How do I live between the two of them? I cannot, Florence. I am afraid to leave the house, I am afraid to stay in. I can't bear it."

"Emmeline, you must try to calm down. I do not think..."

I took both her hands in mine. "We could move away – that's what we could do. Why don't we do that? It would be one way of escaping."

"But where to?"

"You speak a little French, don't you?"

"You mean move abroad?"

"Yes, why not?"

Florence thought for a moment, then shook her head. "It's too drastic, Emmeline."

"Our situation is drastic."

"Our situation could possibly *become* drastic, but it certainly isn't yet, and we must not therefore act as if it is."

"But, Florence..."

She squeezed my hands. "Look, Agnes has vented her fury and has walked away from us quite satisfied that she won her argument. Let's give her a few days to calm down, and then I will speak to her. I'm sure that by then she will have settled into a more rational temper, and I can persuade her to give the letter back. As for your uncle, well, we still have no reason at all to think he is anywhere near finding you, nor that he ever could."

I shook my head. "You don't know him, Florence – he is relentless. For all we know he is the new patron of the WLSC. Imagine him and Agnes working together – I would be absolutely done for."

"Well, I suggest that we stay indoors – keep ourselves to ourselves for a few days."

"That means we will miss the charity ball on Saturday," I said. "Do you mind?"

"Not at all – I wasn't going to go anyway with this ankle. I can still make my donation – I'll have Nellie take a cheque round to their offices."

"But even so… even if we stay indoors for the next month, it all feels so precarious – I don't like it, Florence, I don't like it at all."

"There's nothing else we can do."

"Well I… I can think of one thing," I said.

"What's that?"

"We could pack some cases – all the essentials for a few months, and then we could have them taken round to some stables – not ours – I don't know which ones – perhaps the Bird Cage stables on Sloane Street. I mean we could have a carriage set up there – everything in readiness for a swift departure, just in case we should be forced to make one."

"Would that make you feel better?"

"Yes."

"Then we can at least do that, Emmeline – of course we can."

52

His Stamping Face

"**B**ut, Florence, to travel swiftly is, almost by definition, to travel lightly," I said.

"Two trunks each then?"

"No – *one* trunk each, and not the big ones either." I was now sounding like an ungrateful child, and Florence scratched her nose awkwardly.

"But we don't know what sort of weather we might be dressing for," she said.

"Then you take three main outfits – a warm weather, a cold weather, and something between the two."

"Well, we do need to add something for evenings, but… but I'm sure we can still fit it all in a single trunk."

"Oh… but what about Ming? Damn it." I pushed the trunk away and covered my face. "I hadn't thought of that – why had I not thought of that?"

"We would take him with us of course."

"But what if he is not here when we go? We can't leave him, Florence, we can't. We must keep him indoors from now on – tell Nellie not to let him out at all."

Florence pulled herself over to me, despite her ankle.

"Emmeline, you must stop this. You have no reason to be in such a panic. We can keep Ming in the house if you think it wise to do so – of course we can, but please," she held my hand, "we are a long way from danger yet.

314

Remember, I'm going to talk to Agnes, perhaps on Sunday, and we need only keep ourselves out of view until then. As for your Uncle..." she looked gently into my eyes, "...he cannot find you, Emmeline."

"I'm sorry, Florence, I don't mean to be sharp." I looked at the pile of clothes on the floor. "Running away when you have lots of things is surprisingly vexatious, isn't it?" I tried a half-smile. "I certainly never had this trouble living out of a carpet bag."

"Remember, Emmeline, we are not running away – we are taking a small precautionary measure so that we *could* run away, if ever the need arose."

"Yes, you're right." I smiled and let my shoulders down a little. "And I hardly need worry about being able to find Ming when it's raining like this."

Florence laughed, "Yes, doesn't he hate it?"

"Geronimo was the same – all cats hate the rain, I think."

* * *

The rain continued into the evening and grew ever heavier. I couldn't sleep for the noise and stood at my window for a while, watching the steady inundation of the Brompton Square park.

At the corner of the square I could see the night-watchman, Mr Paul – he was standing at the top of a stoop, taking shelter under a balcony.

At one point, a hansom came past, and I have never seen such a miserable cabbie – he looked as if he had just been dragged out of the Thames. A young woman got out of the cab with her beau, and squealed as she ran into one of the houses. The beau pointlessly hunched his shoulders against the deluge as he paid the cabbie.

As the cab left the square, Mr Paul waved it off, and the effort seemed to spur him into making a round.

He first walked into the park itself, which surprised me, as it looked precariously muddy, but then he walked up to a tall tree and opened his flys.

I looked away, along the park, feeling that it was impolite to watch him add his little drizzle to the flood, but then I saw another figure, obscured by the trees and bushes – a man, no umbrella, just a greatcoat, and he was looking towards the house.

I jumped back and ran into Florence's room.

"Florence, wake up, there's a man – quickly, Florence."

"In the house?"

"No, the park, please come and see. I think it's him – I'm sure it's him."

Florence got out of bed and hobbled into my room.

"There look – he is the right shape, the right build, I am sure it's him, Florence."

"Where? I see nothing."

I pointed. "Look – just between the…"

"Oh yes, I see him."

"And look, here comes Mr Paul, poor fellow – he cannot know the danger he is in."

"Emmeline, you cannot be sure who this man is with such an obscured view. There look, he seems to be talking to Mr Paul in a perfectly civilised manner… and see, now he's leaving, and with a parting wave to Mr Paul. Hardly the maniac you imagined was it? Silly girl." She kissed me on the nose.

"But why was he here? What good reason does a man have to be standing in a park in torrential rain in the middle of the night? And looking at our house. I can't bear it Florence, this constant apprehension – I can't bear it."

* * *

The following morning, Florence had Nellie summon a very damp Mr Paul before he went home, and she spoke to him on the doorstep.

"Yes, Ma'am?"

"Last night, Mr Paul, I was unable to sleep and was watching the rain when I noticed you talking to a gentleman in the park."

"Oh, yes, Ma'am – queer fellow, standing there, all wet. Well, I enquired after his business, so to speak, and he was quite a pleasant chap as it turned out. Not quite a toff, but not a man down on 'is luck, for sure."

316

"What did he say?"

"Well, not a great deal – he alluded after a family matter – 'You know how it is,' he says, and off he went. I had the distinct impression that he pines for a lost love, Ma'am. Either that or he suspects a loved one of some duplicity." He glanced at me, perhaps wondering if I was the duplicitous party.

"What would you guess his age at?" I asked.

"This side of fifty I should say – forty five perhaps?"

"And a bent nose?"

"Didn't notice."

"Stocky though?" I said. "I mean, did he look a solid fellow, like a rugby player?"

"Perhaps... yes, quite stocky."

I looked at Florence, my eyes all alarm.

"Well, thank you, Mr Paul. Please take this for your trouble," she said, as she tipped him.

"Much obliged, Ma'am." And off he went for breakfast and a good day's sleep.

"It sounds just like him, Florence – stocky, bent nose."

"There look, your fears are playing tricks on you – Mr Paul said he didn't notice what the man's nose was like. And... and you have to consider it from a statistical perspective – the chance that this mysterious person, of all the stocky men in London, is actually your uncle, is really so remote that... well, we'll keep an eye out, but I'm quite sure that we should not be unduly worried about it."

* * *

I slept a little on the sofa during the day, trying to catch up on the night before, and as the night approached again, I pretended to myself that I wasn't dreading it. I made myself go to bed at the usual time, but I was up again within the hour, and I took a blanket to the chair by the window so that I could sit and keep guard instead.

Yet again, it was raining heavily. I couldn't see Mr Paul on the stoop this time – in fact, he did not appear to be in the square at all.

Florence limped in about midnight and watched with me for a little while, but unable to stay awake, she got into my bed so that I wouldn't be alone in the room with my thoughts.

I stayed in the chair for the rest of the night, falling asleep every so often, only to keep waking back up with a start.

Mr Paul did not appear all night as far as I could see, but nor did the uncle-ish man.

* * *

When dawn finally appeared, Florence got up, and I fell straight into the warm pineapple nest she had made in my bed.

The next I knew, it was mid afternoon and she was rousing me for a very late breakfast.

"Honestly, Emmeline, look at your eyes."

"I did sleep a little… in the chair… well mostly I didn't sleep, but there was still no Mr Paul after you went to bed – he was not in the square all night. Is Ming in the house?"

"Yes he is. Now, come and have something to eat before you worry yourself out of an appetite. Nellie's gone to the shops, but she has made breakfast for you."

"No Mrs Dockerill?"

"It's her Saturday off."

"So it is… actually I'm not particularly hungry."

"Well, come and try."

I managed a slice and a half of toast with some effort, and filled the remaining space with tea instead.

"Look, the rain has stopped at last," I yawned. "Perhaps I'll take a turn around the garden – see if I can't wake myself up a bit."

"I should think that's a very good idea," said Florence.

* * *

I stood just outside the French windows and drew in the air. The smell of the garden was wonderful – fresh, wet, muddy and green, and although the rain had stopped, fat drops plopped onto the path from the gutters, and every so often a breeze would shake a shower out of the trees.

Then one of the fat plops splatted on the back of my neck and I jumped away from the house. The icy wet ran down my back as a shiver ran up it.

I looked up to see where it had fallen from (a joint in the gutter) and then I looked down to see where it would have landed but for my neck.

There were footprints – two footprints, not mine – big ones, squashed into the mud, the toes towards the French windows.

I stared at them, frozen – Uncle Walter's footprints – the footprints that had stamped themselves into my body, that had tried to stamp out my very life.

Then I looked at the window itself, and I could see his face in it, as if he had left his reflection behind, and it stared back at me – his dead eyes, his stamping face. I shook my head. "FLORENCE."

"Dear God, Emmeline," she said, limping into the garden as fast as her ankle would allow. "What is it? Are you hurt?"

"He was here, Florence, he was here." I pointed to the footprints. "Last night, he came for me, he came to get me, and I see him Florence, I see him – in the window."

Florence grabbed my face by the cheeks and turned it to hers.

"What do you do with the visions, Emmeline? Look at me and think, what have I told you?"

"Let them run their course... they... they cannot hurt me."

"That's right – do not fear them, only watch, and let them pass."

"But we must leave, Florence, we must leave."

She looked at the prints.

"There look," I said, now pointing out a whole line of them running back to the garden fence. "He came through the gap by the plum tree."

Florence put her arm around my shoulders and almost pushed me back into the house before locking the windows shut.

"We need to think this through, Emmeline, and we need to do so calmly.

Firstly we can't be sure that…"

Nellie rushed into the room with her muddy boots on, and the shopping basket still on her arm.

"Nellie?"

"Sorry, Miss – there's horrible news, Miss."

"What is it?"

"Mr Paul has been murdered, Miss – done to death. I got it from Mrs Bridges at the corner house. They found him at home – his face all stamped in. Horrible, Miss – in his own home."

Florence and I looked at each other.

"My God," said Florence, quietly, almost to herself. "Nellie, go and see that the back door is locked will you."

"Yes, Miss." She hurried away.

"Well then," said Florence, with a deep breath, "we'd better get ready to leave, hadn't we."

I had not seen this facial expression before – it was pale and grey, and it snuffed the sparkles out of her eyes.

"I am so sorry, Florence."

"I'll have none of that. Now then, first things first – what shall we do with Nellie?"

"We could send her to her aunt's."

"Yes, that's a good idea, but let us not alarm her any more than we need to."

Nellie rushed back into the room, eyes wide, and slightly out of breath. "It's locked, Miss."

"Thank you, Nellie," said Florence, forcing a sleepily calm tone. "Look, I don't want you getting all upset about Mr Paul. These things can happen in a big city, but in truth they are very rare."

"Yes, Miss." Nellie didn't look at all convinced.

"Now then, I want you to go round the house and make sure that all the windows are locked too. It's nothing to do with Mr Paul, Nellie – the reason is that Miss Stanton and I are going to go away for a little while."

"Yes, Miss."

"We have been planning it for some time, and what with all this dreary weather... anyway, you can stay with your aunt for a while, yes?"

"Yes, Miss."

"Very well. Go and put the house in order – I want everything tidy for when we return."

"Yes, Miss." And off she went.

53

Additional Complications

Had you watched us prepare for our journey, you might have mistaken us for completely different sorts of people than we really are, for we dressed ourselves in a coldly detached manner, talking of boots and practical clothing, and not at all about Mr Paul or my uncle.

"Is that more rain, Emmeline?" said Florence.

I went to the window. "Yes – heavy again."

Everything outside was wet and grey and spoiled – the park was a quagmire, and the sky was so overcast that there was barely enough light to make the soaking ground glisten.

"What a horrible day," I said, and looked back at Florence. She had stopped dressing now and was sitting on my bed, drumming her fingers on her lips and frowning.

"But are we being realistic, Emmeline?"

"How do you mean?"

"I mean can we actually hide in Paris? I have the impression that many people journey there regularly on business. We'll be hardly more hidden than if we stay in England."

"Well… if Paris is too close to home… perhaps… perhaps we should go further afield."

"The South of France? Nice perhaps?"

"Here's an idea, Florence – how about leaving Europe altogether? How about Japan?"

"Oh Emmeline, I wouldn't have the nerve."

"But what's the difference? I mean really, apart from the journey taking longer."

"Well, for a start, we can't speak any Japanese… apart from arigato."

"We could learn," I said. "And I'm sure there would be English-speaking people there – diplomats, businessmen and the like."

"But how on earth does a person get there? I mean how do you arrange such an expedition? I wouldn't know where to begin."

"It's easy, Florence – journeys to the far East are advertised on the front of every newspaper. You must have seen them."

"But there is no time to think about it, to arrange it – we have to go today." Her voice was quite hard, as if she were cross with me. "We don't need additional complications, Emmeline."

"You're right," I said, "I didn't mean to… Sorry, Florence. We will head for Paris. Please don't be cross with me."

She let out a little sigh of exasperation. "I am not cross with you, Emmeline. I am never cross with you." She held me in her eyes long enough for the reassurance to stick to me. Then she said, "Go and have another look out of the window – see if the rain is easing at all."

"No, not at all. And the square is quite deserted… except for… damn it." I jumped back. "It's him, Florence."

"Are you sure?"

"Yes – it's him. He walked past the house – a sideways glance, and walking slowly. We're trapped, Florence, we can't get out."

"But what if we leave anyway? What can he do to us in broad daylight?"

"He will follow us at the very least – wherever we go he will follow."

Florence frowned for a moment, then her eyes lit up. "Well, if we can't get out unseen, then perhaps we can get out… unsuspected."

"How do you mean?"

"It's Saturday – tonight is the Ragged School charity ball that we had abandoned."

"Yes."

"So, if we were to leave the house, in ball gowns, laughing lightly, taking no luggage, just two ladies out for an evening, he would surely expect us back, and in our beds tonight... which is surely what he is waiting for since he doesn't attack now."

"I don't know, Florence... maybe... yes, it might work. But what about Ming? We can't take him to a ball. I mean, it would look a bit suspicious wouldn't it? Leaving in ball-gowns, with a cat in a basket."

"Nellie could take him to the stables when she leaves."

"But wouldn't that look suspicious too?" I said.

"I don't see how else we can take him. Unless Nellie keeps him until we return."

"No, we must take him – I'll not leave another cat behind."

Florence rang for Nellie and went to her writing desk.

"We must be very calm in front of her, Emmeline, act lightly, as if you are looking forward to a little holiday."

"Yes, Miss?" said Nellie.

"Ah, Nellie," said Florence, a picture of normality. "Everything in order?"

"Yes, Miss."

"Good. What is the time now, Emmeline?"

"Half-past six, I think."

"Now then, Nellie, you can leave in few minutes. We are going to take Ming with us so could you pop him round to the Bird Cage stables in Sloane street? Take him in his basket, well covered against the rain, and he will make a better traveller if he can see no one, and no one can see him. Tell Mr Bird to put him with our other things, and tell him we'll come this evening."

"Certainly, Miss."

"After that, I want you to pop this letter round to Mrs Dockerill at her father's house, so that she knows not to come tomorrow. I will send notice to you both when we are going to return, but it may not be for a few weeks. You will both be paid of course while we're away."

"Very well, Miss."

"Now then, Nellie, this next part is very important – we will need the brougham carriage at seven-thirty – that's in precisely one hour, so please let Jenkins know. It is very important that you do this, Nellie, and if, for any reason, he can't bring it, I want you to come straight back here. Is that clear?"

"Yes, Miss."

"Good. Off you go then."

"Thank you, Miss Bright, Miss Stanton. And may I say, I hope you both have a very pleasant evening and a wonderful time away."

54

For Better, For Worse

An hour later, we were dressed and ready.

"That's the carriage now," I said, calling down the stairs to Florence.

"Can you see the driver?"

"One moment… I think… yes, it's Jenkins."

"Are you certain?"

"Yes, I see him quite clearly. He has Peggy."

"Oh dear," said Florence, "I would have liked a more reliable horse tonight."

"He's coming to the door."

There was a knock.

Florence whispered up the stairs to me: "So it is safe to answer then?"

I ran down to join her. "I don't know, I don't know."

Florence opened it anyway.

"Your carriage, Miss."

"Thank you, Jenkins, we will be out presently."

"Very good, Miss."

Florence closed the door smartly and looked at me in silence for a moment, then she put her hand on my cheek, and with her eyes, she asked me if I was ready.

I took a breath to say 'yes' but instead said, "No… just a moment longer."

I tried to think through the mechanics of it all – first we walk out of the door, laughing lightly, then we climb into the brougham, no rush; we roll down the square, giggling – just an evening out, nothing to excite Uncle Walter's suspicions.

Can it be so simple? I thought. I mean what if… what if he stops the carriage somehow? We will never outrun him in corsets and skirts, and Florence cannot run at all with her ankle.

I could see it so clearly – He pulls open the door and grabs Florence, dragging her into the road, and then… and then he stamps on her – he stamps on her face, and he kills her, my Florence… he kills my Florence.

"We can't, Florence, we can't possibly – it's too dangerous."

"But we have no choice," she said.

"But can't we..? Damn it… This is all my fault – I am the one who has brought this upon us – upon you, and… and I… I want to go alone. I must – yes, that's what I must do – I'm going to go alone."

"You most certainly are not."

"Of course I am. This is absurd – these are my troubles, not yours, you did not ask for them, you do not deserve them – of course I will go alone."

Then I slumped to the floor, in horror of the consequences that I was setting out for myself.

"I don't know what to do, Florence, I just don't know what to do." I began to cry.

She crouched down beside me, her eyes were full of tears too.

And then she kissed me, and it was a strange kiss, full of love and fear, and made with trembling lips.

At the end of it, she wiped her eyes and pulled me to my feet.

I took a deep breath, glanced at the door, then nodded my readiness.

We stepped outside.

Jenkins came forwards with an umbrella and walked us towards the carriage.

"I do hope the rain stops before tomorrow," said Florence, quite loudly, "I was hoping to take a walk in Hyde Park in the afternoon."

I could see Uncle Walter standing in the shadows near the entrance to the square.

"Well who knows," I said. "Perhaps it will even have stopped before we get back home tonight." This sounded wrong – too much what we wanted him to hear – a sort of strained normality. But then again, I had no idea how I was managing to talk at all.

We climbed inside.

"Very good, Jenkins," said Florence, and we set off, rolling towards my uncle, and gripping each other by the hand almost to the point of snapping fingers.

We stopped at the entrance to the square, while Jenkins waited for a gap in the traffic.

It was only the briefest pause, but Uncle Walter was not ten feet from me.

I laughed aloud, and then attempted a random snippet from a conversation I wasn't having:

"In that case, I hope I won't have to spend the evening warding of Archie – you know how he is."

Florence laughed too, and as we pulled out she replied with, "Well, we don't have to stay too long."

Perhaps fifty yards from the square I looked through the back window.

"Is he following?"

"I can't see anything through this bloody rain. I think we should go straight to the stables – what do you say?"

"No, we should keep to our plan – if he is following us, by whatever means, then it is better that we take our charade all the way to the ball. Once inside, we can disappear through a back door, and leave him waiting for us at the front."

55

Here I Am, and There You Are

A few minutes later, we pulled up at Morley's Hotel in Trafalgar Square where the Ragged School Ball was taking place.

"Jenkins," said Florence, "I don't think we'll need you again tonight, but would you mind waiting here until ten?"

"Certainly, Miss."

"If we are not out by then, you may leave."

"Right you are, Miss."

The door burst open.

I screamed.

"Calm yourself, for goodness sake." It was Agnes. She climbed into the carriage, showering us with rain as she brushed it off the sleeves of her coat.

"What on earth are you doing here?" said Florence.

Agnes ignored her and spoke directly to me: "If you value your safety, Mr Stanton, you will come with me."

"What do you mean, her safety – what's going on?"

"I have decided to save him, Florence, but only for your sake, which is certainly more than you deserve."

"Save her from what?"

"Yes, what do you mean?" I said.

She looked at me directly again. "There is a man on his way here right now, Thomas – he is coming for you, and he does not wish you well. It seems that your Neapolitan misdemeanours have finally caught up with you."

"My god, then he is following."

"And that is why you are best advised to come with me."

"That won't be necessary, Agnes," said Florence, hesitating before confessing, "we already have a plan."

"Yes, yes – the stables, the carriage, Dover – he knows all about it."

I clung on to Florence's arm as Agnes continued: "So, once again, Thomas, I suggest you come with me, and leave Florence here in safety."

"No, I come too," said Florence, and she put both her arms around me. "We will not be separated."

"Well, you are very foolish, but I've no time to argue about it." Agnes knocked on the carriage roof. "Jenkins"

"Yes, Ma'am?"

"Take a cab home, I'm taking the brougham."

There was silence for a moment.

"Beg pardon, Ma'am," said Jenkins. "Your instructions, Miss Bright?"

"Can you even drive a carriage, Agnes?" said Florence.

"Don't be so bloody stupid – of course I can drive."

Florence looked at me, but I had no answers, so she winced and said, "Very well. Jenkins, go ahead, take a cab back, Miss Grendle will drive the brougham."

* * *

We headed West, and at the fastest canter that Peggy could muster – The Mall, Eaton Square, Kings Road, then left down to the river, following the water Westward a little way.

I glimpsed a sign – 'Lost Road' I think it said, and Agnes now slowed the carriage down. It was a quiet, residential area, and I wondered if she might have access to one of the houses, but instead of pulling up, she continued right to the end of the road, where we dropped onto a dirt track, leaving both light and civilisation behind. We then bumped across a small bridge over a stream, before pulling up on an expanse of boggy marsh.

Agnes climbed back into the carriage with us. She spoke quietly, despite our isolation:

"I am fairly sure that this is the spot. However..."

"The spot for what?" said Florence.

"...However, I can't be completely sure in the darkness. Thomas, get out of the carriage and..."

"My name is Emmeline."

"...and follow the stream down to the river. There should be a small house there. If so, then whistle, and we will follow."

"Why can't we all go together?" asked Florence.

"Don't be foolish – you can hardly walk on a pavement with that ankle – let alone a mud path in pitch darkness.

"She's right, Florence," I said. "It can't be far to the river from here, and I can move quicker than both of you."

I climbed out of the carriage.

The rain had finally stopped, but the air was so thick with darkness that I could hardly breathe.

"A house, you say?"

"Yes. Go," said Agnes.

I looked at Florence and told her that I loved her with my eyes, then I pulled up the skirts of my ballgown and set off.

To my left was the stream I was to follow, or perhaps it was a small canal – it smelt of sewage and bad breath. To my right, a scribble of bushes and small trees were reclaiming the footpath, and in several places I had to kick my way through scratchy wet shrubs to make progress.

After a minute or two of stumbling, I reached the river Thames itself. It had been gorging on the heavy rain for days, and I had never seen it so fat and so roaringly swift. The water was pallid with silt and detritus, and a log tumbled past, reaching out with its arms for help that didn't come.

A man...

A thick arm crushed my chest, and a hand clamped my mouth shut.

He dragged me backwards, thumping me down onto the wet earth, then lay his full weight on top of me.

"Yes, Thomas, here I am, and there you are."

He sealed my mouth tight with his palm and pinched my nose shut.

I could not breathe.

He glanced down at my body then he pushed his nose into my face and sniffed.

My lungs screamed against the suffocation.

"Oh my little tease, you couldn't resist me could you? With your come-hither theft, and your soft pretty dress."

Everything now began to disappear in stars and pain, but at the very last moment, he let my nose open, and the world rushed back in.

"I promised I would fuck you before I killed you, my filthy invert," he whispered. "And I always keep my promises."

As he let go of my mouth and turned me face-down, I managed to scream, so he clamped my mouth shut again.

Florence had heard me – she screamed my name back at me, and I could hear Agnes arguing with her.

Walter froze for a moment.

"Damn them – stupid bitches."

The sound of Florence's voice now fired every muscle in my body to fight him, but he answered by twisting my head to the edge of a broken neck, and the pain made me once more still and silent.

I heard Florence again, closer now.

"Damn them," he growled, pulling up my skirts in frantic snatches.

I did not want her to come – don't come Florence, don't die too, please don't die.

The back of his hand was wet against my buttocks, his fingers convulsing at the buttons of his trousers.

"How dare you make me do things, you filthy wretch," he whispered, "how dare you."

He pushed my legs apart with his knees.

"Dirty. Fucking. Thieving. Bitch."

BANG.

He leapt to his feet.

It was Agnes, gun in hand.

"No," she said, not shouting – a calm, teacherly, 'no'.

He stood still for a moment, his trousers down, frowning, and his mouth slightly open, as if he were right upon the edge of an answer.

She cocked the gun again. "You said you would arrest her, not rape her."

Blood began to run from his nose and ear. He looked confused for a moment, as if he couldn't quite focus his eyes, then he fell backwards, collapsing across the water's edge, his head and torso underwater, his legs still on the bank, and his flaccid penis looking up at his belly, in the same dead pose of its master.

Silence...

Agnes trained her gun on him, and waited. The water lapped, and his arms flapped gracefully in the current.

"Emmeline." Florence limped into the scene at last, and fell on me. "Are you hurt?"

I couldn't think of an answer.

She searched my eyes. "Are you hurt, Emmeline?"

"No... I... I think I... I think perhaps I am all right."

She pulled my skirts back down and helped me to a path-side log, where she sat with her warm arms around me.

"There he goes," said Agnes.

The lapping lips of the Thames reached down to his waist and sucked him quietly into the water. He didn't float, but went straight under, as if his belly were full of rocks.

Agnes inspected her gun, but her hand was trembling.

"Are you all right, Agnes?" asked Florence.

"Of course."

"Thank you, Agnes," I said. "You surely saved my life."

"It was my mistake."

"To save me?"

"No, Thomas, to have trusted a man. But I'll confess one thing – when I saw him on top of you – when I saw you suffer as women suffer, as I have suffered, I did, at least for that moment, see you as a woman."

"She is a woman, Agnes, you did see her – that is who she is."

We were quiet for a moment, watching the river tumble past. I felt no urgency to leave the scene. Perhaps it was just that for the first time in such a long time, I had nothing to run away from, and I wanted to mark it by staying still for a while, even despite the cold and the wet.

In my mind's eye, I watched him disappear under the water again.

"I'm sure I should feel some sort of horror at watching a man die," I said, "but I don't feel anything at all – I really don't. I only wonder where he'll wash up."

"His body?" said Agnes. "Who can say, but his soul is already in hell."

She took a deep breath, and inspected her gun again. "So, this how my mother felt," she said, more to herself than to me. "I can't say I care for the sensation." And with that she threw the gun into the river.

"But why the river, Agnes?" I said.

"What do you mean?"

"How could he have persuaded you to bring me to this place?"

"Oh, international law or something – he said he had to arrest you on an Italian boat. Quite clever really."

She reached into her bag and pulled out a piece of paper, then she turned to leave. "I'll wait for you both in the carriage. Don't be long – it's getting rather cold." Without looking at us, she dropped the paper at our feet and walked away. It was my letter.

"Thank you, Agnes," I said, but she made no answer.

* * *

I put my arms around Florence, buried my face in her shoulder, and we held on to each other in silence, until the clouds dispersed to reveal a setting half-moon.

"It's funny how it can be so wet upon the ground and yet the sky so clear," said Florence with a little shiver.

I looked up to see the moon hovering just above the rooftops of London.

"Do you think that right now, in the land of the rising sun, they are watching the moon rise just as we are watching it set?" I said.

Florence stood up and smiled at me.

"Astronomically speaking, it seems plausible," she said, then she reached out her hand to help me up. "Shall we go?"

56

Florence's Worried Face and Geronimo's Nose

A month later, we stood beside the brougham on Harewell green, looking up the long high street into my home town. I wore a hat with a veil over my face, just to be sure I wasn't recognised by anyone.

"It is such a strange feeling, Florence," I said.

"What is?"

"To be here, all these memories – I have a memory for every stone and tree stump."

"Pleasantly nostalgic perhaps?"

"Yes… no, not really. It feels a little sad – a feeling of loss I think."

"No one can go back, Emmeline – the past is lost to all of us."

"I know, and it's not that I wish to go back as such, but this part of my past is a world that exists right now – a world that Mother and Elizabeth still inhabit. It's not so much a lost past, as a present from which I am excluded."

She climbed back into the brougham and offered me her hand. "Come on now, let's go and see if we can find him, shall we?"

* * *

Approaching my road, I was expecting to feel more sadness, but as we pulled up, a few yards from the house, I found myself more fascinated than upset. I examined it intently through the brougham window, completely preoccupied with the small details of the building – seeing what was the same, and what had changed since I left.

"I think they might have painted the front door," I said "It's nice. And look, that's my bedroom... or *was* my bedroom. New curtains and... there he is, Florence look – oh my goodness, there on our path, sitting, all pleased with himself. Quick, give me the cat basket."

"Go slowly, Emmeline – make sure your veil's down and don't draw attention to yourself... and don't frighten him off."

I walked up to the garden gate very casually. There was, as expected, no sign of life from within the house on a Monday afternoon.

I made some little kissing noises at Geronimo to draw him over.

"Brown?" he said, and trotted towards me.

He had always been a friendly cat, and would trot to anyone, so I cannot say that he came because he recognised me, rather than for a little fussing from a stranger, but I like to think both that he knew me, and that he was happy to see me.

I scooped him up and buried my nose in his neck, and in his faint smell was all the comfort of home.

"Did you miss me, little friend? Did you miss me?"

I could not seem to absorb enough of him, and found myself aching between the need to hold him gently, and the urge to squeeze him with all my might.

"How would you like to move to Japan with me and Florence, eh? It's going to be a wonderful adventure. It'll be like going home for you."

I looked over at the carriage in triumph and Florence was already waving me back. He seemed quite happy about being held, so I didn't bother to close him in the basket, but as I was about to leave, I noticed grains of rice strewn on the ground. I looked back up the path and there was more lying in the gaps between the paving slabs.

Geronimo twitched now, so I took him straight to the carriage.

"Here he is, Florence, my Geronimo. Isn't he absolutely perfect?" I climbed in with him.

"He's lovely, Emmeline, but put the windows up, quickly, and we must have him in the basket for the journey."

* * *

I did not even look back as we turned out of my road, but played with Geronimo's nose through the basket door.

"There was rice on the path, Florence – quite a lot of it."

"A wedding?"

"Must have been Elizabeth, I suppose. What a thought – my sister, a married woman. I feel quite… sad about it."

"But why sad?"

"I'm not sure exactly. It feels quite a lot like anger too – something like that."

A little way ahead, we passed St Thomas' church and I had Jenkins stop the carriage.

"Wait here," I said. "I'm just going to have a quick look – they put notices up in the church porch."

"Is that wise, Emmeline? You don't want to run into that horrible vicar. And anyway, do you really want to know?"

"Don't worry, I'll keep my veil down – I just want to see."

On Friday the 6th of January at 10 O'clock,
The wedding of Miss Elizabeth Stanton and Mr Herbert Palfrey.

I sat on the bench opposite the noticeboard to take it in for a moment. What a thought – Elizabeth and Palfrey's son. Well, why not, I suppose, but what a strangely empty feeling to have not been there.

I could see them all walking past this very bench but three days ago – bride and groom, Mother, Auntie Pollard, and all the relatives that I rarely saw, and will never see again.

They were all smiling – hopeful, happy - a family all belonging to each other, and I wished with all my heart that I could have been one of them – the real me, Emmeline, with her family, at her sister's wedding.

How I missed them, how I still wanted them. Why couldn't that be the world? I thought. It required no great re-ordering of the cosmos to make it true – it required only a little more love.

I heard footsteps inside the church, accompanied by the flat singing of the Reverend Thomas Thomas. He seemed to approach the door, but then carried on past.

The sound of him took me back to the night I was caught in Elizabeth's clothes. It was the sound of that world as it was then, but also as it is now – the world that should have been better, but isn't.

Then I lifted my veil and looked back at the carriage – at Florence's worried face and Geronimo's nose, and the world was just as it ought to be.

About the Author

I am a novelist, singer-songwriter and facial analyst, who just happens to be trans (she/her). I also have ADHD, but no one has convinced me yet that it's a disorder rather than a difference.

As a self-published author with no agent (at the time of writing), I need your help, so if you do enjoy this novel, please consider reviewing it on Amazon, mentioning it on your social media, or perhaps recommending it to a friend.

Thank you ♥

You can connect with me on:
- 🌐 https://www.alexandrasaurus.com
- 🐦 https://twitter.com/alexandrasaurus
- 📘 https://www.facebook.com/Alexandrasaurus
- 🔗 https://www.instagram.com/alexandrahamer

Printed in Great Britain
by Amazon

81354361R00202